# DAYS *of* WONDER

ALSO BY CAROLINE LEAVITT

*With or Without You*

*Cruel Beautiful World*

*Is This Tomorrow*

*Pictures of You*

*Girls in Trouble*

*Coming Back to Me*

*Living Other Lives*

*Into Thin Air*

*Family*

*Jealousies*

*Lifelines*

*Meeting Rozzy Halfway*

# DAYS *of* WONDER

*a novel by*

## Caroline Leavitt

ALGONQUIN BOOKS
OF CHAPEL HILL
2024

Published by
ALGONQUIN BOOKS OF CHAPEL HILL
Post Office Box 2225
Chapel Hill, North Carolina 27515-2225

an imprint of Workman Publishing
a division of Hachette Book Group, Inc.
1290 Avenue of the Americas
New York, New York 10104

Printed in the United States of America. Design by Steve Godwin.

Cataloging-in-Publication Data for this title
is available from the Library of Congress.

10 9 8 7 6 5 4 3 2 1
First Edition

*For Jeff and Max forever*

# DAYS *of* WONDER

# PART ONE

# ONE

# New York State
*April 2018*

Ella stepped through the prison gate, blinded by the sun and the hard blue of the sky, frantically searching the crowd for her mother. At twenty-two, she still felt so, so young, but certainly not the fifteen she had been when she had first arrived here. Freed as if from a box, she stumbled forward but kept her eyes on her feet. If she fell, she knew she wouldn't be able to get up.

Ella clenched the paper bag containing her belongings—everything except for her old cellphone, which the police said they were keeping indefinitely. She craned her neck and rose on tiptoes, searching past the cameras, the shouts, for her mother.

The air felt buttoned too tight about her throat. Colors vibrated, knocking her off balance. The gaping sky looked as if it might swallow her. What scared her the most were the news vans, the reporters rushing toward her, their voices like thorns. *Ella. Ella. Ella*, they shouted. *Ms. Levy. Ms. Levy*. And then *Mrs. Levy*—that one aimed at her mother, Helen.

Though she was surprised by the media's presence, their frenzy was nothing new. They had roiled up public opinion against her from the start. The *New York Times* had blared: QUEENS TEEN PLOTS MURDER OF UPPER EAST SIDE JUDGE. The *New York Daily News*

had been even worse: QUEENS KILLER-CUTIE'S ATTEMPTED MUR-
DER. BOYFRIEND'S DAD FED TOXIC TEA. REDHEAD CAUGHT
RED-HANDED.

Back then, after the incident, not a day had gone by that she wasn't
in the papers, that there hadn't been TV trucks parked on the street
at her mother's home, or reporters hounding her mother, shouting at
her, picking at her past to find the juiciest morsels, acting as if Helen
were to blame too—because in their view she had been a rule breaker
with no morals, a single mother who had been banished from her
Hasidic community when as a teen she had gotten pregnant. The media
searched through everything, finding pictures of Ella from *Help*, her
high school literary magazine, and from the French club, which she had
joined to strengthen her résumé. The papers had published photos from
Ella's Facebook account, along with the messages she had so carefully
crafted—especially those she'd put on Jude's page, including the one
she regretted most: *I'd do anything for you.*

"Ella!" a reporter now shouted. Ella avoided her gaze. "Ella!"
someone else cried. "Hey, Red!"

And that was when Ella saw Helen pushing through the crowd, her
spine stiff, dressed in heels and a blue business suit, her hair covered by
a scarf that also obscured much of her face. "I'm here," Helen said, and
even though it was a warm spring day, she guided Ella into a raincoat
with a hood, pulling it over Ella's face as she led her to the car. Ella
tried to ignore the reporters banging on the roof of the coupe. They
were acting as if she didn't deserve to be free at all; and what terrified
her more than their pressuring presence was that maybe, just maybe,
they were right.

"How do you feel now?" a woman with a microphone shouted.
"Has justice been served? What will you do now? Are you going to try
to find that boy?"

*That boy.*

Another reporter jammed his body against the front of the car, shouting and pointing at Helen. "How much did you really know? How could you let all this happen?"

"Will you ever make tea again?" another reporter called.

Helen's mouth twitched.

"What about a garden?" yet another reporter shouted. "Gonna try to grow more foxglove, are you?"

Helen got in the driver's seat and locked all the doors, ignoring the slap of hands on the windows, the way fingers left prints, like evidence.

"Bunch of vulturous jerks," Helen said. "Buckle your seatbelt, please."

Ella did, trying to make herself as small as possible, burrowing down, and then Helen pressed on the gas and jerked the car forward until the reporters got out of the way. Their shouts continued to bounce against the windows.

"Are you happy now?" a woman called after them.

"Screw the whole lot of you," Helen muttered.

To Ella's relief, the media parade didn't follow them for very long. The whole drive to Brooklyn, Ella stared out the window, stunned at the world. How easily people strolled the sidewalks, the young girls busy living a life that she had missed, all of them ambling in and out of shops or just plunking themselves down on a bench, tilting their faces to the sun and taking this wide-open life for granted. The Free World. That's what they had called it in prison, but everyone knew you still wouldn't really be free if you didn't have the right persona, the right chances.

Did she? Would she?

She didn't know how she felt about going to live with her mother. Right now she needed her, but Helen's apartment wasn't really Ella's home. Helen had moved twice while Ella was in prison, trying to get away from the media and the threats, first deeper into Queens—from Flushing to Bayside—and then deep in Southwestern Brooklyn, in Bay Ridge, a place Ella had never seen.

"Your whole life's ahead of you," Helen said now. "Such a miracle! No probation, no parole. Isn't that something? A clean slate!"

Ella wasn't so sure. "I'm still a felon," she said.

Even after crossing the Hudson, it took them an hour to reach South Brooklyn. The neighborhoods blurred into one another, and they finally arrived in Bay Ridge. (Bay Ridge! Who lived in Bay Ridge?) Maybe she wouldn't have to be on such high alert here, Ella thought as she cracked open the car window. She might be left alone.

They drove by the Alpine movie theater, specialty grocery markets, and an array of people, mostly teens or families, walking on the scrubby sidewalks. She thought she heard people speaking in Russian, or maybe it was Polish. And then there were bars and lounges with signs advertising happy hour, and just a few doors down, a mosque on one of the corners. She could see the Verrazzano-Narrows Bridge, the bay and the harbor. In prison, she had known every corner of her cell, every pockmark in the prison hallways. But here, she didn't know what to make of what she saw, or how to feel about it.

"Want some music, honey?" Helen said as she switched on the radio.

Ella had had a radio in prison and mostly listened to the news, but the stories had all sounded as if they were happening on another planet. There had been snipers in Georgia. A school shooting in Indiana. An outbreak of E. coli.

Helen punched a preset and unleashed Childish Gambino's "This Is America." Ella had danced to that song when they'd told her she was getting out, her cheap commissary radio blasting. Now she didn't feel like dancing, didn't feel anything but guilt.

"Want it louder?" Helen asked, and Ella shook her head. The world was too loud for her as it was, which was both wonderful and terrible at the same time. Through her open window, she could smell an exotic mixture of curry, garlic, and something she couldn't identify but that made her mouth water.

They drove past large homes, with stone facades and slate roofs, and then drove farther down Fifth Avenue, where most of the shops had Arabic signage. The streets were busy with women in hijabs, one of whom had tucked her cellphone between the fabric and her cheek so that she could talk hands-free while she pushed a stroller. There were all these new stores that Ella didn't recognize. People were talking to one another in English, but when she tried to latch on to a word, it sounded like a foreign language she could no longer speak. How would she ever know what to do, what to wear, or even how to act?

They passed falafel stands and red-sauce pizza joints, and all the smells and noise and color filled Ella with wonder—but then her heart sank when Helen turned down 70th Street and the view morphed into something straight out of that old movie *Saturday Night Fever*. Ella was swept back to a different time, with Helen on the couch, watching, laughing; a time when they shared experiences. The buildings here were mostly dilapidated three-story multifamily homes, many of them displaying American flags.

As they got closer to her apartment, Helen kept up a cheerful patter about what would come next.

"This won't be forever. We can sit down together, think of where we can move," Helen said. "Maybe to the middle of the country? Or what about some small town upstate where we can change our lives? Anywhere but here, right?"

"I can't think about anything yet," Ella said. "I'm a little shell-shocked."

"Of course you are, baby." Helen patted her hand. "We have all the time in the world."

Helen slowed by a three-story dirty redbrick building. Three lidless trash bins and a green skateboard kicked upside down graced the tiny patch of lawn.

"Here we are," she announced. The sidewalk was crumbling and there weren't many trees, but as soon as she parked, Helen seemed to come alive. She drew Ella into the building, a dark entrance hall with three mailboxes and a rubber-padded stairway. "You get used to the climb," she said, leading Ella up two flights of stairs, puffing a little when she got to the top. She opened the metal door onto a two-bedroom apartment with carpeted floors the color of a tongue depressor.

Ella immediately felt as if the walls were moving toward her, yet somehow there was too much space, too many things to look at: books tossed on the couch, clothes breeding on chairs, tissue dress patterns puckered with pins on a side table. In prison, Ella had kept her small cell spare so that it would seem larger—or maybe it was just to give herself a sense of control. She had cleaned it obsessively, trying to find some semblance of pride.

She moved to the kitchen and spotted the familiar vintage diner clock, ticking loudly. She had looked at it every day growing up, but now it seemed different, like one of those what's wrong with this picture games she and Helen used to play. Her hand trailed over every surface. She opened up the cabinets. There were the cups she had painted in grade school, garishly glittery—the ones that Helen said she loved but had insisted were too pretty to use. But the fancy French roast coffee Helen used to buy was gone, jars of instant Nescafé in its place. Helen used to cook, but now the cupboards were stacked with Campbell's soup and packaged noodles. Other things were either broken or missing, like the chair with deep blue paisley upholstery that Helen had loved.

She roamed toward the back of the apartment, where she saw a small blue bedroom with a big double bed that was surely Helen's, a patchwork comforter spread across it. She passed another room, probably a second bedroom, but now with shelves full of dress patterns, a long cutting table, and a sewing machine by a window. Through the window, she could see a small backyard, all scrubby grass and an anemic-looking tree.

"I fixed up the bedroom for you," Helen said.

"What? No! It's your room—"

"That living room couch pulls out!" Helen said. "And it's comfortable." She touched Ella's face. "I bought new sheets for you, and I sewed the comforter myself. I wanted everything to feel just right for you." Her mother's face was so bright, her eyes so sparkling, that all Ella could do was nod. "There are clothes for you too, in the dresser."

Ella moved to the window and looked out on the street. No one was there, but she could hear the quiet now, as if silence had a deafening sound of its own. And then she heard some kids screaming with laughter, from blocks away, and she thought how amazing it was that they could laugh like that without looking over their shoulders, searching out danger. It was startling to think that they could just live in the world.

"Come, sit down," Helen called. "I want to show you something."

Ella stiffened when she saw the computer on the dining room table, an iMac instead of the semi-broken PCs she'd had access to in prison. She'd always had someone standing over her, supervising.

Helen waved as if at a fly. "I use it for designs," she said. "To see what's trending out there."

"Okay," Ella said.

"This? This is for you," Helen said, tapping the mouse. A new page opened, showing the special investment account she had started the day Ella was incarcerated. Forty dollars a week taken from her job managing a dress shop in Queens, and now, after all these years, the account had grown to twelve thousand dollars, a small fortune, enough to allow them to start over. Helen had bookmarked sites about different cities: Santa Fe in New Mexico; Gloucester in Massachusetts; small towns in upstate New York, near an actual lake where they could swim, which made Ella think about the Woodstock house that Jude's family had owned.

"It'll be a whole new world," Helen said, but Ella couldn't stop thinking about the old one. "You check out all those places and see what calls to you," Helen said. "I can find work most anywhere, and maybe you could, too."

"Maybe," Ella said. But what jobs could a felon get, even one with a psychology degree? She could be a cashier at the Thrift-T-Mart. Or she could clean houses.

"You could change your last name to Fitchburg, like I did. It's just paperwork and going in front of a judge."

"No," Ella said. "I can't do that. No more court. Not ever."

Helen was quiet for a minute. "You can change your first name, too, if you want. The first step to a fresh start."

Ella nodded. Maybe Helen was right. Maybe it would help her feel more like a new person, if that could be possible.

Ella clicked off the investment fund site and then powered off the computer.

"I'll go make dinner," Helen said. "Is pasta okay?"

While Helen bustled about in the kitchen, calling out that maybe, since Ella was an adult, they should have wine, Ella turned on the computer again. She knew what she had to do, and she had to do it right now before it was too late. She quickly typed in the words: *closed adoptions through New York lawyers.*

Names of attorneys tumbled onto the screen. But which one had Helen used? Her mouth dried. Her throat felt as if she had swallowed stones.

"Rotini or linguine, honey?" Helen called, and Ella felt her heart skittering so fiercely that she thought she might throw up.

"Linguine is good," she replied.

Next, she entered her name, and there it was—a multitude of articles about her. The latest news articles were about the journalist who had shown up five years into her sentence. Terrance Grapler. She would never forget him—his checkered shirts with solid ties, his hair just a little too long—or how he had helped her. His series on botched cases had stirred up enough trouble in the district attorney's office that the governor herself had gotten involved. It had been an election year, and the governor had a vested interest in showing that she supported a project that reopened questionable cases. Sixty percent of all confessions were forced, maybe even more, Grapler had told Ella, plus there were a number of holes in her case. He had also found out that the judge who had sentenced Ella to all those years had been getting kickbacks from the prison for funneling offenders into their cellblocks. Ella had already been condemned by the media, which hadn't helped. She had been charged with attempted murder, as an adult and not a juvenile, even though she had no prior record. Her lawyer, a friend of a friend of her mother's, had arrived too late, before he could instruct Ella not to say a word. The cops had told her if she just signed the confession and gave up her right to trial, if she threw herself on the mercy of the Court, she'd get much less time than the maximum twenty-five-year sentence. But she received that sentence anyway. Her lawyer, who had no real criminal experience, did not appeal the decision.

When she was arrested, she had been held in a windowless room for nearly sixteen hours while the police badgered her to confess to the alleged crime. Even the way her Miranda rights were read was twisted, implying it was better for her to talk rather than to stay silent until her attorney arrived. Those had all been breaches in procedure, Grapler had told her.

"Plus," he said, "Judge Stein had a pacemaker. He had a cardiac condition. The doctors I spoke to said he often didn't show up for checkups, that he'd constantly reschedule appointments. The foxglove could have exacerbated his condition, but he wasn't in good health to begin with. He was overweight. He smoked cigars and drank. And yet no one checked his pacemaker for irregularities. Even the toxicology report was contaminated."

"I don't understand," Ella had said.

"I'm not saying that's the truth or that you're not guilty," the journalist said. "That's not what this is about. But let's talk about justice. You were railroaded into writing a confession and taking a guilty plea. That's what I mean."

And then *boom, boom, boom* again. Because of the technicalities and the governor's ire, Ella's twenty-five-year sentence had been sliced

down to the six she had already served. She wouldn't have to report to a
parole or probation officer. But she would still be considered a felon out
in the Free World, and if she ever wanted to be exonerated, she'd have to
go back to court—and who knew what would happen then or how long
it would take. And did she want to go through that? No, she did not.

"Just finishing up, darling," Helen now called. "Almost ready."

Here it was, the last part of her search. She couldn't help herself.

*Jude Stein.* She typed in his name. And then she thought, *What if
he's changed his name, too?*

*Are you going to try to find that boy?* the reporter had shouted, and
yes, yes, she was. She had to try to find Jude, whom she had loved and
who loved her back. She wanted to ask him why he hadn't come to see
her or even written to her. Why he had abandoned her.

*Just tell me what happened*—that was what she always wanted to
ask. *Just tell me so I know, because you were there with me, and whatever you say, I'll believe.*

The lawyers and the cops had told her that Jude wasn't allowed to
see her, that he had given her up, but she had kept trying, had kept
asking Helen when she visited if there had been any news, until Helen
told her she had to stop.

But she hadn't been able to. One-sided conversations played out in
her mind. *Tell me what happened. Tell me where you are. Tell me why.*

He had never answered her letters, never signaled her in any way.
She couldn't bear the thought of how he must have blamed her—how
he must still blame her—though it couldn't be more than she blamed
herself. She had told herself over and over to move on, like Helen had
wanted. She had never had him visit her in a dream or whisper in her
mind. Instead, sometimes, lying on her prison cot late at night, she had
sworn that she smelled baby powder, that she heard a baby babbling
her name, calling her mama.

The prison hadn't allowed any internet access, but some people
had illegal cellphones, and Ella had traded food from the commissary

for a half hour on one of them. She had searched Jude's old screennames: Botaneasy, Bloomwhereplanted, Hey Jude, Jude the Obscure. She searched for all his old accounts: Twitter, Instagram, Tumblr. She also looked at the accounts of mutual friends, just in case they posted a selfie with him. A mention. She hadn't been able to post anything or to respond to anything. She had only been able to look. And there had been nothing to see.

"Forget him," the lawyer said.

"You were a kid. He gave you up for attempted murder," the other inmates would tell her.

*No,* Ella had said. She believed that couldn't be right. *No, he didn't give me up. He would never do that to me. We would never ever do that to each other. No matter what.*

"Well, he did it. You went to prison, and he went free. And you confessed."

*Let me see him,* she kept asking. *Let me just talk to him.*

"He doesn't want to talk to you. And you know why."

Every once in a while, the prison counselor had requested Ella to come see her, and the counselor kept probing. "Do you regret what happened? Do you want to be better, to have a better life?"

"I don't remember!" she had cried. "How can I atone if I don't remember?"

"You remember some of it," the counselor had assured her. "You confessed. And now you need to process it."

"What if you hypnotize me?" Ella had asked, but the counselor had told her that wouldn't be admissible evidence, because the mind is as malleable as clay and everyone knows you could tell someone in hypnosis that they are a chicken, and they'd believe it and start flapping their arms like wings.

*Remember, remember,* the counselor had kept telling her.

*I would if I could.*

Now Ella heard Helen humming, the way she used to when she

cooked. She heard the water running, the fridge door opening and closing, and garlic sputtering in a pan.

She had more time to explore.

But Helen came into the room too quickly, holding up two candlesticks, taking Ella by surprise. "I thought candles would be nice," Helen said. "You must be starving." And then she peered at the screen and grew still.

"What are you doing?" Helen said carefully, setting down the candlesticks. When Ella didn't answer, Helen reached over her and clicked off the computer. "You're being dangerously foolish. They could throw you back in prison."

"For what?" Ella said.

"For anything they want." Helen put her hand lightly on Ella's shoulder. "You know what they said. You cannot go near that boy again. Not after what happened." She took her hand away, and Ella yearned for its warmth again. "You can't possibly still love him—"

"I don't," Ella insisted. As soon as she said it, though, she felt overwhelmed by the past, how giant her love had been, how it had swallowed her whole and then dimmed—but it had never really gone away. "I just want to know where he is," she said.

"Why? For what?"

"I just want to know," Ella said.

Helen sighed heavily. "You know, honey," she said slowly, "it's been really hard for me, too." She stroked Ella's hair. "Come on, let's eat something delicious."

Ella couldn't imagine eating anything, but she switched seats from the computer chair to a place in front of the flickering candles. Helen brought out pasta aglio e olio on a platter, and a salad of field greens tossed with chopped pears and walnuts. A celebration dinner.

That night, alone in her mother's bed, the door as wide open as Ella could get it, she couldn't rest. She sat up and looked out her window. The room faced the sidewalk, but the street was dark and empty. She shuffled to the living room, where Helen was on the couch, reading. She met Helen's eyes and then snuggled on the couch beside her. Eventually her eyes drooped shut, and she finally felt safe enough to sleep.

THE NEXT DAY was Saturday, and though Helen was happy ("We have all this time together!"), Ella just wanted her mother out of the house so that she could freely search the internet.

She tried to get time alone. She asked her mother to buy her eight skeins of blue worsted wool and size eight bamboo needles so that she could make a sweater. The prison had offered supervised knitting classes, believing that small motor skills would reduce anxiety, and that it could offer the women a sense of accomplishment. The whole time Ella had been in prison, no one had even thought of using the circular needles as a weapon—but the instructor kept a close count of the needles anyway. Ella had thought she could never do anything remotely crafty, that her mother was the creative one, but she had gone to the class because it had broken up the day, and she could get lost in the sound of the clicking needles. Plus, she had loved the feel of the yarn running through her hands. The yarn in prison had been cheap and all the same color, an odd synthetic green, but after she had made a garter stitch scarf which she shyly gave to Helen during a visit, Helen had begun to bring her more and better yarn—linen, cotton, soft wool—and special bamboo needles with a silky feel to them. Ella had become so fond of knitting that it began to feel like a drug that helped her forget where she was and why.

But today Helen shopped faster than Ella expected. She was home before Ella could really make any progress in her search.

The next day she asked for a box of brown hair color, and again Helen came home too quickly, with a box of color called Lush Chestnut and a new cellphone for Ella with an unlisted number.

"So you can always reach me," Helen said, and Ella threw herself into her mother's arms. There it was, another tool of the Free World.

She took the hair dye into their bathroom and, using Helen's sewing scissors, chopped her orange curls to her chin, then painted on the new color. Forty minutes later, she washed it out. In the mirror, she saw a different person. *Reborn a brunette,* she thought. All those names the media had called her—Red Hot, Red-Handed—wouldn't fit her anymore. Her newly dark, cropped hair made her blue eyes look enormous, as if she could see everything she had missed before.

"I don't think I can get used to this," Helen said, staring at Ella's new hair.

"You will," Ella said, even though she wasn't so sure herself.

All that afternoon, Ella played with her new phone, roaming the different sites, playing games while Helen floated around her, making it impossible for Ella to concentrate. Surely Helen's phone would ring, or the intercom would buzz, but things remained quiet. Ella had noticed while growing up that Helen never really had friends because she was always with Ella or at work, but now Ella wondered why her mother hadn't made any new friends all these years, why she hadn't seemed to try.

But Ella knew why. It was all her fault.

She felt her mother watching her, smothering her like a heavy coat she couldn't manage to shake off. When Ella walked into another room, Helen followed. When Ella was in the shower, Helen knocked on the bathroom door and asked, "Everything all right?"

That night, Ella heard Helen quietly glide into the bedroom, then stand there, staring at her. Ella froze, pretending to be asleep until Helen crept away.

THEY SPENT ALL day together on Sunday, shopping for summer clothes and sandals. When a pedestrian accidentally bumped into Ella, she stopped, tense, the way she would have in prison, but Helen took her arm. "It's nothing," Helen said quietly. There was too much noise now, Ella thought, too many strangers glancing at her, and when Helen suggested going to eat Chinese food Ella asked if they could take the food home.

"Of course, darling," Helen said.

Finally, it was Monday morning, Ella's first day all on her own. Helen was going to work at the dress shop in Bay Ridge, where she would do tailoring and some dressmaking.

"Stay inside. You can read! Or watch TV," Helen told her. "There might not be any more stories about you now, but still, I wouldn't go near the news channels, especially anything local." She put a hand on Ella's shoulder. "Protect yourself, honey," she said.

"What about you?" Ella said. "Are they going to ask you questions about me at your job?" she asked, and Helen waved a hand.

"Don't be silly. They love me there," she said. "I work in a back-room, and they won't let the media near me. Anyway, I know how to handle them. And don't you answer the door or the phone unless you know it's me." Helen leaned over and gave Ella a kiss. "It's still you and me against the world, honey."

As soon as Ella heard the front door close, she went to the window facing the street and opened it, letting in the air, the sounds. Below, two guys were arguing, gesturing angrily. A young mother walked by, holding a little boy's hand and swinging it as he sang a nonsensical song. Ella watched as the young woman bent and kissed the boy's head.

Her stomach twisted with grief.

Closing the window, she approached the table and turned on the computer, which somehow seemed easier to operate than her phone. She began to snoop again: local adoption lawyers. There were so many names, how would she know which one Helen had gone to? She wondered too if an adoption lawyer would even talk with her, a felon. She felt something wrench in her throat.

Maybe this wasn't the best way to do things. She knew Helen was a packrat, so maybe she had saved something. A bill. A business card. Ella searched the entire apartment, probing the bottom of a closet that had cards from Ella's first birthday, and another closet with files filled with old income tax returns and payment documents. She had to ferret through until she found a confirmation letter from the adoption attorney, and then, heart thumping, a name and address: Aileen Santiago, 145 West 34th Street, Suite 710.

SIX YEARS AGO, she had lost everything. Jude. Her freedom. Her future. And her baby. Everyone at the prison had urged her toward adoption. "You cannot raise a baby in here," the warden said. "You can't live from visit to visit."

Ella stubbornly resisted, but even Helen pushed and pleaded with her to give up her child.

"Think of your life," Helen urged. "By the time your sentence is served, that baby will be a woman. What do you think will happen when you get out, and she has her own life, her own apartment?" Had she wanted to be a single mother to a daughter she would be able to see only on visits, traumatizing them both? Had she wanted to bathe her own daughter in shame? Better to be invisible, Helen insisted. "Please," she said quietly. "Consider adoption."

Ella cried then, and Helen held her hands tighter.

At the prison, Ella had watched people leave the visiting area as if they couldn't wait to get out of there, couldn't wait to go back to their real lives. The few children she had seen had looked shy and crumpled. Maybe Helen was right, but maybe she wasn't.

"No," Ella said. "I won't consider it."

"I can't take care of your child for you. I can't do it on my own. And I don't want you to have the same struggles that I did. Plus I have to work, every day. I can't afford to take care of a child."

"You won't have to," Ella insisted, because even then, she kept holding out hope that Jude would finally come find her, that he'd call, send a letter. They'd always talked about starting a family together and she knew that—no matter what—he'd never do this to her, to their child.

Helen cleared her throat. "Jude signed papers relinquishing any claim to the baby."

"What? That's not true. When?" Ella said, panicking. "When did you hear from him? Why didn't he contact me?"

"I was told," Helen said. "I thought you knew. I didn't want to upset you by bringing it up."

Ella stared at her, astonished.

"You know, we got lucky. The media doesn't know you're pregnant. Now we can keep it quiet."

"What are you even saying?"

"You didn't get to have a father," Helen said. "Do you want that for your child? Shouldn't she get to have two parents who love her? Maybe a beautiful home and money, too? Opportunities?" She pressed closer. "Shouldn't she have that? And shouldn't you?"

Ella felt the world, the life she had dreamed of, slipping away. "Yes," she finally said quietly.

Helen, against prison rules, swept Ella into her arms. "Darling," she said, "I swear this is the right choice—the only choice—for us to make."

*Us?* If there was an *us*, then why did she feel so alone, so abandoned?

"No one will ever have to know," Helen said.

And she was right, because while the media seemed to have dug up every ugly thing about Ella that ever existed, no one mentioned her pregnancy.

IT WAS DIFFERENT now. Ella's daughter would only be six—not twenty-five. They could still have a life together. The yearning Ella felt was so intense, it doubled her over. She believed that this was a real way to right some of the wrong, to grab some connection. Maybe the only way she had.

IT TOOK ELLA four days to gather her courage and call the lawyer, making an appointment, asking for a free consult, just fifteen minutes. Helen would be at work. She wouldn't have to know.

On the following Monday, Ella gathered all the lunch money that her mother had been leaving her—money that was always left over because she had no appetite and usually just foraged snacks from the fridge. She was eager to get out, though she wasn't sure how to face the Free World on her own. Today, though, determined, she went outside and headed to the subway station. She got the first train that came, the R local, huddling in her seat, trying to make herself as inconspicuous as possible, all the way up to 34th Street—Herald Square.

Emerging into the pulse of midtown Manhattan, Ella was terrified. Every sound made her skitter on the sidewalk. The air had a kind of fierce energy. When a woman bumped into her, Ella flinched, sure she had been found out, or that the woman would yell at her for getting in her way. Instead, the woman smiled at her and apologized.

The law office was in a uniform midtown skyscraper, close to the hubbub of Broadway. Ella felt too young, too nervous to be out on her own like this. She had borrowed a dark blue skirt suit from Helen's closet and slid her feet into a pair of Helen's heels. She had smoothed her wild hair as best she could, using some hair spray she found in the bathroom, but all she had to do was look at other girls on the street to know that she stood out, that she looked like a kid playing dress-up.

When she got off the elevator on the seventh floor, she immediately saw a pair of big glass doors etched with the attorney's name, a young receptionist staffing a desk behind them. As soon as Ella walked in, the receptionist looked up. "Hello. And you are?" she said, and when Ella told her, she told her to take a seat.

Ella had barely settled into the buttery leather couch when a blond woman with a wolf's face came toward her.

"I'm Aileen Santiago," the woman said, shaking Ella's hand.

Ella followed her into an office, then carefully perched on an uphol-stered chair while Aileen sat behind a steel desk that had nothing on it but a computer and a box of tissues. "Go ahead, tell me," she said, and then Ella stammered out her story.

"Your mother had a point," Aileen Santiago said when Ella had finished. "Did you want to raise a baby in prison? A child who would eventually know what you had done?"

Ella flinched. *What she had done.*

"I didn't know what I wanted," Ella said. "Everyone kept telling me to think of myself. To try to move on. To do it quickly so the media wouldn't find out. They kept telling me that the baby would never look for me and even if she did, she might not be happy with what she found. She might consider my life an unhappy story she would never want to tell. They told me the greatest kindness was for me to free her. What was I supposed to believe?"

"But you did give her up. You signed the papers. Why?"

Ella tried to swallow the lump in her throat. "My mother urged me to do it. She said it was best. She wouldn't—couldn't—raise another child on her own."

"And she was right. And you made the choice." Aileen turned to her computer, positioning the monitor so that Ella couldn't see. "And the father signed relinquishment papers, too."

Ella's mouth trembled. For the first time, Ella saw a flash of sympathy in Aileen Santiago's eyes. It softened Ella, made her remember how for months after her baby was gone, she had kept her hands on her stomach, as if trying to feel for something that wasn't there anymore.

But now, impossibly, it didn't seem such a fantasy.

"Why have you changed your mind?"

"Because I made a mistake. Because I never knew I was going to get out so soon. Because I just want to see if there is anything I can do to fix it, to get my child back."

Aileen shook her head. "You know there isn't."

"I just want to know if she's okay, know who has her—"

"I can't give you any information about the adoptive parents." Aileen leaned toward Ella. "It was a closed adoption. What is it you want to do here?"

"Why did you let me come here if you weren't going to help me? Why didn't you just tell me when I called to make the appointment?"

"My receptionist booked this as a consult. I couldn't have known what you wanted until you told me. And I don't give legal advice over the phone to people who are not my clients." Aileen sat still. Ella looked past her and saw photos lining a shelf against the wall. In one, Aileen held two babies on her lap, smiling happily. There was a beach photo of children playing, of a man who looked overwhelmed with joy. When she saw Ella staring past her, Aileen sighed. "My husband and I adopted our children from China," she said.

"You adopted kids," Ella said quietly, looking at the photos. "Was it hard? Did you ever wonder about their birth mother?"

"We're not talking about me," Aileen said.

"You never wondered about their mothers?"

Aileen bristled. "I did. And I sympathized. But many female children in China were being abandoned because of the one-child rule. Or because of poverty. My children needed homes, just like yours did."

Aileen shifted in her chair. "You did the best thing, giving up your rights to that baby. And the father did the right thing, too. So why are you here?"

Ella swallowed hard and began to cry. "Maybe I want her back."

"Maybe?" the lawyer said quietly. She pushed the box of tissues toward Ella, who grabbed two and held them to her eyes. "No one is going to give that child back to you. Not now, not ever. You understand that, right? You may be out of prison, but you're still a felon. And your daughter's been with another family for years. You have a new lease on life, and you should count your blessings. Let that child continue to have her own."

"Don't I have the right to even see her? To know her? To make sure she's happy?"

"You don't have the right to disrupt someone's life, hers or her parents'. You don't even know what she's been told. She might not know she's adopted." Aileen sighed again. "When that child reaches eighteen, if she wants, she can find you."

"Oh my God," Ella said, grabbing more tissues. She looked up. "May I have some water?"

Aileen glanced at her watch and then stood up. "I'll get you some water and then I'm afraid I have another appointment."

The lawyer walked out of the room, closing the door behind her, and Ella froze. Her daughter was now someone else's. She wanted to barge in and take her back and figure out the rest later—how to support her, where to live. Maybe Aileen was right, but what killed her was that she might never see her child again.

She drew herself up, anxiety flaring. Every time she heard footsteps, she tensed, worrying it might be Aileen with the cops, ready to strong-arm her back to prison for any reason they chose.

Ella jumped from the chair. She went to the attorney's computer and clicked on History, and there it was, her name on a file that the lawyer must have checked before their appointment. She clicked on it, and there was the information about her. And there was this, too: *Infant girl. Ann Arbor. Mark and Marianna Shorter.* An address and a phone number. She guessed people could adopt from different states, because here it was. Or maybe they had just wanted to make it harder for her to reach her baby. She knew these people could have moved, but it was something, a start. *Put it behind you,* the lawyer had said, but Ella knew she couldn't. She knew if she didn't go see her daughter now, she would die from longing.

She grabbed a pen from the desk and scribbled the info on the inside of her hand. She heard footsteps and quickly clicked off the history. Heart pounding, she headed for the door, almost crashing into Aileen.

"I changed my mind," Ella blurted. "I'm not thirsty." Then she fled, her fingers closed over her prize.

THAT EVENING, WHEN Helen got home, Ella told her, "I know where I want to live. Ann Arbor, Michigan."

"I never thought of Ann Arbor," Helen said. Ella couldn't tell her that she hadn't thought of her mother there with her, either; that she saw only herself there, alone, finally being an adult. And finally free.

When Helen asked her why she had chosen Ann Arbor, Ella said it was because it was a college town. "It's supposed to be magical there," she said, though all she really knew about it was that it was far away from Brooklyn.

"What will you do there?" Helen said.

Ella knew it wasn't going to be easy finding a job. She had gotten her psychology degree in prison as part of an innovative program from Bard College, but she wasn't sure what she could do with it. She had even taken classes on how to present herself to a potential employer, how to dress, how to speak. But in prison, it didn't matter if you made mistakes. Now it would.

"Apply to everything," the women in prison had been told. "You never know what a job you think you don't even like can lead to. And some jobs may look the other way on a background check."

Ella promised herself she would try, but she still needed time to heal.

ONE MONTH PASSED, and then another. Helen kept her promise and helped Ella change her last name to Fitchburg, even going with her to stand in front of the judge to get it done. "My brand-new girl!" Helen had said, and Ella felt she just might be. By then she could sleep alone in Helen's bedroom, with the door closed. She swore she felt herself getting stronger—older too, in a way. Red roots began to thread into the brown, her curls growing longer, more unruly. Helen offered to take her to a hair salon, but Ella shook her head. She didn't want any-one controlling any part of her in the way they had in prison. For her, that included letting someone else try to tame her curls.

Journalists somehow found their unlisted numbers, so Helen changed them again. Ella knit while she looked online for jobs. She read articles on her phone about what it was like to work a job, how you had to create a separate, professional self. There were also articles from women who wrote that they had been wrongly fired, or hit on by their bosses. One of them had sued her boss in court—and won.

*No court. No lawyers. Never again.*

"What's it like to work?" Ella asked Helen that evening.

"I can take you with me one day, if you like—"

Ella shook her head. "I don't want to make things hard for you. Anyway, I'd rather you tell me."

And so Helen did, telling her how every morning she would remind herself that she could do this. How she had to pay attention to everything around her, how she had to learn to read how people were feeling.

"But most of all," she said, "you have to believe in yourself." Hearing that, Ella bit back tears, because how could she do that?

She also knew that being told about an experience was not the same as having it. Ella might be frightened of not having Helen around to protect her, but she was more frightened of not being able to protect herself, of not knowing how to be a grownup in the outside world.

The next day, Ella donned a baseball cap and took the R train back into the city. *Be brave*, she told herself, but the hordes of people crowding past her overwhelmed her. A man with a tree branch strapped to his back waved at her, shouting, and she cringed away from him.

She wandered in and out of stores, daring herself to respond when a clerk asked, "Can I help you?" Finally, she began to relax and headed for a tall, silver office building on Broadway. It felt instantly different when she went inside, and her fear stepped back up. Everyone looked so polished, so sure of themselves, dressed in suits or silky-looking shirts, so well groomed that Ella pulled her hat over her hair a bit more. She tried to make herself a shadow. Two men were standing by the outer door, both studying a folder.

"I still think we can push that percentage," one of the men insisted.

"Let's put a pin in it and talk at lunch with Claire," said the other man. Then a woman in a dark suit, her glossy hair pinned back, rushed toward them.

"The client was late again!" she said. "But I'm here now. What's going on with these files?"

"We'll talk at lunch," one of the men said, opening the front door. Then he said something else that Ella couldn't hear, and the woman threw back her head and laughed, as if they were friends, too, and not just coworkers.

Ella walked deeper inside, closer to an elevator bank, and stood next to a woman, young like Ella, who was reading from a sheet of paper and biting her lip. If this woman could do it, maybe Ella could too. "Rough day?" Ella forced herself to say. She wanted to flee immediately, but the woman looked at her and brightened.

"Oh my God," the woman said. "You know how it is. They want everything yesterday."

"The day before yesterday," Ella blurted, and the woman's smile grew. "Take the time you need," she continued, parroting what Helen had told her about finding a job.

This time, the woman touched Ella's shoulder, and she felt a small electric shock at the contact. "I wish you were my boss," the woman said, and then the elevator came and she got on.

Ella, however, turned away, not wanting to extend the interaction. "Oh, I forgot something!" she said. The woman in the elevator waved goodbye and Ella waved back.

The elevator left and Ella laughed. Maybe she could do this after all. She could keep practicing until it felt more familiar to her.

She made her way over to Eighth Avenue and down to the Village, feeling the neighborhoods change as she got farther downtown. Manhattan had always seemed to her like a kind of house with different rooms. While Jude's Upper East Side had seemed like an expensive living room where you had to be careful not to touch anything lest you break it, Hell's Kitchen was more like a motley den, where there were wildly competing food smells and louder voices. The West Village felt like your best friend's furnished basement, where you could smoke weed and listen to music and talk about everything and no one would give you funny looks.

On 14th Street, she stopped at the Good Hearts Thrift Store, filled more with hipsters than people who looked like they really needed to shop there. She browsed the ten-dollar suits, because she planned to dress the part—if she ever landed an interview. She stopped when she found a black jacket and skirt—because black was New York cool, or at least it used to be—and a pale peach blouse to go under it. She also snagged a pair of five-dollar black pumps that weren't too scuffed and a small purse that looked professional. *Look like you mean business,* they had told her in prison. *Shoulders back. Keep your head and chin and hopes up.*

Ella bought the clothes, holding the bag close against her chest all the way home.

THAT EVENING, SHE told her astonished mother what she had done. She even modeled the outfit for Helen.

"Ta-da!" she said, but Helen looked as if she would cry. "What, Mom?"

Helen swiped at her eyes. "I could have gone with you," she said.

Ella shook her head. "I had to do it on my own."

"I could have made you something brand new. You didn't have to buy clothes."

"You still can," Ella said. "I'll need other clothes for work, won't I?" And then Helen seemed to practically glow.

ELLA SCOURED LINKEDIN and Glassdoor for jobs in Ann Arbor. There were job openings for school helpers, for clerks in various shops, and for orderlies at an assisted living facility, but when Ella saw the check box on the application forms about being a felon, she began to feel desperate.

By the end of July, she was beginning to worry that she would never find anything. She hadn't even gotten an interview yet. "It's okay," Helen said kindly. "You will. And there's no need to rush." But then, as if by another miracle, she found a job that asked for a writing sample before an application, a job writing an advice column for a new Ann Arbor newspaper called the *Grapevine Arbor*. It paid five hundred dollars a week, something she could live on if she was careful. She could rent a room. Or a tiny studio in a bad part of town. She'd live on peanut butter and saltines. The paper wanted to use a fake name, a fake photograph, and that suited Ella just fine.

At first she didn't tell Helen about applying for the newspaper job. She didn't want Helen's help, because she knew her mother's hovering would just make her more unsure, more frightened. Instead, she worked on the sample letter prompt that the owner, a woman named Pearl, sent her: *My partner gives me the silent treatment. What do I do?*

In prison, the women would withdraw into themselves when they had been deeply hurt, such as when a partner hadn't come for visiting days three weeks in a row; when a prison friend had been released and they had to stay; when there had been a loss of friendship, of company, maybe of hope. It wasn't that the women hadn't wanted to talk. Rather, they couldn't, just for self-preservation. They had to keep still so they wouldn't break. They had to honor their boundaries.

Ella reread the prompt five times, considering. Then she wrote about how people who feel they have no power sometimes mistakenly think that there's control in silence, in denying others their voice, when in fact, the real solution is to talk, to communicate, even if all you can do is sit beside someone and hold their hand.

Ella sucked in a breath. She attached her reply to the email, hit Send, and put her hands over her face. *Please. Oh please.*

Pearl emailed back almost immediately, wanting Ella's cell, relaying her own, and asking Ella to call her. Ella waited until Helen was at work to make the call. Then she sat with her phone in her hand, trembling. She did some deep breathing to calm her voice, and when that didn't work, she put on the suit, the shoes. *There*, she thought. *There I am. A little bit more brand new.*

When she called, to her shock, Pearl's voice was bouncy with enthusiasm. "I love what you wrote!" Pearl said, "Let's you and I have a talk next week. It's important to me that I hire someone I feel simpatico with. And in the meantime, I'd like to give you two more assignments to see how you might do with our tougher questions. Short, pithy answers, please. We don't have a lot of space."

"Of course," Ella said, and then she hung up the phone and cried.

The assignments came that evening, two different letters, one from a reader who bluntly asked why the fuck a columnist could answer questions that he himself could not. Ella could tackle that one. She knew from prison that sometimes you were just so deep in a problem, you couldn't find a way out; that sometimes it didn't even matter if another person could give you an answer, because just the pure act of talking—and of listening—could open a door.

She was happy with that answer, but the next question made her want to give up.

*I adore my older brother, but he was sent to juvie two years ago for arson. After he came home, there was a fire in his neighborhood and I think he did it. But when I asked him, he threatened to hurt me if I told anyone. He said I'd better have proof if I'm going to accuse him like that. He says he can't go back to prison. What do I do?*

*Signed, Hopelessly Devoted*

*Dear Hopelessly Devoted,*

*I don't question that you love your brother, or that you want the best for him. But right now, you have no proof that he caused that fire. His saying that he cannot go back to juvie doesn't mean he's guilty, but it does sound like he's afraid, and that fear generated an immediate reaction.*

*Now let's talk about the other issue, his threatening to hurt you. Has he ever done this before to you or anyone else? Is this the brother you adore talking or is it his fear? You didn't mention how old you are or where your parents are in this, but you might want to talk with them if they're around.*

*Try to stay calm. Stay loving. Listen to your brother and be present for him. Don't assume he's guilty; the world already does. That's how we tend to see the formerly incarcerated. Don't let your own fear and anxiety change your relationship with him in the absence of evidence. It's up to you to be the person who upholds the great ideal: innocent until proven guilty.*

Ella didn't know if that was a decent answer, but it was one that felt right to her, especially with how confusing guilt and innocence really were. She sent the responses off, and two days later Pearl called her.

At first, they just talked. Pearl asked her what advice columns she read, if any, and what books she liked. She asked how she might react to being called bad names, which made her laugh, because wasn't that what prison was all about most of the time?

"I have an iron skin," Ella said.

Pearl steered the conversation around to herself, talking about painting her house, every room a different color, about how cold Ann Arbor winters are. "You'll need a really warm coat," Pearl told her.

"I love the cold," Ella lied, a warm, hopeful light building in her stomach. "The more hats and scarves, the better."

"Ha, you say that now," Pearl laughed, and then she cleared her throat. "Well, you know, the other applicants have much more experience than you do—though some, of course, aren't crazy about the salary—"

"The salary is fine—"

"But I like talking with you," Pearl continued, "and that's important. And I like how fast you are. Do you know some of the applicants haven't even turned in their first assignment yet? That just won't do. And I like your answers, which manage to be honest and yet compassionate. And short, too. Like I asked for."

Ella's heart beat faster.

"Let me think about it," Pearl said. "I'll call you in a week. We have a small office on the university campus, but you can work from home if that's okay."

"I'll start knitting my mittens," Ella said. She felt like an idiot for saying that, but Pearl laughed.

IN THE FIRST week of August, Pearl offered Ella the job. "You can start the second week of September," she said. "Give yourself time to move and settle in, and give HR time to process all the paperwork."

As soon as Ella hung up, she sat there, unable to move, her breath quickening.

But when the *Grapevine Arbor* emailed her the employment forms five minutes later, wanting her to sign, scan and send them back, there it was, glaring up at her, the box you had to check if you were a felon. Ella's stomach roiled. If she checked yes, she wouldn't get the job. She wouldn't get to see her daughter. What if she didn't check it? What if she could lie and say she hadn't seen the check box? She could make it vanish, just like she was trying to forget her prison sentence. What if she made herself so invaluable that by the time they found out—if they ever found out—it wouldn't matter?

She filled in *B.A. Psychology*. They didn't have to know it was a prison program. It was still a degree and from an accredited institution, something to be proud of, not defensive about. Then she checked the box that read, *No, not a felon.* One truth and a lie.

She was sweating now, but she filled out the rest of the form, scanned it, and then hit Send before she could change her mind.

"WILL I LIKE Ann Arbor?" Helen asked that night. "I imagine there'll always be work for a good dressmaker."

Her face was open and hopeful, her eyes bright. Ella could see her mother scanning the apartment as if she were deciding what to take and what to leave behind, and how exciting that would all be. Ella felt a whip of sorrow, or maybe it was guilt, because didn't Helen deserve more, too, than to be left behind again? Hadn't Helen given up so much for her?

"Mom," Ella said, "I need to go out there on my own."

Helen froze. "What?" She reached behind her for a chair and sat down. "I just got you back, after all these years. I just got you back and you want to leave me?"

"I need to see what it's like to be on my own, to see if I can make it." Ella heard the tremor in her voice. Her mother looked so sad and small that Ella wanted to fling herself into her mother's lap and apologize, but instead she steeled herself.

Helen rubbed her forehead and blinked hard. "All these years . . . ," she said.

"You know you'll always be welcome in my home."

"Your home," Helen repeated quietly. She ran a hand under her eyes. "I thought *this* was your home. I thought wherever we were together was home."

"You can visit. I want you to visit," Ella said. "Please, Mom. I need to do this. It doesn't mean I don't love you or need you. And the job doesn't start until September, so I'll still be here for a while. I just wanted to tell you." Ella bit her lower lip. "So you can share my excitement."

Helen looked at Ella. "Of course, baby," she said quickly. "You're an adult now. It's probably right that you should at least see what it's like to be on your own."

"I'm still going to have you visit," Ella said. "It's not like I'm cutting you off here."

"Well, then," Helen said. "I can't wait to visit."

"Maybe you'll be relieved when I'm gone," Ella said. "You can have your life back!"

"Oh yes," Helen said. But she didn't look at Ella when she said it.

That night, when the lights were out and Ella was trying to sleep, she heard her mother crying. She lifted herself up. She could go to her. She could tell her the truth about her fear. She could say that she'd stay longer, and then Helen would relax. Helen would wrap her arms around her, holding her just a little too tight, a little too long.

Instead, Ella settled back down in the bed, her eyes wide open until Helen's crying stopped.

HELEN HELPED ELLA find an Ann Arbor apartment online that she could afford, just two low-ceilinged rooms in a shabby two-story duplex. She would have the top floor, and her own private entrance at the top of a staircase on the side. Helen offered to help with the rent. "Your first apartment," she said, but her voice was tinged with sorrow.

Ella had been among adult women in prison, women who'd told her about their home lives, about paying bills, managing kids. But these had just been stories to Ella. She hadn't lived any of that herself.

Helen showed Ella how to set up a budget, but Ella was already looking for ways to conserve, to make the most of what she had. When Helen gave her money to buy their weekly groceries, Ella compared the prices of things, always going for the least expensive brand. She used to love to buy paperback novels when she was in high school, to own them, but now she began to use the library because books felt expensive, like an indulgence. And then, amid the lingering fear, a new feeling began to take hold: pride.

ONE DAY, HELEN came home with a second car, a creamy yellow beater with red upholstery.

"You bought another car?" Ella asked.

"It's used," Helen said. "Very used. But it runs. And it's for you because it's best to learn on a car you're going to be using. You need to learn how to drive. You can't go to a place without a subway system and not know how."

Ella blinked at the car. She slid into the driver's seat, her hands shaking. Helen buckled herself into the passenger's seat and put her hand on top of Ella's. "Don't be nervous," she said. "You've got this. Step on the gas and turn right."

Ella practiced driving for the month of August, until she began to feel like she was part of the car, that it could reliably do what she asked it to. The day she passed her driving test, she drove through the entire city—Ella steering confidently, Helen blinking back her sorrow. Ella drove carefully through the thickets of families strolling in Park Slope, over the Brooklyn Bridge, and into Manhattan. She drove up the east side, from the East Village through Murray Hill, then Turtle Bay, and up to the Upper East Side where Jude had lived. When they passed his home, Helen looked away.

"You can relax a little," she said gently, tapping Ella's knuckles on the wheel. But Ella had to make sure she was taking in everything—the crooked tree on the corner, the red door on a brownstone—because this might be the last time she would ever see it.

FINALLY, ON A freakishly hot September day, Ella and Helen stood out on the street in front of Ella's packed car.

Helen's mouth wobbled. "I could squeeze in the trunk," she said.

The heat was coming in waves. The car didn't have an air conditioner, so Ella had all the windows open. She had gone into prison a teenager, and here she was now, something else—not exactly an adult, but maybe on her way to being one. She reached for Helen, wanting to rest her head against her mother's shoulder one more time, to inhale the lemony scent of her mother's shampoo. But Helen stepped back, her hands flying up, her eyes watering.

"You can do anything now. Be anything you want," Helen said quietly.

"You helped me."

"You helped yourself, honey."

"Mom," Ella said. "You have to let me hug you."

"I don't like goodbyes," Helen said. "I just want us to say, 'See you soon.'" Her hands were shaking, and for the first time, Ella noticed the blue veins in her mother's hands, the dry, wispy edges of her hair. *She'll still be here. Any time I want to come back.*

"See you soon," Ella said quietly.

"I'm going inside so I don't have to watch you go." Then Helen lurched toward Ella, holding her tight, breathing against her neck.

"Call me every day. Be safe. Be happy," she whispered. "That's what I want for you." Helen let go first.

"That's what I want for you, too," Ella said.

"My Ella."

"Mom—" Ella said again. For the first time she realized that she wouldn't see her mother every morning, and a bloom of panic rose in her throat. "I'm going to miss you."

"Don't you know that I'm always with you?" Helen said quietly. "Wherever you are. Wherever you go. I'm there."

Helen tapped Ella's heart and then her own. "Us against the world, remember?" she said, her smile wobbling again. "Always was, always will be. Check the glove compartment." Then she turned and walked back into the apartment.

Ella got in the car and drove. She didn't check the glove compartment until she was out of New York State, at a rest stop parking lot, so sweaty that her shirt was sticking to the upholstery. She snapped the glove box open. There it was, a white envelope, probably a letter full of advice Ella would never consider taking—but when she ripped it open, a check fluttered out. She stared at it. It was for the money Helen had saved while Ella was in prison. Ella hadn't even thought to ask for it, because she knew that Helen could use that money. She felt like a thief—stealing from her mother, on top of the crime of leaving her behind.

# TWO

# Brooklyn

*October 2018*

> *Dear Clancy,*
>
> *I caught my mom snooping on my phone and let's just say she saw things I didn't want her to see, including that I was skipping school and sneaking out at night to be with my boyfriend, a boy they don't approve of because he is older than I am. I'm 14 and he is 16, but we are both VERY mature for our ages! She now wants to drive me to and from school so I won't have a chance to see my boyfriend AT ALL. And she's grounded me unless I'm with girlfriends and am under adult supervision. I am in PRISON here! What can I do?*
>
> *Signed, Desperate Inmate*

Helen was hunched over her computer, reading her daughter's column, which Ella's editor had decided to call Dear Clancy. Ella had been gone only a month, and at first Ella had called her every other night, always with a story about how busy Ann Arbor was, how delicious the food was, how she loved her job and her apartment, and no she never saw her landlady. But lately, Ella's calls were truncated, evasive almost. Helen had kept asking Ella over and over when her first column would be out, and all Ella told her was soon.

Now Helen was sitting alone in her apartment, reading the column over and over again.

*Desperate inmate.* She cringed at those ugly words. What did that letter writer know of prison to even dare to make a comparison like that?

Missing Ella hadn't gotten any easier. She knew all the wisdom about being a parent. You don't have kids to keep them. Your kids are only on loan. They don't really belong to you, at least not forever. But in the Hasidic community in which she had grown up, kids were the seeds that rooted people even deeper in the community. They were always close by, sometimes in their own place but across the street from family, so it seemed as if they never left. She ached just imagining such a thing. She felt the same fierce love that she'd felt when she'd nestled Ella in her arms as a baby, when Ella and Jude had been part of her household, when Ella had come home from prison to her. She loved Ella more now, even though she sometimes thought that Ella loved her less.

Sometimes Helen would swear she heard Ella humming in the other room or clattering in the kitchen. She missed her daughter when she was food shopping, and still caught herself buying the chocolate cookies Ella liked, or the frozen yogurt, and she couldn't bring herself to eat any of it. All she had to do was look at these groceries and her appetite would vanish. She had made roast chicken dinners for Ella, pork chops and fresh veggies, but on her own, she stuck to cheese and bread, or sometimes just a bag of potato chips for dinner.

Helen sighed and walked to the window. She kept thinking that reading Ella's column might create a connection, that maybe she would find clues as to how her daughter was coping or even feeling. Why had Ella chosen to respond to that particular letter? Why would she want to be reminded of that word, *inmate*? Helen certainly didn't. No, Helen wanted to be able to kvell over her daughter, the newspaper writer. A columnist! But she couldn't. Ella's column came out under a different name, with a ridiculous photo of a woman who looked nothing like her beautiful daughter. Still, she knew that Ella had gotten lucky landing this job.

"Are you guilty?" she had whispered to Ella when she had first been allowed to see her at the police station. "Did you do this?" But Ella had just stared at her and then down at her confession, and when Helen saw it was written in Ella's own hand, she had felt punched in her heart. Her daughter's whole body was shaking; her mouth was locked shut. After that, nothing else mattered except that Ella was her daughter and there wasn't anything she wouldn't do for her.

But how strange that Ella was working for a paper, especially when newspapers hadn't been kind to her, splashing the story across New York like a spill of sticky beer, everyone reading, wanting more, more, more. By the time Ella was trending on Twitter, Helen had shuttered both of their accounts in disgust. The journalists acted as if they knew her daughter, and they attacked Helen in their sordid articles, too, blinding her with the lights from their cameras, making her face look small and white, like a torn petal. She wanted to just forget, when all those people out there wanted to remember, and to have fun doing it.

Helen had asked Ella to take photos of her new apartment, to send her pictures of Ann Arbor. She kept checking her phone, but there weren't any photos. Once, she had taken her cell and had snapped a shot of the living room table. She sent it to Ella along with a text: *The table misses you!* She had thought Ella would think it was funny, but she hadn't received a response, so then she had typed, *You okay?* Ella had typed back, *Yes! Love you!* And that had been that.

She reread the answer Clancy had given:

> *No one can completely make your life a prison. I am betting your parents are worried simply because you are so very young. First, there are all sorts of ways to exert freedom in a confined circumstance. Dig deep within yourself to find something that comforts you, something not under your parents' lock and key. Maybe it's a journal where you write your feelings. Maybe it's the act of making plans for the day when they will no longer be in control of your time. If you cannot talk to your parents just*

*yet, write them a letter showcasing how responsible you have been in the past, and how your new love will not derail that. Ask them to trust you, even a little bit more. Could they meet your boyfriend and see then what you see in him? Tell them the visit can be like a test drive. Work something out, bit by bit. Free them in order to be able to free yourself.*

Helen felt stung by the words *talk to your parents*. Ella didn't talk to Helen anymore, so how could she be giving out that sort of advice?

The next letter asked whether a woman should sell the family home she loved and move somewhere warmer. Helen could never imagine selling a home, especially if she were lucky enough to own one, but Ella had answered that new starts were important. Was that what was happening to Ella out in Ann Arbor, a new start?

Helen's grief taunted her. Every time she saw a dark cap of curls, reminding her of her daughter's, she froze in pain. One night, she found herself watching one of those dumb television movies, about an estranged mother and daughter who find their way back to each other. The plot was stupid, but she was glued to it until the final embrace. When she turned off the TV, she seemed to discover herself alone, and haunted because the TV show was not her life. She felt she was slowly going mad.

She stretched, trying to shake off this darkness. It was only eight at night. She could go out, get dessert, walk around. There were so many things she could do besides worry about Ella. But of course, she would be doing them alone.

She had always had friends growing up in the Hasidic community. Maybe not close ones, but she had people around her. Before Ella went to prison, Helen had focused all her energy on her daughter. Now, though, what she had were her job at Nan's Superior Tailoring & Clothing, and the two women who worked there: Nan, the owner, and Betsy, her assistant. Superior Tailoring was in a cozy brick building on 5th Ave, not far from Helen's apartment. The shop was painted a soft salmon pink, with a decal on the window of a woman using a sewing machine, pins fanning out from her mouth like an exotic flower. Inside the shop the atmosphere was airy, colored the same pale pink, with racks of hand-tailored clothing for sale (it always thrilled Helen when someone bought one of her dresses or shirts), design magazines, and a triptych mirror. The workroom in the back was where Helen spent her hours. It held two sewing machines, one fancier than the other; a step-up fitting stand for clients so that Helen could pin whatever they had on into the right shape; and another triptych mirror.

Helen had gotten the job when she first moved to Bay Ridge. She had experience, but better than that, she was wearing one of her own designs when she came in, a floral-printed sheath cut on the bias with a lace hem, and as she was talking to Nan about a job, a client came in, pointed at Helen's dress, and exclaimed, "If that's for sale, I want it!"

Nan blinked in surprise, but Helen was prepared. "I can make you one," she said. "If you want to put down a deposit, we can take some measurements now."

"Sold," Nan had said, holding out her hand to Helen. "Start tomorrow."

AT FIRST, HELEN hadn't wanted to make friends, or to have anyone in the shop really know her. Plus, she was so busy she didn't have much time for chatter. She kept to herself in the backroom, designing, altering, only occasionally coming out into the main area to talk to a customer about a dress or shirt that wasn't draping properly. Helen ate her lunch alone, the same cheese sandwich on a roll, and an apple, every day. On her breaks, she walked around the block. It suited her.

Since Ella's departure, though, her routine no longer satisfied her. She began to venture into the main room more, to talk to the other women. She didn't know what to say at first; she just asked about hems and zippers, sleeves that were either set in or not, whether a dress should have a lace panel. It was Helen's idea that they should also stock hand-knit sweaters and scarves. Maybe gifts, too. Impulse buys. "Great idea," Betsy said.

Helen felt the words bursting from her. "We should all get lunch."

Nan's face bloomed into a smile. "Now you're talking," she said.

They went to a diner, just a block away, and settled into a red plastic booth. Helen was glad that Nan was so easy about spilling out her life. Nan was married and had a son in college who never called. Betsy, in her thirties, was engaged to a doctor who was never home, and wondered aloud if that was going to be a problem. When Nan asked Helen if she had kids, Helen swallowed. "Grown daughter," she said simply, because how could she tell them the truth, or any of her history? She was just lucky that after two years of working there, no one had recognized her yet. And why should they? She had her new name. She had colored her hair. How would anyone know her when she didn't even recognize herself?

ONE DAY, HELEN was out on the shop floor. Nan had listened to Helen's ideas for the shop, and they now had a small table piled with small gifts like leather gloves and handbags. There was another table filled with gorgeous mohair hand-knits and some woolen scarves, arranged so that all the colors showed. Helen wasn't looking forward to going home alone and was debating whether to ask Nan or Betsy if they wanted to go out after work with her for a quick dinner, when a man walked in, looking confused.

For a moment, she thought she had seen him before, but she couldn't be sure. In any case, the store didn't get very many male customers unless they were wandering in with their wives or girlfriends, which was the reason for the two upholstered chairs set in a corner, near a small table with some magazines. But this man was alone, smartly dressed in a dark suit and tie, and he tilted his head when he saw her. For a moment, Helen worried that he knew who she was, that he was going to dredge up the past and ask her all sorts of questions she couldn't answer. She busied herself folding sweaters and felt him approaching.

He smelled like pine.

"I'm looking for a gift," he told her.

Helen's shoulders relaxed. "What's she like?"

Helen loved the way he brightened. What a lucky woman, she thought, to be loved so hard that your lover would buy you something lovely.

"She's funny. She loves baseball. Neutral colors."

"What else?" Helen said.

"She's sixteen, my niece. What do I know about women's clothes?"

As soon as she heard the word *niece*, Helen felt buoyant. That made him even more special, that he was buying for his niece. "You don't have to know, because I do," she said, warming to him even more. She helped him pick out a mohair hand-knit the color of cream. "Who doesn't love mohair?" Helen said. "This was hand-knit by a local artisan. And cream goes with everything." When he paid for it, she saw his name on the credit card. "Morris," she said.

He laughed. "Actually, my name is Mouse. That's what I'm called. It stuck and now it's me," he said, and ran one hand over his head. "It's awful, isn't it? But then again, it's better than Morris, my given name."

"Morris is a nice name," Helen said.

She was just completing the transaction when she noticed his expensive-looking leather gloves, the fine weave of his suit. He was handsome, but surely out of her league, and surely not from this neighborhood, either.

"Where do you live?" she asked, trying to sound casual.

"Upper West Side," he said.

"What are you doing all the way out here?" she asked, surprised. "That's quite a trek."

"I just like exploring different neighborhoods," he said, smiling.

When she handed him the sweater in a gift box, his hand grazed hers, and she felt a jolt of heat. He must have felt it, too, because he pulled his hand back, hesitating, watching Helen rub her fingers.

"So," he said awkwardly, and then he turned and walked out of the store.

That night, Helen called Ella, and to her delight, Ella picked up. "Darling!" Helen said.

"You sound so great," Ella said. "What's going on?"

Helen sighed. It suddenly felt too soon to tell Ella she had met someone nice, someone who brought a bit of sun in her life. "I had a nice day today, that's all," Helen said.

MOUSE CAME BACK to the shop a week later, and then two other times, always looking a little lost. He always bought something, and somehow, she knew what he wanted. She showed him a gorgeous cashmere scarf and wrapped it around his neck and spun him toward the mirror to show him how it accentuated his gray eyes. Another time he came in and all he said was, "Brrr, I need a new jacket," and Helen showed him one she had made of soft dark wool. Each time, he stayed a little longer.

She kept finding things to show him: a new wallet on the gift table that he might like because of its slim, sleek shape, or a tie she had hand sewn herself. He bought both, and as soon as he left, she wanted him to come back in. She began to realize how much she counted on his visits. It became a joke between them, the reasons he gave her for being there. Once he told her that he had read about a fancy new cheese store down the street from the shop and he had to try it out. "What, there's no good cheese on the Upper West Side?" she said, making him laugh.

"Not like this," he said, meeting her eyes.

HE WAS BACK again a week later, and this time, he looked nervous. Mouse drew himself up. "Please forgive me for being brazen, but have you had lunch?"

She loved that he had used the word *brazen*. It made her think he was educated, that he read. But she could hear the warning signals in her mind. Men lead to trouble.

"I don't know—" She hesitated. "Maybe another time."

He stepped back, deflated. "Of course," he said, straightening his shoulders, and he left shortly after.

As soon as he was gone, she regretted thwarting his request. She had to admit that she was lonely.

How lucky some people were to have a big, noisy family. How lucky she had been to have known that joy herself, if only for a little while, when she had been young, living in the Williamsburg community in Brooklyn. She had once been someone else. Her name had been Shaindy. She still loved the sound of it, but now when she said it to herself, she felt a stab of pain. It used to be a name that was said with love.

She missed the crowd of relatives she'd had as a child, the grandparents on both sides, and the great-grandparents, too, because people in the community often became parents as early as eighteen. And of course, the cousins and nephews and nieces, all part of the tight-knit Hasidic community in which she had grown up. Such a wealth of family in Williamsburg! The joyful family meals. So much food and laughter. Always groups of girls, her friends, gossiping about the matches and marriages they might have, the kids they would raise, how they would have nine, ten, maybe twelve. Helen had been very happy then.

She had known from the time she was very young that her community was separate from the rest of the world, and hers was one blessed and chosen by God. They were special and protected! She knew, too, that she didn't ever have to worry. There was a path for her to follow, and if something made her stumble, the community would help her. They'd bandage her knees before she had even skinned them. She had seen it—how when her parents couldn't afford the rent one month, word had spread, and all the other families pulled together and paid for the next two months. When her sister was sick, another family came and took her to the right doctor, one from the community. There were so many volunteer organizations. One took care of new mothers, sending over cooked meals, used baby clothes, seats and cribs, and organizing carpools for whatever the family needed. Another group helped put together weddings for families who couldn't afford the huge events everyone wanted. They rented out beautiful wedding gowns, made loans at no interest, and even helped with the purchase of the bride's first *sheitel,* the wig worn for modesty, or the groom's expensive *shtreimel,* the fur hat worn on high holidays.

Those who lived outside the community—those who were not Hasidic, not even Orthodox, who dared to parade in shorts and bare heads, the ones who believed in nothing—were to be pitied because no one would do the same for them. The outsiders were to be shunned. Hashem didn't love them. And back then, neither did Helen. Just the thought of being an "other" terrified her.

Helen knew how outsiders could hurt her, staring and snickering at her and her family, sometimes shouting *Jew,* twisting the word into a curse. The outsiders wanted to eradicate her community, to break them apart and banish them from the world. She herself had known their looks of hatred.

"We take care of our own," her mother had told her.

The community had their own ambulance, their own police, their own doctors, and if they did sometimes deal with non-Hasidic people, it was because friends, people they trusted, had recommended them and said they were fine. No one could destroy the community, though they tried, with their secular libraries full of lies, their sneers, their taunts.

Living in the community brought joy, but as she grew older, she began to realize that some aspects of the community were not so joyful. The songs they sang were wonderful, but girls were not allowed to sing them along with the men, so Helen sang them to herself when she was alone. The one song she was permitted to sing was a Yiddish singsong that listed dozens of things she must never do.

Her mother was always in the kitchen, usually tired. She would cook even when she was ill and coughing into a cloth. At meals, her brothers were served first, and they never had to help out the way Helen did. If she hadn't followed those rules, there'd be gossip about her, and she would have had to face sideways glances every time she stepped out into the street. She couldn't even confide her dissatisfaction to her girlfriends because of that fear.

Her brothers had separate, different lives—lives that had nothing to do with her. Her younger brother Yankel had a happy celebration when he was just three, when he got his first tallit katan, with white strings and knots at the corners that would hang over his hips forever. His beautiful soft locks were cut for the first time, except for the long tufts from above each ear, which her mother lovingly twisted with a rag and sugar water into curls.

Her brothers didn't learn English, only Hebrew, Yiddish, and Aramaic, all of it to labor over learning the Talmud and Jewish law. But girls could learn English, enough to be able to function in the world, because they had to do that for their husbands and families.

Helen had known all the things banned to her and she had pretended not to be eaten alive with curiosity about them: secular books, dating, forbidden foods like the glossy red lobsters she sometimes saw in the markets. A cheeseburger because you couldn't mix milk products with meat, no matter how delicious it sounded. You had to be careful because people here loved to gossip about others, especially if you dared to do anything different.

Helen had never married, but she was supposed to. When she was seventeen, right on track, a matchmaker met with her parents, the same one her older friends had used, a woman famous for the fruitful matches she made. She had interviewed Helen, asked whom she knew, how she prayed, how she helped her mother.

Oh, it was so exciting! Her future, unfurling in front of her.

There was so much to look forward to, like the kallah classes that prepared women for marriage. But then, as she thought more about married life, she had felt so confused about what it was going to feel like to sleep next to a man, to see him undress, to let him touch her. She wondered if her curiosity was immodest, if it was wrong to wonder and want to know. She knew that her purpose was to bear children, but just thinking about sex was so dark and confusing that she felt her mind shut down.

But Helen's chances weren't as good as other girls'. Her little sister Esti had to take insulin shots for diabetes every day, which was a continuing expense a boy's family might feel would be a burden. The boys the matchmaker found for her all seemed to have issues, too: their parents were divorced, or there was also illness in their family.

The boys she met seemed so much younger than her brothers, so much more awkward, like they had stones on their tongues. Their long black coats were made from less expensive material, often shiny or frayed from wear. Sometimes their side curls had food caught in them or were poorly kept—so unlike her brothers, all of whom took pride in their appearance.

Helen's suitors seemed more juvenile than she had expected a possible husband to be. One boy had bitten his nails until they bled. Another had kept snorting for some reason and hadn't even said excuse me. She had been so excited, so full of hope, but as she looked at them, one by one, sitting across from her at her parents' dining room table, she felt nothing but boredom and foreboding. She couldn't imagine marrying a single one.

Her mother had disagreed.

"It's you that's the problem, not them," her mother had said. "Other girls would kill to be matched with such fine, righteous boys." She nagged her to brush her hair more carefully. And next time, don't slouch in her seat the way she always did.

The matchmaker had told her parents that each of the boys Helen met with had passed on her as a potential spouse. There were always reasons, which the matchmaker phrased as things Helen could improve on. Did Helen have to joke so much? Not everyone appreciated her humor. Did she have to so readily express her opinions? No boy wanted a wife who brought nothing to the marriage but stubbornness and trouble.

The gossip about her brewed and spread, reflecting badly on both her and her family. Her parents and siblings were all furious with her.

"What about *our* matches?" her younger sisters had asked. "Already everyone is talking."

People began to whisper that Helen had turned away from the righteous path, and even when she told them point blank that the accusation was ridiculous—that her faith and her community were her life—she felt no one believed her. If this kept up, her parents warned, they wouldn't be able to marry the rest of the children.

"The next match will be it," Helen had promised, tired of the looks, of the gossip. When her mother had suggested they go shopping in Manhattan, at Macy's because they needed something special to make Helen stand out, something to catch a nice boy's eye, Helen agreed.

Ultimately, her mother had chosen a heavy navy skirt that came to midcalf, with white piping on the bottom, and a white blouse with a slightly ruffled high collar.

"This will work!" her mother had said. "Just look at you."

On the subway ride home, Helen had carried her package like a treasure. But then, when her mother had closed her eyes, someone across from Helen got up and left a paperback behind on the seat. *A Tree Grows in Brooklyn.* Helen was used to reading Jewish books, with characters who wore wigs like her mother, or payes like her brothers. These were books about girls who had adventures no more thrilling than figuring out how to be happy with what they had, or how to turn the mishap of carrying money during Shabbos into a mitzvah by leaving the coins on the street for someone who needed it. She had known that all secular books were forbidden, but the cover of this book whispered to her. It showed a girl in an immodest skirt sitting in a tree and reading, looking like she was dreaming up the most amazing future. It was about Brooklyn, where she lived, and she couldn't imagine the harm in just looking at it. Besides, she most likely wouldn't have another chance, and no one else was paying attention to it. As they got off the train, she scooped up the book and hid it in her jacket.

She had told herself she would read just a page and then dispose of it, because she had known it was wrong. Everything she'd read before in school had a clear moral to the story. This didn't seem to be the case with *A Tree Grows in Brooklyn*. Francie wasn't content with only what she had. She yearned for more, and she yearned a lot. When Helen started to read it, she couldn't stop. She carried the book everywhere, enthralled by the story. Francie had felt like a friend—Francie, who yearned for a bigger world and didn't seem to mind if people thought she was different. When Helen finished the novel, she read it again. Suddenly, when she looked at her life, the colors she had loved now seemed dimmer, the people seemed faded and they blended into one another, all looking the same. Her life felt torn, and it was all her doing. She couldn't go to a better school like Francie did. She didn't have parents who would push her to be better than they were.

She shouldn't have read that book. She shouldn't have dared. And now look what had happened. This yearning was punishment. She had been on another path to another future, meeting with the matchmaker, waiting for her whole glorious future like a banquet she couldn't wait to taste. And now she hungered for something completely different. With the seed of doubt firmly planted, another world opened for her— but she had lost her family.

Helen always told herself that she never regretted the break with her early life because it had led to Ella. But sometimes now she had to cover her ears because she was sure she heard her father and brothers singing at the table. She felt her father's hands blessing her head. She had to shut her eyes because she remembered the glow of the Shabbos lights, the bustle in the kitchen of her mother and sisters cooking meals together. How special it had been to be a part of that family. To feel so loved. How wonderful not just to believe in a path but to see proof of its righteousness everywhere. *We'll always be there for you.*

And now here it was again. The yearning. She had told Ella the story of her past with all its rules because she wanted her daughter to grow up differently, open to the world around her, to the many experiences she could have. Helen had been such a free and easy mother to Ella, but now she wondered if letting Ella grow up without a framework was one of the things that led her to the trouble that would be the beginning of the end for them both.

Maybe, she thought, that nice man, that Mouse, would come back again, and she wouldn't be so lonely. But maybe he had changed his mind about her, found someone more suitable. Maybe, too, Ella would visit soon.

Maybe. All these maybes.

A FEW DAYS later, Helen was in the backroom designing a dinner suit out of purple crepe when Nan peeked in.

"There's a man looking for you," she said, beaming.

Helen walked out into the shop, and there was Mouse, shifting his weight from foot to foot. Helen felt a spark of joy.

"Mouse," she said, delighted. "What brings you to the neighborhood this time? A new restaurant? A bakery?" She winked at him, wanting to tease. "A bowling alley?"

"Just you," he said, laughing. "I would have come sooner, but I got so busy at work, and then I started second-guessing myself about whether you'd really want to see me again." He looked down at his tie and straightened it. "I'm probably a fool, coming back here to find you, to ask you to a lunch you already rejected—"

Helen had just finished her cheese sandwich and apple, but now that she had this second chance, she felt braver. She didn't want him to leave. She looked up at his kind face, and she decided in that moment that this was the time for her, like Ella, to make a new start.

"Why?" she asked.

"Because you're intriguing. Because you're different from any woman I've ever met."

"In that case, I'm starving."

# THREE

# Ann Arbor

*October 2018*

Ella returned to the blue house on Third Street, crouched down behind two bushes, then watched and waited for the little girl to appear. The neighborhood was unusually empty today, with only a few cars and a battered white truck.

She had walked here from her apartment in Kerrytown, the way she always did, taking different routes so that no one would begin to recognize her. It was just a short walk, an easy half hour, even quicker if she took her bike. This neighborhood was eclectic and becoming gentrified. Two-story historic houses, with real porches, walkways to the doors, and even turrets on the windows, mixed with two-story clapboard homes that looked as if they had seen better days. Her daughter's home looked like a combination of both, with its white wraparound porch badly in need of a paint job. The windows weren't fancy either, but they allowed her to see snatches of the rooms from her crouched position behind the bushes. And some days, like today when no one was around, she could stand up and casually explore.

It was only October, but already she shivered from cold. She wished she could afford one of those expensive sheepskin coats so many of the college kids wore. Well, they probably had trust funds, rich families. All Ella had was herself—and the check Helen had given her, but she couldn't bring herself to use it unless she had to. Unless one of those coats found its way to the Salvation Army store on campus—so marked down that she could afford it—she would never have one.

She had been in Ann Arbor less than two months, arriving in September with the onslaught of students, and here it was nearly Halloween. When she realized how walkable the city was, she had sold the car Helen had given her and bought a bike, socking away the money, not telling her mother. That cushion of cash made her feel better, and having a bike helped her blend in with the students.

She came to the Third Street house almost every day, always at different times. She told herself over and over that she was twenty-two years old, not sixteen. She kept hearing that lawyer's voice in her head, and Helen's, too: *They will never give your child back.* But her yearning pulled at her like a rubber band, constantly stretched to the edge of snapping. She had to know her daughter. Even if all she did was see her, she had to somehow be close to the one beautiful thing she had created in her life.

She didn't see the family every time she came here—not even most times. The first time she had seen them had been a chilly day in September. They had come out the front door, and Ella had stumbled backward, almost falling. She figured that the burly man in the baseball cap taking the front steps two at a time had to be Mark. The woman with the long curly hair had to be Marianna. And oh! That child! In overalls and a green velour T-shirt, her chocolate hair in pigtails. "Carla, let's go," Mark said, opening the car door, and then Ella knew her daughter's name. Carla. A name so beautiful it almost made her cry.

She had watched as Mark reached for Carla's hand. "What, you lost another mitten?" he said. Carla then showed her father her free hand wearing a sky-blue mitten. "One does no good," Mark said, scolding, but his voice was gentle, and Ella liked the way that Carla grinned and then wrapped herself around her dad, putting her hands in his jacket pockets. She had a good daddy, then. That was something to hold on to. Marianna was laughing. That was something to hold on to, too. They seemed like a happy family today.

The family piled into a white Honda Accord and then sped away, while Ella stood, hugging herself tight, waiting for her heartbeat to slow.

She spotted them again a week later, when she was biking across campus. They were walking home, everyone carrying a bag, and she circled around the block twice, then three times, for another glimpse before they vanished.

Ella came back the next day and the next, and each time she saw them, she learned something new. The man had a collection of baseball caps, a different one every day, each one festooned with the name of a sports team. *Does he like them all?* she wondered. She once heard the man snipe, "Please, not gluey spaghetti again tonight," and the woman dipped her head, so Ella knew she wasn't such a hot cook. And the girl! The little girl could whistle songs. She could hop on one foot for the count of fifteen. She was always saying, *Look at me! Look at me!* And Ella always looked, snatching these moments from odd angles through the windows.

But the truth was, she didn't know how she might parent her own child. She hadn't had siblings or ever really been around kids. She had never babysat. This gave a new purpose to her watching: she'd take her clues from Carla's parents to figure it out.

After a while, she noticed a pattern. During the weekdays, the family left the house each morning at eight. They bounded home around three. The little girl went to Green Tree Elementary School, just a block and a half away, and sometimes to one of the two neighborhood playgrounds: one next to the school on Fifth Street, and then a larger playground where kids played soccer next to a big hill that she knew had to be great for sledding come winter. On weekends, the family walked to campus to get frozen yogurt, always at Get Spooned, or to a movie, or sometimes just to the dollar store. She didn't think they had ever noticed her, though she could never be sure, and one time, she was almost certain that Marianna had been looking right at her.

One night, Ella followed Mark, letting him lead her to the Old Town Tavern off West Liberty Street, where he worked as a bartender. While Mark served drinks and cleaned glasses, Ella sat at a booth and nursed a glass of red wine, waiting. She leaned forward so she could catch bits of his conversation, not relaxing again until she heard him tell someone his wife was an accountant and maybe she could look at this guy's taxes for him. Ella returned to her drink.

The bar closed at eleven, but Mark stayed, cleaning up. Ella waited a block away until she saw him locking up, and then she followed him home, waiting yet again until he had gone into his house before she wound her way back to her apartment.

Ella climbed the side stairway up to her apartment on the second floor, quietly opening her door with her key. The people downstairs had their TV blasting, and she knew it would come up through her floor. But she was used to noise. Plus, to her surprise, it made her feel less alone.

She had a fold-out couch to sleep on, a table for her laptop, a chair, and a tiny kitchen, and she loved it. Her own place! She could lock the door when she wanted privacy, and she could open both her windows when she wanted noise: the churn of motorcycles, the buzz of people.

She had tried her best to make it homey. She had bought supplies at Ann Arbor Arts for a vision board, hanging it right over her little table, pinning up photos of what she hoped her life could be. A little house by the Arb and the Huron River so she could smell the trees all the time. In the corner was a tiny photo she had surreptitiously taken of Carla. She reached up and gently touched it.

THE WEEK SHE arrived, Ella had walked over to the ground-floor office of the *Grapevine Arbor* on North Division Street. There were several rows of cubicles filled with people, phones ringing, and in the back, a glass office. There was Pearl, looking out through the glass wall and waving her over. She looked to be about the same age as Helen, and she seemed surprised when she saw how young Ella was. "Ah, well," Pearl said. "Sometimes the unexpected can be good."

Pearl asked someone to bring them lattes, and then led her into the office, talking nonstop. She learned that Pearl drove a Mercedes and lived in the village of Barton Hills, on an acre of land, in a house you couldn't even see from the road, with her husband, a banker. She showed Ella a photo of her house, which looked like a mansion—all woods and dormer windows.

"People think that because I live in the Hills Village, I don't do anything but golf, but I'm different. Some of the women there have a lot of money and they just need things to keep them busy," she said. "Not me. I admit I aspire to greatness. And I don't want this paper to be just for people who have third homes here. I want it to be for everyone. Reader-friendly and all that. And I assure you, the newspaper is so much more than a hobby."

She continued, "So. Let's talk about your being our Clancy Brown. After my know-it-all aunt, whom I loved devotedly and who died two years ago. I'm still not over it." Pearl wanted to use a doctored photo of her aunt for the column. "No one knowing who Clancy is just adds to the intrigue. And I like to think it's making the real Clancy happy somewhere."

The process would be simple, Pearl said. Dear Clancy would run every Sunday, and all Ella had to do was make sure she had everything emailed to Pearl by Friday. Pearl would edit the column herself and pass it on for web upload. Ella would have a special email address for the digital letters, and an assistant would forward mail from the Dear Clancy post office box for the readers who preferred to handwrite their queries.

Ella was sent on her way, flustered but excited.

SLOWLY, QUESTIONS BEGAN to trickle in. The first few letters were easy to answer—about getting a cat when your boyfriend was allergic ("There are hypoallergenic cats," Clancy suggested), or whose turn it was to do the dishes ("Make a chart," Clancy said)—but Pearl told

Ella not to worry. "They'll deluge you soon." In the meantime, she recommended that Ella get to know her "inner Clancy" and settle in.

Ella started a second vision board, this one right next to her first board, both in her bite-sized kitchen—just a half fridge, a two-burner stove, and one cabinet. Since her meeting with Pearl, she had begun the process of becoming Clancy, starting with the doctored photo of Pearl's aunt. In the picture, Clancy was a striking middle-aged woman with a dirty-blond shag and a bobbed nose, smiling empathetically at the reader. Ella had found photographs of what she thought Clancy's personality would be like, slowly building a vision of who she imagined her character to be. A photo of a woman striding down a gravel road in cowboy boots represented Clancy as an ass-kicker. A couple holding hands showed that Clancy knew love. A woman accepting an award for writing meant Clancy was acclaimed before this, so of course Clancy could do this job easily.

It felt good to be Clancy. To be someone else. It felt safe. And every day, once she stepped into that space, she knew just what to say, just how to respond to people.

THE DAY AFTER she met Pearl at the newspaper, Ella was back by the blue house, crouching for hours, waiting for the family with no success. She walked home through the Diag, the square in the middle of campus, then past a huge block sculpture resting on a point. People looked at her as if there was nothing wrong with her striding among these college kids. She didn't want to go home just yet, so she wandered to her other favorite places: Literati, a bookshop with a black-and-white painted checkerboard floor she loved. She loved too, that the owners, Mike and Hilary, always said hello and let her browse. She stopped at Wooly Bully, a yarn store, and then at Rad Threads, where the students shopped. She studied the purchases of other young people so that she could buy the same things and look even more like them. And finally, before she went home, she wandered over to Vicki's Wash and Wear Cuts on Murray Avenue, a maple-lined street with cozy two-story homes that looked like they came from *It's a Wonderful Life.* Helen had always trimmed her hair growing up, and then Ella had learned to do it herself in prison. But now she wanted to treat herself, and if that meant giving up a little control, so be it.

Ella had heard women at the yarn shop talking about Vicki, the proprietor and stylist, how much they liked her, how she could coax your hair into turning somersaults if that's what you wanted. As soon as Vicki came to the door, slender as a swizzle stick, her hair rambunctiously curly, her face bright with a smile, Ella liked her. "Come on and sit and we'll talk hair," Vicki said.

There was a confident gentleness in Vicki's hands on her scalp, a soothing cadence to her voice. "I see your natural color growing in," Vicki said. "Red as a russet apple!" Vicki told her to leave it alone, not to coat it with dye.

"It doesn't look stupid like this?" Ella asked, and Vicki assured her that the only thing it looked like was real, and real was always beautiful.

The scissors seemed to whisper by her, and Vicki kept talking, all the while helping Ella build a new lexicon. *A Squared* was shorthand for Ann Arbor. *The Ugly* meant the UGLi, the undergraduate library. She now knew not to go out when the Michigan football team had a home game because the streets would be clogged with frat boys in team jerseys and hats, their faces painted half yellow and half blue, and crazy fans pumping their fists into the air and shouting. Vicki told her about the town of Ypsilanti, how it was cooler than A Squared and so close, but also full of crime.

When she left Vicki's, her hair trimmed, her scalp feeling like it was glowing, she walked back home, studying how girls her age acted with one another, how they threw their heads back and laughed, how some girls moved as if they owned the street.

It was later now, almost dusk. She knew she could go to the bars, pick someone up, go home with him, and then leave before daylight. But she didn't feel ready. Maybe she never would.

She turned a corner and there was Wood You, the handmade furniture shop on State Street. She needed a chair for her apartment and
this store always had strange things in the window that drew her eye.
A punk Barbie on a blue-painted wood stool. A dog perched on an
intricately carved end table. She entered the shop and noted a few customers milling around; Ella could tell by the way they were dressed
that they had money. She knew she couldn't afford to buy anything
here, but she kept running her hand along the smooth wood anyway.

A guy with floppy hair and a porkpie hat came over to her. "Hey,"
he said. "What can I show you?"

"I love your stuff, but it's priced too high for me," she admitted,
and he studied her.

"You a student?" he finally said, and she shook her head. She
thought of the college catalog she had picked up one day on impulse,
but she wasn't sure if they would take felons and she didn't want to
ask. Still, she had taken it home and read it, as if it had been a menu
and she was starving.

"Me neither," he said. "My dad says I was born with tools in my
hands and wood on the brain. And that's probably why I own this
shop." He laughed. "But not everything is expensive, you know."

He asked what her apartment was like, how much room she had,
and what kind of chair she was looking for.

"You're being kind, but—" Ella said, and then he told her he was
just going into the backroom, and he'd be right back.

When he came out, he had a bright blue chair. The arms were
curved, the legs delicately etched with small vines, and as soon as Ella
saw it, her hand flew to her stomach. "I think I need that chair," she
said. "How much?" Maybe she could pay for it in increments.

He studied her again. "Do you work?"

"I have a job," she said. "I write."

"Ten dollars then," he said.

"Come on. You're joking."

He lifted the chair up and settled it into her arms. "I'll tell you a secret. This was my old office chair and I recently made myself a new one. No room for this anymore, so if you take it, you'd be doing me a favor."

"Can I at least give you twenty-five?"

"Take the offer of ten before I mark it down to five." He tipped his hat at her.

"You're so kind," Ella said.

"Sometimes I am," he said. "I'm Henry. See you next time."

And she said it back.

THAT EVENING, ELLA settled into the chair to begin work. How beautiful it was! How comfortable! She loved the feel of the wooden arms as she stroked them. She couldn't stop looking at the graceful contours of the blue-painted wood.

When Ella had started her job, there had been only five letters. After a few weeks, there had been twenty and then thirty. Circulation of the *Grapevine Arbor* had gone up, and Pearl had called her to thank her, which had made Ella glow. If she could help others, then maybe she could help herself.

Ella scanned today's letters. Most came by email, but a few had been forwarded from the post office box. For some reason, the handwritten ones were the saddest. Some of the pages had been stained with coffee or wine, the handwriting crumpled with emotion, smeared from tears maybe.

*I feel you. I know this pain.*

There were recurring themes about one partner wanting sex more often than the other, in-law clashes, horrible bosses, troubled kids, and nasty siblings. She knew enough about psychology to intuit that most of the writers already knew what they wanted to do, they just wanted Ella's approval. For her to say: *You are not as bad a person as you think you are.* That was what most people wanted to believe.

She'd do just two letters tonight, she decided, and she opened the first. Immediately she felt the desperation rising from the words like steam:

> *My sister told me that I am "dead to her" because her ex asked me out. She believes I coerced him to want me instead of her (I don't want him at all and said no to him!) and that I did it deliberately to hurt her. I love and want my sister back. I sent her an expensive designer dress for her birthday, and she sent it back to me, scissored up into squares with a note thrown in that said: "You like this. I don't." How can I have a relationship with her again?*

Ella rubbed her temples.
She started to write:

> *Sometimes people vanish from your life and we cannot know why. Sometimes they vanish, like your sister, because she was so hurt that it might be easier for her to believe that you were the siren that drew her boyfriend to you, rather than for her to admit that maybe things just weren't going well in the relationship. Or maybe her ex isn't who she thinks he is. Let her feel her feelings. It's probably safer for her to displace her rage because she knows you will always be there for her. While him? Probably not. Tell her you hope she forgives you, even if you think you have nothing to be forgiven for. Tell her you love her. That's what really matters.*

She lost her momentum. How could she tell a stranger how to keep someone in her life when she had been unable to do the same with Jude? With Carla? She'd have to finish that one later.
She opened the next.

*I know I am homely. Don't try to convince me that I am not.*
*I know that I am, and people have told me so. I'm not enclosing*
*a photo, so don't ask. Don't tell me that photos lie. Even so, I*
*am desperate for love and since I know I cannot have it, I want*
*to know how to learn to live without it and still be happy. Can*
*you help?*

This one was hard. Ella knew all about learning to live without
love, but her personal lessons weren't for this guy, even if she did feel
for him.

*How brave to write a letter about something you believe*
*about yourself that causes you pain, and which may not be true*
*at all. But you know honesty, bravery, are much better qualities*
*than a button nose or big blue eyes. Those are the things people*
*will respond to if you let them. And to prove this, I want read-*
*ers who might like to get to know you to write to you here at*
*Dear Clancy.*

Ella knew she'd get responses. She wasn't asking anyone to do more
than write to him, and just a few letters of interest or support might
be enough to give this man confidence. She couldn't really tell people
how to live their lives, especially when she had made such a mess of her
own, but she didn't really have to: the whole secret was to let people
know you were listening, that you were bearing witness, helping them
see there could be new versions of themselves.

Her cell rang and she picked it up.

"Baby girl," Helen said. "How're you doing?"

"Busy," Ella said. She waited for the onslaught of questions, the
familiar feeling that she was a safe that Helen was trying to pry open.
Ella hated herself for it, but sometimes she would cut her mother off
completely, telling Helen she had a deadline when she didn't. Other

times she didn't answer the phone. But this time she sounded so lonely, like she had become a dry, twisted sponge that could no longer expand.

"I read your most recent column. It was great. When can I visit you there?" Helen asked.

"Soon," Ella said. Her hands ran down the lovely arms of her new chair. "What have you been up to in the city?"

But as Helen began to answer, Ella heard something different in her voice, a brightness. She told Ella that she had gone to hear the Philharmonic earlier that week. Another afternoon, she had gone to a museum to see a Van Gogh exhibit and had stood in front of a painting for so long, a guard came over to her, suspicious. When Helen paused, Ella could hear something in the background. Music, she thought.

The conversation didn't really go anywhere, but something felt strange about it and Ella couldn't place it. "What made you start going out?" she said.

There was a moment of silence, and Ella braced for what her mother might say next.

"Oh, I don't know," Helen said. "Don't I deserve to? I miss you so much I feel eaten up alive sometimes. I just try to keep busy, so I won't feel it as much."

Ella looked around her small room, glancing outside at the rusty dirt of the yard below. She loved her mother, but she wasn't ready to share her solitude, to open up her new world to her mother's scrutiny.

"You can visit soon," Ella promised.

Helen wasn't really falling apart without her, and wasn't that a good thing? Wasn't that what Ella wanted? Still, it unsettled her a little.

"What are *you* doing these days?" Helen asked, and Ella could feel the wire of tension in her mother's voice.

"You know what I'm doing. Working. Living. Why would you even ask me that?"

"Because I worry. Because I'm your mother. Because I know you."

"You think I'm going to screw things up?" Ella said.

"No, baby. Of course not. That's not what I meant—"

Ella felt herself snapping shut.

"There's my doorbell," she said, a lie. "I have to go." She hung up and shut down her computer, then picked up her needles and the yarn she had bought at Wooly Bully. She thought about Carla, her small cold hands, the missing mitten, and she began to knit a pair for her. She'd use a special yarn, a soft blue that looked like the mitten Carla had lost. She'd leave them at the door. No one would have to know she was the giver.

ON THURSDAY, WHEN her columns were finished and Carla's mittens were done, Ella walked over to Carla's house. The car was gone, so she carefully placed the mittens in the mailbox.

Then she walked to Green Tree Elementary, hoping Carla might be on the school playground and she could watch her. See if her daughter had friends, if she was a runner, or if she stayed quietly in a corner by herself. She didn't see Carla among the spill of children coming out of the school, running to their parents or caregivers, but she kept waiting.

As usual, she pretended she didn't see the ALL ADULTS MUST BE ACCOMPANIED BY A CHILD sign. She ducked down to a bench, sitting among all the nannies, the harried young mothers, and the occasional father.

She reached into her bag and took out her knitting—a sweater for Helen, which she planned as a kind of peace offering. It was a seed stitch in burnt orange that she knew her mother would love. Helen would say that every time she wore it, she would feel Ella, and maybe that was okay for now. In any case, she could knit away her nerves. She anxiously scanned the playground for Carla. She craned her neck. She got up and walked around. She sat at three different benches, finally settling into her knitting.

She was finishing a row—concentrating so hard that the laughter and yelps of the kids, the calls of their nannies or parents, blurred into a kind of music—when she felt something bounce against her leg. Surprised, she reached down to pick up a red ball.

"Hey, that's mine," a voice called out, and she looked up to see a little girl coming toward her, her dark hair in braids, a bright canary yellow coat thrown open, wearing gloves that were way too big. As the child came closer, Ella realized with a shock that it was Carla. Had she been here this whole time and Ella had missed her?

Ella's hands were shaking but she held the ball out to Carla, willing her to come closer. She wanted to touch her hair, her arms, hold her hands. She wanted to burrow her face in her neck and smell her. Carla was the image of Jude, slim as a straw, with his almond-shaped eyes and long lashes, and Ella struggled to swallow the pain of that realization. She was about to reach out and touch her, but then another voice interrupted, and there was Marianna running to them.

"Oh my God, I'm so sorry," Marianna said, her long black curls casually corralled into a ponytail. A black leather jacket, Mark's most likely, was falling off her shoulders.

Carla exuberantly flung herself into Marianna's arms.

When Marianna sat down next to her, Carla stared at Ella, and Ella realized with a start that she had no idea what to say to a kid. But then Carla said, "Mommy, watch me," and ran off to the swings, and Ella felt she had missed her chance.

"You look familiar," Marianna said, scanning Ella, her face suddenly serious. "I'm so bad with names. Do we know each other?"

"I don't think so," Ella said. She kept knitting to calm herself down.

"I'm so sure I know you. Do you know Mark?" Marianna said, and then her voice turned pointed. "My husband? He works at the Old Town Tavern nights?"

Ella rested her knitting on her lap, staring at the stitches before she looked back up at Marianna.

"It's such a small town—maybe I have seen him around."

Marianna gave her a deeper look and then seemed to relax.

"Yes, of course. There's this one guy I always see around with this long white beard, but after all these years, I still have no idea who he is." She stuck out her hand. "Hi. Sorry. I'm a little on edge today, I guess. I'm Marianna."

"Ella," Ella said.

Marianna craned her neck, watching Carla. "Which one of these little hooligans is yours?" Marianna said, and Ella stiffened.

"I don't—" she said, and stopped, because saying none wasn't true. But Marianna just nodded and then studied Ella's knitting.

"This is gorgeous," she said, reaching out, touching the yarn. "I wish I had time for something like this."

"It's easy. I can show you."

"I still wouldn't have time. I work full-time most days as an accountant. And then I have that one over there running around like a racehorse— Carla. And, to be honest, my husband is a full-time job himself . . ."

She smiled when she said it.

"I used to have so many friends when I was younger," she continued. "I miss them, I really do. But everyone's so busy that when you do have time to do something, well, you're just too exhausted."

Ella started another row, the click of the needles soothing her. "You're lucky," she said quietly. "You have a husband, a child."

"Ha," Marianna said. "You think so?"

Ella looked closer. Marianna had lines like parentheses by her mouth. Her eyes, beautiful and green as they were, were beginning to be hooded. She hadn't known Marianna's age, but she must be forty, Ella realized. Closer to Helen's age than to hers. Closer to Pearl's.

Marianna was now looking at her as if she had read her thoughts. "You're so young. And if those are things you want—a husband, a kid— then you have plenty of time. Just don't rush things. You a student?"

Ella shook her head. "I write. I sell pieces here and there."

"Anything I've seen? Would I know your name?"

"Probably not."

"Ah, not famous yet," Marianna said.

"I don't want to be famous. Fame is overrated," she said.

"What's your byline? I'll look out for it."

"I use different ones," she said.

"Well, what's your name then?"

"Ella Fitchburg," she said. Her new last name still felt funny in her mouth, as if it were a marble rolling around her tongue.

A group of older students walked by, chattering and laughing, and Marianna looked up, her face full of yearning.

"Sometimes I look at all these students and I wish I were one of them. I wish I could talk to them, but no one has time for an old mom like me." Marianna laughed.

"You're not old," Ella said.

"Oh, you're being kind," Marianna said. "I like that in a person."

Ella felt something roiling in her stomach. Marianna spun her wedding band on her finger and sighed. "Oh well, what're you going to do?" she said, half smiling. "It is what it is. And everyone's lonely sometimes, right?"

Ella studied Marianna. Just because you got to know someone didn't mean you had to tell them every secret you had. You could have companionship, someone to sit and talk with, someone to join for coffee. Plus, the more she could see Marianna, the more she could see Carla.

"I have time," Ella said. "I just moved here a few months ago and I don't know many people."

Marianna tilted her head. "Well then, I hope I see you around here again." She waved her hand at Carla, who was zooming down the yellow plastic slide.

"Carla!" she called. "Time to go, baby tiger! We need to go get dinner ready and I'm going to need your help." Marianna turned to Ella conspiratorially. "She makes more of a mess, actually, but I love the company. And Mark's so old-school he never really helps, either. He thinks male cooking is restricted to tossing a salad and grilling."

"At least he does that," Ella said, a knot unraveling in her stomach. This was a good family, she thought, a good way station for her daughter. She pictured them sitting around a table tonight, maybe talking about the surprise of the mittens, which might lead to how Marianna and Carla had met a woman in the park who was knitting. Maybe Marianna would talk more about her, and what would that be like? Would Mark say, "How wonderful, I want to meet her." She tried to imagine it, a place for her at their table, too.

"Carla doesn't always listen," Marianna said, beckoning to her daughter.

"How do you get her to, then?" Ella said, curious, and then Marianna dug around in her purse and pulled out a five-dollar bill and waved it in the air for Carla to see. *Bribes*, Ella thought, tucking the information away.

And it worked because Carla galloped over, grabbing the bill and skidding to a stop.

"Oh, that's pretty-y-y," Carla said, her fingers finding the knitting. "Can I try?" She tugged at the needles.

"Don't pull at it, baby," Marianna said, grabbing Carla's hand.

"It's okay," Ella said. "No damage done. Maybe next time, I could teach you?" She hated the way it sounded like a question, the way her voice seemed drenched in yearning.

Carla's face brightened. "Really? When?" she said. "When can you teach me?" She looked at Ella confidently. "I'm a very good learner."

Marianna stood, gathering her things. "Another time, baby," she said. "Now it's time to get you and me home."

After grabbing Marianna's hand, Carla turned back to Ella. "What are you going to dress as for Halloween?" she said. "I'm going to be a space alien. I thought about it for a long time and that's what I'm going to be. A space alien from Saturn because that's my favorite planet. Because of the rings."

"I don't know yet," Ella said.

"I could help you think up an idea," Carla said. "I'm very good at ideas."

"There you go," Marianna said. "But we can think them up for her later. Time to go. Come on, kitten."

Ella watched the two of them as they walked away, hand in hand. *Another time*, Marianna had said. *Next time*. And Carla had offered to help her think up a costume.

Ella knit another row, the sun warming her face. Next time maybe she would bring another color yarn, show them how she could weave it in. Yellow might look good against the burnt orange. Or maybe the surprise of blue. Maybe she could do a fancy stitch. Basketweave. Or intarsia, crossing colors to craft a spray of roses in the pattern.

A teenaged couple walked by, holding hands. The boy stopped and kissed the girl so passionately it looked as though he would devour her. Embarrassed, Ella concentrated on her knitting, dropping a stitch and picking it up. When she looked up again, they were gone, but she couldn't stop thinking about them.

Love, she thought. In prison, women turned to other women for partners and lovers and sometimes seemed happy. Some even had prison weddings. Ella had attended one event, bringing ramen packets from the commissary, tied together with yarn—a makeshift bow. There had been singing, and dancing, too.

But Ella couldn't trust love, no matter how inviting it might seem. You thought it was going to last forever because you had been so changed by it, like a shower of diamonds had fallen over you. She and Jude had been so in love, like two runaway cars without brakes, with engines that had roared too fast. But though she wasn't—she swore she wasn't—pining over him, she couldn't let go of the wondering, the need for some sort of closure. She wondered where he was now, if he still thought about her. Maybe he hated her. What would he think if he knew Ella had found the little girl they had made together? How would he feel if he knew she still thought about him, about the night she lost him?

*You'll get over him*, Helen had told her. *Young love doesn't last.*

But sometimes it does.

# FOUR

# Manhattan

*April 2011*

Ella held her breath, tugged up her skirt to shorten it, and then, along with her two best friends, Suze and Christina, walked toward the high-rise on East 76th. She looked up at the ornate carvings on the limestone building and felt dizzy. Everything in the Upper East Side seemed so clean and empty compared to other areas of the city, particularly Queens. The sidewalks looked bleached; every tree was surrounded with bright flowers and gated with wrought iron. People here were so dressed up they looked polished, wearing fancy fabrics and walking fancy dogs who sometimes had jeweled collars and even little rubber boots over their paws. Ella had no idea what to think of any of it.

She had no idea what to think of this event, either. Billy, Suze's cousin, had told Suze that his parents were in Tahiti all weekend. He was throwing a party, putting it on his dad's card, and he wanted her to come. "Bring your friends," he said.

*Just what any party needed,* Ella thought anxiously, *three outcasts,* and Ella felt like the biggest one of all.

At school, the kids called Ella Lobster because of her bright red hair. "Did you stick your finger into an electric socket?" one boy liked to ask her, tugging at her curls. She was so pale, even a little bit of makeup made her look like a clown. *Casper the Friendly Ghost*, kids taunted her, and she flinched as they sang the theme song over and over again until she just wanted to die.

Suze was ostracized because she had a birthmark, a prominent port wine–colored stain across her face, which no makeup could hide. But Suze also suffered for her reputation as a nerd: she was so smart and serious that she had taken college courses at NYU over the summer. Christina had been the subject of ridicule for as long as they could remember because of a limp caused by her mild cerebral palsy. And because she insisted on confronting people who refused to acknowledge it.

"Are we dressed okay?" Ella said, adjusting her clothes again. She wanted to be among people who didn't know them tonight. Desperately desiring to look older than fifteen, older than a sophomore, she had swiped on three coats of mascara and a slash of Riot Red lipstick and hoped for the best. She was tired of feeling less than, of being the girl whose mother made all her clothes, and who could never assemble them to look like those of the other kids her age.

"What do you care what anyone else thinks? They all have single-digit IQs," Suze said.

*I care,* Ella thought.

In front of them loomed a doorman in a gold-buttoned jacket and red cap.

"We're here for a party. Penthouse," Christina blurted.

"Go on up," he said, pointing behind him.

"Go," Christina said, gently shoving Ella.

"Here goes nothing," Suze said. "Just don't embarrass me and start snapping stupid selfies."

Ella flinched. She actually liked looking at other peoples' selfies. She roamed the popular kids' social media, jealous because they all looked like they were having the best lives anyone could imagine. She knew that there was an artifice to this, and that no one's life could measure up to the way they presented it online. For example, that summer, Suze had posted a photo of herself under the Brooklyn Bridge wearing a glamorous new lipstick, while Ella knew she had spent the entire morning crying over something mean a boy had posted. Ella felt a little cheated—her life was so boring, she didn't even have any secrets to hide.

Inside, the lobby was all rose marble floors and dark wood railings. A chandelier glittered from the ceiling and real art hung on the wall, a far cry from Ella's mother's apartment. And then she noted with a start: You couldn't smell anything cooking. You couldn't hear anything here.

In the mirrored elevator, the girls glanced at one another with trepidation, and Ella smoothed her hair for the fiftieth time. After what seemed like forever, the doors opened directly onto a high-ceilinged loft with gleaming wood floors and dark blue walls, black leather furniture arranged in casual groups. Servers in white shirts wandered about with trays of hors d'oeuvres and flutes of champagne. The kids here were in jeans and hoodies, some of the girls wearing what looked like just their bras. Now Ella knew: her red dress screamed loser, a girl who didn't know how to dress in the casually mussed way of the teenage elite.

"Hey, great hair," a tall, slim girl said, gliding past and nodding at Ella. Ella pulled back, shocked. A fashionable girl at this party liked her hair? Imagine that.

There were glasses of what looked like wine on a table by the window and Christina grabbed two, handing one to Suze, who immediately downed it. Ella also took a glass and drank. It tasted like metal, but she drained it. Music was blasting from speakers, and some kids were lazily dancing.

"I'm going to find Billy," Suze said. She gave Christina and Ella a gentle nudge. "Mingle," she ordered. "We'll meet up here later."

ELLA WANDERED THROUGH the rooms as if she were a spirit, thinking what a terrible mistake she had made coming here. She had never been to a party like this, and certainly never one without parents present. There were huge pieces of abstract art along the wall, and even a bronze sculpture of what looked like a woman screaming.

In the corner of a sitting room, Suze was talking and laughing with one of the rumpled-looking boys. *That must be Billy,* she thought, and she considered joining them, but what would she say? She searched for Christina and found her standing against a wall in the huge kitchen, looking terrified. Ella could join her, too, but then what? There would be two terror-stricken girls being ignored instead of just one.

Ella almost grabbed another glass of wine, and then stopped herself. What was she doing? She was already buzzed.

She wandered into another room, and then she saw him. He was in a corner of what seemed like a study, sitting against a book-lined wall, reading. His sandy hair was so long he could have tied it in a ponytail if he wanted. He was so shockingly lovely, Ella had to look away. She wasn't the only one who thought so, though. Girls were watching him, clearly talking about him in barely subdued voices. "Hey, Jude," she heard one of the girls trill. He glanced up and smiled, and went back to reading.

Ella couldn't move.

She crouched down to see the title of the book. *Looking for Alaska.* She had a copy of that herself. It was a book she loved. All of it. It had made her cry, but in the best way. How intriguing it was to see him reading it, surrounded by these glamorous people. He seemed oblivious to them all. She walked closer to him, gathering her courage.

"That's my all-time fave book," she said.

He squinted up at her. "Mine too," he said.

"I don't believe in fate, do you?" she said. She felt suddenly ridiculous. What a stupid thing to say. Her voice sounded thin and way too squeaky. "What I mean is that we create our own fate, right? We can escape what people put on us."

He looked up as if he had known her all his life. *Oh, there you are. I've been waiting for you,* his eyes seemed to say.

"I hope we can," he said, then told her his name was Jude and asked for her name. She liked his voice, deep as a baritone, smoky sounding.

He made room for her to sit, and then he was talking to her about why he was here because he almost never went to things like this, but he knew the kid throwing the party and he hadn't realized it would be so boring (*Boring until now*, he said to Ella, who flushed), but to be polite, he wanted to stay another half hour.

"Oh, look at this," Jude said, and then he showed her the book, talking about how it was both sad and beautiful. And then because it felt so easy, so natural somehow, she was talking, too, telling him about living in Queens, and when he didn't make a face of dismay because Queens was so uncool, she told him more. How she loved the pizza on her block because the crust was perfectly burnt and how her mother designed dresses, which sounded nicer than just saying she worked in a tailoring shop.

Then it was his turn to speak, and the more he did, the more she realized the differences between them. She lived in a two-bedroom apartment on the second floor of a prewar building in Flushing; he lived in a fancy Upper East Side townhouse not far from Billy's. She went to public school; he went to a prep school called Dalton. Ella had grown up without a father, grandparents, aunts, or uncles. But Jude's father was a prominent superior court judge, and his family parties apparently used to be the stuff of legends.

"Well, he doesn't have them anymore," Jude said flatly. "And anyway, legends are unauthenticated. They weren't that great." She was just about to ask him why when he impulsively reached for one of Ella's curls. "I like your hair."

Ella flushed because this was the second time someone had complimented her, and from this boy, it seemed even more special.

"I've never seen you at Dalton," he said.

"I don't go there," Ella said, and then she blurted out where she did go to school, because she was still feeling the alcohol. But instead of making him laugh, her admission only made him more interested. "What's that like?" he asked.

"Like a school." *What a dumb thing to say,* she thought immediately.

But he must not have thought so because he kept talking to her, shaping the air with his hands, and she felt like she had drunk too much wine, that her whole face was moving and she couldn't control it. To her amazement, he kept talking to her, even when she spotted desserts coming out, carried on trays by the same servers, then even when the servers seemed to vanish and kids started heading to the door.

"This is so weird," he said. "I feel like I've always known you, like we grew up together or something. I've never felt so easy with a girl."

She felt it too, only she had never been with a guy before, so she had nothing to compare this to. He could just be toying with her. Her throat tightened. "Me too," she said, and his smile grew, and she suddenly wanted to touch his cheek.

She could see other kids at the party staring at them, staring at her like they suddenly noticed her because Jude had. She liked that feeling. She wanted to sink into it—but then she heard her cellphone blare. It was her mother, probably wanting to know where she was. To her amazement, she saw that hours had passed, and she had spent most of them talking with Jude.

She got up and Jude took her wrist. "Wait," he said, and then he took her phone and put his number in. And then he asked her to put her number in his phone, and when she handed it back to him, he was smiling. "Please, let's talk again," he said.

She found Suze, talking to another boy, and Christina, laughing in a circle of girls.

"I have to go," Ella said, and they nodded and joined her, the three of them shuffling toward the elevator.

The whole subway ride home, Suze talked about how much fun the party was, how she and Billy were going to start doing more things together. Christina talked about the girl she had met who was a painter and how much fun she had.

"You have a good time?" Christina asked Ella.

The night felt too tentative, like it might vanish if she talked about it.

"Sure, I did," she said.

Ella's friends had no idea she had spent the whole party with one person. They hadn't seen her.

But Jude had.

SHE THOUGHT JUDE would text her right away, but when he didn't, she worried he was ignoring her. And if he was, she couldn't text him herself because ignoring her meant he didn't want anything to do with her. But then she started worrying that something might have happened to him. Maybe he had gotten sick and was in the hospital. Or what if someone had jumped him by the subway? Her heart thundered in her chest, and she reeled with nausea.

Ella saw Jude in everything. At Fro-Yo the next day, she remembered how Jude had turned away the chocolate desserts because he was allergic. And at night, rustling in her bed, she wondered if Jude slept with two pillows the way she did, if he slept in pajama pants or nothing at all—and then she couldn't sleep at all.

When she found herself on the Upper East Side again, one day after her school had let out early, she told herself she was just walking around because the neighborhood was so clean, so quiet. When she passed Dalton, the school Jude had talked about, she told herself it was just coincidence. Rich kids attended Dalton. Kids whose lives were as smooth as a newly paved road leading to a dazzling future. Someone who went to Dalton couldn't possibly have any desire to hang with someone like her. She stopped, hesitating, wondering if she should swivel back around and go home.

She saw a group of kids in some sort of enclosed garden on the side. Most of them were leaning against the fence, smoking, laughing, looking stoned and reckless, but there in the corner, carefully, almost tenderly patting down the soil, was Jude. She didn't call out to him, but he looked up suddenly, as if he knew she was there. When he saw her, his face lit up.

"You found me!" he said, as if he somehow knew she had been looking. The other kids were wandering back inside, tossing their cigarettes onto the ground.

"Why didn't you find *me?*" she blurted. "Why didn't you text?"

He looked at her, surprised. "I did text," he said, "I never got a text back." He recited her number back to her and she felt suddenly buoyant. "The last digit isn't mine," she said. "It's a six, not a nine. I must have put it in wrong." Then he smiled back at her.

"Well, here we are," he said.

"I love these plants," she said, and she was quiet while he told her about how one kind needed a lot of light and that was why he was planting it in this corner, while another didn't do well in this climate, but he was going to hope for the best.

"My father thinks it's stupid to do this," Jude said. "And, well, you see the other kids. They couldn't give a flying fuck."

"Your dad's wrong. It's wonderful." She reached through the fence and touched one of the leaves of the plant he was tending.

He glanced at the door to the school, probably realizing he was the last kid still outside. "I have to go, but can we meet again?"

She looked at the tiny green shoots pushing their way up, at the careful way he had arranged them in rows.

"Yes," she said. "Yes, we can."

HE TEXTED HER the next day. She met him after he finished weeding and watering the community garden, and after his guitar lesson (*I suck at it, but my dad wants me to learn to play an instrument*, he'd told her). After her lit magazine meeting.

Every day, she and Jude met at a different location: in the Village, at the Sheep Meadow in Central Park, in Gramercy Park. They read books together, including *It's Kind of a Funny Story*, about a kid who checks himself into a psychiatric institution for five days and finds that love is his cure. Ella said it was the best book ever written because it could make you laugh so hard you felt like you were about to pee your pants. The story broke your heart and then patched it back together. She and Jude made up stories about people in the park, giving them lives with adventure. A young woman with a briefcase was crying on a bench, and when she got up and left, Ella nudged Jude. "She embezzled money from her company, a job she hates, and she's decided she's quitting her job and moving to the Caribbean where no one can find her," she said.

Jude pointed to an elderly couple holding hands, leaning on each other for balance. "They met when they were fifteen, like us," he said, and then he took her hand. "What a life they had! He forgave her when she cheated on him, and loved her even more for coming back to him."

"She cheated on him?"

"She was testing their love."

"How silly," Ella said. "To test love."

JUDE WAS ALWAYS stopping to touch a petal, to feel a leaf, and all he could talk about was how he was going to be a botanist, that maybe he could work at the botanical gardens in the Bronx.

"What about you? What are you going to be?" he asked. Ella wanted to say she would be whatever he wanted her to be, but instead, she told him she liked writing, that she kept a journal—and no, he couldn't see it.

"Soon, though, you'll let me?" he asked, and she nodded.

He would bring her flowers, telling her the meaning of each. The iris, her favorite flower, meant hope. The lily meant joy. Fresh basil was good for your skin, good for what ails you. She pressed every flower and plant that he gave her into her copy of *Looking for Alaska*, so that she'd have them forever and she'd see them every time she reread the book, which was often. She wanted to tell him she was in love with him, but it seemed too scary, too dangerous. Instead, she looked up which flower meant love—lavender. When she put a stem of lavender into his hand, he looked at her, startled. He pulled away a sprig, and with his eyes locked on hers, gave the piece back to her. And so she understood.

One night, at home in her room, she felt his presence and went to the window. There he was on the sidewalk, looking up at her. *I was just thinking about you.* She swore she heard him saying that right in her head. She grabbed her hoodie to go downstairs, throwing it over her T-shirt and sleep shorts, but when she got to the door, there was her mother in her nightgown, frowning.

"Where are you going this time of night? I heard you get up," and then Ella had to make something up and go back to bed. She still hadn't told her mother about Jude. She was afraid she wouldn't approve.

By the time she looked out the window again, Jude was gone. But it didn't matter. She had seen him, and he had seen her.

Jude surprised her by showing up outside her school one day. He was dressed in a black T-shirt and black jeans, and he looked so beautiful that Ella's heart leaped. For a moment she couldn't breathe. She heard the girls around her talking about how hot that guy was and wondering whom he was here to see.

"How do I look?" one blond girl said to another, fluffing out her hair. Ella started to walk toward him, and one of the girls bumped her pointedly with her elbow, sending Ella to the ground.

While the girls were laughing, Jude strode over and helped her up. By the time she caught her breath, everything had changed. Kids were staring at her as if they were retaking her measure.

She took Jude's hand and he draped his arm over her shoulder.

"I wish you hadn't seen that," she whispered, and he shook his head.

"You're a thoroughbred," he told her. "Those girls are just carousel ponies."

The next day in school, the same boys who had mocked her now looked at her with interest. They called her by her name. In the bathroom, Paula, one of the popular girls, offered Ella a lipstick to try. "This would look good on you," she said. "It's totally your perfect shade, Pink Passion." She waited while Ella put it on and then nodded. "That's definitely your color," Paula said, and Ella flushed, pleased by her reflection, and the name of the lipstick, too.

But Suze and Christina weren't so happy about Jude, mostly because Ella was never around anymore. She had promised herself that she would make time for them, but she never did, because every spare moment she had, she was with Jude. At the end of April, Christina and Suze came to her locker for what they said was an intervention.

"Who wants a girlfriend who puts her boyfriend first?" Suze demanded.

"Come on," Ella pleaded. "It's not like that." She felt a moment of panic because she loved her friends. They had stuck with her, but every moment she wasn't with Jude, she was still filled with reveries about him, his face, how he talked, his hands on her face.

"All you do is spend time with him. I'm sorry we ever went to that stupid party," Christina said.

"You are so unfeminist," Suze said.

Ella felt merged with Jude. He might come from money, but they shared so much. Every time she mentioned something she felt, he seemed to feel it, too. When he talked about what he wanted for his future—a garden, a home, decent weather, a bunch of kids (*Imagine a little one with your face!* Jude said, tilting up her chin), she told him she wanted what he wanted.

Sometimes she knew what he was going to say before he said it, and other times he would finish her sentences. She felt like she had always known him, like they had grown up together. It was both wonderful and terrible. Wonderful because of how she felt. Terrible because when they were apart, she felt unmoored. Love was pinballing inside her, crashing and zinging. She kept waiting for a moment when she could catch her breath, but it always eluded her. At night, she filled the pages of her journal with poems and stories about him.

ONE DAY, HE was so quiet that she worried he was suddenly tired of her. "It's not you," he said, but when she tried to kiss him, he pulled back. It was a hot day for late spring, and he picked at the long-sleeved shirt he was wearing.

"Want to borrow a T-shirt?" she asked. When he refused, she said, "At least roll up your sleeves," and she started to undo his cuff. He flinched and pulled away, but not before she saw the bruises flowering on his arm.

"What happened?" she said.

He waved his hand dismissively. "I got clumsy and tripped. Forget it. Really."

And, of course, she did. She took a selfie with her phone, making a funny face, and sent it right to him. He laughed. He took her phone and took a photo of the two of them together, forehead to forehead.

The next day, they cut school and went to Prospect Park. While Ella ran through the new grass to the ladies' room, she returned to find Jude reading her journal. She was usually so careful with it, hiding it in her locker so that no one could grab it and make fun of her. She froze, terrified. Days ago she had written a short poem about Jude, about how he made her feel, and she knew it would be close to the last page. *Every star alive is burning in you, Jude*, it went. *You are every sun.* Maybe it was a dopey poem, but it was the way she felt.

"No one's ever written me a poem before," he said quietly. "No one's ever taken the time. Or the care."

"It's not very good—"

"Can I please have it?" he said, and when she nodded, he gently tore out the page and put it in his backpack. "I'm going to memorize this," he said. "For when I don't feel like myself." She saw him swallow, hard. "For when I forget that I can be loved and love back."

Feeling woozy, Ella shut her eyes. Love. He said *love*. He kissed her, and he was like a drug. She wanted more, more. He took her hand and they walked deeper into the park, off the beaten path and behind some hedges, like it was their own private universe.

He pulled her down to the grass, which felt soft against her face. Ella shut her eyes and looked up at the patches of sky above the trees, feeling as though she could reach out and touch the blue. She could hear the plants whispering around her. Jude touched her shirt, lifting it up a little.

"Is this okay?" he asked, and she reached over and unbuttoned every button. He sat up and took off his shirt and then his pants, and she saw how his hands were trembling. She was amazed; she had thought he was in charge, that surely he was more experienced than she was, and she had no experience at all. She put one hand on his bare chest and he lowered himself down beside her. "I want you to know there haven't been many others," he said. "I want you to know this means something. Everything."

"I've never—"

"Okay," he said. "That's okay. I'll go really slow."

Jude embraced her, then kept asking, "Is this okay?" and she kept answering with her mouth, her embrace, her legs wrapped around him. When it was over, they lay in each other's arms, laughing.

She kissed his mouth. She felt as if her whole body had melted.

He helped her up. They helped each other dress, and the whole time Ella had her eyes locked on him, and she couldn't stop smiling.

After the first time, they began making love every chance they could, in public parks, in the gym at her school when it was empty. But what she cherished most was afterward, when they would talk, when he would tell her things. He lived with his father, whom he loved, and she learned that his mother had died. But when she asked him about it, he grew silent.

"Is it okay if I don't talk about that?" he said, and Ella could only nod.

"Let's talk about us instead," Jude said, coiling one of her curls about his thumb and tugging her to him to kiss. "What if tomorrow we hang at my house?"

"What about your dad? How can we do that?"

"My dad doesn't get home until late. We could have the whole place to ourselves."

"I'm in," Ella said.

SHE HAD KNOWN that Jude was wealthy, and she had expected his home to be in a posh apartment building, like Billy's. Instead, he stopped in the middle of 74th Street in front of a three-story white limestone townhouse with a carved dark wood door, and a separate basement entrance, the yard ringed by an intricate wrought-iron fence.

"Here's home," he said.

She looked at him, stunned. "You live here? This whole place? All three floors?"

"Basement, too. I'll give you the tour."

She stepped into the foyer, onto the gleaming wood floors, past a white marble fireplace. Light flooded in from the south-facing windows, warming her. In the corner, a marble staircase curved up to the next level. "This is like *The Great Gatsby*," she said.

"They made you read that in English, too?"

Laughing, he led her into the kitchen, with an island so huge it had eight chairs around it. She couldn't believe how spacious this place was. Upstairs, one room led into another: a study, a bedroom, and one of the home's three baths, all with showers and fancy tubs with gold hardware. By the time they reached the top floor, Ella felt a stab of longing to live in a place like this.

"My dad says the house has good bones. We've had it forever."

"Your place is amazing," she said. "Your dad's bedroom is the size of my mom's whole apartment."

"It's not a big deal. It's just a house."

But Ella could see that it wasn't. The top-floor bathroom, tiled in what looked like natural stone, featured a claw-footed tub. "Come see my room," Jude said, and he led her to a closed white door at the end of the hall.

"Ta-da," he said, opening his door. "My inner sanctum."

It was a mess, but a glorious mess. She loved that there were books spread on every surface, his deep-green walls covered with photos of the rainforest and other flora that she had never seen before. She skimmed her fingers across sheets that were so soft she wanted to bring them home and have her mother make a dress out of them.

"Wait, no plants here?" she said.

Jude shrugged. "My dad thinks they bring bugs." He took her to his window and showed her their small, iron-gated patio in the backyard. "The only garden he has is a rock garden. He says it's inspired by his time in Japan, but he never even goes out there."

"This house has everything," she said quietly. "What more could you possibly want?"

"You," he said. Then he lowered her to the bed, sweeping the books onto the floor.

AFTERWARD, HER LEGS twined with Jude's, Ella felt buoyant with joy. Sex, she decided, was so much better in a bed. Especially when it was his bed, his room, his home. There was so much intimacy even in his sheets, and she wrapped them around them both like a cocoon. She never wanted to leave here. Never.

"All of this is just ours," she said, and he kissed her.

"I'm starving," Jude said, and led her two flights down to the kitchen.

He was rummaging in a cabinet, looking for snacks, when Ella saw a package of Yahrzeit candles.

"We have these too," she said, pointing.

"We never use them," Jude said.

"We don't either. I don't even know why we have them."

"Are you religious at all? I'm not."

She shook her head. "My mom doesn't believe in God anymore. She doesn't fast on Yom Kippur because she said people are punished enough just by living their lives."

"Wow. That's harsh."

"Sometimes she lights candles on Friday nights, even though she's not religious. She gets really quiet and thoughtful about it, like it's something she needs to do. I have to admit, somehow, the candles make me feel holy, just for a moment, but my mom gets so quiet afterward, so sad. Like she's remembering her past, and the ritual doesn't work the way she hoped."

"Wow," Jude said. He admitted that he had never had a bar mitzvah, and when Ella asked why, he just shrugged.

"Do you believe in God?"

"I don't know," he said. "My mother told me that no one knows the truth. If I wanted, I could believe in God, and what kind of God that was would be up to me. My father believes in nothing and no one except himself." He paused. "I wish I had your upbringing."

"You do?" she asked, startled. She began to tell him more, how Helen believed in education, so she had often bought Ella books about God, about being Jewish, always telling her she could choose what to believe. For a while, Ella had imagined that God was like the father she didn't have, a kindly man who supported her when she messed up, who looked down on her with love. But after a while, her connection with God had faded, and she thought about it less and less.

The Jewish holidays came and went without much notice, and the main reason Ella had even known the days were special was because Helen would get silent on those days, as if she were mourning.

In elementary school, most of the kids were Christian. They had brought in Christmas presents for show-and-tell. Her teacher used to call Ella "our Jewish friend," which made Ella's stomach flip because she didn't feel like anyone's "friend." The teacher made her stand up and talk about Hanukkah, even though Ella had only a foggy idea about what the holiday was. One kid in the back even shouted, "You're supposed to get eight gifts!" That left Ella even more confused because she knew nothing about that. The whole experience had been humiliating. When she had asked her mother about it, Helen had told her that the Hanukkah she had celebrated growing up in her Hasidic community was actually a solemn, serious holiday, based on history rather than on gift giving.

"Are we Jewish?" Ella had asked. Helen had sighed, then said, "We can be whatever we want to be."

Ella told Jude how when she ten, she had insisted on attending Hebrew school, jealous of the Christian kids who got to leave school early on Wednesdays for catechism classes, wanting a faith of her own. She had been so excited and full of hope, but the class had turned out to be a boring recitation of the histories of people she had never even heard about, like Abraham and Moses, although everyone else already seemed to know everything about them. The kids weren't friendly to her and she thought they were whispering about her behind their hands.

When she came home from the class, Helen had asked, "How was it, darling?"

"I'm not going back," Ella had said, and her mother never brought it up again.

Still, she had wondered about religion. Her mother's endless stories about growing up in the Hasidic community hadn't made her yearn for that particular life. She knew how hard her mother tried to give her a different upbringing than she had had. Her mother had insisted that Ella make her own choices about everything, something that filled Ella with glee, but it also made her wonder if her mother would eventually step in and take back the controls. She hoped not. She really appreciated that her mother didn't censor anything Ella read, and had sent her daughter, at just eight years old, to the library with a note that said she was allowed in the adult section and could take out any book she wanted.

"Really? My dad would never give up control. Your mom must really love you," Jude said wistfully.

"I don't know," Ella said. Sometimes Ella felt weird rather than triumphant in these freedoms. Helen had always gotten so excited when Ella did something that Helen had never been allowed to do, like choosing her own outfits and hairstyle, once even going to school with her hair braided into twelve different pigtails tied with twist ties. Helen had taken Ella to see movies that were meant for adult audiences and spoke to her like an adult. As a child, Helen had been denied children's games other than playing house or playing school, or an occasional game of checkers with her father, and by the time she was nine, she spent most of her time caring for her siblings. She wanted more for Ella.

"It made it hard to shock her," Ella admitted to Jude.

"What if you stole something?"

"I'd never do that," Ella said.

"So, you have your own code or faith, a sort of self-created limit."

"I don't know. I guess you could say that I made up my own religion," she said. "To be kind and loving to everyone, and that if I did something bad, I'd try to make it better."

"I like that. That's going to be my religion now, too," Jude said.

Ella didn't mention that these days, her religion was really just Jude.

"I wish I had someone like your mother in my life," Jude said. He opened another cabinet and pulled out a new bag of chips, holding them up for her okay. When she nodded, he found a crystal bowl and filled it to the top.

"Dining room," he said, leading her. In the hallway, they passed photo after photo of a beautiful woman, her eyes big as planets, her hair a sheet of caramel blond; and Jude, stopping in front of one, seemed pained. "My mother," he said, and then he went silent. Jude continued forward, but Ella lingered behind him, eyes on the photo, trying to figure this woman out.

Just then, she heard the front door open and Jude stiffened. "Come on," he said, and led her from the dining room into the foyer. There at the lip of the door was a man, large and imperious in a dark suit, his hair slicked back.

"Dad. I thought you were working late again."

"Who's this?" he barked, his gaze snapping to Ella.

"Ella. His girlfriend," Ella said, when Jude seemed tongue-tied by the question.

Jude's father looked at her more closely. "I'm Judge Andrew Stein," he said pompously, emphasizing the word *Judge*. He began asking questions. He wanted to know if they went to the same school, if he knew her parents at all, and then, after she told him her single mom was a dressmaker and that they lived in Queens, he seemed to lose all interest.

"It's almost dinnertime," he said to Jude, and then he turned to her. "I know you must be getting home, Ella."

When she was almost out the door, she saw Jude mouth, *Come back here tomorrow.*

She did, of course. How could she not? She came back every day. They usually had a few hours before his dad got home, and, after their first encounter, they always managed to make the most of it, so his dad had never caught them having sex. Instead, he came home to find them watching a movie on the giant plasma TV or having tea and cookies at the kitchen island.

Still, Ella could sense that Judge Stein didn't like her. He never spoke to her directly, and when Jude pointedly talked about Ella— like how she was getting straight As this semester—Judge Stein only shrugged. One evening he mentioned the time, how late it was getting, that he and Jude had plans; but the next day, Jude said they had only ordered a pizza and then his dad had vanished into his study and closed the door.

Then one day, Ella and Jude misjudged the time. In the throes of passion, they hadn't heard the front door open, or his father's shoes on the stairs. Jude's father found them in bed, naked.

"Get up. Get dressed. Get downstairs. Now," he said.

Once they were in the living room, he began his lecture. "What is it you think you're doing? You're just kids. And you're way too close. You both have schoolwork. You should be hanging out with your friends."

"We *are* friends," Jude said. "Best friends."

"You're acting obsessed. You could ruin your lives."

"We're saving our lives," Jude said.

"Oh, so dramatic," his father said dismissively. "And you," he said to Ella. "Go on home. No more of this." He pointed a finger at her, glaring until she felt herself pale. "Does your mother know what you're doing?" he asked. "Must I call her?"

"My mom lets me make my own decisions," Ella said. She wasn't ready for her mom to know about Jude. She didn't want to share any part of this story she was living.

Jude's father snorted. "Well, I make them for Jude. And I don't want you over here ever again when I'm not home."

"I'll just take you home," Jude said to Ella.

"To Queens? No, you won't," his father said. "And did you hear what I said?"

"Fine. I'll just walk her to the subway, then," Jude said, and he yanked open the front door, striding to the edge of the sidewalk, waiting for Ella.

At first they just walked, not speaking. And then Ella stammered, "D-Do you think he'll really call her?"

"My dad likes to use threats," Jude said bitterly.

"I haven't even told my mother about us yet," Ella said, cringing at Jude's surprise. "I want this to be just us, just in our world." Part of her didn't want to tell him that she was afraid of her mother knowing, of her taking over, wanting to be a part of it, the way she always did. The whole "us against the world" thing might have been fun when Ella was little, but now it made her feel smothered. She also dreaded her mother talking like Jude's dad about how she hoped they weren't "moving too fast," which everyone knew meant having sex.

"Is that okay?" Ella said finally.

Jude nodded, so silent that Ella grew uneasy. She clenched his hand, walking downtown with him, all the way to the 7 train at Grand

Central. Jude hesitated. "We don't have to put you on the train here," he said. "Fuck him. Let's keep walking. I want more time with you."

They started to walk crosstown, to the West Side, through Times Square, and then wandered farther west and then downtown through Chelsea. When they reached the Village, Ella finally felt at home. When she would go into the city with Suze and Christine, this is where they'd hang out, hoping some of the area's cool would rub off on them.

On 8th Street, they passed a tattoo parlor, Think In Ink. Through the window, they could see a young guy, skinny as a cigarette, his arms and neck covered in flower tattoos.

"We should get one," Jude said.

"What? A tattoo? My mom would kill me."

"I thought she let you do whatever you want—"

"Sometimes."

"We should get the same one. Like we're marked. Like we're forever joined, and nothing can erase what we feel for each other. And even when we're apart, we'll know we're still together in some way because we each have the same tattoo."

Ella hesitated.

"Don't we have to be a certain age?" she asked, and Jude laughed.

"Look at the guy doing the tattoos. Do you really think he's going to care?"

Ella frowned. The guy looked up and waved, and then went back to work.

"We'll do them high up on our arms, so we can hide them with our sleeves," Jude said, already pulling open the door to the parlor. "No one will even know unless we show them. Come on, we'll just look."

Inside, a young woman was leaning back in a chair, a twining snake tattoo taking shape along her arm. The woman wasn't crying or yelping, so maybe it didn't hurt.

"I'm just finishing up," the guy said. "Take a look at our designs while you're waiting."

In front of her, on one sweep of white wall, was a crowd of images. You could choose flowers, wild animals, or really anything you wanted. She was tempted by the various cursive fonts, imagining a line of poetry linking them forever. But then she noticed there were beautiful birds, too, and she couldn't tear herself away from them, almost as if they were calling to her. "What do you think of these?" she asked Jude, who came closer to her.

"As long as it doesn't look like the Twitter logo," he joked.

She studied the designs. "This one," she said, pointing to a gold-and-green hummingbird, its wings pointing up as if the bird were flying high. "I saw one once and I almost couldn't believe it. They're so small and beautiful and they make such a cool sound."

Jude went first, rolling his sleeve to his shoulder and grinning at her the whole time. "Easy as pie," he said. When it was Ella's turn, she kept her eyes locked with Jude's, and when the pain came, it was surprisingly exquisite, just like love.

Both tattoos were a little lopsided, but Ella didn't care. And it didn't matter that they always had to hide them from their parents, because they, the two of them, would always be connected now. They left with plastic bandages covering their arms, sample packs of antibacterial ointment in their pockets, and a sheet of instructions.

Jude walked her to the subway station, and then kissed her good-bye. "My dad can't stop us from seeing each other. We'll find other places to be together."

The whole subway ride home, Ella was terrified that Jude's father had called her mother. She worried that somehow Helen would know she had a tattoo. But when she entered their apartment, Helen never said a thing.

After that, Jude and Ella tried to find other private places to have sex. The school janitor found them half undressed in the gym at Ella's school and threatened to tell the principal, and for days afterward they worried, but the janitor never did rat on them.

"Look," Jude said, after an agonizing week without a quiet place to be together. "Do you think we could hang at your house?" He nudged her with his shoulder. "I should get to know your mother, shouldn't I? I mean, you know my dad."

"I don't know," Ella said. She thought of showing up with him, a beautiful boy who loved her. And really, was there any other way for them to be together all the time?

"Fine," she said reluctantly. "I'll ask. She might say no, though."

THAT EVENING ELLA told her mother that she had a boyfriend and she wanted her to meet him. The whole time she was talking, she couldn't read her mother's expression.

Ella expected a lecture from her about how she was too young to date, have her repeat the same warning about how many opportunities had been wrested from her as a teenager, and did Ella want to end up like her, alone and working long hours to make ends meet? Instead, Helen grew still, as if she were considering something.

"What kind of boy is he?"

"Don't you trust me? I think you'll like him," Ella said. "We read together, we're friends. He's super smart, too, and he's studying to be a botanist. You have to trust me. I'm not going to do anything stupid."

"What's his name?" Helen asked, and Ella told her.

"What's his family like? What do they do?"

"His father's a judge. His name is always in the papers."

Helen's face lit up, and Ella felt a flicker of irritation.

"Mom, this isn't about money—"

"Of course it isn't. It's about where he comes from, his family, whether he deserves *you*." Helen studied her nails and then put her hands in her pockets.

"Bring him to dinner," she said finally. "Friday night. Let me see for myself what kind of boy he is. Then we can decide."

Ella nodded. But she and Jude had already decided. They had promised each other: *We'll be together forever.*

# FIVE

# Philadelphia

*November 2018*

Jude, deliriously happy, woke up next to his wife, Angie. He couldn't believe how beautiful she was, how lucky she made him feel. They had been together for only a year, but he still couldn't get enough of watching her in the morning: the golden silk of her hair across the pillow, the tilt of her nose, her mouth so red it made him want to never stop kissing her.

"Mmm," she mumbled in her sleep, and he kissed her gently on the shoulder.

After the pain of losing Ella, he had never expected to be partnered up again at twenty-two. Never thought he would wind up in Philadelphia, either, but after the mess in Manhattan, his father had decided a fresh start was needed. His father had become the dean of Penn Carey Law School, a job as prestigious as his judgeship. He had arranged for Jude to change his last name from Stein to Miller, though he said his own name carried too much weight to change. Jude had been too stunned, too paralyzed by what had happened, to do anything but let his father take control.

"Things are going to change," his father had said, and in some ways they had. His father hadn't hurt him physically since they left New York, though sometimes Jude noticed his father's mouth tightening into a line, his hands becoming fists, and Jude thought he might still want to beat him. Instead, his father had started attending AA meetings. Every week, and whenever he got a chip, he stuck it in a pocket and later made sure that Jude could see it, like a promise he wouldn't break. Mostly, he kept a respectful distance from his only child.

But to Jude, his father's silence had been its own kind of abuse. His father never mentioned what had happened. It was as if his father had shoved the past into boxes and sealed them with super glue.

"Everything I do, I do for you," his father had insisted. He had pulled strings to get Jude into a fancy private high school, had tugged more strings to get him into Penn's early admission program. But Jude hadn't ever wanted to be a lawyer, despite how much his father pushed. He hadn't even studied botany, because after everything that had happened, Jude hadn't felt he deserved to. When he finally had to pick a major, he chose computer science—something with cause and effect, like lines you knew not to color outside of. As soon as he had finished college—a year early because he had taken a double course load—he landed a job at Take Tech. It paid well enough that when a one-bedroom had opened up in East Falls, he had signed the lease, painted the rooms blue and green, and found some cheap furniture that looked adult enough. Work had filled his hours and his days, and he hadn't expected, or even wanted, anything more.

And then, almost a year ago, in a happy accident, he had met Angie, a massage therapist he went to see after he had wrenched his back. She hadn't been anything like what he expected. She was willowy and pale and younger than he was and so slight that he couldn't imagine her being able to get out the knots in his muscles. Her long hair splashed down to her waist, and she smelled like lavender. She had asked him plenty of questions, but she never pried if he didn't answer. She just moved on to another task. He had signed on for six sessions, but he found that he liked being around her. The more he saw her, the more time he wanted to give her.

He would never have told her that her he was falling in love, because that idea terrified him. Love was dangerous, especially when it was so quick like this. Look how it had turned out with Ella. With Ella, being together, falling in love, had been stormy and dramatic and intense. Having sex with Ella had been like a thunderclap. *You're the air I breathe*, they used to tell each other, as if at any moment they'd suffocate. *Without you I'd drown.* But the first night with Angie, after dinner and wine, when they finally fell into bed, making love had been more like floating in a lake where you could see clearly down to the soft sand on the bottom. After, he kissed her shoulder, so intoxicated that he had never wanted her to leave.

And to his joy, she hadn't. She'd moved in with him as seamlessly as she had arrived.

Now, Angie shifted in bed and her beautiful eyes opened. "I have something to tell you," she said cheerfully, and then she sat up.

He guessed that she had a new client, or had seen a new restaurant she wanted to try, but instead her smile grew. "I think we should take in a boarder," she said.

"What? Are you kidding? Why would we do that? I don't want anyone else here—" They had moved to a larger apartment, so they had more room now, but a boarder was out of the question.

"They'll be no real trouble," she said, her smile widening. She put her hand on top of his and led it to her belly. "Though I bet this one will be a real crybaby."

He stared at her.

"Get it?" she said, studying him. "Crybaby? How come you don't look happy?"

"We're too young—" he said, immediately hating that he was parroting his father's words.

"We're not too young," she told him. "We both make enough money, and we love each other. We have space. We can do this."

How could he tell her they couldn't? A baby was permanent. There'd be so much more to lose.

"Don't you want to have kids?" she asked. "Didn't you ever think about it?"

He had, but with Ella, lying on the grass in Central Park, staring at the sky and concocting their futures.

"A little one with your face!" he had said to Ella, although he had actually hoped they might have two, maybe three—their own little circus. The fantasy had buoyed him so much that he had believed they could do it.

*Oh, Ella.*

He rubbed his eyes. He couldn't be a father. He and Angie had talked about everything in their life—a home by the ocean one day, trips to Paris—but never about kids. He realized he had avoided that topic with her. How could she be pregnant?

"You were so careful about taking the pill—"

"Jude," Angie said. "Nothing's one hundred percent. And I'm pregnant. It's sort of a done deal." Her face was full of doubt now.

"How pregnant?" he said carefully.

"Just three weeks," she said.

"But that's hardly anything. Are you sure?"

"I tried three different tests. All positive. Doctor confirmed it, too."

"So fast? Just like that?" He looked at her, astonished.

"Is this really not something you want?" she said. "I know we never talked about it, but I thought it was just because we were so busy—"

He touched her lovely face. He didn't know how he felt except that his life felt upside down. If he had a child with Angie, did that mean Ella was really and truly gone?

"What do you say, bucko," Angie said quietly.

"We're going to be parents," he said, and then she smiled and rested her head on his shoulder.

Angie nudged him. "Gus if it's a boy. Giselle if it's a girl."

THAT NIGHT, AFTER Angie went to bed, Jude sat down with a sheet of paper and made up a list of all the things his father had done that were right and good, things he could easily repeat for his own child:

He taught me how to ride a bike.
He took me miniature golfing.
He read to me.

Then he wrote down all the things that his father had done that were wrong:

Drinking
Hitting
Not listening
Blaming
Judging
Controlling
Not forgiving
He loved my mother more than he ever loved me

Jude stared at the list. He certainly would never hit his child. He always listened, and he didn't talk much. He would never blame or judge anyone, least of all a child, and he knew all too well that he couldn't control anything because he had tried and look where that had gotten him.

But that had been a long time ago.

And he wasn't that Jude anymore.

And he wasn't his father.

He crumpled the list. He could redo. Redeem. He could be the best, most loving father and husband, a man so good people would look at his family and think, *What a lucky wife. What a lucky child. What a lucky life.* He would never leave his son alone with his dad, either. He would make sure that his father knew he was an adult and could make his own decisions, no matter what anyone else thought. He was the father now.

He went into bed and curved his body around Angie's. He placed his hand on her stomach, on their child to be, growing inside her.

HE CALLED HIS father the next morning to tell him he was going to be a grandfather, not expecting much. When he first introduced Angie to his dad—a special dinner at a fancy restaurant where Jude never quite felt at ease—his father had been polite, even charming. But as Jude told him the news of their unborn child, he felt a charge through the line.

"You're too young to be a father," Judge Stein said. "You have no idea how to raise a child."

"And you do?" Jude said.

Then Jude shut down. He refused to let his father hurt him anymore. His dad was either going to be happy for them, welcome their child, or be totally shut out of their lives. *I'm going to be a dad*, Jude thought, and then he felt his despair about his dad's hostility vanish, replaced with a new sense of wonder.

JUDE'S EUPHORIA QUICKLY gave way to a claustrophobic unease, thick and sticky as honey. He dreamed that he was back in the kitchen of his father's Manhattan townhouse, so bright and gleaming he was wearing sunglasses. One of the white cabinets was open to a row of clear glass teacups. He felt a cup in his hands, carefully lowered it onto the matching glass saucer, and turned to see Ella right beside him, her smile a beam of light that lit up the room. He startled awake.

*Shake it off*, he told himself. He jumped into the shower, and then pulled on clothes for work, a Ramones T-shirt and his favorite jeans. As an IT consultant, every day was casual Friday, and the people he

worked with didn't care what he wore. They were just grateful that
he could fix whatever they couldn't. He was confident and collected,
because when it came to computers, he had all the answers. And he
stayed calm when others panicked.

In these spirals of despair, Jude couldn't escape the feeling that he
was doing everything wrong. He was clearly a mess, and no matter
what he did or how hard he tried, he couldn't forget that night, or fix
it. He couldn't unlock any sort of atonement. Instead, he had just tried
to protect others from himself by never getting too close. Even with
Angie, he had fought that desire for closeness. Maybe he didn't deserve
forgiveness, love, or even luck. Because even though Ella had done the
crime, he knew that he had been the impetus. *I would do anything for
you.* That's what she had said. That's what she meant. And when he
said it back, he thought that he meant it, too. And look how wrong
he'd been.

He had ruined Ella somehow, turned her into a person who would
be sent to prison at fifteen. He had ruined his own mother, who had
loved and doted on him and who had paid for it. And he constantly
worried that, without meaning to, he would ruin Angie, too.

He could remember his father loving him when he was little. They
had played catch in the park. Judge Stein had taught him how to ride a
bike, running beside him, assuring his son, "I've got you! I've got you!"
until the boy had safely soared down the street.

JUDE MADE COFFEE and sat at the kitchen table, remembering his
mother, a familiar ache rising in his chest. She had taught him to love
plants and had challenged him to name the wildflowers they saw.

He was twelve when it happened—celebrating his birthday, the
whole family at their house upstate in the town of Woodstock. They
had been so happy back then. While his friends' parents all seemed to
be going through divorces, his parents had adored each other more
and more. His mom stuck love notes for his dad all over the house. She

fussed over him, cooking his favorite meals, buying him special cuff-links to wear in court. Every night they spent upstate, after Jude had gone to bed, his parents would sit out on the porch, laughing, talking, and drinking wine. Sometimes back then, Jude thought he could see a look of surprise on his father when he looked at his son, as if Jude were a gift he never expected.

One weekend Judge Stein had to stay in the city to work on a case. Jude and his mother drove up from the city anyway, conspiring about the fun things they would do without him. That Saturday they had gone out for ice cream and, alone on a country road without another car in sight, Jude pressed his mom to teach him how to drive.

"You goof!" his mother cried, her blond hair ruffling in the air from her open window. "You're not even old enough to get your permit."

"It's deserted here," Jude said. "You can even put your hands on the wheel by mine."

She laughed, shaking her head.

"Please," Jude said. His mother always enjoyed being spontaneous, so unlike his father. "It'll be an adventure!"

She hesitated and then threw the car into park. She jumped out of the car and traded places with him.

"You little smartass," she said affectionately. "Just for five minutes, then. And only because no one else is on the road."

Jude gripped the wheel, then stepped on the gas jerkily, then a little more, and the car began to gain momentum smoothly. It felt as if he were flying.

"Slow it down, buddy," his mother said. Then, "Okay, time to stop. Lighten up on the gas."

"Okay, okay," he said, but he didn't—the speed felt so intoxicating. He swiveled around to look at her, beaming, lifting his hands, just for a second.

"Jude!" she cried.

What happened next was a blur. Jude looked down to find the brake as a blue car came out of nowhere, racing toward them. Then there was a terrible slash of sound, followed by darkness.

From that moment on, everything had been his fault.

IN HIS KITCHEN, Jude lifted his head from his hands. *Breathe*, Angie was always telling him, her voice soft, a gentle lasso.

He breathed. He was going to have a new family now. The one from before, with Ella and Helen, no longer existed. Maybe it never really had.

# SIX

# Queens
### *May 2011*

Two days after Ella told her about Jude, Helen was setting the table for dinner for the three of them, excited by the thought of company, of another person being in the house. She had stopped lighting Shabbos candles a long time ago, but that didn't keep her from lighting regular candles, and as she did, she felt a sense of holiness in the room. Maybe that was a good omen.

Even though she had suggested this dinner, trying to be open in a way her parents had never been, the truth was she wasn't thrilled about entertaining Ella's boyfriend, a kid she didn't know. Maybe by getting to know him, she could coax Ella back a bit. For the past few weeks her daughter had been drawing away, always dreaming, shutting everything and everyone out. She frequently didn't hear Helen when she asked her a question. Ella was coming home later and later from school, always with a flimsy excuse. At night, Helen heard her prowling around, and one night, Helen had gone to Ella's room to find her leaning out the window, looking at the sidewalk below. Helen had crept downstairs to see what was drawing her daughter's attention, and that was when she saw a boy with long shaggy hair staring toward Ella's window, his face lit with love.

She couldn't let things go on this way. Helen kept imagining all sorts of terrible things, such as Ella getting pregnant like she had, or

Ella running away with that boy and ending up panhandling on the city streets. Hadn't her daughter listened to her stories, how her friends and family had shunned her? Even if she had wanted to walk into her family's shul on Shabbos, she knew she wouldn't be welcome. So many things could be taken away from you.

And then she thought of herself, alone in the house, without her daughter, and all she could think was *Too soon, too soon*. She was desperate for every second of these last years before Ella would inevitably go off on her own. Helen hadn't gone to college and it would be wonderful if Ella could be the first generation to do so, but she would have to depend on scholarships for that. Plus, Helen didn't know if Ella wanted to further her education. When she asked, Ella just shrugged.

Helen checked the clock. Ella and Jude were coming after their school activities, and they'd be there soon.

She had researched this boy's father, Andrew Stein, a superior court judge. He was wealthy and privileged, and they had a huge townhouse on the Upper East Side. Worried how her place would look by comparison, Helen had taken a whole a day off from work to clean. She couldn't do much about the faded velvet couch except brush it. She couldn't replace the chipped wainscoting or the horrible, old-fashioned gray wall-to-wall carpeting the landlord had installed. What she could do was run out and buy flowers—bright, showy gladiolus—and put them around the apartment.

She paced, waiting. Then she changed her dress from her workaday blue denim to one she had borrowed from the dress shop, a navy silk. Deciding that was too fancy, too obvious, she changed back into the denim and added dangling earrings. She put on lipstick.

Ella and Jude arrived by six, holding hands, their love palpable. Jude put out a hand politely.

"I'm so happy to know you," he said. When he walked to the living room, he turned to her and told her how much he loved the velvet of the couch. He admired the wainscoting, and then he asked if he could help with dinner.

"So polite!" Helen said.

And then Jude noticed the flowers and his whole body seemed to relax.

"Gladiolus," he said. "They represent strength, remembrance."

"Jude knows all about botany," Ella said proudly.

Jude sat down on the couch, Ella beside him, Helen on her favorite blue paisley chair. He began asking Helen questions about her life, about what books she read, while Ella sat there awkwardly. He told Helen how he loved plants and wanted to be a botanist, how his mother used to drive him along the back roads outside the city, stopping so they could look at the wildflowers. She had taken him foraging in Central Park, showing him how you could make soup out of the greens they found. She had pointed out marigolds, lilies, even purple foxglove, which was not only gorgeous but that some herbalists would brew into a calming tea.

When they sat down for dinner, Helen worried about the store-bought pasta with jarred sauce, but Jude had second helpings, and when she got up to clear the table, imagining that Jude must have a maid for that, maybe a cook, too, Jude sprang up, gathering plates. And then Ella joined him in washing and drying the dishes. Helen couldn't help herself; she came into the kitchen to help, too, all of them laughing and talking. For a moment, Helen felt like she was back in her parents' home, except there, the men would never have done the kitchen work. Helen grabbed a towel, shimmering with pride. She had cooked a dinner people enjoyed. She was making the kitchen shine. Letting the evening just happen. That was true holiness.

When Jude left, Helen turned to Ella. "I like him," she said, and Ella beamed. "He's welcome here anytime."

AFTER THAT, JUDE began coming to their apartment more and more, sometimes every day. Helen would hear him in the background whenever she called Ella's cellphone. He'd be there when she got home. Only a fool could miss how happy Ella was. It was as if she had relaxed into her own skin finally, and that made Helen relax, too. But it wasn't just Ella who had changed—it was Helen's home. It felt noisy with life again. Maybe not the swarm of people from her childhood, but there was always someone in the kitchen, someone bringing out a chessboard. Even the air felt different, lighter.

"Make yourself at home," she told him, and he did, and wasn't that something? She felt good when she saw his socks in the laundry curled up like commas; and of course, she'd wash and fold them, the same way she would Ella's, because what were families for? And wasn't this what it was beginning to feel like, the three of them? She bought him a toothbrush and always put clean sheets on the velvet couch for when it got too late and she didn't want him taking a subway or even a cab home, not when he seemed so tired.

"Make sure to let your father know you're here," she said, and Jude always nodded.

She loved his laughter, the low buzz of talk, the life in her house. Jude had even come to the shop, alone, because he had wanted to see where she worked. She had been beaming, proud. She had showed him her workroom, she had introduced him to coworkers, and when he left, one of the saleswomen had said, "Your son is a darling!"

"He's not my—" Helen said, and then stopped and smiled. "Thank you."

ONE NIGHT, HELEN awoke to the sound of the two of them having sex in Ella's room. She froze, and then got her robe. She didn't think it was right for them to have sex in her house. Was it right for them to have sex at all? When she was Ella's age, no one she knew had had sex unless they were married. No one had talked about it. And then Helen had had sex—only once—and that had been her ruin, her never-again moment. But if she said no to Ella, what would happen? They'd have sex anyway. So she waited until the next day, when Jude was gone, and offered to take Ella to a doctor to get the pill or an IUD.

"Mom . . . ," Ella said warningly.

"You're risking your future—"

"Oh my God, that's what his dad says," Ella said. "I'm not discussing this."

"You are if you're having sex in my house. Having overnights. You have to be protected. Both of you."

Ella's face turned steely. "Fine. We'll take care of it."

"How?"

"We just will."

"You prove it to me, and then he can sleep here. I'd rather you do it here where you're safe than outside where you won't be."

Ella sighed heavily, but two days later, she purposefully left a box of condoms displayed on her desk. It wasn't protection enough, but at least it was something.

Even after that, Ella was stiff around Helen, and Helen knew that the subject was closed.

There were other closed subjects. One day, Helen saw how Jude and Ella were talking secretively at the kitchen table, practically whispering. She noticed how sad Jude looked, how he was wearing a long-sleeved shirt buttoned to his wrists. He looked like he was crying.

She waited until Jude headed for the bathroom and then quietly asked Ella if this talk was something an adult should know about, because there were resources for all kinds of things.

Ella grew alarmed. "It's nothing," she said. "And it's not your business. It just has to do with Jude and me." Ella frowned. "And what are you doing, hovering over him?"

Helen sighed. "Honey, he doesn't have a mother, and he needs mothering."

That night, Ella and Jude were watching *Fame* on the small TV in the living room. Helen came in and said, "Oh, I love that film!" and sat beside Jude. As soon as she did, she felt Ella watching her.

"Didn't you say you had to finish a dress?" Ella said pointedly.

Helen felt the air around Ella chill, so she left the two of them to watch alone.

Helen fretted and worried over Jude. She sat in her bedroom, which was also her sewing room, yearning to be with the two kids. Jude didn't seem to mind her presence. She gave him advice and he listened to it. He seemed genuinely interested in what she had to say. Almost once a week, he brought her a new plant. And not only was Jude not turned off by their shabby home, he seemed to want to be there all the time. He made himself comfortable, treating the fridge as his own, sprawling on the couch. But he gave back, too, making dinner without being asked, cleaning up the kitchen after meals so that it gleamed.

She couldn't resist. She got up from her sewing machine and pressed her ear against the door to hear what the kids were saying.

"Soon as we graduate, we'll leave the city," Jude said.

"Let's go live on the beach."

"We can get married in a field of flowers and build our own log cabin. I'll have my own plant store and you can help me, and maybe you can become a writer, since you like stories."

"Two kids," Ella said. "Or maybe six."

"Not six!" Jude said, and they both laughed, and Helen, listening, thought of her home growing up, how six was never too many children, just as there was never too much happiness.

Jude told Ella that they would have their life. They'd have everything and it would go on forever and ever and ever.

Helen picked up the sleeve she was working on again, part of a dark green velvet suit that she knew could sell at the shop. She told herself that Ella and Jude were just dreaming, that there was no danger in their relationship. None at all.

LATER THAT WEEK, Helen was listening to Jude talk about the books he was reading. "I just finished *One Flew Over the Cuckoo's Nest*," he was saying to Ella. "You have to read it!"

Helen grabbed a pencil from an end table and wrote the title down. She wasn't familiar with that title, or any of the other books Jude mentioned, but she could check them out from the library.

His face glowed when he talked, and he turned to smile at Ella. The kids. She thought of both of them as hers somehow.

"I bet you have a nice garden at home," she said, imagining it spreading across a rooftop, or potted along a sunny balcony. But Jude shook his head.

"No, actually. My father says plants draw bugs."

"Does he now?" Helen said, and then she had an idea. This was her home, and she could do what she wanted, and if that included making that home more welcoming to Jude, especially with that father of his, well then that's what she would do. It would be a mitzvah. A gift from her to the kids.

"I want to show you guys something," she said, and then she led them down a set of stairs to the back of the building. "Ta-da," she said, opening the door. And there it was, a square patch of dirt in a corner, overgrown with grass, buzzing with insects. A shared backyard that no one ever used.

"Well, what do you think?" she asked. "You could have a garden here. I know it's little, but it's something. And there's a lot of sun back here."

Jude threw his arms around her. She couldn't believe that she, Helen, could do something for this wonderful boy that his own father wouldn't, and she felt a special thrill knowing that it would be yet another thing that would draw him to her home.

Ella hung back, uncertain, but Jude grabbed her hand. "We can go together and choose seeds tomorrow," he said. "We'll get a shovel and some fertilizer. It'll be our garden. Thank you, Helen. Thank you, thank you, thank you!"

It was the first time he had used her first name.

"I'm sorry—I didn't mean to be disrespectful—" he started to say, but Helen raised a hand.

"It's actually more respectful for you to call me Helen."

The next day Jude and Ella got to Helen's apartment early, carrying packets of seeds, a shovel, and a watering can. Every day that week, they met at the house after school, first to clear and then to dig the garden and seed it.

"Our garden!" Ella kept saying when they finally tromped inside, tired and grinning, dirt on their clothes and under their nails. Helen knew that *our* meant that she wasn't invited to help, but that was okay, because when the kids weren't tending the garden, they were sitting next to it on rickety lawn chairs, talking. All Helen had to do was look outside her kitchen window and she could see them there, her radiant children. And afterward, the kids would come inside, and she'd cook them dinner, and her house would be flooded with life again.

Most of the seedlings took ten days to germinate, three weeks to grow. And grow they did, and Jude began coming to Helen's more and more often to nurture them, to be with Ella, and to see Helen, too. Eventually bigger greenery poked up. Butterflies and bees and birds came. All that summer, there were marigolds, tomatoes, bright bursts of sunflowers that Jude said could grow to beanstalk height. And plenty of foxglove, the purple flowers Jude had asked to plant, the blooms she thought were so pretty.

IT WAS JULY, and so hot that Helen wanted to get to work early, if only for the relief of air-conditioning. The kids had already gone out to a museum and Helen was just about to leave for work when someone buzzed her apartment. She looked outside and saw a man in a business suit.

"Who is it?" she said into the intercom.

"Judge Andrew Stein," he said.

Surprised, she buzzed him up.

As soon as he came in, he looked her apartment up and down as though entering had been a mistake. She offered the couch, but he sat on a wooden chair, brushing it off first. She offered him a glass of water, and he looked offended.

"Judge Stein," she said finally. "I'm betting this is about our kids. Am I right?"

He sliced one hand through his hair. "I was going to phone you about this before, when I caught them at my home, in bed together."

"What?" Helen said.

"I told them Ella wasn't welcome in my home anymore. Now I find out he's over here all the time instead," he said. "They're seeing too much of each other. It's not healthy. Jude has a future to think about."

"Well, they're kids. Puppy love," Helen said, but Judge Stein shook his head.

"My son is at your house all the time. He sleeps here. He eats here. He's taking advantage of you."

"No. No, he isn't. I love having him here. He's a perfectly good, polite boy. A nice boy."

Judge Stein sighed. "Well, truthfully, I'd like for you to help me stop it. They can see each other, but not like this. It's—obsessive, wouldn't you say? He's practically living with you. They're still children. Don't you think this is wrong?"

Helen could see Jude's sweater tossed in a corner. She now stocked his favorite lemon yogurts in her fridge. Already this morning, she had changed the sheets on Ella's bed—and done a wash so there would be fresh linens for Jude on the couch. And there in the kitchen was the chess game she and Jude had played for long, comforting hours.

"I don't, actually," Helen said, standing. Her head felt full of bees. And then she motioned him to the back window, where he could look out and see the garden. "See that?" she asked, and he peered past her. "The kids built that garden. They dug the dirt. They planted all kinds of things."

"My son is always trying to get me to buy plants," Judge Stein said. "But I know what would happen. No one would care for them."

"But look how they care for this garden!" Helen said. "It's full of flowers and herbs."

"Jude knows how I feel," Judge Stein said, turning from the window. "I believe your daughter knows as well. This isn't a good situation, and I am going to do my best to nip it in the bud."

"Try that and it'll just get stronger," Helen said. "Believe me, I know. Let it burn out."

"Fire burning out is one thing. Wildfire is another," he said shortly.

Helen sighed. "I trust my daughter to make the right decisions," she said.

"So I've heard."

"Thank you for coming by." She walked to the door, firm but polite.

As soon as he left, Helen went back into the kitchen, simmering with rage. *How dare he?* she thought. She had a full house here now, a family. There was warmth and laughter and love. And she was going to fight to keep them.

# SEVEN

# Brooklyn

*December 2018*

Helen wandered through Williamsburg, feeling as if she had a tenacious flu, and desperately hoping that reliving a bit of her past might cure it. Even bundled up, she felt the biting chill, but she couldn't go home yet. Maybe she would run into someone she had known. Someone who would know her still, and who would have forgiven her. Maybe they'd even welcome her back. She searched every face she passed, but she didn't see anyone she knew from her old community.

Helen passed a street that was so dangerous when she was young that she never dared approach it. Yet now, to her surprise, Hasidic women—in heavy beige tights under long skirts, wearing wigs—were traveling in groups, pushing strollers, holding kids' hands. They were all so young, and here was Helen, forty years old—an ancient age in her community, a shanda that she wasn't married. *I was once one of you.* She felt a pang of longing as she watched her people, but with no way to approach them, she kept walking.

Everything looked so different. The outskirts of the Hasidic community had changed—gentrified with fancy cafés, an Ethiopian restaurant, a Greek one, hipster kids in ripped jeans with those man buns and tattoos creeping up their necks.

When Helen passed a real estate office, she stopped and doubled back. It was as if the listings were calling to her. Williamsburg. Even if the Hasidim wouldn't speak to her now, maybe they would when they saw she was part of the community. And other people, like that boy who had given her directions, might too. This whole area felt like bounty, busy with all kinds of people, full of noise and color and smells. Her quiet Bay Ridge neighborhood had been perfect for Ella when she'd come home from prison, but now Helen felt that quiet slowly killing her.

Glancing at the listings in the window, she quickly realized that Williamsburg was significantly more expensive than where she was now. But maybe Helen could make do with less, a one-bedroom instead of a two. Or even a studio, because all she really needed for her work was a table. Plus, it didn't seem likely that Ella was coming back. Maybe she could get a better job right here and it would pay more. It wouldn't hurt to look.

She walked into the real estate office. There were large photographs on the wall, one showing a couple looking out at the twinkling city below them. Another showed a family with a baby on a white living room rug.

"So, how can I change your life today?"

Helen startled, and then looked up. A woman in a red printed dress addressed her again. "Where you make your home can make all the difference in the world, don't you agree?"

"I want to rent a studio," Helen said, surprising herself.

THE LAST WEEK of December, Helen found a new job in Williamsburg. The shop was called The Fabric of Life, and it even paid her a bit more money so she could save a little. She found, too, a studio on Bedford Avenue, tiny but bright, with one large bay window that looked out onto the street. After she signed the lease, she enlisted Mouse—whom, to her delight, she was seeing more and more often—to help her move. He happily helped her paint the place a cheery soft yellow to make it even brighter. "Is this farther for you?" she asked him, worried.

"It's actually closer," he told her. "Especially via Uber. I'm always happy to order one for you to come visit me. I'd like that."

She hung photos of Ella, and one of Helen's family when she was twelve and they had all been photographed together, smiling, proud, happy.

She still spoke and texted with Ella. She had the beginnings of something with Mouse. And right now, being here in this neighborhood again, felt right to her—as if an empty space inside her were slowly being filled.

ONE NIGHT, HELEN stopped at a store she remembered from childhood, attracted by the silver candleholders in the window. She thought back to how a similar candleholder had graced her mother's kitchen table. She couldn't afford one like that, so she bought something simpler, made of polished wood, along with cream-colored candles.

The first thing she did when she got to her apartment was set up the candles and light them. Shabbos meals and holidays had been so extraordinary, the table set so beautifully. There had been all that love for her, for the whole family; but that was gone now, shut off the day they kicked her out of the house. They had never really known her. And they had never known their granddaughter.

And now here she was in her little apartment. She looked around, taking in the way her furniture looked by the window, the light splashed on her table, the flames danced atop the pretty candles. She would make her own blessings, her own life.

She thought about the grandchild she'd never known—hadn't wanted to know. If she had, maybe the child would have been with her now. Maybe she could have raised the girl herself. She thought about how full and happy she had been while Jude was with them, the feeling of having a family. But she also knew that raising the child from infancy would have been impossible.

Every time Helen saw Mouse, their connection seemed better than before. Mouse took her to see *Wicked*, her first ever Broadway show, and he bought her a copy of the Gregory Maguire novel on which it was based, so that she could read it before seeing the play. She felt him staring at her, and when she turned to him, his whole face lit up.

"What?" she said.

"I love how excited you get by everything," Mouse said.

Helen blushed. "I know, I'm a rube."

"Never a rube!"

"No, no, it's okay. I'm not well educated and I'm probably not what you're used to. I know that your neighborhood is filled with sophisticated, well-educated women. They probably take all of this for granted because it's their world."

"Maybe they do," Mouse said. "I've dated a lot of people who came up the same way I did. Nothing surprises them. But what I love about you is that you're not that way. It's like all your cells come alive when you experience something new."

He took her to restaurants she would never have thought to choose herself, introducing her to Ethiopian food, vegan sushi, Indian food so spicy that her mouth seemed to catch fire. But she loved the flame. They went to concerts, and as they walked into venues, he would put his hand on the small of her back, and his warmth would spread through her. He held her hand, interlacing their fingers, letting her know, *I've got you.* Helen still felt as though people were looking at her, but for once it was not because she had done something wrong. Instead, they might be thinking: *Look how he adores her. What a lucky woman.*

Best of all were the regular, quiet times they had. Grilled cheese at a diner, served with french fries, extra salty. A trip to the Guggenheim to see a new Picasso exhibit. He bought her brand-new hardcover books, and as soon as she finished one, he'd bring her another. Since Ella was born, she had never had much time to read, but how could she not read what he had bought her? She loved getting lost in the stories and found that reading everything by a particular author felt like they were speaking directly to her. She read and loved all of Sue Miller and

Elizabeth Strout. She devoured Toni Morrison and relished the dark, smart terror of Dan Chaon.

"More, more," she told Mouse, and he obliged. She arranged the books on her lone shelf, and every time she looked at them, she felt a jolt of pleasure. It was the first time in a very long while that someone had focused on her so intently.

By New Years, Mouse widened their circle, introducing her to his friends. He held a dinner party at his apartment, a huge two-bedroom on West 86th Street. As soon as she entered, she felt at home. There were comfortable throw pillows on every seat, a cushiony couch. Even the lighting was soft, giving the pale polished floors a glow. He led her to his dining room, with a long wooden table covered in tapestry cloth, and seated her between him and an orthodontist with a great sense of humor. Mouse's friends kept including her in conversations, not giving her even a moment to feel nervous.

The woman sitting across from her, a fashion copywriter, said, "Mouse tells us you're a dress designer!" Her eyes shone with interest.

"Oh, it's nothing," Helen insisted. "I tailor things. I do almost of it in a backroom. And some of it at home."

"I want to see that backroom!" the woman said. "Name a day. I'll come over and then take you to lunch. How does that sound?"

Helen, astonished, looked over at Mouse, who had been listening and who was now grinning at her.

"Why, it sounds amazing," Helen said. Of course when she told them where it was, the woman said, "Wow, that's quite a hike. It takes a lot to get me below 14th Street these days, let alone across the river!"

Some of the other people laughed knowingly, but Helen shook it off. That journey was nothing to Mouse, which made him all the more special to her.

HE WANTED TO know everything about her. How she had started to sew, how it felt to make all her brothers' and sisters' clothing when she was growing up—but almost never making anything for herself. He cooked her dinners, something no one but Jude had ever done—and he had been a kid at the time, courting her daughter, so that didn't count. Mouse was so chivalrous that he never pushed for more intimacy, even though Helen found herself thinking about the curve of his neck, the smooth slope of his shoulders. Other times, she saw the way he was watching her, drinking her in.

"C'mon," he said one night, after a romantic dinner at his apartment. He drew out a checkers set, and as soon as she saw it, Helen felt a pang. She thought of her father, teaching her how to play, then playing game after game with her, against the backdrop of laughter and noise in their home in Williamsburg. She thought of her mother cleaning, the older kids taking care of the younger ones. She thought of all that love stitched together in one place. It had been a treasured time for her, playing with her father, having all his attention focused on her as she moved the checkers about the board. She hadn't played that game since she was nine.

"Oh, I don't know . . . ," she said now.

"Wait until you see my strategy!" he said. He laid out the board and pieces, and Helen held her breath.

"You make the first move," he said, and when she did, she looked up and saw him smiling at her.

A Mozart symphony was playing softly from the stereo, and she remembered that she once told him that she loved Mozart. He had remembered.

"A most excellent move," he said, and Helen relaxed.

IT WAS THE end of January when Helen realized, with a shock, she was in love. It was such a strange sensation, like the lingering scent of lavender. She kept thinking about him. She was forty years old and this was her first time in love. What a thing!

She couldn't tell him. He might not feel the same, and then she would be crushed. Instead, she decided to show him her feelings in a subtle way. She'd make him a shirt, and every stitch would be a message to him. If he felt the same spark that she did, she was sure he'd know just what that shirt really meant. She brought home bolts of cloth he might like, including a silky cotton in dark gray, which would accentuate his gray eyes. She had to measure him, so she brought out the tape measure and stood so close she could feel his breath on her shoulders. She had thought he'd be astonished, but instead, he grew still, and she felt her heart clutch. When he cleared his throat, Helen stopped.

"What is it?" she asked, alarmed.

"I don't talk about it a lot, but I'm a widower, six years now. I took care of my wife for years before she died," he said. "I didn't mind. I loved her. I'm fifty years old and I've dated and dated, but all the women I meet seem to want something from me. Money, usually. Sex. Security. Expensive dinners." He tipped up her chin. "What do you want from me, Helen? I don't think you want anything. I think you just give and give without thinking of yourself."

He was so close that she could see where he had cut himself shaving. She put one finger up to cover the cut. He bent and kissed her.

Stunned, Helen put her hand to her mouth. In all of her reveries, she hadn't planned on a kiss like this, so deep and soft and warm. She shivered.

"Too soon?" Mouse said.

"I haven't—" Helen said. "It's embarrassing, but I haven't been with anyone since I was a teenager."

Mouse gave her a long, thoughtful look. He stroked her hair and looked deeper at her.

"Something's wrong, I can see it in your face. Please, won't you tell me?"

Helen waved her hand. "I don't know—"

She studied the intensity of his gaze. She had never heard him insult anyone. He never even seemed to judge people.

"I grew up as a part of the Hasidic community," she said. "My first name was Shaindy—"

Mouse opened his mouth to speak, but Helen raised her hand.

"No, no, listen," she said. "How I grew up is still who I am. Why I am like I am, I suppose."

"I like who you are."

"I was supposed to get married when I was eighteen."

"Jesus. How could you even know what kind of husband you wanted at that age?"

She shook her head. "I didn't have to know, because they were going to choose for me. They set up meetings with prospective matches. And I wanted to meet them. I was so excited about it, so hopeful about the way my life was going to change. It was the way we did things.

"But the matches they made for me were so bland—closer to boiled potatoes than men. I looked at them and I couldn't imagine spending my life with a single one. Of course, my mother disagreed. 'It's you, not them,' she told me. She thought I had studied too much in school, but honestly, I knew nothing about the way the world worked. Works."

"But you're in the world now. You're making your way."

"I could be more educated. A lot of what I know is self-taught," she said. "No one told me or showed me what to read. I just read. If it was in front of me, I grabbed it. I read my grandmother's *Reader's Digest* in the bathroom. I once took a copy of *A Tree Grows in Brooklyn* that I found on the subway and practically memorized it, hiding it under the covers at night, reading with a flashlight. When I left home each day for school, I wanted to learn everything there was to learn. But then I went into Manhattan one day and got into trouble. Big trouble."

She waited, but Mouse was quiet for a moment, watching her. "What happened?" he asked.

"I've never told anyone. I wasn't supposed to take the subway by myself, and certainly not to go into Manhattan. But I wanted to. Something kept calling me, pulling me outside the bounds of the community. I tried for weeks to go down the subway stairs, but I was so afraid. What if something happened to me? I knew there were people out there who would want to hurt me or even kill me, just because I was different."

"But you went. What made you able to finally go?"

Helen swallowed. "My mother. She was angry with me because she found the book—*A Tree Grows in Brooklyn*—hidden under my mattress. I told her it was a wonderful book, that there was nothing wrong with it, and she tore it up, page by page, and threw it into the trash."

"Knowing you, I'm surprised you didn't pull out all the pages and sew them together somehow," Mouse said.

"I wanted to, believe me, but she would have just ripped them apart again." Helen told him how she stormed out of the house, how her anger had fueled her dash to the subway. At first, she was just hoping to find more books left on the seats. She had already planned to find better hiding places for them. She kept telling herself how brave she was, like Francie in the book. But she ended up riding the M train all the way to 34th Street because she had been too terrified to get off at any of the other stops.

"That must have been so scary for you," Mouse said.

"You have no idea," Helen said. "I couldn't find the courage to ask anyone where I should go. Even though I spoke English, just like most of the people there, somehow when I heard them speaking, I couldn't understand a word. I couldn't speak it back. Plus, I believed the people there were tainted, not like those in my community. And I knew that they might do terrible things to me, just like my mother had warned me. So, I started small, although to me it was daring. I went into Macy's, the same Macy's my mother had taken me to to find presentable things for me to wear for my matches. This time, I tried on a sleeveless shirt and pants! I wore pants! But just for a moment because it was too immodest for me. It wasn't normal." She swallowed hard.

"I knew I couldn't tell anyone, but I kept going back. It felt like a fire had been lit inside me, strengthening me, yet capable of consuming and destroying me if anyone from the community found out. One day,

I went all the way up to Central Park. I sat on this bench, so terrified my whole body was shaking. I was just watching people, imagining the lives they might lead. Then a man came and sat on the bench, too close to me. I was frozen in place. In the community, you aren't supposed to even look at men. Yet here I was. I wanted to run, but I couldn't move."

Mouse gently put one hand over hers.

She told him how she jumped up from the bench; she needed to find the subway, but quickly realized she didn't know which way to go. The man was looking at her, but in a kind way. "Are you lost?" he asked.

Feeling a growing panic, she walked back to him. "Excuse me," she said. "Where is the subway downtown?" Her voice had sounded tinny in her ears.

"Oh, it's close," he said, pleasantly. He pointed toward a pathway. "Right through there. Can't miss it."

But she was still scared, and he must have seen her terror because he then said he'd walk her to it.

"It's just a little way," he said, standing and gesturing. "Follow all the people. They're all going the same way as you."

She walked beside him. He told her that his name was Edward, that he was a lawyer. And then he touched her arm, and her stomach roiled. She stepped back, nearly stumbling.

"Hey, hey," he had said kindly. "We just head left here. That's all."

He steered her into a wooded area, then suddenly pushed her to the ground. She begged him to stop, but he was so much stronger than she was. She made her hands into fists and hit him as hard as she could, but that only seemed to make him stronger and more determined. She started to scream and he clapped his hand over her mouth so that she had to struggle to breathe. And then a bolt of pain seared through her, and then it was over, and suddenly he was gone.

Helen finally looked up. She saw Mouse's hands on hers before she allowed herself to feel them again.

When she met his eyes, she saw they were damp. "Why are you crying?" she whispered.

"Because what happened to you was so wrong."

"No. I was so stupid," she said. "I should have known better. I should have listened to my parents—they told me what would happen."

He squeezed her hands. "How could you know? How could you even imagine it was your fault?"

"I talked to him! I went with him. How could it not be my fault?"

"Helen," Mouse said gently. "You were a young, innocent girl, attacked by a stranger who took advantage of you. It was *rape*. It was *violent*. He is to blame, not you. He should be in prison. You . . . you did nothing wrong."

Helen began to weep, swiping at her eyes until Mouse handed her a tissue. Her shame was so consuming, she felt like she would die.

"It wasn't your fault," he repeated. "None of it."

Helen could hear his words, but they seemed to be floating above her, like balloons she couldn't quite grab.

"I brushed myself off," Helen said. "I found a cop and asked him where the subway was, and when he told me, I found it and took the train home."

"You didn't tell him what happened? What that man, that monster, did to you?"

"It was my fault," she said.

"Helen, listen to me. It wasn't—"

"I wasn't supposed to go into the city by myself, to talk to or even look at men, especially ones I didn't know! There are rules, Mouse, for a reason. And look what happened when I disobeyed them! I got what I deserved." She felt herself tottering on the edge of hysteria, but then she saw Mouse's shocked face.

"No one deserves to be attacked," he said quietly. "No one deserves to be raped."

"That's such an ugly word," Helen said.

"That's what it was. Rape. An ugly word for an ugly crime."

There was a long silence between them.

She told him how from then on, people in her community noticed something was off about her, sensed that she wasn't right. At home, she no longer wanted any part of the household chores she had done before, including watching her younger siblings. The only time she felt at peace was when she was at the sewing machine, the whir of it soothing her. She felt split in two.

A week later, she had gone to meet another match, a boy her mother had approved of. She had seen him at the butcher helping his mother, being polite. But when Helen met him, she only stared sullenly at the tablecloth and bit her lips. She could tell by the way he quickly averted his eyes that she revolted him, the same way she was revolted by herself. She said goodbye as politely as she could.

Her world had changed. She felt as if she might ignite from shame.

"You had no one to talk to?" Mouse asked. "No girlfriends?"

Helen shook her head.

"God, Helen," Mouse said. "I'm so sorry."

"Don't say that," Helen said. "You can be sorry that that happened to me. I am. But that encounter gave me my daughter, my Ella. And she has been my life ever since."

She told Mouse how she hadn't even realized that she was pregnant until three months later, when she hadn't been able to keep any food down. She told him how she finally went to her parents and threw herself at their mercy. She was their daughter, and despite everything, she knew that they loved her, that they wanted to protect her. They had always taught her that family was everything. Maybe she could accept a second-tier match, a leftover boy. No one would have to know she was pregnant. They could pretend the baby was early.

But her mother had put her hands on Helen's stomach and then recoiled. "It's too late," her mother said. "All anyone has to do is look at your belly and then they will see. It's a shanda. You are a disgrace."

Helen told Mouse how her parents announced to her that she was no longer their daughter, that she had not only shamed herself, but also her siblings. She had ruined their chances of a proper match. Everyone would gossip if word got out. No one could know, not even the rabbi. Certainly not her siblings. She would have to leave the community before her disgrace ruined the entire family. Better to make up a story that others might believe—that she'd been sent to Israel to visit cousins, that she might even find a match over there and stay—than to let her stay with them.

"I saw how I had made them suffer," Helen said. "My father looked shattered. 'You were my jewel,' he kept saying. My mother made my siblings stay in their rooms, and even though I was crying, and she was crying, she told me there was nothing to do but throw me out; that it killed her, but she had to protect the rest of the family, my siblings."

Helen sighed. "I had nowhere to go. I slept in an alley that first night, sure that in the morning things would be better, but somehow news of my pregnancy had gotten out, and no one would even look at me."

"Couldn't you have given the baby up for adoption?"

"I didn't know how," she said. "And my family had tossed me away. How could I do the same thing to my child?"

She told Mouse how she had again taken the train into Manhattan. The city seemed like a sleeping dragon, ready to devour her. Nothing and no one could help.

"I saw homeless people sleeping in Penn Station, and so I napped there during the day. I ate food people left behind in restaurants, ordering coffee at diner counters and taking scraps from un-bused tables when no one was looking. I was sure I was going to die, that I would be punished for stealing food, but then, to my shock, nothing happened. Nothing!" she said, amazed. "So I ate more traif and stole hours of sleep in public places.

"Finally, about a week after my parents kicked me out, someone saw me scavenging from the dumpster behind the diner and approached me.

I was afraid and ready to run, but she spoke softly. And, in a blazer and slacks, she looked wealthy to me. This Good Samaritan told me about a place called Covenant House, where I could go and they would help me. She even paid a cab to take me there."

"I know that place. Good people," Mouse said.

"They, that place, they helped me. For the first time, I met people of color, talked with non-Jews, spent time with the people I had been warned against and had always avoided. They talked to me, and I found out many had stories like mine. Some were also dealing with drug abuse."

"Everyone has a different story, Helen."

"Well, telling mine at Covenant House saved my life. And that place certainly saved Ella's. They showed me this whole new world. And they even found me a job sewing in Queens.

"I stayed until Ella was born and by then I had saved enough for a one-room basement apartment. No real windows, hardly any daylight, but it was ours. I changed my name, too. I became Helen. My old name, my old person, Shaindy, was gone."

Helen felt scraped raw, as if there were nothing left inside her. She didn't realize she was crying until Mouse brushed her tears with his finger.

"It's okay," he said. "It's all okay." He took her hands and kissed them. "I'm so glad you told me. It makes me care for you even more. What you've been through. How you've triumphed over it all."

"I don't know if I'd say that," Helen said. She felt like an iceberg, smooth, showing serenity above deep, dangerous waters.

They lay on the couch, Helen in his arms. He stroked her hair.

"You really think it wasn't my fault?"

Mouse hugged her tighter. "Okay, try this. Think of this as a story about another person. A young girl who goes to the park in the daylight to ask for directions. There's nothing wrong with that. Think about a man who violently, without her permission, attacks her. There's no way for her to stop him. He's bigger, stronger. He forces himself on her. There's everything wrong with that. Think if this had happened to your daughter."

"I would go and find and kill that man," Helen said.

"The point is you wouldn't think for a second it was Ella's fault. And this was never your fault, Helen. Never."

She rested against him. He was a good man, she knew that, and if a good man thought she was innocent, then maybe she really could be.

"I was stupid," she decided, but Mouse shook his head.

"You were brave and tough. Look where you are now, with a job and a daughter and a home!"

"It wasn't easy," she said.

Feeling she might as well tell him everything, she recounted the months after Ella was born, how she had fallen into a black hole. She was in this tiny apartment and everything was so hard, and she missed her parents, her family, so, so much, and she had kept thinking how easy it would be to take her life. She could swallow a whole bottle of aspirin. She could walk in front of one of those buses that sped by with seemingly no regard for pedestrians. One day while Ella was sleeping, she had actually put on her coat, had her hand on the door to meet that bus, when Ella began to cry from the open dresser drawer Helen used as a crib. It was then that she knew she couldn't do it, not to her daughter. She had taken off her coat and gone to her baby.

"I'm here," she had promised. "I'll always be here."

Now Helen sighed. Maybe Mouse was right. Maybe it wasn't her fault, just a terrible thing that had happened to her. She felt herself growing lighter.

She didn't want to move from Mouse's arms. He treated her as if she were something rare, like he was the lucky one, not her. She tilted her head and this time she kissed him. Deeper, with more passion. He didn't move. She kissed him again, her breath quickening, and he drew back, watching her. "Helen, are you sure this is what you want? I'd never push you."

"I want to," she said quietly. "With you, I want to. But I don't know what to do—" She covered her face with her hands. "Since then, I've never—"

He gently took her hands away from her face.

"We'll figure it out," he said. "And you can be the one to initiate everything. We'll get there, together."

She took his hand and led him to the bedroom. And that night, Helen slept in Mouse's arms. He never tried anything, never even moved to unbutton her blouse.

When she awoke, she stared at his face. How beautiful he was. How kind. He had just let her be herself, and she was so thankful.

"It's morning," he said, opening his eyes sleepily. "Should we have breakfast? I make a mean pancake."

Helen didn't want pancakes. She put her fingers against his mouth, then started to unbutton his shirt, and next her own. "Is this what you want?" he asked her, and she nodded, and then he touched her breast.

She shivered.

He was slow and tender and when she saw how he kept his eyes open the whole time, watching her, she began to cry.

"What?" he asked, alarmed.

"I'm just happy," she told him.

# EIGHT

# Ann Arbor

*January 2019*

Ella was in the Diag, enjoying the clear, bright day as she watched the students, dressed in boots and coats and scarves, tromping through the snow between classes. Some of them smiled at her, as if she were another student, and impulsively she followed a group of them into Angell Hall, a building constructed in the style of the Greek Parthenon, with columns running up its front. Inside there were beautiful mosaic tiles on a vaulted ceiling, and she tipped her head back to drink in the view.

Ella meandered, finding her way into a lecture hall, and on an impulse took a seat near the back, her heart thudding. What if someone approached her and told her she didn't belong here? What if they booted her out? She looked at the girl next to her, dressed in carefully ripped jeans, and imagined tearing her own jeans in the same style. She looked at the girl's textbook, *Ancient History for the Ages*. Okay. That was what she'd learn here. Most students had laptops, but the girl next to her had a notebook, a pen.

She leaned toward the girl. "I forgot my notebook," she said. "Can I borrow some paper, and a pen?"

"I hear you. I do that all the time," the girl said. She ripped a few pages from her notebook and handed her a pen.

Ella watched the students settling in, flirting, talking, then growing quiet. Not one of them looked as frightened as she felt. She watched the professor, dressed in loose jeans, his hair long and tousled, talking about Caligula and how he had wanted to make his horse part of the Roman Senate. All the students were laughing, and Ella laughed, too. She had spent so much time practicing being an adult, learning to think like a working woman before she had even gotten to Ann Arbor and started her job. Now she realized that she also wanted to know what it was like to still be a kid. A college kid—something she had never been.

When the class was over, the girl next to her said, "See you next time," and Ella stood there for a moment, stunned with joy. She could come back if she wanted. And next time, she'd have a notebook and pen. She could talk more to this girl; they might even become friends.

ON THE WAY home, she stopped at Wooly Bully to browse their selections of yarn while she happily waited for her meeting with Marianna and Carla, for Carla's very first knitting lesson. Sometimes when she didn't have a project in mind, she visited the shop just to touch the materials, and to imagine those luscious wools and cottons knit into something special. Today, though, she thought about what Carla might like for her first project.

As soon as she walked in, she felt warm. She loved this store. There were always a few people sitting around one of the blue tables knitting, getting a lesson, or just enjoying the vibe. There were stacks of knitting magazines on a rack by the window, and rows upon rows of blond shelves filled with yarns of different colors and textures. Knitting samples hung from some of the shelves so you could see what the yarn would look like in specific patterns.

Ella crouched down to pull out a skein of deep blue wool when she felt someone beside her, and then she was startled to feel breath against her ear.

"Boo!" Carla said, and she wheeled to see her daughter leaning down beside her. Marianna was looking on from several steps away, as dazzling as a mirage.

"I'm so glad we're finally able to do this," Marianna said, smiling.

Carla hopped on one foot, tugging at Ella's hand. And then Ella remembered how Marianna had caught her attention on the playground, bribing her with money. Well, yarn wasn't money, but, to Ella, it was close.

"Hey, Carla," Ella said. "You can help me choose a yarn if you want to. You pick any color you like."

Carla scanned the shelves, her face so serious that Ella had to smile. And then Carla looked at the yarn in Ella's hand.

"That's the same color as my mittens!" Carla said, splaying her hands.

Marianna looked from the mittens to Ella, and then frowned, as if she were trying to figure something out.

"Lots of yarns look alike," Ella said quickly. "Lots of stitches do, too." Marianna was holding Carla's mitten against the yarn, comparing them. "Is something wrong?" Ella said.

Marianna waved her hand. "Nothing," she said. "It's just that someone left a pair of mittens for Carla a while ago, and they were made from this yarn."

"Wow. That's a nice gesture. Or do you not think so?" Ella said.

Marianna shrugged. "I just don't know who to thank."

Ella relaxed. In the end, she bought more blue yarn for herself, and a pair of short, thick plastic needles for Carla that would be easy for her small hands to handle. She also helped her pick out a pattern for a scarf she could make from some rainbow-colored yarn that Carla selected after much deliberation.

"A very wise choice," Ella said, and Carla beamed.

"Can you teach me now, like right this very second? Like right, right now, this very very very second?" Carla asked.

Ella had never taught anyone else how to knit, but she remembered learning in prison, the teacher telling them a little singsong saying. "The mouse goes in, he gets the cheese," the teacher had said, pulling up a stitch and then sliding it off the needle. "Then he runs away."

Everyone in prison had knitted easy things. Potholders first, then scarves. A lot of the women had given it up after a while, bored. Ella, though, had quickly become addicted. She loved the hypnotic click of the needles, the way squares of knitting could be built into something new.

Ella looked at Carla's open face. "Let's sit at this table by the window," she said.

Ella cast on stitches for Carla, promising to teach her how to do that step later, that the important thing now was to just get going. She even cast on some stitches for Marianna to try, offering her own needles from her purse.

"I'm making a scarf for Georgie," Carla said.

"Her stuffed moose," Marianna clarified.

Ella sat so close to Carla she could smell her hair, a faint strawberry shampoo. She could feel a kind of warmth radiating from her. Marianna gave up on her knitting after a while and just happily watched. As she pulled stitches from one needle to the other, Carla was filled with questions. Who made the yarn and why? Did the sheep ever know that the yarn was from them and how did they feel about it? Could you knit with your fingers if you lost your needles?

Ella knew what she was really asking. "Honey, if you lose your needles, I'll buy you more. You don't have to worry."

"I won't lose them," Carla said, but the whole time they were knitting, Carla kept her fingers gripped on the needles.

By the time they left, Carla had a whole inch of scarf, and even though Marianna tucked it into a bag, Carla kept fishing it out.

"Just making sure it's still there," she explained.

All three of them were walking through the park when, to Ella's surprise, there was Mark in the distance, coming toward them. That was so lucky, she thought. She could finally meet him. She had won over Marianna, and she could win over Mark, too. But as she got closer, she saw his face darken.

"Oh, fuck," Marianna said quietly.

"Mommy said a bad word!" Carla said.

"What's the matter?" Ella said. But before Marianna could tell her, Carla was running to Mark. "Daddy!" Carla shouted, hurling herself into his arms, not letting go. Mark put a hand on her head and said something to her.

"I'd better go see what he wants," Marianna said, and it was as if all the joy had been squeezed out of her.

"I should go—" Ella said, but Marianna held up one hand and Ella saw it was trembling.

"No," Marianna said. "Stay. This will only take a moment."

"Should I come with you?" Ella said, and Marianna's face tightened.

"Please, just wait here," she said.

Marianna's walk was different when she approached Mark. Slower, almost slumped, but when she got to him, she drew herself up. Carla was behind her father now, her arms wrapped happily around his legs, but Marianna was shaking her head no, no. Again, no. Then Mark shoved Marianna, and she stumbled, catching herself. He shoved her again and this time she fell, sprawling in the snow.

Ella felt a stab of fury. "Hey!" she shouted.

Carla jumped back, biting her thumbnail, staring down at the ground where her mother was slowly gathering herself.

Mark loomed over Marianna threateningly. Without thinking, Ella ran toward them. Mark glared at her and then abruptly turned and strode away.

Carla folded herself around her mother, not speaking. Ella crouched down and gently helped Marianna to her feet.

"Are you okay?" Ella asked, but Marianna ignored her. "Marianna?" she repeated. "What's going on? What just happened? I thought that Mark—"

Marianna lifted her hair up from her collar and smoothed it. She brushed the snow off her jeans and looked down to survey the damage, then took a deep breath.

"Nothing's going on," Marianna said. She stroked back Carla's hair. "Everything's fine, baby," she said.

Ella saw the scrapes on Marianna's hands, the rip in her collar. "Marianna—" she said, but Marianna turned to Carla.

"Who wants hot chocolate?" Marianna said abruptly.

"Me!" Carla took her fingers out of her mouth.

"Who wants some nice numbing caffeine?" Marianna said wearily.

"Me," Ella said quietly, and she took Marianna's arm.

THEY WENT TO Child's Play, a local café that had a special play area for kids, with blocks and crafts and plastic toys. They waited for Carla to get settled and then sat down in the seating area for parents.

"I wish you hadn't seen that," Marianna said. "It's nothing. Really. He came home and we weren't back yet, so he came to find us. Of course he got mad and blamed me." She pushed out a breath.

"I want you to know that I'm excellent at minding my own business," Ella said. "But is everything okay?"

Marianna's shoulders drooped. "He wasn't always like this," Marianna said. "When I first met him, he was head bartender at the Jordan Hotel, with a 401(k) and benefits, not to mention regular, healthy tips.

"The first time I walked in—I know this sounds stupid, because he didn't know me at all—but he became protective. I was there in the crowded bar, but somehow he made sure none of the guys at the bar would bother me. Drinks would appear in front of me without my having to order. I started to like it and so I came more often, spending time with him, flirting. And then one day, when I was ready to go, he politely asked for my number."

It was easy after that, Marianna said. They started seeing each other, going to movies, taking walks. He was so intensely loving, buying her flowers, telling her over and over how pretty she was, how smart. She had never had attention like that. He looked at her like she was made of stardust. She had grown up in a household of yellers—both her father and mother tearing her down for tiny missteps, somehow unable to show their only daughter that they loved her. With Mark there was never any yelling, only tempered, constant support, and a kind of unbridled adulation that felt like a drug to her.

"He shoved you," Ella said.

"His weapon of choice is usually words," Marianna said.

The coffees came and Marianna reached for hers. "He doesn't really hit me."

"Marianna," Ella persisted, "what about in the park?"

Marianna chewed her bottom lip. "He knows that if he ever hurts Carla, I'm walking."

"What if he puts hands on you again?"

"I promise, it's really not an issue."

The coffee was dark and bitter, but Ella drank it in gulps. "What did he want?" she asked.

"I guess some women might be flattered, but I'm not. He's just jealous," Marianna said. "Sometimes I think he follows me, making sure I'm not flirting with other guys. But I never can catch him at it.

"Today, he found a note on my dresser, a note I had scribbled to remind myself to call my boss. *Call Tom.* That's all it said. *Call Tom.*"

Marianna's cell rang and she tugged it out of her purse and then showed it to Ella. MARK. She clicked it off.

"There it is. The apology. Well, let him wait," she said.

She sighed and rubbed the damp table with a finger. "Want to know something? Our romance was the stuff of fairy tales. My friends were all jealous because even after Carla arrived, we were still holding hands all the time, looking at each other like . . . Well, you know. There was no one else I wanted to be with. I used to rush home just to talk to him. Just to see what little surprises he had for both of us."

"What happened?"

Marianna shrugged. "After Carla started in day care, I got a job as an accountant. Before I got that job, we could barely afford our bills, even with Mark's tips. But when I started working, things started to change. I suddenly had money to buy nicer shirts, more professional skirts. I even had people looking up to me, coworkers inviting me out to lunch. And suddenly Mark didn't like that. He wanted me to quit my job, to be a fifties wife, someone who'd have dinner on the table when he wasn't working, who'd keep a clean house. That's not me. It never was, so why would he suddenly expect it?" Marianna took a sip of her coffee.

"My life got fuller and his began to thin," she said. "He lost his job at the Jordan Hotel for talking back to their manager. But he landed his job at the Old Town Tavern so quickly, I didn't worry too much. But it was definitely a step down, and he started drinking more and bringing the bar home with him."

"Mommy, look!" Carla shouted, holding up a drawing of a house and a huge smiling sun. Marianna blew a kiss to her.

"Marianna . . . ," Ella said, "could you leave him?"

"You think it's so simple? We have a nice house, but it's his—his parents left it to him. It's in his name. And Carla adores him," Marianna said. "She's a child. What does she know except wanting everyone to love her, especially her daddy? It breaks my heart to see the way she yearns after him. She's as desperate for his love as I had been at first." She lowered her voice. "Before I knew better."

"Was he good with her when you were . . . pregnant?" Ella said. The coffee burned her stomach. She knew she shouldn't have asked, she felt her face heating, but Marianna tilted her head.

"We adopted Carla as a newborn."

Ella couldn't meet her eyes. She dug her hands deeper into her pockets. "Did you know the birth parents?" she asked carefully.

"A closed adoption. A precious baby girl. But closed was better for everyone, we were told." Marianna smiled, remembering. "I didn't see her birth, but I always imagined it. You know that saying, you didn't grow in my belly but you grew in my heart? It was like that. And she knows she's adopted. We told her very calmly, matter-of-factly. That the mommy who had carried her, the daddy, couldn't keep her and so with the greatest of love, they let her go."

Ella pushed the coffee away. Words jammed in her throat, and she felt dizzy.

"Did she ever ask more about her parents?" Ella said.

"We're her parents," Marianna said.

Ella felt sick. She got up from her chair. "I need to go. I didn't realize the time—"

Marianna pulled herself up and smiled. "Oh, of course. And I want to thank you so much. For hanging with us like this, for adult conversation. I work with adults, but you know, work conversation isn't the same. It seems like all my friends have drifted away over the years." She waved to Carla. "It's hard sometimes." Marianna pulled out her phone again. "I feel embarrassed telling you all this."

"No, no, I'm glad. It makes me feel close to you, like we're friends."

Marianna handed her the phone, brightening. "We are friends, aren't we? Here, put your number in. That way we won't have to wait to run into each other. Carla clearly likes you. Maybe next time, we can take her to the bookstore. And I'll put my office number into yours. You can call me there." She cast her eyes down. "That's best."

"Why is it best?" Ella said, but before Marianna could answer, Carla suddenly ran into her, wrapping her arms around her waist.

"I think you've made another friend," Marianna said.

Ella dared to stroke Carla's hair. After a moment, Carla ran to Marianna and plopped herself onto her lap.

Ella's hands hung by her side, useless now, yearning to have the girl back. Carla snuggled into Marianna and bounced off her lap again. Maybe, Ella thought, that was just part of having a child. You keep grasping for them to stay, and they keep moving farther and farther away from you. Maybe that's what she had done to Helen—and she immediately felt a rush of guilt.

"Are we going to see Daddy now?" Carla said.

"Can't live without her daddy," Marianna said thoughtfully. And then she said quietly to Ella, "Can't live with him, either." Her forehead buckled. "Maybe you're right. What you said. Sometimes I think I *should* just leave."

Ella froze. "Would you?" she asked. What would that mean for Carla? How would it change her own relationship with the little girl?

Marianna grew still. Then her eyes met Ella's. "I feel terrible even saying a thing like that."

"Can't live without Daddy," Carla repeated, tugging on Marianna's sleeve. "Come on, Mommy, let's go."

Marianna said quietly, "How would I manage on my own? What would that even look like?"

She looked so scared, it scared Ella. She wanted to tell her that you could surprise yourself by your own strength when you were forced to. But then she'd have to tell her how she knew that, and she couldn't.

"Mommy, let's go!" Carla said.

"We'll talk more," Marianna said, and then she took Carla's hand and they left.

ELLA TRUDGED TOWARD home, feeling as if she were swimming, drowning. She didn't notice the snow seeping into her cheap boots, her fingers so cold she couldn't move them. She was insane getting involved with Marianna, letting her confide in her. Sure, she liked her, and the more she got to know Carla, the more in love she was, but neither one of them was really hers to care about. Plus, there was Mark. She had liked him at first, from what she had seen while spying, but today she was horrified. She knew what people who hit were like. Someone who hit once would surely hit again, and she couldn't bear thinking of Marianna or Carla being a target. She'd have to talk to Marianna again. And she'd have to keep watch.

She walked around, winding in and out of stores. She headed for Wood You, because the things there were so beautiful—the shining maples, the dark walnut tables, the tall dressers with carved edges that she ached to touch. She could dream of saving for them, of having a table like the chair in her home, but she always knew it was just a dream, that she'd never have the money. And maybe she was also going there because she hoped to see Henry, his presence friendly and calming.

When she got to Wood You, it was closed, but the lights were still on. Henry was inside, waving at her. He opened the door.

"Hey, there," he said. "How's the chair?"

It was the first time she had seen him without his hat. His hair was curly, in need of a cut, but she liked it, how wild it was—full of possibilities.

"The chair is wonderful."

"Come on in," he said. She walked inside and he looked like he was going to say something more, but then he seemed skittish, like he'd changed his mind. He stepped farther into the store and then stooped, and she didn't know what he was doing until he grabbed for a cup and a slice of cardboard. And then she saw the roach, as big as her thumb, racing right toward her.

"Oh God!" she yelped, jumping up and then away.

Henry was moving closer to the roach, calm and steady. "I know I'm probably the only person on the planet like this, but I just can't kill roaches," he said. He crouched down and put the cup over the insect, and then slid the thin piece of cardboard beneath it.

"There you go," he said. Then he took the cup and cardboard outside, freeing the roach back into the city.

"Safe travels," he called after it.

Ella felt a flush of warmth.

"There," Henry said when he came back in. "Now he'll go back to his community and tell them how kind I was, and his whole roachy family will probably come tomorrow and I'll have to lead them out, too."

She felt an invisible hand on her back, nudging her toward him.

"Come see the back," he said, his face perking up with excitement, and she followed him into his workspace. There was a large dining table with curved, claw-footed legs, and she thought, *How beautiful.* For a moment she remembered how Jude had been so passionate about plants, but Jude had never been calm like Henry.

Henry ran his hand over the tabletop. "It needs to be sanded and stained. Want to help? It's great for stress."

"Do I look stressed?" she asked, curious.

He shook his head. "Everyone's stressed, aren't they? Just make sure to go with the grain, not across it."

He handed her a square and she began to sand, rubbing harder and harder, and though they didn't talk, she felt that the rasp of the squares was a kind of communication in its own way. The smoother the wood became, the more she felt the stresses of her life begin to recede. Her yearning for Carla was still there, but now the anxiety was gone. Her complicated feelings toward Marianna had loosened, and suddenly it didn't seem so terrible that she was friends with a woman who was almost twenty years older than she and mothering her daughter. She ran her fingers over the area she had smoothed, smiling, and moved over to sand a new section.

"I've been thinking," Henry said, and Ella looked up, pulled out of her trance. "We should go out sometime. What do you think?"

Ella thought about going back to her lonely apartment, about all the voices in her letters clamoring for her to answer.

"I think Friday would be good."

THEY BEGAN SEEING each other, and the more she saw of him, the easier their friendship became. One week passed, and then two and three, and then it had been an entire month. What she liked most about Henry was his excitement about furniture. They could be in a dive bar, and he'd show her a curve built into the corner of the table, or point out how a chair was made of three kinds of wood, and where each began. She started picking things up about furniture, almost by osmosis, noticing the flared dovetailed joints, feeling a surface to see if it had bubbles in the lacquer.

She liked talking to him, and when she repeated to him the same lies that she had told so many times now, they felt like the truth.

He told her how his parents had wanted him to be a doctor, like his dad, but then in eighth grade he had taken a woodworking class, and that was that.

"All the other kids were making square lamp bases, but I carved a dog," he said. She liked that he loved wood, that he was happy in his work. She liked that he didn't ask her too many questions, which made it easier to talk. She told herself Henry was just someone to talk to, someone who paid her attention when she most needed it. He never asked for more, never pushed her for anything, and she liked that, too.

She began to feel him everywhere in Ann Arbor—if not his very person, then his designs. She couldn't figure out why she felt so comfortable at a new restaurant until she bent and looked down at the table legs. Delicate carvings—Henry's signature. She stroked the arm of the chair, and when she left, she told the waitress, "I'll be back." Truthfully, the food wasn't very good, the eggs had been too runny, but that chair—that chair beckoned her as if it were saying, "You are always welcome here."

ONE EVENING SHE was helping Henry sand some new pieces in the workroom in the back of the shop when she got a splinter. "Ow, ow, ow," she said, putting her finger in her mouth.

Henry dropped the sandpaper and took her hand, studying it. "Oh, that's a beaut," he said. "You sit right there."

She sat on the chair and felt him studying her fingers. She started to think about the curve of his throat, the funny way his ears sometimes poked out from his hair. She started to want to touch him, to feel a tug of desire. She looked at him, waiting, but he was still teasing out the splinter. He wasn't sharp and jagged like Mark, someone who could hurt. He wasn't Jude, either. His life seemed more contained, with less of Jude's darkness.

"Henry," Ella said. And then she bent toward him, like a flower on a stem, and kissed his mouth. Not like a friend. Like a lover.

"Not here," he said.

They walked the three blocks to his apartment building, which looked more like a two-story house with an attic. He opened the front door and she followed him up the stairs into his apartment, a two-bedroom with bay windows, and, of course, lovely furniture.

When she saw his bed, the headboard carved with stars along the top, she touched the stars with amazement. "This," she said, astonished, and he smiled and touched her face.

"This," he said, and kissed her.

AFTERWARD, THEY LAY in his bed, the sheets crumpled on the floor. He reached over for one of her curls and wound it around his fingers.

"Well, that was a surprise," he said, and Ella laughed.

"Surprises can be good," she said.

"Do you want me to walk you home? Or do you want to sleep here?" he asked.

Ella thought about going home, being alone in her apartment. It called to her, a siren song, but then she thought, what if she did leave, and left Henry ruminating about the evening? What if he decided he didn't want to be with her anymore? That she was too quiet? Too strange?

"I'll stay," she said.

That night, she couldn't sleep. She had known she wouldn't be able to, not in a strange bed. She watched him sleep for a while and slipped out of bed and walked to his living room. She saw his wallet on the floor and, unable to resist, picked it up, opening it to see a photo of a woman, young and beautiful. She peered at the writing on the bottom of the photo: *Love always, Alice,* and to her surprise she felt a pang. Well, who was she to talk? Hadn't she kept a photo of Jude for years in prison? By the time she was released, she had worn it down so much you couldn't even make out who it was anymore.

She crawled back into bed, and Henry stirred.

"Hey, you," he said sleepily.

"Who's Alice?" she said. "Oh my God, I'm so nosy. I was just in the living room and I saw a photo and—"

"It's okay," he said quietly.

She waited.

"She is just someone from my past. That's all." He sat up, and there was that calm again. "I was supposed to marry her . . . until she ran off with my best friend."

"Jesus, I'm sorry—"

"That's why I didn't bring you back to my place at first, why I waited a whole month, biding my time," he said. "I'm slow to trust."

"But you do trust—"

"I think I trust you," he said.

"But you still keep the photo," she said.

He looked pained. "Maybe it's there to remind me to be careful."

"You don't have to talk about it," Ella said. "Let's go back to sleep."

AFTER THAT FIRST night, she began staying over more and more, though she could never sleep through the night. She awoke at three, and then at five, her heart pounding. Not wanting to disturb Henry, she would carefully slide out from under the sheets and walk around his apartment, or sit in his living room, reading one of his books until she started to drift off again. She never told him about her nighttime jaunts, and he never mentioned them.

Henry was the only man she had been with besides Jude, and Jude had been everything to her. Still, being with Henry was so different than being with Jude. Jude and she had what felt like a telepathic connection, in each other's head all the time. But she never could be sure what Henry was thinking, and when she asked him, he would shrug and change the subject. She liked being at his place, working, reading, listening to him. She even liked it when she got up in the middle of the night and she could just be quiet and still, reading through the books on Henry's shelves.

One morning, at Henry's, her own shouting woke her.

"What's wrong? Are you okay?" Henry said, hovering over her.

"Nothing," she said. "I just had a bad dream."

"Tell me."

"I can't remember it." She tried to look cheerful because she did remember things from the dream. Her bed in prison. A teacup filling with hot water. The garden behind their shabby apartment building in Queens—the earth loamy and dark. The garden smell, the way the plants had poked up their green heads. The way Jude had tilted his chin up when he was upset.

"It was just a stupid dream," she said, and then she saw Henry's shoulders relax. He held her closer.

He tumbled into sleep, but she lay awake. It was dangerous not to be in control here, to give someone knowledge of things you had kept secret, a weapon they could use against you. She knew, too, how love could make you do things you never would have imagined. She struggled to keep her eyes open.

She didn't know how much of her real life she could share. Certainly not the past. Her present was a different story. Henry hadn't seen her with Carla or with Marianna yet. He didn't know how important they both were to her or why, and if he found out, she had no idea what he might think. She couldn't figure out how she would defend herself or even explain what she was doing.

She thought of the day she had given birth, how they wouldn't let her hold or even see her baby. How no one could be in the room with her except the doctor and a nurse. How she had cried for her mom, then for her baby, and then for herself. How she had tamped most of that memory down because it was so painful.

She couldn't tell Henry.

She couldn't open everything up again like that. The stakes were simply too high.

# NINE

# Queens
*June 2011*

ometimes Jude thought he was dazzled in love not just with Ella, but with her mom as well. Not the same way, of course, but she made him feel protected somehow. He had liked her immediately, at the first dinner, and that feeling never changed. She acted like he was worth her while, that he might even be special. And more importantly, she treated him like family. Sometimes it was difficult, because it made him remember his own mother, and then he'd feel himself crumbling. He'd walk out of the room to compose himself, and Helen always noticed, saying something like, "Hey, where you going? I have fresh muffins here."

"Stay over," she'd always say, making up the couch for him, turning on a nightlight so that he wouldn't have to stumble if he wanted water or the bathroom. For the first time in years, he had known deep, dreamless sleep.

It was summer now and he didn't have to work, and Ella didn't have a job either, other than Helen's insistence that she finish her summer reading, which she had mostly done her first week out of school.

Helen gave him a drawer in a dresser for his things, so he didn't have to worry about clean underwear. She began buying things he liked: ingredients for oatmeal raisin cookies, hard pretzels with extra salt. "Make yourself at home," she told him, and he did, and he loved it.

Ella, though, wasn't so happy. She was always pulling him away from Helen, grabbing for his hand at dinner, kissing him on the mouth in front of her. He tried to explain it: "It's so peaceful with her," he said. "I love your home."

"This dump?"

"It's a home. Unlike my dad's place, it looks lived in. I love how the stove doesn't always go on the first time you hit the gas. I love the feel of this apartment, like I belong here." He hesitated. "I love the way your mother makes me feel. Like I'm a good person."

"You love my mom?"

"As a mom," he said. "I love you as my girl."

"Your girl," Ella said, blushing. "I can be your girl and my mom can be your mom, then."

BEING IN LOVE made Jude careless. The world now felt so shined up, so brand new. When he returned to his townhouse the next day, his father started yelling about dishes being in the sink, about responsibility. His father's voice had a twang to it, and Jude knew he had been drinking. He crept upstairs while his father was still shouting and closed himself in his bedroom, sprawling on his bed.

His father would eventually get silent. Then he might drink more. Or he might fall asleep. But either way, Jude was safe up here.

The drinking hadn't always been an issue, and Jude knew it was his fault. It had started after his mother died. Jude's father would polish off whole bottles of wine every night. And then he moved on to harder stuff. One drink. Then two and then three. Drinking had turned Andrew Stein into a person Jude didn't recognize. Once drunk, he would become violent, tearing apart the house. He would curse and weep until he'd fall asleep with one of his wife's dresses in his arms. As the months wore on, he began to turn his anger on Jude.

The beatings never lasted long, especially if Jude curled himself into a ball, his face protected by his arms. Sometimes his father would stop abruptly, his whole body shaking, as if suddenly realizing what he was doing. He would apologize, ashamed, and then he would try to help Jude get cleaned up, assessing the damage evenly, the way he would have considered a case. "You're fine now," his father always said.

People kept telling them that the grief would ease, the pain would loosen, but it never really did. Two months passed, then six, and his father was still coming apart. Andrew had even sold the Woodstock house because it was too painful to return to the place where he felt his life had ended.

One night Jude had heard his dad sobbing, cries knotted with pain. He looked from the top floor down at Andrew, who had Jude's mother's dress, a favorite red-and-white floral, clutched in his hands.

"Come back," his father had cried into the dress. "Come back."

Listening to the sobs, Jude had gone into the bathroom and pulled the blade out of a razor and sliced two horizontal cuts across his wrists. Mesmerized, he watched as the blood flowed. Then he felt two hands grabbing him.

"Jesus, Jude!" his dad said, his face leached of color. "We're going to the hospital."

The doctor there patched him up and asked him if he wanted to talk to someone, and all he could think was, yes, he would, but that person would be his mother.

The doctor sighed. "You know," he said. "Life is precious. Don't fuck it up."

He stood to leave, lingered in the doorway, then turned. "But I don't think you wanted to. Not really."

"Why not?" Jude asked.

"Because if you had, you would have cut deeper."

Defeated, Jude crept back to his father in the waiting room. He hadn't killed himself. He had ruined even that.

NOW, JUDE STRETCHED on the bed. The house was silent. He was tired but hungry, and he made the mistake of creeping into the kitchen. His father was still there, glowering.

"Dad—" he said.

His father turned and slapped him across the face so hard, Jude stumbled, hitting his arm against the island. Jude's father covered his own face and then began sobbing, turning away from his son.

Jude left the townhouse, limping out into a heavy rain, rolling his sleeves down to hide the new bruises that were already forming. He wanted kindness now. He wanted Ella. He wanted Helen. He wanted to be with them, but how could he go there? They'd want to know what had happened and why. They'd find out and they wouldn't want him around anymore. He'd ruin everything all over again.

But maybe it was better to go now, to get it over with, to put a finish on it and sink back into his own misery, alone. All he knew was that he had to see Ella. He had to talk to her, to be with her, no matter the cost.

The subways were running late, and they were crowded. He stood the whole time, leaning against a pole, wet and miserable without a seat. As the adrenaline wore off, he started to feel the full weight of the damage inflicted on his body. He doubled over and hugged himself.

By the time he got to Ella's, he was crying. As he approached the apartment building, his cell buzzed. A text from his father. *Call me. Wherever you are.*

*Fuck you*, Jude thought, and put the cell back in his pocket. He pressed the buzzer to be let in.

He climbed the stairs, wincing, and there was Ella at her door. She looked shocked to see him in such a condition, and pulled him inside. "What happened?" she cried, and he shook his head and wrapped an arm around her for support.

"Is Helen here?" he asked, newly afraid. Ella knowing was one thing, but telling Helen was another. How could he know whose side she might take? If she knew the reason for his beatings—what he had done to his mother—might she blame him too?

Ella shook her head. "She's not here. Working late," she said, and he grew weak with relief. She guided him to a kitchen chair.

Ella got a dishtowel and wet it, and then gently cleaned his face. "Who did this?" she asked. Then she crouched beside him and took one of his hands in hers. "It's okay. We'll call the cops. They know these kids in the neighborhood—"

Jude lifted his face. It would be so easy to lie, but there she was in front of him, her body leaning toward him. "It wasn't kids," he said.

"Adults did this?" she said, shocked. "Why? Oh my God—"

"It was my father," he said, shaking his head.

"What?" Ella held his hand tighter.

"It's only when he drinks," Jude said. "My dad cares about me. He doesn't mean to do this."

Ella's body seemed to harden. "Then why does he do it?"

He couldn't answer that. He couldn't tell her the why, couldn't tell her the whole story because then she'd know that his father wasn't the only monster, and she might turn from him, and he couldn't bear that.

Jude said, "Please. I don't want to talk about it."

"He can't do this to you. We need to go to the cops."

Jude snorted. "The cops. My father's a judge. He has the system in his pocket."

"Maybe if they saw you. Maybe if they talked to him or saw him—"

"Saw him do what? He's a drunk, but in the outside world no one knows he's like this. Everyone loves him."

"I don't—or, didn't," she said. "And if they see you, no one can say this didn't happen."

Jude shook his head again.

"Then what do we do?"

Jude pressed his forehead against Ella's. *Here it comes. This is when it all ends.* "He beats me because I was responsible for my mom's death."

"I don't believe that for a minute," she said, and then he told her, like a test, sure this would end things, and when he was done, she leaned forward and hugged him for a long time.

"No way was that your fault," she said quietly into his ear. "You can't ever think that it was. And I'm so sorry. That all sounds horrible."

"I wish I wasn't alive," he whispered.

Alarmed, she touched his face. "You can't say that. You can't ever say that."

"I tried before." He pulled up a sleeve and showed her the ridged marks, the scars he had told her were an accident when he was trying to carve something out of soap, just for fun. The scars she had kissed because she had believed him.

"What? Why would you do that? Why wouldn't you tell me the truth?"

He was quiet for a moment. "Because life got too hard," he said finally. "Because I was afraid."

"If you die, then I die, too," she said.

"Sometimes, after he hits me, I think about killing myself, but then I think about you."

"Keep thinking about me, and then you won't do it. And it's your dad who needs punishing, not you. I wish the cops would get him."

"I could kill him sometimes," Jude said.

"I know," she said, smoothing his hair back from his head. "I think I could, too. I hate that he's been doing this to you." She kissed his face, his neck, the tips of his fingers. He leaned against her.

"Maybe he'll stumble on the stairs when he's drunk and break his neck. Maybe he'll choke on a fish bone," she said, kissing him again.

"He has a bad ticker. Maybe he'll take too many heart pills," Jude said. "Or his heart will give out. Nature will do what we can't."

"I knew something was going on with you, something deep, and I hoped that you'd trust me enough one day to tell me."

"How?"

"Because I imagine that relationships are easy when everything is all lovely and bright. It's when there's real trouble that your true self comes out. Hardship, not joy, makes love deeper." She placed a hand on his cheek. "I love your true self. I want us always to tell each other the truth."

"Please," he said. "Please don't tell anyone. Not Helen. Not anyone."

"Are you sure? Maybe she could help—"

"No. It has to be just us. You and me."

"Just us," she repeated. "Helen isn't a part of this."

They cleaned the kitchen, and then Jude slipped out, promising her he'd be okay now, that his father was done for the night.

He had been gone only half an hour when Helen came home, and there was Ella at the kitchen table, thinking about Jude.

"Everything all good?" Helen asked cheerfully.

"Everything's great," Ella said.

IT WASN'T, OF course. Jude's father began to notice how often Jude was out with "that girl." He kept warning Jude, his voice taut with anger. Now, not even the refuge of his bedroom offered him a buffer from his father's rage.

"Get down here," Judge Stein routinely shouted up the stairs. "I'm tired of you not listening to me." And then things would always escalate into another beating. His father made his apologies in the form of gifts: video consoles, a ten-speed bike, a new computer. But still he would wind back to his old self and say yet again, "I don't want you seeing that girl."

Jude left the gifts untouched.

No matter what his father thought, Jude and Ella were meant to be together. Jude knew it. Ella knew it. Maybe Helen knew it too, but Jude never asked her. As soon as they were eighteen, they'd get married. Nothing special, just a justice of the peace with Helen as a witness, and Ella in a filmy dress that Helen would have hand-sewn especially for her. They'd buy some land upstate and have a little farm; they could even open a stand to sell their excess produce.

"We can have dogs," Jude told her. "And cats and goats and make cheese and sell that, too."

"How many kids?" Ella said. "Still six?"

"Two. One with your face. One with mine. Or two with your face because it's so gorgeous. And mine is just funny."

His father couldn't stop them. No one and nothing could.

AND THEN, AT the end of July, Jude's father made an announcement.

"We're moving," he said. "I have a new job in Philadelphia."

"What?" Jude said. "When?"

"Early September. Right before your school starts."

"I don't want to move. Why are we moving?"

"I'm stepping down from my seat on the bench. They've hired me as dean of Carey Law School at Penn."

"Why can't you teach here in New York?"

"Because I don't want to. Because we both could use a fresh start. Things will be better. You'll see. You'll be able to start your junior year fresh."

"We can't move," Jude said, panicking, thinking about Ella.

"It's a done deal. We're leaving in six weeks. The semester starts right after Labor Day, but we need to get settled."

Jude felt a dizzying shift under his feet. He tried to convince his father to let him stay here, that he could live at Ella's, that Helen would be thrilled to have him, that she thought of him as her own son. He would continue school with his friends at Dalton.

"That's not going to happen," his father said dryly. "You are not her son."

He told his father that maybe Ella could come with them, that she wouldn't be any trouble.

"There will be plenty of other girls in Philadelphia. You'll forget her."

"Is this why you changed jobs?" Jude asked.

"This isn't up for discussion," Judge Stein told him. "This is what I want. And you and the girl are too young. This is a good move for us all."

"That's what you think," Jude said, storming upstairs. His father didn't bother to stop him.

JUDE GRABBED SOME cash he had stuffed in his sock drawer and took a cab to Ella's. Crying the whole long way, he thought of how he'd tell her. When he arrived, she wrapped herself around him.

"This can't happen," she said.

"I'll never leave you," he told her. "He can't make me do this."

"We'll talk to my mom. She won't let you leave, and neither will I," Ella promised. "She'll go talk to him. He'll listen to another adult."

They went to Helen, who was beading a dress.

"What happened?" she said. "You look like you lost your best friend." She put her sewing down beside her.

As Ella told the story, her mother's face puckered with confusion.

"You could talk to my dad," Jude said. "You could tell him I could live with you, that I could finish school here and that I'd visit him all the time—"

"Did your dad say that would be okay with him?"

Jude and Ella were both silent, and Helen sighed.

"I know he doesn't want you two together," she said. "He came to the apartment to tell me, in no uncertain terms."

"What? My father came here?"

"It's okay. It *was* okay. I asked him to leave," Helen said.

"And you didn't listen—" Ella said. "You love Jude. I know you do."

"Yes, I do. But this is different. I can't just take in his son without his permission."

"What if I go live with them?"

Helen knit her brows. "I can't let that happen."

"We'll find another way," Ella told Jude.

Helen sighed heavily, her eyes full of sorrow.

THEY WENT OUT to the garden behind the apartment building. "Philadelphia isn't that far away," Ella said. "It's a short train ride."

"But it will be difficult," Jude said. "It'll be harder for us to spend the night together—almost impossible." Frantic, Jude shoved his hair back from his face. "I wish he would just die."

Ella watched him, silent.

"Maybe one of the criminals he put away will off him," Jude said.

Ella half smiled. "That's just in the movies," she said.

"Or maybe he'll forget that you aren't supposed to stick a fork in a plugged-in toaster."

Ella brightened. "Or maybe he'll be walking to the car and a rabid dog will bite him."

"He's going to fall down the stairs," Jude whispered.

"We'll run away. We'll find a way. If he touches you again, I will kill him myself. All I know is you can't leave me."

Plotting his death was a fantasy.

Until it wasn't.

# PART TWO

# TEN

# Brooklyn

*February 2019*

Helen was going crazy missing Ella. She had hoped to spend Thanksgiving with her, and then Hanukkah—either in Brooklyn or Ann Arbor—but Ella had put her off, claiming she was drowning in work, that she could neither take time off to travel nor host her mother. Not yet. Always not yet.

"You know I love you. You know I wish I could," Ella said, and something tight in Ella's voice made Helen know not to press her.

Meanwhile, Helen's new joy was Mouse. After the New Year, they went to see the giant Christmas tree at Rockefeller Center, their noses nipped with cold. They went to more concerts and readings where they sat holding hands. Helen loved it all; it was such a strange and exciting time.

"Tell me more about you," he kept prodding, but Helen could only dole out pieces of her life for fear he might leave if she told him all of it at once. She couldn't help being afraid.

And, too, she couldn't help feeling how even though this might be a new start, it could be a bad start, too. Sometimes she thought she should back out of this relationship now, before she was too deeply invested. She began studying him, trying to find fault, justification. But the few things she found seemed so trivial. He sometimes spoke so fast, he spoke over her. He sometimes scraped his fork on the plate without even knowing it.

"Tell me about you," Mouse repeated.

Hesitantly, she told him more about raising her daughter, skimming the story, revealing only that Ella was now in her early twenties and living in Ann Arbor, writing a column for a weekly newspaper.

"She sounds interesting," he said. "I hope I can meet her sometime."

"You will," Helen said, but she couldn't help wondering if it was a mistake to make that promise.

One night, during a snowstorm, they were at his place watching the news, and it was followed by a ripped-from-the-headlines movie about Gypsy Rose Blanchard, a wheelchair-bound, chronically sick teen who discovers, to her horror, that her devoted mother had fabricated her illnesses to get attention, sympathy, and medical procedures that would keep Gypsy sick. In an attempt to free herself from her mother's clutches, Gypsy Rose and her secret boyfriend brutally murder her mother.

"All those secrets," Mouse said. "Nothing good ever comes from keeping a secret."

"Sometimes people feel they have no choice," Helen said.

Mouse shook his head. "Secrets have weight, and they just keep getting heavier and heavier. And anyway, Gypsy should have gone to the authorities first," Mouse insisted.

"And what if they wouldn't help?" Helen said. "And look at what she suffered! She felt helpless. You can't say she was guilty—she was out of her mind and desperate."

Mouse shook his head. "People like that are crazy. Yes, she should have had justice, but what she and her boyfriend did to her mother was far worse than what was done to her. It was murder. Sometimes things actually are black and white, you know. There's a right thing to do and there's a wrong thing."

"And how do we know what the right thing is?" Helen said, her voice rising.

"Right is right," Mouse said. "It's as simple as that."

"What about shades of right?" Helen said, practically shouting now. "What about that? What about circumstances we know nothing about? Gypsy's mother might have done terrible things, but she loved her daughter! And Gypsy loved her mother even though she got her boyfriend to help kill her!"

Mouse looked at her with concern. "Wait, wait. Why are you getting so upset?" He tried to take her hand, but she pulled it away. "Why are we talking about this terrible case?" He shut off the TV. "There. Now, how about if I make us some tea?"

Helen stood quickly and got her coat.

"I don't need tea," she snapped, and fled his apartment.

She saw his texts on the subway but didn't respond. They kept coming that night and she ignored them. She didn't calm down until the next day, and even then, she felt as if the brightness and hope she was finding in their relationship had faded a little. He was judgmental, she decided. That meant he would inevitably judge her, and maybe she had had enough of that.

Men. They had never done her any good in life. Certainly not the man who had violated her. Not even that boy Jude. All that talk about how he'd do anything for Ella. But her daughter had been sentenced to twenty-five years, and he got off scot-free. She had misjudged Jude so badly. And she was beginning to understand that she had misjudged Mouse, too. Who needed any of them? All these men were so nice at first, you didn't notice the danger. Thank God she hadn't told Ella about Mouse, because Ella would surely be asking her all sorts of questions.

Yet, despite herself, she kept expecting him to call. She sat at home waiting, but she heard nothing. She was furious with herself for getting into an argument she could never win, because she could never explain herself to him. A thousand times she had picked up the phone to call him, but she always put it down again.

She missed him. She missed how he smelled like pine, and even though she knew it was his aftershave, she liked thinking it was just how he smelled. She liked waking up and seeing his head on her pillow.

Well, all that was in the past now. She could yearn for him all she wanted, but she'd have to fill the time now with something else.

AS MORE WEEKS passed, she kept busy. It was a snowy winter, making it hard for her to even imagine braving the outside except for going to work. So, she did things indoors. She spent long evenings putting together five-hundred-piece puzzles, and when those grew too easy, one-thousand-piece puzzles. She rearranged all the photos in the house so that wherever she looked she would see Ella and herself. She often traced those faces with her finger.

After that, she was cleaning her sewing space, gathering embroidery threads and bits of fabric to put them in some order, when she had an idea. She carefully embroidered a message on a thin strip of orange linen: *Dream Big.* Then, she took one of the dresses she was working on for the shop and carefully picked open the hem, tucking the cloth inside. She wouldn't tell the shop what she had done, but she loved the idea of the secrecy, how someone might feel that strip of cloth and read her message. And even if they didn't, maybe the message would act as a talisman.

She began doing this more and more. The next day, she bought pale yellow wool and made Ella a dress, long sleeves with fake pearl buttons at the wrist, a V-neck that would graze her clavicle. She embroidered a strip of cloth: *I will always love you and always be proud.* She was about to sew it into the hem when she took her tiny gold-plated hoops from her ears—the ones she always wore because she thought they were lucky—and put them in the hem, too. They'd add weight to the dress. Ella might feel something in the hem and open it to see what it was, and then she'd find the message. She thought of Ella wearing her earrings, carrying that luck. She was packaging it up carefully to send to her daughter when her cell rang.

"Ella," she said happily. "I was just thinking of you. What synchronicity."

"I need to ask you something," Ella said, and Helen settled in her chair. Maybe she wanted to find a day for Helen to visit. Maybe she needed money—and of course, any money Helen had was Ella's.

"Did you get to see my baby when she was born?" Ella said abruptly. There was a strange current in her voice.

Helen felt as if a crack were forming along her spine. "Why are you asking me this now?" she said quietly.

"Because I want to know. Because I was thinking about it. They wouldn't let me see her when she was born, so the only way I knew her was through my belly. Shouldn't a mother get to see her baby?"

"I think you know it isn't a good idea to talk about this."

"Why isn't it?" Ella said. Helen could hear Ella's ragged breathing.

"It's the past, honey. All we have is our present. Our futures."

"Well, I'm doing some wondering in my present. Why did you make me give her up? Why didn't you take her? Don't you regret that?"

Helen pressed the cell against her ear. She didn't know what she was supposed to say. She had always thought that when Ella was married and giving birth she would be there, holding her hand, and then holding her grandchild. But those dreams had been crushed, along with her daughter's. She had never seen the baby, let alone held it, which was a good thing, because if she had, she would never have let that child go and that would have been a mess that neither she nor Ella would have been able to handle.

"Why can't you tell me the truth?" Ella said. "Why can't you just say you didn't want to? That it wasn't that you couldn't, it wasn't because of time or money, the way you said. Was it because it was Jude's baby?"

"You were going to be imprisoned for twenty-five years! What happened that you're asking me this now?" Helen said. "I didn't have the resources to be a single mother. Not again. And I wanted something better for you."

"Better." Ella snorted.

"And you got it. You have a new life now and you should be happy living it." Helen swallowed. "Are you looking for someone to blame?"

As soon as she said it, she felt ashamed, because if anyone was pointing fingers at anyone, it was Helen, blaming herself.

"Fine," Ella said. "I made a mistake calling you."

"Wait—" Helen said, but Ella hung up.

# ELEVEN

# Ann Arbor

*February 2019*

Ella stamped the icy snow from her boots and tugged off her hood before she entered the office building where Marianna worked as an accountant. Her whole face felt chapped and red, but Marianna had sounded so terrible in her last text that Ella braved the clinging cold to come to her office and go have lunch. At least this building was warm.

Marianna's office was two floors up, a large, lively loft space with people sitting at open cubicles. As soon as she opened the glass door and approached the receptionist, she saw Marianna talking and laughing with a tall man in a dark suit, who was beaming at her. Then she heard someone shouting. The cubicle workers were standing, craning their necks, and then Ella froze, because there was Mark striding through the room in a puffy jacket, a wool hat pulled low over his forehead, his hands balled into fists. "Marianna!" he shouted, and grabbed her by the elbow, shoving the tall man out of his way.

"What do you think you're doing?" the man said angrily.

"Wait," the receptionist said, but Ella sprinted toward them.

"Do you take me for a fool?" Mark said, and Ella could hear the anger in his voice. Marianna put a hand on Mark's shoulder, and he shoved it off.

"Leave her alone!" Ella said, but both Mark and Marianna ignored her.

"What's this supposed to mean?" he shouted. "I come here to surprise you for lunch, and this is what I see, you canoodling with some man!"

"I think you need to leave," the tall man said. "Now. Before I call security."

"You know he's my boss!" Marianna said to Mark. She made her face look as pleading as possible. "Can you lower your voice?"

"I'm so sorry, Tom," Marianna said to the tall man. "He's leaving now—"

"Get out of here," Tom said quietly to Mark. "Now."

"This is my wife. Why are you talking to her like that, smiling like you share a secret?" Mark's mouth narrowed. "I'm her goddamned husband."

Ella motioned toward Tom but Marianna locked eyes with her and shook her head. She lifted her hand like a stop sign.

"I told you to leave," Tom said. "I repeat. Do I have to call security and have them escort you out? I can if you like."

"If I like?" Mark drew himself up, glowering at Marianna, his arms folded, his mouth tight. He took a step closer to Tom, but when Tom didn't move or step back, Mark deflated, turning to his wife.

"I'll see *you* later," he said, jabbing a finger at Marianna, his face dark; and then she began to shiver.

Mark strode to the elevators and vanished. After pausing a moment, Tom turned to Marianna, clearing his throat.

"Are you okay?" he asked. She nodded. "Are you sure?"

By now, there was a crowd of people standing, whispering to one another and watching, and Tom waved his hand. "Please, everyone, go back to work. Everything's all settled now."

He waited for people to slowly sit down, to settle, and then he turned back to Marianna. "This can't keep happening."

"What? It's happened before?" Ella said, stunned, and Marianna turned to her.

"Please—" Marianna said quietly. "You need to go."

"It disrupts everything in this office," Tom continued, ignoring Ella. He put his hands on his hips and shook his head, staring at the ground. "Come to my office."

Ella watched as they entered his office and he closed the door.

BACK ON THE street, bundled up again, Ella began to worry. She pictured Mark's face, the veiled threat in his every movement, every gesture. And worse, she had seen the fear in Marianna. The same pain, the same whipped look she had once seen in Jude after his own father beat him. She hadn't been able to stop the brutality and she had been too afraid to stand up to Judge Stein, but she had been a kid then, and now she was an adult with agency. She wouldn't let this happen to Marianna if she could help it.

*Maybe they'll call the police*, Ella thought, *and make sure Mark can't come back.* But there was the house they shared, which Mark owned. He could make things difficult for her there. Ella wrapped her arms tightly about herself, shivering.

Later that afternoon, she texted Marianna.

*Are you okay?*

*Yes.*

*No.*

*I don't know. I fucked things up.*

*Mark went to get Carla.*

*I'll have to see him when I get home.*

*No, you didn't fuck anything up.*

*Can I do anything?*

*About Mark.*

*No. Not a good idea.*

*Then let me buy you dinner.*

Yes.

*Diosito's. Twenty minutes.*

ELLA GOT THERE first, winding through the colorful Mexican prayer flags to one of the blue vinyl corner booths in the back, where it was more private. When Marianna showed up—her faux fur coat that she called "the creature" buttoned up to her throat—her eyes were red.

"I got fired," she said, sitting down, slouching out of her coat.

"What? How can that be? It seemed like your boss was on your side—"

"He was at first. But this keeps happening. And my work was suffering. Apparently, other people have been complaining to HR." Marianna bowed her head. "He said Mark has come to the office when he knew I wouldn't be there to ask my coworkers all these personal questions. People were pretty creeped out. I can't even explain it to myself. It can't get worse than this, can it?"

Ella scooted closer to Marianna and put an arm around her.

"Where's Carla?" she said quietly. "Because if she's with Mark, I'm thinking maybe we should go get her right now."

Marianna shook her head. "He would never hurt her. Never. It's me he wants to pummel. And she worships him. How can I deny her that?"

"Do you even still love him?" Ella asked.

Marianna stiffened. "I don't know anymore," she said. "He watches me. He's jealous of everything. I don't know what's happened to him. He blows up for no reason." She bit her lower lip. "He can gallivant all over Ann Arbor, talking up women at the bar—I've fucking seen him! But I can't even work with a guy without him getting all fired up. I don't know what to do anymore."

Ella swallowed hard. "We talked about this before. You could leave him."

Marianna looked at Ella, astonished. "Talking and wanting to do something is one thing. Actually doing it is another."

"You can leave," Ella said.

"With what? I lost my job, remember?"

"You'll get a new job."

"Sometimes I forget how young you really are," Marianna said quietly. "What's that like? To have all that hope."

"Don't you have dreams of something better?" Ella said. "It isn't just young people who have dreams."

"Of course I do. I have crazy dreams about living in a cottage by the ocean with Carla. Of hearing waves crashing as I curl up with her. Sometimes I imagine opening a bakery that sells only cupcakes. I think about coming home to Carla, the two of us being alone together, happy and safe. None of those dreams have Mark in them."

"See?" Ella said encouragingly. "That doesn't have to be a dream—"

Marianna scoffed. "Look, it's not that easy. You'll understand when you've lived as much of life as I have. Nothing works out that way."

"I want to help you," Ella protested. "Let me help you. Any way I can."

As soon as she said it, she felt terrified. She didn't know how she could help or what it might cost her. Only that she would.

# TWELVE

# Manhattan

*September 2011*

Ella held Jude's hand so tightly she was sure she was leaving marks. "Wake up," she told him. "Don't sleep."

He nodded at her, drawing his shoulders up. It was early morning and so hot and humid, their sweaty T-shirts were pasted to their backs. Central Park was alive, especially where they were, by the Columbus Circle entrance, surrounded by people hawking bike and city tours, the vendors selling ice cream from carts, the stream of tourists already steady. The more noise the better—they couldn't risk falling asleep. They needed each other, and the time they had left was slipping away.

In four days, Andrew Stein would be moving himself and his son to Philadelphia. From the moment Jude's father had told him about the move, Jude had decided that he and Ella would spend every minute together that they could, to have more time to think what to do, how to stop this. Fueled by adrenaline and need, they usually stayed up most of the night on their cellphones. Other nights, Jude snuck out to be with Ella at her apartment, the two of them prodding each other awake whenever one of them drifted. Jude even bought some Adderall from a Dalton classmate, but when it just made them more exhausted, he tossed the rest. When they were apart, they practiced telepathy, Ella concentrating so hard she sometimes gave herself a headache. They set their alarms so they could take catnaps at the same time. Fifteen minutes. No more than twenty.

Now though, with just days left, with school starting soon for both of them, they were desperate.

"My mom keeps harping on the dark circles under my eyes. She keeps reminding me that there are trains to Philly, that it doesn't take that long to get there." Ella scoffed. "She doesn't get it. Or she doesn't want to."

Now the park bench felt as if it were whispering to Ella, pulling her down to lie on it, so she stood up.

"Wait," Jude said. "We've been skimping on sleep since July. And we got through the last two days without real sleep. That means we can do another."

Ella put her hand against his face. "We can do anything," she said.

He pointed to a cart. "Espresso," he said. "Maybe this time it'll work."

They gulped down several, until Ella's heart was pumping in her chest. She placed a hand on her ribs. "Fuck," she said. "It feels like it's coming through my skin." *Four more days,* she thought, and she went to buy another coffee.

"C'mon," Jude said. "Let's go to your place. If we keep moving, we'll stay awake."

AT HELEN'S, THEY went out to the garden so that Jude could water the plants, which were wilting in the steamy weather. He sprayed them carefully, spreading the water evenly. "I'm going to miss this," he said.

"No, don't say that," Ella said.

Jude squinted at the garden. "Oh my God, I swear I'm hallucinating from lack of sleep." He smacked a hand against his head.

"What's the record for not sleeping?"

"I don't know, but I bet we beat it."

Ella blinked. She plucked some red flowers, the petals like little faces. Jude was pulling up plants and putting them in plastic bags, saying he was going to replant them, put them in pots instead of the ground if he had to.

"I'll call you constantly," Ella said, leaning closer to the flowers, her hair brushing the ground. "We'll text. We'll telepathize." She laughed. "Is that a word?"

"We'll be eighteen soon, and then no one can stop us."

"Not that soon," she said.

"Maybe the elevator will malfunction, and he'll be in it," Jude said.

Ella knew this game, all those possibilities swimming around them like a school of playful fish. Sometimes they made her feel better. Sometimes they didn't.

"I can't stand it," Jude said. "I can't do this. I can't be without you." His eyes grew red with tears. "I'll run away. He can bring me back and I'll run again. And you can run with me. You will, won't you?"

"Jude—" she said. "You know the answer to that. I would do anything for you. Anything. You know that."

Ella watched him stuff basil into a plastic sandwich bag, then rosemary, and then foxglove leaves.

Jude frowned. "He can't separate us." He looked suddenly stern, then almost afraid. "Come to my house. We'll give it one last try. Maybe today is the day he'll listen to us, together. He'll see what this is doing to us."

The sun was going down, but the humidity lingered, making Ella feel like a wrung-out dishrag. She couldn't remember if they had eaten lunch, but now it must be past dinnertime. "What time is it?" she asked, and Jude showed her his phone. Seven.

They stood, woozy, and held hands. Ella thought of what she had learned in science, that everyone is made of atoms, but that the subatomic particles that comprise them never really touch one another. No matter how tight she held Jude, there would always be space between them.

WHEN THEY REACHED his townhouse, Ella realized she was so exhausted she couldn't feel her feet anymore. Their subway car hadn't been air-conditioned, and it was so crowded with people, she had felt the steam of their breath cooking her.

All she could think about was Jude's bed, the expensive down comforter, the soft pillow. *Stop*, she told herself. As they entered through the carved wood front door, Ella felt the shock of the central air-conditioning against her sweaty face. And then, there was Jude's father, standing in the midst of boxes. She could only think how much she hated him.

Judge Stein didn't yell. Instead, he just stared them up and down.

"What is she doing here?" he asked quietly.

"I need to talk to you," Jude told him. "We both need to talk to you."

"You look terrible," he said.

Jude didn't move. Ella waited.

"So, who's hungry?" Judge Stein finally said. His shoulders relaxed. "Let's have a last supper?" He grinned when he said it. Ella wanted to hurl herself against him, to beg him to reconsider moving.

"We both need to talk to you," Jude said again.

"After dinner," he said. "Not on an empty stomach."

His father ordered pizza, but not the kind she was used to—the greasy dollar slices you could grab just about anywhere in New York—but something fancy, with artisanal layers of vegetables Ella didn't recognize. They sat in the grand dining room, the table set with china plates and cloth napkins. *It's just pizza*, Ella thought. She didn't need to be afraid.

She heard herself chewing. She felt her lids closing and she jerked them open again. She concentrated on Jude, how beautiful he was, how she loved him.

"I know what you want to talk about," Judge Stein finally said. "Let me save you the trouble. We're moving. I already got you into a good high school, Jude, and it starts soon. And Ella, you'll be starting school, too. No more of this nonsense. You're too young to be in a relationship like this. I won't change my mind. End of story."

Ella blinked hard. His words seemed to cut a path through the air, a road leading to nowhere she wanted to go. Then she thought of a movie she had seen once in which the closing credits read: *The End? Or is it just the beginning?*

"Wait," Ella said. "Listen to us."

"We have a lot of packing to do, and I could use your help, Jude. Let's just have tea and dessert—I've got some black forest cake here—and then off you go, Ella."

*He knows my name*, she thought. He had never addressed her by name before. She wondered what it meant that he did so now. And the *off you go*, like she was a child who'd obediently do his bidding. It made her feel madder and more helpless.

"We'll make the tea," Jude said. "But then I have things to say to you."

"Make sure it's decaf," Jude's father said.

"It'll be herbal," Jude said, and he looked at Ella when he said it.

They were in the kitchen alone. She could hear his father in the other room, leafing through the newspaper, the rustle as he turned the pages. Her mind flooded with opportunities.

"Let's just run away," she said, grabbing his arm. "Right now. No one will find us."

Jude was putting water on to boil. "He'll find us. And it will be worse when he does."

"What are you two doing in there?" Jude's father called from the other room. "Let's get this show on the road."

*This show.* That was all it was to him. Beginning. Middle. End.

"I wish he would just die," Jude said. The words hung in the air. They both froze.

"Me too," she whispered.

She was so tired, so, so exhausted. Every surface looked like a place she could sleep, but she knew there was so little time left with Jude. When she thought of him gone from her life, all she could envision was an endless trail of black stretching out forever. She didn't want him to go, and she didn't want to go back to school without him. She grabbed his wrist and saw his scars. He wouldn't try to kill himself again, would he?

What if he did? What if he couldn't live without her?

"What's the point?" he said, rubbing his eyes.

"Us. We're the point." She touched his wrist, then his scar, and brought it up to her lips and kissed it. "You won't try again, will you? Promise me you won't. Without you, I'll die, too. I swear it."

He started taking things out of his pockets. A flower, the petals flattened. The sandwich bag filled with herbs. He took out the sprigs of foxglove and gently smoothed them on the counter. "I grew these," he said.

"I know. We did."

"I thought it would help his heart. The right dose could help it . . . the wrong dose could stop it."

The kettle boiled and Jude shut it off.

"He has no heart," Ella said.

"We have to do something," Jude said, his voice cracking in desperation.

Ella sat for a just a moment before she leaned her head against his back. She was so tired, so very, very tired, but she pinched her thigh to hurt herself awake, to stay there, with Jude.

TIME JUMPED, AND she was suddenly upstairs on the third floor of the townhouse. She couldn't figure out how she had gotten there. Or when. Did she tell Jude where she was going? She felt her bladder, heavy in her body.

This whole top floor seemed to have changed. She couldn't remember which door led to the bathroom. She kept one hand on the wall until she opened a heavy wooden door at the end of the hall, and there it was, the big tub, the skylight wedged in the white ceiling so you could look at the stars while you were bathing.

She couldn't find the light switch, so she peed in the dark, then washed her hands, trying to make out her face in the dark mirror. She sat on the edge of the tub, huge and claw-footed. She had never been in a tub that large, so she stepped in and pulled the curtain from the rod and spread it over her like a blanket. She reached for her phone. To her surprise, Jude had sent her a dozen texts and she wanted to read them immediately and text him back, tell him where she was. She settled against the tub, and as her fingers found the letters, her leaden eyelids seemed to crash down. *Jude*, she thought. *Jude*. And then the phone tumbled, and she slept.

SHE AWOKE WITH a start. She couldn't remember when she had come upstairs. How much time had elapsed? She had stopped checking the time, because she didn't want to know how fast time was passing, how every second was against them.

She crept down one flight of stairs and then another. When she was just above the first floor, she crouched and looked down. She could see the dining room from this angle, the table cleaned up—but who had done that? Then she crept down the rest of the stairs, and she even checked the basement, but no one else was home.

Maybe Jude was outside. She went to look, but to her horror, as soon as she opened the door, it closed behind her, automatically locking.

*Fuck*. She didn't see either Jude or Judge Stein anywhere. In fact, she didn't see much of anyone out here. It was so dark and still, and she still wasn't sure what time it was. The Upper East Side seemed to get to bed earlier than any other part of the city, the quiet over the neighborhood like a comforter. She didn't even see the usual pet owners walking their dogs, didn't hear the usual noises from windows—music, conversations. She blinked hard, thinking maybe she was asleep. Maybe she was dreaming. She hadn't learned much in school this year, but she remembered science, the teacher telling the class that some quantum physicists believed that there was no time, that it was a manmade construct. When the teacher had told the class time would start to go backward and eventually it would stop altogether, that everything was happening at the same time, someone in the back had quipped, "Oh, imagine the never-ending blow jobs!" and the teacher, disgusted, had ended the period.

What if it were true, though? What if she and Jude were here right now, and at the same time she and Jude were married in California with a baby and a dog and no one to bother them? What if she and Jude were both ninety-nine and holding hands on their porch, rocking in their chairs, remembering the gorgeous, beautiful life they had shared?

ELLA REACHED FOR her phone to text Jude, but it wasn't in her pocket anymore. Panicked, she searched herself again, and then she remembered. She had been about to text him when she was in the bathtub, and then she had fallen asleep. Her phone must have fallen to the floor, or into the tub, and she hadn't seen it with the light off. She dug in her pockets, finding only her MetroCard—she had nothing she could use to even leave a note.

She hit her fist against her thigh, to test again if she were dreaming. It hurt. There was nothing else to do but to return home before Helen started to worry.

She walked over to Lexington and into the subway station, asking a tired-looking woman in the customer service booth what time it was. "Two a.m.," the agent said, and Ella, stunned, stood there, not knowing how it could be so late, how much time had passed. Her mother would be livid, but she wasn't scared of anything now except not seeing Jude.

She had no memory of how she got home from the subway to her bed in Queens, how her comforter had snuck up to her chin. She lay on her back, begging Jude to hear her thoughts, to come stand under her window again. She'd know if he was there. She'd feel his presence.

"SLEEPYHEAD," HELEN SAID the next morning when Ella stumbled to breakfast. "Where were you for dinner? I tried to wait up for you, but I conked. What time did you get in?"

Ella shrugged, said she was packing boxes with Jude.

"Next time, call," Helen told her. "You know how I worry."

Ella waited until Helen left for work. They didn't have a landline, so all she could do was try to text Jude in her mind. *I'm sorry. I miss you. Where are you?* She dragged herself through the morning, washing her face, throwing on clothes, sure that Jude would come to the house. He'd be worried she hadn't called—although maybe he'd find her phone in his bathroom. She knew she very much did look like shit, with shadows like half-moon stains under her eyes, her hair matted because she hadn't yet showered, but she didn't care. Jude, she knew, would always find her beautiful.

She kept staring out the front window down to the sidewalk, waiting for him. There was the usual traffic, the sprawl of people on the street, and then she saw it from the front window: a black police car double-parked on her street; two men in dark jackets and suit pants coming toward her apartment building, one tall and burly, the other so blond he looked whitewashed. The burly cop stared up at her and beckoned her to come downstairs. Ella felt his eyes on her, like rubber ink stamps punched on her chest.

*Something happened to Jude,* she thought, and she felt herself go white with terror.

She ran all the way down the stairs, remembering to lock the outside door. The two cops looked at each other. "Ella Levy?" one said, and she nodded.

"Let's go to the squad car," the burly officer said, and Ella followed.

"Is my mom okay?" she asked.

"Sure, she is," he said. "But we need you to come with us." The blond cop opened the car door.

"We just need to talk to you at the station," the burly cop said. Ella felt her mouth drop open. "About an attempted murder."

"What?" she said. "I don't understand. Is Jude okay?" She looked around her, panic rising in her throat.

The burly cop's eyes were steely. "This is about you trying to poison Judge Stein."

"Jude's dad?" she said.

"In you go," the cop said, his hand on her head, guiding her into the backseat. Then they got in, too, the pale cop driving.

"I have to call my mom!" she said, starting to cry. "I need a lawyer!"

"First, you need to talk to us."

"We're going to read you your Miranda rights," the driver said once the car was moving. She stayed silent and he began in a monotone, but she couldn't focus on the words. "Do you understand the rights I have just read to you? With these rights in mind, do you still wish to speak to us?"

She stumbled on the word *still* because she couldn't tell if that was a bad thing or a good one. "I want a lawyer," she blurted. "I want my mom."

The whitewashed cop sighed. "Of course," he said, "but like I said, you need to talk to us first."

AT THE POLICE station, they fingerprinted her and then brought her into a cramped room, empty but for a metal table and two chairs. Two glaring lights hung from the ceiling, so bright they made her squint.

The detectives gave her a Coke and a package of cheese crackers. When she was finished, the burly cop pulled a latex glove over his hand and gingerly took the can. She wondered why but was afraid to ask.

It was then that they began to batter her with questions. *I want my mom. You have to call my mom.* The things they kept asking made no sense. How did she feel living in a poor Queens neighborhood? What did she think of Judge Stein's huge townhouse? How did it feel to be there? What was Jude doing that night? Why did she hate his father?

"I didn't hate him—" she said, but they were peppering her with other questions, their faces grim. They kept asking her, again and again, insistent. *What did you do? What did you do?* And sometimes they said, *We know what you did. We know.*

And then they began to tell her, over and over, like a story they seemed to believe. *You put the foxglove in the cup, didn't you? You gave it to Judge Stein, didn't you? You made him drink that tea and then you skedaddled out of there.*

The interrogation went on forever, and she was afraid to ask them anything. The two detectives came and went from the room, but she stayed at the table. When she started to fall asleep, the burly cop prodded her arm to wake her.

"I want a lawyer! I want my mom!"

"Are you really sure you want that?" he said. "Because a lawyer means a trial, and a trial is difficult. A jury. A judge. All of that. It never turns out well."

She froze. *Was this true?*

"If I were you, I'd waive my rights to a lawyer, to seeing your mom and upsetting her. If you tell us what you did, we can make this a lot easier on you. We're here to help you. If you bring in a lawyer, the first thing he'll do is try to stop us from doing that."

She blinked, confused. "I want to talk to Jude!"

"Well, he's right next door in the next room, and, I'm sorry to tell you this, but he already told us what happened. What you did."

"What happened? What did he say?" She shut her eyes, trying to feel Jude in the next room, but all she could feel was her heart ramming against her chest.

"You know what he said. You were there," the burly cop said.

She had no idea how many hours had passed when they thrust a paper under her nose and handed her a pen, insisting that she write out a confession. "You could be sent away for a long time if you don't," one of them said.

"I don't understand," she said. "I don't know what this means."

"We have your phone," the burly cop said, and Ella started. He took it out of a jacket pocket and slid it toward her. "Unlock it, please," he said.

She did, punching in her passcode—the day she and Jude had met. She handed it back to them, watching as they swiped through her messages. The blond cop raised his eyes at the burly one, who nodded. The blond man stood and carried the phone out of the room.

"Can't I have it back?" she said.

"It's evidence. You're not getting it back any time soon."

"How is it evidence?"

"*I would do anything for you*," the burly cop said. "*I hate your father.*"

He sighed. "It's incriminating stuff . . ."

She stared at him, stunned. "Do you have Jude's phone too?"

"This isn't about Jude."

She looked down at the paper and saw her name, and then Jude's—Jude's!—but everything else looked like hieroglyphics. "What is this?" she asked, sobbing.

"It's for your confession. We need you to state what you did. In your own words."

"I want to call my mother!"

"You can call her after we're through here," he said.

There were no windows in the room. No clock on the wall. She wanted to sleep so badly, to vanish into a dream, where she could be with Jude. But every time she started to fall asleep, one of the officers would wake her with a question that made no sense to her.

"It'll look better for you if you just cooperate with us. Judges always look kindly on cooperation. And under the circumstances, no judge is going to be on your side here."

Every time she heard a noise, she tensed expectantly, sure it would be Helen breaking into the room, coming to rescue her.

But her mother never showed. Instead, the officers kept badgering her, goading her to pick up the pen. They told her it was nearing nighttime already, that everyone had news of this now, including the media who had condemned her, and that was all it took to send her away for years and years. No jury would buy her story because she had no story. There was only the truth.

"What truth?" she said.

One cop leaned over her. "We know it was you. We'll put in a good word for you if you confess." He tapped the paper. "Go ahead now. Start with *On the night of . . .*"

They kept telling her what to write, over and over, until she began to doubt her own memory. But every time she said, "Wait, that's not true," one of the cops would say, "Really? Write it down and I bet it will jog your memory." They kept assuring her that they knew what happened. She and Jude had been at the house. They had a small bag of foxglove. Jude had confessed that he hadn't done anything, that it was Ella who had urged him to boil the water. And then she remembered the gurgle of the water, those pretty glass cups, and she wrote it down. "What did Jude say?" she asked. The words kept scrambling in her mind.

"That you did it."

She felt her body shaking, and she gripped the edge of the table. "He said I did it?"

"Didn't you? Are you sure it isn't true? Are you one thousand percent sure?"

She shut her eyes. She smelled the pizza and then heard the crumpling of the newspaper his father was reading.

"I don't remember! I really don't remember!"

"You tried to kill a superior court judge. You want to put your fate in the hands of jurors? Trust me, no one is going to be on your side here. The judge in your case will probably know Judge Stein personally, will have known him since law school."

That was when her world went dark, when she felt as if her arms and legs were made of cement.

"Judge Stein nearly died. He told us what you did."

"What did I do?" she cried. In her mind she saw it again: Judge Stein reading the paper in the other room, then standing. His anger boiling like the water for the tea. She heard herself telling Jude, *I would do anything for you.* That was true. It had always been true.

"Jude told us you did it," the burly cop said again.

When they fit the pen more firmly into her hands, she tried to let it drop from her fingers, but she couldn't move them. She didn't know who she was anymore, how she could have done such a thing. She started to write, one cop leaning over her shoulder. "That's good," he said, reading. "That's very good."

AND THEN, after what seemed like the tenth time she had rewritten the confession, the cops stood up. "All you have to do is sign."

She scribbled her name.

"I want my call," Ella said, and this time the cop said, "Sure, why not."

HELEN ANSWERED ON the first ring, her voice tense with worry. She had been working late and hadn't heard from Ella since breakfast that morning. Jude hadn't answered, either. Growing more and more anxious, she had called the hospitals, and then the NYPD, and that was when she found out that Ella was in custody.

"I'm on my way, but I'm stuck in traffic," Helen said, her voice wobbly.

"You have to come!" Ella cried.

"I already called a lawyer," she said. "He's a friend of a friend. We'll both be right there."

But it felt like another hour before Helen arrived, her face chalky white. A man her mother introduced as Clark Royton strode in after her, in an ill-fitting suit, livid because he should have been called earlier.

"We have a confession," the burly cop said.

"We'll just see about that," Clark said. He turned to Ella. "Don't say another word, now," he said. "I'll handle everything."

And, terror-stricken, she let him.

TWO DAYS LATER, a petrified Ella was seated in a prison van, her legs shackled, her hands in cuffs, sitting on a too-narrow metal seat so that no matter how she shifted, she couldn't get comfortable. There were four other women with her, none of them speaking, except for one who kept saying she needed to pee. The driver, behind metal meshwork, acted like he couldn't hear her.

Everything had happened so fast. Clark told her Jude had been freed, so she thought she might be, too. Ella had sat frozen through an arraignment, while the prosecutor had read the charges—attempted murder in the second degree—and did she understand the charges and still want to plead guilty? Because she didn't want to go back into that room, she said yes. Yes. Yes.

To her shock, the judge then determined a sentence. Twenty to twenty-five years. She wouldn't be let out on bail—because her guilty plea negated the need for a trial. Instead, he remanded her to the custody of the Department of Corrections, held in the local jail until they could arrange for a transport to a minimum-security women's prison upstate.

"Your honor!" Clark had finally interjected, and Ella sobbed harder. The more she tried to meet her attorney's eyes, the more he looked away.

Ella didn't know what a real prison would be like. She had no idea what to expect. The exterior was squat and brick and industrial looking, spread out on an empty patch of land like a sprawling nightmare. Inside, there wasn't much light. The floors were dark, too, and the whole place had an institutional smell. They gave her dark green pants and a dark green shirt, socks and underwear, and she was brought to what looked like a dorm of eight square cells, each one with a bed, a desk, a sink, and an open toilet. There was a door you could close but not lock. Only the main door to the dorm locked, and that was done by the guards. Her cell was toward the back, and she didn't have a room-mate, but even so, she felt the other women watching her, taking her measure. A few of them snickered, and she knew that couldn't be good.

"You want me to fuck you up now or later, babyface?" a beefy blond woman said to her. Ella cowered in her cell, terrified for days. The tension only seemed to grow. She kept her head down. There wasn't much silence, but when there was, it had a presence, as if it were waiting for her, some unseen force biding its time before it struck.

She missed Jude desperately. She missed her mom. She had only seen her once, before they took her here, her face puffy with sorrow. But when Ella asked her mother to find Jude, to make sure he was okay, Helen's face darkened. She refused to talk about Jude, and instead told Ella that she was going to talk to Clark again and see what they could do, that she was never ever giving up on freeing Ella. She was going to visit every week and write her letters, and fight for her on the outside.

But all Ella could think about was that her mother wouldn't be the one in prison. Ella would. And Jude was nowhere to be found.

SOMETIMES AT NIGHT she could hear screaming. Women got thrown into solitary for talking back to the guards or not moving quickly enough. She had thought that the shower, the gym, the cafeteria would be the scariest places because of movies she had seen, but to her surprise, she felt the most afraid in her own cell. That was when women could just walk in as if they had been invited, slapping her books to the ground just because they could, sometimes slapping her face too, and then leaving. There was a rumor about a guard who liked to rape inmates.

Ella learned to be a loner because it threw the other women off. They didn't know what to make of her. She learned to keep her head down, to look hostile even when she wasn't so that people would keep their distance, keep guessing about what she might do. She spent her time in the library and she watched, figuring out who the other loners were, whom she could talk to, whom she could trust.

The worst of it was the boredom. Every day was and would be the same—every hour accounted for, from waking up to breakfast to shower time to her work detail, which Ella came to dread. They put her in the prison garden, pulling weeds, and all she could think about was Jude. Every plant looked like foxglove to her.

One day, one of the women near her started spilling dish liquid on the floor. Ella watched, tense, sure a fight was brewing. Then the other women stood up and took off their shoes and they began to slide along it, whooping, skittering, laughing—some of them falling on their butts. "Hey, Ella!" one of the women called. "Hey, babyface!" She motioned for Ella to join in. Tentatively Ella took off her shoes. She gathered her breath and then slid, and the women cheered. For a moment, she wasn't in this prison at all. She was flying, and the feeling of wonder made her laugh out loud.

HELEN KEPT HER promise about visits, about sending letters. She'd stuff them with newspaper clippings on things she thought Ella might like—animal stories about dogs who had traveled hundreds of miles to find their owners, cats who seemed to understand language, changes in their neighborhood in Queens. When Helen visited, she brought food and yarn, money for the commissary, and other things that sometimes other women would steal just for spite—and that sometimes Ella would share to keep them from stealing everything. She lost weight. Her hair lost its shine. And she was extremely tired. By the end of September, she was throwing up every morning. It was the other inmates who told her: she needed to get a pregnancy test.

ELLA WAS STUNNED. Her period had always been erratic. She was used to missing it. And Jude had always used condoms or pulled out in time. She tried to remember the last time she'd had it, and she thought, *July*. Maybe July. Maybe August. Maybe she didn't know.

She went to the infirmary and a nurse was with her when she saw the blue line coming in clearly on the test. The nurse sighed heavily.

"We don't do abortions."

Ella's mind shut down. The nurse told her she'd get her prenatal vitamins and set a schedule for checkups. Then she asked Ella if she had family, someone who could raise a baby outside of prison. Otherwise the baby would be adopted through an agency or go into the foster care system.

"My mom," Ella blurted. "I'll see her this week. My boyfriend." She was nauseous with hope.

She didn't know what to do. How to feel. At night, she tried to telepathically get to Jude, to tell him they were going to have a baby, to ask him what he wanted to do. Would he raise their child by himself until she got out? But her telepathic skills felt rusty, and in the end, all she heard was the thump of her own beating heart.

THAT WEEKEND, WHEN Helen came to visit, carrying a bag full of magazines and books, Ella told her.

"Well," Helen said finally. "You'll have to give it up for adoption."

Stunned, Ella stared at her mother.

"Why can't you raise the baby?" she asked. "Why can't you bring it in for visits—"

Helen held up a hand. "You know why not," she said quietly. "I have to work. You have to get through this. It would be so much harder for both of us. And for the child. Twenty years is a lifetime—"

"Jude can be there, too," Ella said. "Find him, find his dad, tell them I'm pregnant. Jude would never ditch his responsibility."

She gripped her mother's hand.

"Please, Mom. You have to do this for me."

She wouldn't let go until her mother slowly nodded.

IN THE WEEKS and months that followed, Ella's nausea stopped, replaced by shortness of breath. She requested looser prison clothes. Her breasts hurt. Everything about her body was a reminder of the baby growing inside her—her baby, and Jude's.

The other women became more approachable, friendlier. She began to know their names. Annie. Susan. Ruthanna. Beth. They were all ages. They were twenty-five or twenty-nine. They were thirty or forty. They gave her their yogurts at breakfast because she needed more calcium now. They wanted to touch her stomach, to try to convince her to keep the child because of the fierce yearning they had for their own children. They showed her photos of their little ones in party clothes, in jeans, sometimes perched on a father's lap. "It's all so worth it," Susan told her. "The throw-up, the poop. The tantrums. None of that matters. You'll never love anyone as much as you will your child."

She didn't know what to believe. Ella had never loved anyone as much as she had loved Jude.

AROUND CHRISTMAS, HELEN came for her weekly visit, her hair damp from snow, her cheeks burnished from the chill. She strode past the fake Christmas tree the prison had in the visiting room, the little green plastic Menorah on a table, and then told Ella the news. Jude would not be helping. He had given up his parental rights. Ella crumpled over the table between them, but Helen insisted that this was a good thing. She leaned across the table and took Ella's hands.

"Clark Royton helped me find an adoption lawyer."

At first Ella didn't understand, and then Helen began telling her how this lawyer had already found a couple who wanted the child.

"What about Jude?" Ella whispered, and Helen slowly shook her head.

"Where is he?"

"I don't know. All I know is that he gave up his rights. All I know is you have to let this go now. Let him go."

Ella's mouth went dry. "Who will take the baby?" she asked flatly. Helen could only tell her it was a closed adoption.

Ella walked out of the room and back to her cell, ignoring Helen's voice calling out to her.

ELLA BURIED HERSELF in books from the prison library, losing herself in other peoples' stories. She was a ballerina in Mexico or a doctor in France, not an inmate. She passed her days in even more solitude than before.

"Hey, Mama," some of the other women called to her when she'd waddle by, hugely pregnant. Somehow, the women on her cellblock learned that the baby was being adopted, and they grew kinder to her, watching her tenderly, leaving little presents for her to find. All Ella wanted was to forget. Their kindness made her remember.

IN APRIL, WHEN Ella was eight months pregnant, Helen came in and told Ella she had an idea. She spread out information about getting her GED. "You could pass that test without even studying, a smart girl like you," Helen said.

Ella sighed. "And do what with it?"

"You could go on and get a college degree if you want," Helen said, "This prison has a program for young people like you, through Bard College. You could learn something and then when you get out—"

Ella laughed sharply. "I don't know," she said. "That doesn't sound possible. It sounds scammy."

"Do something with your time here. Don't wallow anymore, baby girl."

"I'll think about it," Ella said.

And she did, about all the days stretching out in front of her like the same dirty bolt of cloth that could never be cleaned. Doing this might break up the monotony, eat away at the endless time. She wondered if everything she studied, if she started now, would go to the baby too, by a kind of magical osmosis. In any case, it would be something to do, something to distract her from the discomfort of being pregnant day in and day out. She'd have to really think about it.

ON MAY EIGHTH, Ella gave birth via emergency C-section in the prison hospital, a procedure during which she was so woozy she felt as if she were hallucinating. The doctor put up a sheet so that Ella couldn't see anything, but she felt it, as if aggressive hands were rummaging around inside her, rearranging her, making her different—and wasn't that the truth? She had wanted Helen to be in the room with her, but all she had was this rough, efficient doctor.

And then the doctor said, "And we're done," as if it were a triumph, and he quietly lifted the baby. She tried to raise herself up, to see if it was a boy or girl, but a nurse gently lowered her down. She heard the child's cry, a mewl like a kitten, but she saw nothing. Another nurse whisked her baby away.

SHE WAS LEFT with a scar, a reminder, so no matter how hard she tried, she'd never forget, and even if she did two hundred sit-ups a day, she'd never get her flat stomach back. Her breasts hurt, too, and sometimes leaked or sprayed milk without warning, branding her shirts with a yellowish stain that never came out no matter how much she scrubbed. The other women in the prison knew what was going on, and they brought her extra, clean T-shirts to wear, cupcakes from the commissary and cups of tea. Sometimes they just sat quietly beside her, mourning with her as if they were holding a kind of vigil for her baby and for theirs, as if things might get better for all of them. But everyone knew they wouldn't.

It was Helen who came to her rescue again, pushing Ella to apply to the Bard Prison Initiative and get a degree. All she had to do was write an essay and go through an interview. "You can build something here," Helen insisted.

Ella spent days writing the essay and landed an interview with a Bard professor who seemed to like her. To her surprise, she actually got into the program. Instantly, things changed. Night used to be the worst, the loneliest time, but now she couldn't wait for it because the prison got quiet then and she could read or write drafts of her papers— longhand first, to be typed out later in the library. While she was studying, going to school, she could think of herself as a college student, not just a felon. She could stop obsessing about having given up her baby. She buckled down and studied for a degree in psychology.

And when she got it, four years later, in a small graduation ceremony at the prison, Helen was in the first row, crying with pride. Ella happy-cried, too. And then weeks later, the prison made her a peer leader, a position that usually went to the old-timers. Peer leaders advised inmates on how to endure in prison, or steered them to resources for legal research or counsel. What the women wanted from Ella was more private: How to get over a broken heart when your lover didn't show up for visits. How to stop the panic that seemed to close in during the long nights.

And Ella, in a blaze of gratitude, using what she had learned, helped them.

# THIRTEEN

# Manhattan

*August 2011*

That night of the dinner in his father's townhouse, Jude lost track of Ella. She seemed to have suddenly vanished. He looked everywhere, running up and down the stairs calling for her, and he kept texting her. *What's up? Where are you? Why did you leave?* But there was no response. Had she really left him to handle this night by himself? He kept looking, even went outside to see if for some reason she was hanging around the front stoop, maybe talking to his dad. And when she wasn't, he went to the subway station she used, even going down to the platform and calling her name. But she wasn't there either.

He was so tired he couldn't think straight. He sat on the stoop, waiting for her, and found himself dozing and then sleeping, and then he jerked awake. The weather was so humid, so disgustingly heavy. What the hell time was it? He checked his phone for her texts again, and for the time. Nine at night. She wouldn't have left so early.

He went back into the townhouse, for the AC, and into the kitchen. To his surprise, the counter was wiped clean, the tea was gone, the leaves—and how had that happened? He couldn't remember. *Whoosh,* he heard. *Whoosh.* He followed the sound into his father's study, and there was his father, struggling to pull himself up by the filmy window curtains, a teacup smashed to pieces on the floor. His father coughed and gasped. His hands grasped at the air and his eyes locked on Jude.

Jude grabbed his cell and called 911. By the time they answered, he was screaming.

THE WHOLE WAY in the ambulance his father wasn't making sense. The paramedics gave him an EKG.

"Heart rate's low," one said.

Jude told them about his father's cardiac condition, how he was on digitalis. The judge mumbled deliriously that he was seeing halos, and turned his head to vomit onto the floor of the ambulance.

AS SOON AS they got to the ER, the doctor looked at the EKG results and frowned.

"Does he ever mistake his meds? His digitalis? Take too many?"

Jude froze. "He never has," he said. "That I know of."

"Let's get some blood tests, some levels—we'll give him atropine. It'll punch his heartbeat up. And we'll measure his dioxin levels to see what's going on."

His father was just lying there, not moving. Jude took his hand, which felt clammy.

Then his father clutched Jude's fingers. "I'm dying," he said.

Jude's eyes stung with tears. "No you aren't," he insisted, but he felt the cold racing up his spine.

"Your dad doesn't mess around with herbs, supplements?" the doctor asked.

Jude couldn't breathe. "He doesn't believe in that stuff," he said. He pressed himself against the wall.

"Could he die?" Jude asked in a whisper.

The doctor studied him. "You let us do our job," he said. "We'll do a blood panel for toxins to make sure, get the results fairly quickly. Once we get some results, we'll know what to do."

They unlocked the wheels on his father's bed, and Jude followed them to the fifth-floor ICU, where the doctor squeezed his shoulder and told him to wait outside.

He sat alone in the waiting room, watching the clock on the wall. One in the morning. Then two. Then it was three a.m. and still no one came to speak to him. There were some magazines, and a TV was broadcasting weight-loss infomercials soundlessly.

Jude put his head in his hands, feeling his pulse beating through his temples. He remembered vaguely, through a haze, that he had been looking for Ella. He was sure that he had searched for her all over the house, and then outside, even walking a few blocks in each direction, and he couldn't find her. His father must have had a heart attack, he reasoned, and he began to shake. He hated his father, but he loved him, too. He shut his eyes. *Only for a moment*, he told himself.

WHEN HE AWOKE, the room was bright with light. There were all sorts of people going back and forth, a commotion of carts and gurneys, people crying or laughing or just stunned, and everyone was ignoring Jude. He glanced at the clock and then jumped up. Eight in the morning! He felt himself going crazy. Why hadn't a doctor come to tell him anything? He had this idea that if his father was all right, things would have happened quickly; but instead, they were moving through sludge. He wanted to get up, to grab a doctor, but even after his few hours of sleep, he was still so exhausted.

He waited, falling in and out of hallucinatory sleep. Finally, he jolted awake again, not knowing where he was at first. He tried to flag down a doctor or nurse, but no one could tell him anything. The receptionist reiterated that someone should be right out to speak to him. He sat down again and tried to stay awake, waiting for someone to come update him. He moved only to relieve himself in the men's room down the hall, then to grab some food from the vending machine that he was way too tired to eat, and then later just to walk, to try to center himself and keep exhaustion at bay. Each time, he ended up back in the waiting room. Maybe this was all a nightmare and he was still asleep. He sat again, and then kept nodding.

SOMEONE TOUCHED HIS shoulder and Jude awoke, blinking, his throat so parched that he couldn't speak at first. A nurse and two men in suits towered over him.

"Is my dad okay?" Jude asked, standing. He looked at the clock. How could it be five in the afternoon? "Why didn't anyone wake me?" he said.

"Your father's stable now. Sleeping," the nurse said.

"I need to talk to the doctor," Jude said, and then he looked at the men again. "Are you the doctors?" he asked, confused.

"Detectives," one said, opening his coat to flash his badge. *Cops?* Jude thought, panicked.

"You can talk to the doctor when you come back," the other man said. "We need you to come to the station with us, just to answer some questions, get it all down on record."

"Get what on record?"

"You need to come with us."

"I can't leave my dad."

"Yes you can, son. This is a good hospital."

The cops stood firm, so Jude gave in and went with them.

AT THE POLICE station, Jude was put in a room with a lawyer who said that he knew Jude's father personally. He told Jude to call him Frank.

"Your father is a good man," Frank said. Some other cops came in—a woman, and the two detectives from the hospital. "You want some water?"

Jude nodded, and someone got him water and a package of cheese crackers.

"Tell us what you remember," the woman said.

Jude's mind clouded over. "I don't—" he said, then halted.

"Why don't you remember?" she asked. "A kid like you. You don't want to go to prison."

"No need to threaten," Frank said calmly.

"I didn't do anything!" Jude cried.

"I see," one of the detectives said. "You know your girlfriend, Ella, is right in the room beside us. We picked her up this morning."

Jude jumped up. "This morning? When this morning? Why didn't you tell me?" He swallowed hard. "I have to see her." But the detective shook his head.

"The hospital called us because they found poison in one of your dad's labs."

Jude's head swam. "I thought he had a heart attack? I don't understand why someone didn't wake me to tell me—"

Then Jude remembered: the times he had gotten up to pee, to grab candy from a vending machine way down the hall. Doctors might have come while Jude wasn't there. Once again, it was his fault.

"Hospitals are busy places. And your dad could have had a heart event, but you know, the lab tests apparently say something different. And when your dad stabilized a little, he said something interesting to one of the nurses. That last night, he drank some tea you and your girlfriend made."

"Wait—" Jude said.

"Ella told us she grew it in her backyard. That means criminal intent."

"She told you that?"

"Let's just focus on you."

"Please, I'm so tired. Can't I just sleep?" Jude said.

"Yes, let's finish this up," Frank said.

"Soon," one of the detectives said.

But they wouldn't let up. They kept hounding him with the same questions—about Ella, about foxglove, about how he could make this easy for himself or he could make it hard.

It seemed like hours passed, and then another cop came in and said something to the one asking all the questions, who nodded.

"So, your father's going to make it," he said. "He's turned a corner."

Jude collapsed, banging his head on the table. He couldn't keep his eyes open. His lids were burning. The detective hoisted him up again, squeezing his shoulder reassuringly.

Frank gestured to the door, indicating that the detectives should follow him. They stepped into the hallway. When the door opened again, only Frank came back in. This time, every muscle in his face looked relaxed and smooth.

"The cops are letting you go now," Frank said. "There's no real evidence against you. Nothing to charge you with."

Jude braced his hands on the table, weak with relief. His father was okay. He could leave. And then he remembered. "Where's Ella?" he said. "I want to see her—"

Frank looked at Jude and shook his head. "You can't see her. She's in a different boat than you are."

"What boat?"

"The attempted murder boat."

Jude felt himself reeling, so nauseous he thought he might vomit. "That can't be true," he said.

"It's true," Frank said. "She signed a confession."

"What? Confessed to what? When?"

"She confessed. And no, you absolutely cannot see her. Go see your dad." He said it like an order. "We think you had no part in this. You're free to go and you should count that as a blessing."

"I want to see the confession!"

"That's not my call. Not yours, either," Frank said.

Frank escorted him out of the station, then flagged a cab for him, clapping him on the shoulder and telling him to give Judge Stein his regards. All Jude could think was that something was so very wrong. He kept hearing his father's voice yelling at him about his mother. *You are responsible. You did this. You.*

WHEN JUDE RETURNED to the hospital, a nurse was just coming out of his father's room.

"Ah, there you are," the nurse said. "He's so lucky; he nearly died. We'll keep him here with us for a few days so we can watch him, but he's out of the woods. You can go in now."

Jude's father was hooked to an IV and dressed in a faded green hospital gown. He looked wan and tired, so small in the hulking hospital bed. Jude didn't know what to do or say, so he just stood there. And then his father reached for his hands. "My son," he said.

"They told me you're going to be all right," Jude said.

"I will be. They have to monitor me here for a few days for rebound toxicity, and I have to check in with my regular doctor."

Jude swallowed hard. "I had to speak to the police."

"Well, of course," Andrew said. "I was poisoned. They can't ignore that."

Jude felt the room chill, and he started to cry. "I'm sorry!" he said. "I'm so sorry!"

He thought of his father teaching him how to ride a bike, holding on, assuring him he'd never let him fall. Then he thought of his mother dying in that crash, and the way his father's face had changed when he learned that Jude had been driving.

"Jude," Andrew said, pulling his son closer to him. "Please don't talk that way. I know that I don't always act like it, but I do love you." He gripped Jude's hand tighter.

"I know I've been so sad. So angry. I've made so many bad judgments. And I've been a rotten father. If I hadn't been, then we wouldn't be here now."

Jude caught his breath, sobbing. The air was moving around him. *I love you.* His father had said *I love you* to him.

"We're all going to be okay. I promise you that," Andrew said.

"Where's Ella? What's going to happen to her?"

"I don't know."

"They told me she signed a confession. Why would she confess to something she didn't do?"

"Listen to yourself," Andrew said. "Listen to what you just said. There was hot water in the kettle. There were leaves in the cup."

"*I* left the cup!" Jude said. "She wasn't even in the kitchen then! She didn't do anything! I don't think she—"

"You don't *think*—" his father said, interrupting him. "I can see that look on your face. You're not sure, are you? Well, that confession should make you sure."

Jude struggled to remember what happened. No matter how hard he tried, he couldn't figure out the order of events that night. He thought of the missing time, the blank where the memory of that night should be, the moment when he realized Ella wasn't there. He thought: *She'd do anything for me.* And then: *I'd do anything for her.* But oh my God, what had she done?

"I need to hear it from her," he said. "I need to see that confession—"

"And what good will that do? How could that make you feel any better? Besides, the police don't have to show you anything, and they won't."

"What's going to happen to her?"

"What needs to happen." His father's lids began to flutter. "She confessed. That's all I know. And I know that both of us are tired, and we both need to sleep. Especially you."

BUT JUDE DIDN'T sleep. He couldn't. He kept calling the hospital to make sure his dad's condition was still stable. He lay awake alone in their big, empty townhouse. Time began to blur again. Did he visit his father that day or was it the day before? Was it the next day or the day after, when he ran past a vendor on the street and saw the newspaper headlines, blaring at him? There was his photo, his dad's, and Ella's.

## RICH BOY, POOR GIRL. YOUNG TEMPTRESS ATTEMPTS MURDER

And beneath it:

### REDHEAD CAUGHT RED-HANDED

He grabbed several different papers, wondering how it had all happened so fast. He returned home to find a TV truck parked in front of the townhouse, a newscaster saying something into a microphone and pointing to his home. His heart pounded with terror.

"I need a smoke, then let's do another take," the woman said, walking briskly toward the truck. Jude used the opportunity to rush behind her to the basement entrance, and quietly locked the door behind him. As soon as he was back inside, he stuffed the papers into the trash.

He called the police department, but still no one would let him see Ella's confession. It was just as his father had said.

He stayed up, listening to the sounds outside his door, sure a cop was going to bang on it and tell him they had arrested the wrong person, that it was Jude who was going to be locked up in prison, that they knew he had made the tea, that Ella was going free.

Somehow, as always, he was to blame. And somehow, he had to make this right.

HIS FATHER CAME home three days after he had been admitted. The media continued hounding them; the phones kept ringing. Jude kept calling Ella's phone, Helen's too, and both kept going to voicemail. He wouldn't answer any call unless it was from Ella. And when she didn't call or text, he just stayed in his room, paralyzed.

The next morning, while his father slept, Jude went to the police station again, asking about Ella. "I have to see her," he said.

"Then you better travel upstate to her prison," the cop said, mentioning a place Jude had never heard of: Rigley Women's Correctional Facility.

Without fanfare, the officer swiveled his body to talk to someone else.

WHEN JUDE GOT home, his father was sitting up in bed. He smiled when Jude walked in.

"I need to go see Ella," Jude said, and his father's smile faltered. "I know the name of the prison."

"So do I," his father said. "And you won't be allowed to see her. You won't be on any visitor's list."

"I can go there, though. I can stand outside and—"

"And what?" his father said. "Do you think prisons allow people to do that?"

"Did you see to that?" Jude asked quietly, and his father sighed. "Did you pull those strings?"

"Listen, Jude. We are lucky to be rid of her. We can move on with our lives now."

But Jude couldn't move on. He and Ella had telepathy; they could tell what the other was thinking. Alone in his room, he shut his eyes tight, reaching out to her. Nothing happened.

HE WENT TO her apartment in Queens, his second home, his real home. He pushed the buzzer to Helen's apartment over and over but got no response. He wanted to throw himself into her arms, to hug her the way he always used to. But she wouldn't answer. He felt raw with yearning. He wound around to the backyard so that he could look up at the apartment's windows. But when he turned the corner, he stopped dead. The garden was gone. All that remained was plant debris strewn carelessly over a raw patch of dirt. Jude could read the message clearly: *I'll never forgive you for this.*

He had destroyed Helen too.

DID MEMORIES OF Ella fade like his old T-shirts? Did he forget her when he got to Philly with his father a week later, the way he was supposed to? No. Instead, she haunted his dreams, and his waking hours too. Every time he saw someone with curly hair like Ella's, he felt punched in the heart. Every time he showered, he didn't just see the hummingbird tattoo they had gotten together to symbolize their love. He felt it too, as if it were burning on his arm. It reminded him of every bad thing in his life, the terrible fate of the girl he loved.

One day in the early fall, Jude found himself outside a tattoo removal parlor.

"Might hurt," the guy said, examining his arm.

"Good," Jude said, and shut his eyes. *Make it hurt*, he thought. *Make it kill*. He deserved it.

# FOURTEEN

# Ann Arbor

*March 2019*

When Ella got to the park, she spotted Carla first, on the swings. And there was Marianna, on a bench, beaming.

"I did it," Marianna told her. "I took your advice. I saw a therapist and she helped me realize how right you were." She sat up straighter. "And even better, I transferred some of our money into a bank account that is under my name only.

"And soon, I'm going to tell Mark I want a separation. I have to make sure I have a job and money to support myself first. I've been looking at housesitting listings. There are some for a whole year—professors who need someone to water their plants while they're on sabbatical or vacation and they just don't want to give up the house. I could do that, Ella."

Ella felt a stab of worry.

"I couldn't have done any of this without your support," Marianna said.

Ella smiled weakly. What if Mark found out Marianna had her own money? He might be kind to Carla now, but he had been kind to Marianna at first, too. What if his ire turned on her child as well?

Ella couldn't let that happen.

Marianna told her that ever since that day at the office, they'd slept in separate beds, and now he barely came home from work. She said that he was always shouting and angry and when she finally told him quietly that maybe he should get counseling or anger management therapy, he had mocked her for being middle-class and stupid.

Ella's heart pinched.

"If I told him the truth, that I was going to leave him, he'd go ballistic, so instead I told him I was going to move out for a while, to give us some room to breathe."

"What did he say?"

Marianna sighed. "He wasn't happy. He told me I'd never find a place of my own that I could afford, that he'd never let Carla go. He said he was the reason I even had a life, because he inherited our house from his parents. He kept reminding me that it was his house, not mine." She threaded her hands together. "Ella, he got so furious. I told him I wouldn't stop him from seeing Carla, that he could see her whenever he wanted and vice versa."

"Can't you tell him you want a divorce?"

"Jesus, no. One step at a time," Marianna said. "I have to see a lawyer first."

Ella didn't know what to say. She placed a hand on Marianna's.

"You are such a good friend," Marianna said. "I don't know what I'd do without you. Mark's driven everyone else away." And then Carla came running to them from the swings, and Marianna laughed as Carla jumped into Ella's lap. "I don't think Carla would know what to do without you, either."

THAT EVENING, ELLA paced her apartment. She had answered the Dear Clancy letters for the week, one from a man who was afraid to put himself into a romantic situation.

*Me too*, Ella thought, and left the letter up on her screen.

She couldn't help it. She felt like everything was coming to a head. There were too many feelings scrambled inside her—her worry about Marianna and Carla, plus her growing feelings for Henry, whom she had been seeing a lot of. They met for dinner every other night, always at a different restaurant and once at his place, where he proudly made her lasagna. They went to see live shows at the Ark. In the evenings, they went for long walks, braving the cold nights of March in Ann Arbor. She liked him more and more, which felt dangerous, especially because he seemed to be liking her more and more too. She knew what that meant. Sooner or later, she'd have to tell him about her past.

But thinking about him made her miss him, so she grabbed her jacket and walked to Wood You, hoping he'd still be there.

When she arrived, the shop was closed, and she felt a scratch of disappointment until she saw the light on in his backroom. She knocked on the door loud enough to grab his attention. She waved and smiled, and then he grinned back at her and came to let her in.

"I'd invite you in, but I have a cradle to finish," he said.

"Oh, I won't intrude—" she said, a little deflated, but he perked up.

"Wait," he said. "I have something for you."

He went into the back and came out holding a small, intricately carved box. He put it in her hands.

"It's beautiful," she said.

"It's for your secrets."

"Henry—"

"So they won't bottle up inside you. Put them in this box. Honor them."

Ella ran her hands over the lid.

"Will you do that?" Henry asked, looking into her eyes. Ella could only nod.


WHEN SHE GOT home, she placed the box on her desk, where she could always look at it. She knew he'd never check if she actually wrote down her secrets, but she felt compelled to, because look how beautiful this box was, how special. She got a piece of paper and a good pen and wrote, *I really like Henry*. She folded it up and put it in the box, and to her surprise she felt better.

She got another piece of paper and wrote: *I have a daughter here who I gave up. No one knows but me. I don't know what to do about it.*

The notes came quicker: *I tried to kill Jude's father.*

*I need to be part of my daughter's life.*

*I need her to know me.*

And then her cellphone buzzed, and she carefully shut the lid of the box. The screen read PEARL, and for a moment she felt that throb of fear the way she always did when the phone rang. Someone was coming for her. Or something.

*Please don't fire me. Not now.*

"Hey, Pearl," she said, standing up to talk. "Glad I grabbed this before it went to voicemail."

"So," Pearl said, "things are going to change around here now."

Ella dug one nail into her palm. She tried to think of any other job she could get now, and her mind went completely blank.

"Dear Clancy has been syndicated in newspapers across the Midwest and East Coast!" Pearl said, her voice pealing into laughter, and Ella's legs folded under her, dropping her back into her chair. "And there's talk it could go further. You are *so* getting a raise!"

After chatting about the specifics, Pearl hung up, but Ella stayed on, her cell pressed to her ear as if she were holding a conch shell, listening for an imaginary ocean.

Then she dialed Helen, to tell her, to have someone who might truly understand what this meant for her.

DURING THE LAST weekend of March, late in the day, Ella found herself in Marianna's house, helping her finish packing to move into a housesit over by Green Tree Elementary on West Jefferson Street, which wasn't too far from their house on Third. The sky was darkening, and Ella couldn't shake a sense of dread—that Mark would burst in on them.

"He knows I'm moving," Marianna insisted. "I just didn't tell him *when* because I didn't want a scene."

It seemed to have happened so quickly, finding the house and then a job as an accountant for a small business with flexible hours. The house was fully furnished, so there wasn't much that Marianna needed to move—mostly her clothes, some dishes, some things for Carla.

The owners of the housesit had already left to stay four months in France, and maybe even longer, so that the wife could do research for a book she was writing about Paris. All they needed was someone to watch the house, water the plants, and feed their cat, Nora.

"I have two houses now!" Carla said. "I'm so lucky!"

Despite her pretense of calm, Marianna kept glancing at the clock. "We don't need to pack *everything*. I can always come back if I need to."

Ella glanced up from folding Carla's clothes into a box. Carla was pretend helping, but mostly playing with a bright blue Slinky Ella had given her.

"Don't give me that worried look," Marianna said. "Mark knows where the house is because we share Carla, but he's not getting a key. I'm going to make sure this works out."

The house was a medium-sized clapboard, painted green with a red door and set back from a pretty lawn lined with flowerbeds. As soon as they parked, Carla bounded from the car.

Inside was warm and soothing, full of plants and comfortable-looking chairs. Marianna seemed happier, calmer. Nora, a big tabby, wound herself around Carla's legs. Carla talked to the cat soothingly. "This is going to be an adventure. You just wait and see, Nora," Carla said, and the cat purred under her hands.

Carla was studying the bookshelves, then pulled out a book with a bright cover. "Look! The sun!" she said. She showed the book to Ella, pointing to the layers of the sun on the cover.

"The deeper you go, the hotter it gets," Carla said. "More hotter than it gets here."

"Just hotter, honey. Or more hot," Marianna said, and Carla tapped her head as if she got it.

"Hotter. More hot," Carla said, and then she scampered off to find Nora.

"Don't worry," Carla told Nora. "Your owners will be back, and in the meantime you have me to love, love, love you." Then she crouched down and tenderly pecked the cat's head with a kiss.

FOR THE FIRST few weeks, things seemed to be working out. Marianna told Ella about how much she loved the house, her new freedom from Mark. She liked her job, too. Carla seemed happy and told Marianna that Mark had bought her a whole new Hello Kitty bedroom set for her old room.

Even the hours were working out, because Mark would come get Carla early in the morning and take her to school, and then bring her home to Marianna. They didn't speak much, but they didn't argue either, and that was something.

One day, though, Marianna came home from work to find the housesit had been rearranged. New books and toys—things she knew she hadn't bought—were displayed on Carla's bed. When Mark arrived with Carla, he looked at her all innocently. "Hey, you refused to give me a key," he said. "How could it have been me?"

"How did you get in the house?"

"Are you losing it?" he asked her, and then Carla ran in, calling, "Mommy is a stupid head," and Marianna started.

"What did you call me?" Marianna said.

"Stupid head," Carla said.

"That's not nice. We don't say those words."

"Daddy does," Carla said. "He says that all the time." Then Carla romped to her room and Marianna frowned at Mark.

"You leave me for good, I'll make sure you never see Carla again," he said quietly.

She watched him walk out into a light spring rain.

Then she reached for her cell to call a lawyer.

THE NEXT AFTERNOON, Ella took Carla to I Scream, pandering to the little girl's addiction to chocolate cinnamon cones. Ella couldn't believe she had Carla to herself for two whole hours before she had to return her. Marianna had told her she had an appointment with a lawyer because Mark had threatened to take Carla away. And while Ella was relieved that Marianna was finally going, she was also terrified. If Mark won full custody, what would that mean for her relationship with her daughter? A chill ran through her body.

Across the plastic table, Ella couldn't stop looking at Carla, touching her, making her laugh. Already a woman had remarked on what a "well-behaved daughter" she had, and Ella hadn't corrected her. They were just about to go when she felt someone watching her. It was Henry.

"Oh, and who's this charming young lady?" Henry said.

"Carla! I'm Carla!" Carla said, jumping up and down a few times. "Who are you?"

"I'm watching her. For a friend." Ella felt the sweat prickling along her back. She didn't feel ready to tell Henry the truth. She hadn't told Marianna about Henry, either. She wanted to keep those two parts of her life separate, and yet, here they were, the dividing walls swaying, and she'd have to bolster them.

"Henry," he said. "I'm Henry, and I'm so happy to meet you."

"She's Ella! She's family! That's what Mommy says," Carla said, and Ella pointedly looked at her watch.

"Oh no, it's late—I have to get her home."

"I saw the two of you talking," Henry said. "So deep in conversation! You're a natural with kids, Ella."

Ella flushed, partly because it mattered so much that she was good with Carla, and partly because she didn't know how to explain this to Henry.

"Can I see you later?" Henry asked. Ella thought of all the questions he'd have, the answers she'd have to make up. Or maybe she wouldn't. Maybe he'd believe she was just a sitter, that she'd be too young to have a school-aged child.

"Yes, she says yes!" Carla said, as Ella helped her put on her jacket.

"You heard what the little lady said," Henry said.

"I guess I'll see you later," Ella said, because that could mean anything, that she might see him on campus, or she might show up at his doorstep. She pulled gently at Carla's hand, and they stepped outside.

"Bye, Henry," Carla called, and then Ella said it too.

The whole walk to Marianna's, Ella tried to think of what to do, even as Carla chatted nonstop about electricity and plants and her new favorite color of yarn, which was burnt orange because how could you burn a color, and if there was burnt orange was there also burnt red?

"Anything's possible," Ella said distractedly.

AS SOON AS they got back to Marianna's, Carla shouted, "We met a guy! He said I was a charming young lady."

"A guy?" Marianna lifted one brow.

"Henry!" Carla said.

"He's a friend," Ella said.

"Ah, *Henry*," Marianna said.

"Don't you give me that wicked look," Ella said, but she smiled. "I told you, he's just a friend."

"I can't meet your friend?" Marianna said. "Your *special* friend?"

"Of course you can," Ella said, but she didn't look at Marianna when she said it.

"I think it's apple juice time," Carla said emphatically.

"I'll get it," Ella told her. She wound her way into the kitchen. On the fridge was a new drawing labeled MY FAMILY AT THE PARK. There were four people, Marianna with curly dark hair, Carla in pigtails, Mark, and then a woman with red-crayon curls who was surely her. Her breath stopped and she thought she might cry.

"Hey, I'm thirsty!" Carla called from the other room. Ella quietly took the drawing down and tucked it under her shirt. She'd take it home. She'd look at it every day. Sometimes the walk to this house was hard, especially in the Michigan winter, but for moments like this, she'd travel five times as far.

IT WAS MAY now, nearly Carla's birthday. It was a hard time for Ella because even though she'd get to spend the day with Carla (Marianna had told her she was going to bake a cake, have a party and invite a few friends of Carla's, and neither she nor Carla would dream of having a celebration without Ella there), and she could have the pleasure of giving her the hand-knit sweater she had made for her, Ella felt thrust back in time, back to the prison, giving birth to a baby she wouldn't get to keep.

Today, Ella was supposed to meet Carla and Marianna at a park, but it started to rain heavily, dampening Ella's plan to surprise Carla by taking her to a petting zoo. Ella texted Marianna but got no answer, which worried her, so she took an Uber to the housesit. Standing on the stoop in the downpour, she had to ring the bell four times before Marianna answered. Her eyes were bright red from crying.

"I can't do this anymore," Marianna said. And then she opened the door wider and flung herself into Ella's arms in tears.

"Tell me what happened," Ella said, guiding Marianna back inside. "Tell me everything." And Marianna began to talk.

It had started out so innocently. Just the two of them making a chocolate cake, Hershey bars melting and bubbling in a pot, the scent so intoxicating the two of them had been swooning.

When Marianna's cell rang in another room, she had done everything right. She had turned the stove off. She had ordered Carla to sit, to not touch anything.

She never made it to her cellphone. Instead, she had heard Carla screaming.

Terrified, she had run back to the kitchen to find the pot flung across the floor, the walls spattered. Carla was slumped on the floor, drenched in chocolate and sobbing, her skin blistering from the burns.

Marianna had rushed her to the ER. She had shoved her way through the waiting room to get to a doctor, all the while shouting, "It's a child and she's been burned!"

A doctor came out and quickly took Carla in, but not before he had looked at Marianna through slitted eyes, as if judging her. He raised one hand to stop her from following them. "Go sit in the waiting room," he snapped.

She had paced and wept, wept and paced. What were they doing to her baby? The hours thickened and hardened like candy until a nurse with a clipboard finally approached her, daring to ask Marianna if she had ever hurt Carla before.

"What?" Marianna had felt paralyzed. "Of course not!"

"She has second-degree burns—"

And then Carla finally came back out, chewing her bottom lip the way she always did when she was frightened, walking as if there were glass beneath her feet. Both of her upper arms had white bandages on them, which made Marianna want to weep again, but instead she forced herself to be calm, fending off the weight of the nurse's scrutiny. She had stroked Carla's hair, murmuring to her that it was going to be all right, that she loved her, that they were going to go home now.

"Here," the nurse had said abruptly, holding out a bag for her. "Pediatric pain killers, extra bandages, burn cream, and instructions. Let's hope we don't see you here with this again."

*How dare you!* Marianna had thought.

As soon as they had gotten home, she had let Carla watch as much TV as she wanted until she had fallen asleep. The next day, Carla had bounced awake, in a happier mood. Marianna had put new cream and clean bandages on the burns, and she had let Carla stay home from school.

"I want to go," Carla had insisted. "I want to show off my bandages," and that was when Marianna had told her to dress in long sleeves for school because no one had to know that she had been burned, that there was no reason for anyone to talk about it. The whole thing would have been just another terrible incident, faded with time, right along with the burns.

But of course, nothing was ever that easy.

Now, Marianna drew in a long breath.

"The school called child services," she told Ella. "There's this mandate to report anything they think might be abuse. The school counselor even talked to Carla."

"Child services! What the fuck? They can't do that—"

"Yes, they can," Marianna said. "And they talked to Mark first. He told them that I drink, when everyone knows that it's him who gets sauced, not me. He told them I have a temper, too, when he knows damn well that only happens when he provokes me, when he doesn't stop. And even worse, Mark got to Carla first. She adores her daddy, always wants to please him, and that bastard must have coached her, because the social worker told me that Carla said I had deliberately burned her, that this wasn't the first time, either. And they believed it."

Marianna started to cry harder, wiping away her tears.

"Mark made sure to tell them I had moved out, only he called it abandoning my family. I had to let the social worker into my house while she acted like she owned the place. I had to stand there and watch her switch the lights off and on, the water too, to see if I had paid my bills. She checked the fridge to see if there was enough food, and I heard her cluck her tongue when she looked inside. How was I expected to go shopping when all of this was crashing down?

"I kept asking her, are you a mother? Are you a wife? For a second, she looked sympathetic, so I told her that things were even harder for me because I was separated from my husband and we were living at two separate addresses. And then she fucking frowned! She said that I should have told the school we were separated because it was school protocol. And then she said that she had to put this immediate safety plan in place, where Mark has Carla, where I can only be with her if he's there too, because I might be a danger to my own child. Me, who would rather die than see her hurt. It's all another chance for Mark to punish me. He's never there when I'm supposed to come to see her. And when he is he finds a reason for why I have to leave early.

"Child services is investigating me, Ella! Not Mark. Me! This whole thing could take an entire month—maybe even two depending on the investigation. What the hell am I supposed to do?"

Ella felt her breath catch. If Marianna couldn't see Carla without Mark being there, then neither could Ella. That couldn't happen. "Can't you get Carla to tell the truth to the social worker? Can't you tell her how important it is?"

"And confuse her and make her feel horrible about herself, make her doubt her hero dad? Even if I did, he'd just pour on more coaching.

"I love her," Marianna continued. "I would rather cut my own arm off than harm her. I don't even raise my voice to her, you know that. She's everything to me. She always has been. I had wanted a child so desperately, and I couldn't conceive. Six IVFs. And then I had to convince Mark to adopt because he didn't like the idea of 'raising someone else's kid'—his words. But the second they put Carla in my arms, I knew we were meant to be together."

Ella remembered the hospital bed where she had given birth to Carla. The nurse not letting her see the baby. "It's easier this way," the nurse had said, her voice kind. Ella had turned her face into the pillow and shut her eyes.

Now, her throat turned dry.

"I talked to my lawyer," Marianna said. "I got a consultation, but nothing's been done or signed yet. The guy has a shaved head and the scales of justice tattooed on his forearm, but he said without a legal separation, there's no custody agreement and that complicates things. He said that if I need money, Mark can't withhold monetary support, either. But my 'drinking'? The so-called 'rages'? They can't prove it; it's just Mark's word against mine. The lawyer told me he'd talk to the right people, and if a formal complaint isn't filed, the case will be closed."

"But that sounds like good new—"

"The lawyer said child services isn't my enemy. They do give mothers a lot of chances. They don't want to keep parents from their kids unless it's necessary. Oh God, Ella, what if they say it's necessary?"

"It won't be necessary," Ella said. "The lawyer will handle it."

Marianna showed Ella the calendar on her phone, how she had marked the days when she could go visit her daughter at the Third Street house, but it always had to be when Mark was there to supervise, which even though he had changed his schedule so he wasn't working nights, wasn't a lot.

Sometimes, during the scheduled hours, Mark would purposefully leave the house so that Marianna couldn't see Carla. He'd apologize later, make up some excuse, but then he'd always say that this was all her doing. All her fault. She made this happen. When she tried to challenge Mark on why he'd withheld their daughter, he'd say, "I didn't burn her, if that's what you're asking."

"How's Carla holding up?" Ella asked.

"She bites her nails until they bleed. I try to get her to talk to me, but she won't. All she says is that Daddy's sad, and that she doesn't want Daddy to be sad.

"Child services asked to speak to anyone who has seen me with Carla, who knows both of them. They don't usually talk to friends, but you're more than that, and you know her. You love her. Please will you speak to them? Be a reference? Tell them I'm a good mother?"

The uneasiness started in Ella's legs, moving up to her belly and then circling to her chest.

"Will you?" Marianna persisted. "Mark has turned everyone against me, even the people at my old office."

Child services would want to know things about Ella. Who she was. Whether she was a credible witness to Marianna's mothering. What her past was like. Her experience with children. And all those roads would lead to the one place Ella wanted to forget: being in prison.

When Ella got out, she had promised herself that she would never be in a courtroom again, not even for a traffic ticket. She'd never meet another cop's eyes or ask for anything. And even if it wasn't in a courtroom, but a room with a lawyer, or even just someone from child services, she didn't trust any of it. She couldn't. Or maybe she just didn't trust herself. She was a felon, and why would anyone believe her?

But what was just as terrifying was having to tell Marianna that she was Carla's birth mother, that she had hidden that fact since the day they met. She wasn't legally allowed to have contact with her daughter, and anyone who found out could make things so much worse for everyone.

"Please. Will you?" Marianna said.

Ella stayed very still. Her blood pulsed in her ears.

"And if it goes to court, will you testify on my behalf?" Marianna said. "You'd make such a brilliant witness. You speak so well, you know us both—"

Stones formed in Ella's throat. "I can't," she whispered.

Marianna frowned. "What?"

"I am so sorry, but I can't—"

"But why not? You love Carla. I know you do! And you know how she feels about you." Marianna gripped Ella's hands.

"You're like ice!" Marianna started to warm Ella's hands in her own, but Ella drew them back.

"I can't. They wouldn't listen to me—" Ella said, her voice high and skittish.

"Of course they will. Why wouldn't they? You pay your taxes, you have a job, you know us—we're practically family."

Ella couldn't breathe. She started gathering her things, getting ready to leave, when Marianna jumped to her feet and grabbed her arm.

"I told you, I can't!" Ella snapped. Marianna stared at her, shocked.

"What are you saying?" Marianna said. "Aren't we friends? I thought we were. All these talks we've had, these days we've shared—"

"I helped you," Ella said, her words tumbling over one another, "as much as I could—"

"As much as you *could*? What the hell does that mean? Is there some kind of cap, some ceiling on being a friend? You know how vicious Mark has been. How cruel he can be. You're the one who convinced me to leave him, something I should have done years ago. Why are you being like this?"

The roaring in her ears rose and fell like waves.

"Why can't you?" Marianna repeated.

"Because I'm Carla's birth mother!" Ella cried. As soon as she said the words, she wanted to choke them back.

"What?" Marianna said. Ella watched as Marianna seemed to morph into another person, stiffening, the air turning cooler around them.

"Is this a joke?" Marianna took a step back, stumbling, and blinked hard at Ella. "That can't be true. You're too young. You can't be."

"I am. I got pregnant at fifteen."

"We never knew who Carla's birth parents were and we didn't want to know. The adoption was closed and the only way anyone could know is if one day Carla wanted to find you. And if you wanted that to happen, too—"

"I found the records—I went to the lawyer's office and I saw them. I wasn't supposed to, but I did."

Marianna drew herself up, her body twisting with anger. "But why the fuck now? What do you want, Ella? You want to take my child away from me, too? You saw your fucking chance and now you're grabbing it while I'm down?"

"I was barely sixteen when I gave her up. I was desperate. The father vanished and . . . I never forgot." It wasn't a lie.

"The father?"

Ella froze. "I don't even know where he is now—my mother said he gave up his rights."

"So did you. And you did it legally. You don't get to have a do-over here." Marianna's mouth thinned into a line. She looked down at her hands.

"You know what hurts the most?" Marianna said. "That you pretended we were friends. That you cared about me. And I, the fool, believed you. I know we're different in age, but I used to feel understood by you. Like you really got me. More so than I used to with friends my age. I couldn't wait to see you some days. I needed that friendship. I loved it and I loved you. Why did you have to pretend?"

"I didn't—" Ella said. "I need our friendship, too. For the longest time, I didn't have a single friend." She felt a coil of desperation tightening inside her.

"Bullshit. I was just Carla's mother to you. That's all. Don't tell me that's not true. Fuck you, you basically *stalked* us."

Ella swallowed hard. "That was true at first," she said. "I did stalk you. I needed to make sure that my daughter had loving parents, that she was taken care of, that she was happy."

"And then what? What if she hadn't been? You would have tried to take her?"

"You would have too if you were me! Don't tell me you wouldn't. Look how hard you're fighting for her with Mark."

Marianna grew still. "Fine. You care about her. But you don't give a fuck about me," she said finally.

"That's not true and you know it. I listened to you when you cried about Mark. I encouraged you to move on, to get a lawyer, a bank account. I helped you move. Is that what people who don't give a fuck do? I saw from the first how you shower Carla with love. How you look at her like you can't believe your luck. You think I'd tear her away from that, ruin her life? You are the *best* mother."

She paused, taking a deep breath.

"And you're an amazing friend to me. You treat me like . . . like I have worth. Like I matter. You make me feel like we're our own little wonderful family, and for me that has meant everything." Ella slashed at her sudden tears. "I don't want that to change."

"You're not my family. Right now, I'm not even your friend. And neither is Carla." Marianna's eyes flashed with anger. "Stay the hell away from us. I don't ever want to see you again."

It was the *us* that really hurt.

Ella watched Marianna march through the living room toward the front door. She wanted to call out, to say fine, yes, all right, I'll speak to child services, testify, whatever. Because what did it matter now? Why should anything matter more than Carla's welfare? But she was frozen in place, hating herself more than she ever had before because she was putting her terror ahead of her daughter. Maybe Marianna was right, she didn't deserve Carla. Her little girl deserved so much better. She knew she was a terrible excuse for a mother, a terrible excuse for a friend.

Marianna opened the door for her, expectant. "Leave," she said. "Leave now."

ALL THAT NIGHT, back in her apartment, Ella tried calling Marianna, but she wouldn't pick up. In the morning she went back to the house and stood outside, but couldn't catch sight of her through the windows. *Forgive me*, Ella wanted to say. *Forgive me.*

She turned and walked home, bundling into her jacket. She couldn't forgive herself. Not for any of it. Marianna probably thought Ella had completely unburdened herself, but Ella hadn't told her the worst parts, all those terrible memories she wanted to erase. If something in life reminded her, she shut her mind like a trapdoor, barring entry. What good did it do to think about any of it? It changed nothing.

For the first time, she noticed how lonely her apartment was. She had done her best to make it feel homey—hanging a few prints, buying a pretty rug—but it still was the place of one person, isolated, desolate.

A FEW DAYS LATER, when it was Carla's birthday, Ella was still shut out. She felt frantic with longing, as if someone had scooped her heart right out of her body. She couldn't bear the thought of Carla thinking that Ella had forgotten her or, even worse, had deliberately ignored such an important day. She hadn't been able to wrap Carla's birthday sweater, and there it was, lying in a basket, like an accusing finger pointing and blaming her.

She did her job, she walked around Ann Arbor with no destination, and then she came home and stared at the ceiling. She often walked to the house on Jefferson, but no one was ever there. She went to Mark's as well, but his house was always dark. Henry kept calling her, but she couldn't answer. She didn't know what she could possibly say to him.

And then one day, he was there, standing outside her door.

"You have to let me in," he said, his voice insistent.

She did, and as soon as he saw her, his face softened.

"Wow," he said. "You don't look so good." And then he quickly regrouped. "I mean, you always look beautiful, but—are you ill? Can I make you soup?"

"No. No soup," she said. "I'm just exhausted."

"I can see that. Why don't you nap? I'll just sit here and make sure you're okay."

She let him guide her to her bed. She felt him sitting beside her, waiting for her to fall asleep, but she couldn't because of the cascade of worries storming through her. She tried to slow her breathing, pretending to be asleep, and finally he quietly got up and left. As soon as she heard the apartment door close, her eyes flew open.

Everything bothered her. The old movies she tried to watch seemed silly. The books she tried to read spilled their words off the page. She even tried taking an Excedrin PM, but nothing helped.

Ella kept going to the park by Green Tree Elementary, day after day, evenings, mornings too. Even when it was raining. The drenching was a punishment she deserved. She stayed out for hours, and then she went to Literati Bookstore and then the yarn store and then to Marianna's house, but Marianna was never there, nor was Carla. She felt their loss like an amputation. She had had a friend. A real friend. She had had her daughter, at least a little, and she had thought their relationship was blooming into something real, something permanent. And now she had nothing, and she felt as if she were nothing, too.

She bet Mark had been able to fool the social workers the way he did everyone else, putting on his charm, pretending to be warm and loving, one arm around Carla in what wasn't really a hug, but a proprietary hold, a vise. He'd play doting father. He'd show off a clean house filled with dolls and toys. And Carla adored Mark. She'd be ecstatic, getting all this extra attention from him.

*None of this is your business.* That's what Helen would tell her. Sometimes Ella told this to people who wrote to her column. If you couldn't be sure that you could help someone, if there was any chance you might harm them by helping, then maybe it would be better to do nothing at all until you had more information. But how were you supposed to get that information? How were you supposed to know? All she knew was she didn't want Mark to be Carla's father.

SHE THOUGHT THAT spending more time at work might save her. Thinking about other peoples' problems, being able to suggest ways to get out of their labyrinths, had always made her feel stronger, of some value. She was syndicated now in papers throughout the Midwest, and would soon be on the East Coast as well. She pulled up some of the Dear Clancy letters. She'd pull herself out of this slump.

*Dear Clancy,*
*My child is making me crazy and I'm afraid I might hit her.*
*Signed, Smack-happy Mama*

*You don't deserve to have a child*, Ella started to type, and then she stopped, her fingers hovering. She put her face in her hands. There was no way she could say such a thing to anyone. No way that she could concentrate on work tonight. She deleted the file.

She tried to exhaust herself physically, doing jumping jacks in her kitchen, walking ten thousand steps around her building. She drank half a bottle of wine, but that made her throw up, and more tired than before. She knew she was in trouble when she went to the kitchen and for a moment: Like a sign or maybe a warning, she envisioned Helen and Jude there, with Marianna and Carla, and Mark glowering at her, and when she took a step toward them, they vanished. All she saw was an old hoodie thrown over a chair.

THE NEXT DAY, Ella was once again heading for Marianna's housesit, desperate to see her, to make sure she was okay, and to get news of Carla. She had even packed a blueberry jam sandwich, Carla's favorite, just in case. Maybe after checking on Marianna she could go to Mark's again. She might get something on him, something incriminating, so Marianna could get legal custody.

The sky was like hard concrete, the wind smelled like rain, and Ella told herself all she was going to do was a quick checkup and then she'd go home and hunker down.

There it was, Marianna's housesit. She rang the bell, but no one answered. "Marianna!" she called through the door, knocking for good measure, feeling the catch in her voice. She dug in her purse for her notepad and a pencil and wrote *Call me* and slid it under the door. Then she headed toward Mark's.

She had reached the end of his block when she heard Mark's voice. Ella dipped down behind one of the bushes, watching and waiting. There was Carla in a flimsy jacket, holding a big stuffed moose. And walking toward Mark was a woman Ella had never seen before. She had a dark ponytail, and she rested her head on Mark's shoulder as if she owned it.

*Fucker,* Ella thought, watching him crouch down to talk to Carla but still holding the woman's hand. Ella couldn't hear what they were saying, but she saw Carla's face crumple. She saw the way Carla clutched the stuffed animal to her chest. Carla shook her head.

"We talked about this, Carla," he said. "Remember?"

"No—" Carla's voice was a note, falling.

"Honey, you get to watch all the TV you want inside," Mark said. "Whatever show you want to. Pammie and I just have some things we need to take care of in the other room."

"I can help you!" Carla said.

"No, honey, you really can't. Watch TV. Isn't *Blue's Clues* on?"

"That's for babies. And I want to play outside. You promised I could."

"As soon as we're done," he said.

"Daddy—"

"What did I say?" His tone sharpened. "What did I tell you?"

The woman flinched. "Mark," she said hesitantly. "Maybe—"

"Jesus," Mark said to the woman. She took her hand away from his and stuffed it into her pocket, lowering her gaze to the ground.

Ella froze. She watched them go into the house, their heads bent toward each other in conversation.

She got up, her knees creaking, and then the door opened again and there was Carla, her jacket thrown open, winding her way to the backyard.

It was a shocking thing to see, a little girl left outside on her own, even in a backyard. Who allowed that to happen unless they were watching from a window, making sure all was okay? She wanted to text Marianna, but what if she then called the cops and told them Ella was stalking?

Ella walked to the side of the house, by the hedges ringing the lawn all the way to the backyard. Carla was sitting on the ground below the kitchen window, speaking quietly to her oversized stuffed animal. Ella waited five minutes, then ten, hoping maybe Mark and that woman had just run in for something and might be right out. But when they didn't appear, she walked toward Carla.

"Ella!" Carla called, and ran to her, holding her animal by its leg.

Ella saw scrapes on her face. "How'd you get those?" she said. "Are those new?"

Carla shrugged. "I don't know." Then she looked up, smiling. "I missed you!"

"I missed you more," Ella told her.

"That's what Mommy says."

"Where is Mommy?"

Carla looked down at her shoes.

"Have you seen Mommy?" Ella asked, and then Carla scuffed her feet on the ground. "Have you, honey?"

"Daddy says I will soon. But where were you? Why didn't you come see me?"

Ella felt the pinch in her stomach. She crouched down beside Carla, rubbing the girl's shoulders as if she were confirming she was real. Carla's pink nail polish was chipped, and her nails were bitten down to the nubs. It made Ella hurt just to see them.

"Listen, honey," she said, trying to make her voice soothing. "Should you be outside on your own?"

"I'm a big girl. I'm seven now."

"Of course you are. But can you go inside if you want?"

Carla hesitated and then leaned forward to whisper. "I'm supposed to watch TV when Pammie comes over, but sometimes it gets boring. Daddy comes and gets me when he's ready."

"And how long is that?"

Carla dipped her head. "I don't know. Sometimes it's a long time. I'm supposed to be a good girl."

Ella dug in her purse for the blueberry jam sandwich.

"Want this?" she said, and Carla grabbed for it. "Did you have breakfast today?" she asked, and Carla nodded. "What did you have?"

"Crackers."

"And what else?"

Carla shrugged and then stuffed half the sandwich in her mouth. "Take your time," Ella said, and Carla slowed down.

"So you don't get to speak to Mommy?" Ella said.

"Daddy says I will," Carla insisted. "I told you that."

"I bet she must miss you so much."

"I was with her before," Carla said thoughtfully, "and now I'm with Daddy." She looked up again at Ella. "Sometimes I wish I was with you."

"I know," Ella said carefully. She hugged her arms about her. "Hey, I know. Want to play a game?"

"What kind of game?" Carla wiped her hands on her pants until Ella fished out a tissue for her.

"We're gonna learn a little song."

"What song?" Carla asked, perking up.

"A number song. It's a way for you to remember."

"Remember what?"

"Do you know Mommy's cellphone number?"

Carla shook her head.

"Well, then I'm going to give you my cellphone number, so you can call me if you ever need me."

"I can call you?"

"Yeah, if you miss me, or if you think of something you want to tell me. You can call me anytime. For any reason."

"Like if Georgie needs to find her shoe and I don't know where it is?" She waved the moose's foot.

"Exactly," Ella said. "But also, you can call me if you feel lonely or sad or scared even. Or if Georgie does."

Carla frowned. "I don't have a phone."

"But your daddy does."

Carla brightened. "That's right!" she said.

Ella urged Carla closer. And then she began to sing to the tune of "Happy Birthday," because she thought that was something Carla might remember. "Six, four, six, one, two, threeee, five, fi-ive, six, two-oo . . . Six, four, six, one, two-ooo-oo . . . three, five, five, six, two-oo," she sang. "Got it?"

They sang it together, three times, then another, and then Ella asked Carla to sing it all by herself, which she did, her face glowing with pride. "There you go," Ella whispered.

"Daddy says I've got a great memory."

She tapped her chest and then Carla's. "That's good. This is something special, just like my coming to visit you now is special. It's just for us."

"Will you come again?"

"I will. Of course." Ella cupped Carla's little face in her hands. "Let's sing it again, one more time, just for good luck." Then she heard the front door open, and Mark's voice calling Carla's name. Carla frowned. "It's okay," Ella said.

Mark barreled toward them, his face dark. The woman raced out behind him, her hair, loose now, flying behind her.

"Hey! You!" he shouted. "Ella!"

He knew her name. She didn't know what if anything Marianna had told him about her, but anything could bring new trouble. The little girl cowered, not looking at Ella, putting her hands to her face as if to make herself invisible.

"I'm so calling the cops!" he shouted, waving his cellphone. As he was punching in numbers, Ella, burning with rage and grief, ran.

SHE DIDN'T STOP running until she was back at her place, and by then she thought of all the things she could have said. The way she could have stood her ground. *Go ahead, call the cops and we'll see who they feel is in the wrong. Go ahead because I'm watching you. Go ahead because I am calling child services.*

And she could have told him the one thing she couldn't let him know: *Go ahead because I have a right. Carla is my child.*

But she didn't have that right.

She dialed Marianna and the call went straight to voicemail.

Ella couldn't breathe.

*I'm a felon and I can never get her back.*

SHE CALLED CHILD services anonymously. She told them a girl looked uncared for. They wanted to know how. They took the address down. They didn't ask for Ella's name.

THE MAY FLOWERS were beginning to bloom when she finally went back to Mark's house. No one was there, not even in the backyard. She returned to her apartment to wait.

Time stretched like elastic. Ella still felt jumpy. Henry called and she told him she was buried in work. She felt the disappointment coming through the phone, so, forcing levity, told him Helen's favorite joke about a duck who enters a lip gloss store only to tell the cashier to "put it on my bill." She just wanted to him to laugh.

"I'm here, you know," he told her.

"I know."

"You and I can work here side by side, in my workshop. We can be together."

"I know," she said, but she didn't offer to come over.

"Whatever it is, I can help you."

But how could she ask him to start looking for Carla? To watch out for Mark or try to find Marianna? She'd have to tell him everything, and he'd never understand.

She missed him. But she missed Carla, too. The soft weight of her in her lap. The smell of her strawberry shampoo. The warmth of her skin when Ella kissed her cheek. She also ached for Marianna, to be able to talk to her, to explain. How was it possible that she didn't know what was going on? Surely Marianna wouldn't leave Ann Arbor when her daughter remained in the clutches of her abusive husband.

She walked for hours around the city, trying to find the family, but she never saw Marianna or Carla or even Mark—not by the elementary school, the parks, downtown or up. Instead of being exhausted, Ella became more and more wired. She didn't know what to do about it, how to tamp down this growing ache that was taking over her body. She imagined things to make herself feel better, impossible things. Even if she could never see her daughter again, at least Carla might be safe and happy and loved. Maybe that was the best she could hope for.

ONE DAY, SHE went to the Old Town Tavern, where Mark worked, but he wasn't there. There was only one woman bartending, swathed in black, her hair in a long braid down her back. Casually Ella asked about him.

"Fired," the woman said, swiping a clean rag across the bar.

"Why?"

"The usual reasons. Drinking on the job. Hand in the till," the bartender said. "That's a big no-no around here."

"I thought he owned this bar," she said, and the bartender hooted. "As if."

"Do you know where he is?"

The bartender peered closer at Ella. "Why would I?" she asked. "You gonna order a drink or what?"

Ella shook her head and left.

WHEN SHE ARRIVED home, everything seemed so out of control that she listlessly rearranged all her books, dusted her tiny place, and even did the dishes. Then, because there was nothing else to do, she sat down to work on her letters, clicking on the first one.

*Dear Clancy,*

*When my daughter was little, she clung to me like Velcro.*
*Now that she's sixteen, it's all closed doors and buttoned lips.*
*I know this is supposed to happen, but it's breaking my heart.*
*Will she ever love me again? And if she does, will it be the same*
*way or something different?*

*Signed, Brokenhearted Mom*

Ella typed, *Dear Brokenhearted Mom,* and then stopped. How could she possibly tell this woman—or anyone—anything anymore? She shut the computer down, even though she had a whole backlog of letters to sift through. She couldn't concentrate and already Pearl had texted her and asked her where the column was. Ella didn't know what to say. She used to be so good at giving advice, relying on her experiences, her hardships, her thoughtfulness.

If she hadn't been able to escape her own mistakes, at least she could manage to help other people. Now, all she wanted to do was answer every letter with the same advice she told herself: *Get used to the pain. Treat it like a splinter. It might work its way out, or it might work its way deeper, festering. There is nothing you can do.*

She forced herself to write a column and, restless, watched one bad movie after another on TV, until it was suddenly six in the morning. She couldn't sleep so she rearranged her tiny kitchen. She considered trying a hot bath, even though she didn't particularly like baths, when her phone rang. No one ever called her, except Pearl and Helen, and neither one of them would be calling this early.

Unless it was Marianna. She grabbed her cell.

"Marianna—" she said, catching her breath. There was a rustling sound on the line, someone waiting, fidgeting. Through the receiver, she heard a small cough, and then a voice.

"Ella?" Carla whispered. "I remembered the number song. I got all the numbers right. Because I'm smart."

Ella snapped to attention. "Honey. Honey, are you okay?"

"I don't know," Carla said. "I'm on Daddy's cellphone."

"Daddy's there? Who are you with, honey?"

"Daddy. I was with a lady, too."

Ella thought of the woman who had been with Mark, the one he had scolded. "And where is that lady now?"

"I don't know. She left."

"And where are you, honey?"

"A hotel."

"What hotel?" she said.

Carla was silent.

"Honey," Ella said. "What are the numbers on the hotel phone, tell them to me." She heard the little girl shuffling, shifting the phone, before reading them slowly. Ella wrote them down. The area code was California. What were they doing in California? Did Marianna know? Was Mark even legally allowed to do this?

"Is there a number on the outside of the door? Can you go and look? Or is there a key, with a number?"

She heard the clatter of the cellphone falling, and then Carla came back. "Six-one-seven," she said. "It's on the key."

"Now, is there a name on the key? Can you read it to me?"

She could hear Carla breathing. "Fairfax Inn," she said finally.

"Good job," Ella said, trying to calm her. "Honey, where's your Daddy now? Did he go out for something? Did he say when he'd be back?"

Carla started crying. "I tried to call Mommy, and no one answered!"

"Honey, don't cry. I'm right here. Where is he?"

"On the floor! He woke me up when he came back!"

"Wait, what do you mean?"

"He gets mad if I wake him."

Ella felt her body tense. She glanced at the clock. It'd be three a.m. in California. What was going on? *Drunk on the job*, the bartender had said.

"Honey, listen to me. I want you go to where he is, and put your hand on his chest." Ella tried to make her voice calm and casual, as if she were telling Carla something no more important than that she should make herself some soup. "Go on, I'll wait for you to do it."

She could hear Carla's steps. "Okay," Carla said.

"When you put your hand on his chest, does it move up and down?"

"No! He's bleeding! It's on my hands!"

"Honey, can you shake him? Try to wake him up? Or is there a cup in the bathroom that you can fill with water and toss it on his face?"

"He'll yell at me—" Carla said, protesting.

"If he does, you put him right on the phone with me and I'll take care of it."

She heard Carla calling, "Daddy, Daddy, Daddy," louder and louder. And then Carla picked up the phone. "He's not moving," Carla said, starting to cry. "I'm scared. I don't know what to do."

"Sit tight," Ella said. "Everything's going to be all right."

"Is Mommy coming? Are you coming?"

"Someone is," Ella insisted. She'd call the police and not leave her name. Or the hotel and tell them. "I just have to get off the phone and call them—"

"Don't leave me!"

"It's just for a minute," Ella said. "I'll call you right back. I promise."

"No, don't go—"

"Have I ever broken a promise to you?" Ella said quietly, waiting.

"No," came the small voice.

"Then listen," she said. "You keep that phone in your hand. You count to two hundred and then the phone will ring. Do it now, honey. Start counting. Let me hear you."

She waited until she heard the click of the phone. She found the hotel online, and thank God, there was only one with that name in that area code. She called and a woman answered, and Ella said that there was a little girl in room 617 and her father had been injured, and someone should get up there right away, and before they could ask who she was, she hung up and redialed Carla.

"Mommy?" Carla said.

*Yes. No.* "It's Ella. There's going to be someone coming to the room very soon to help you, honey. And I'm going to stay on the phone until they're there with you, okay?"

She didn't want Carla looking at her father, so she asked her if she could see outside the hotel window, if she could describe what was there. She asked her what she wanted for dinner, for breakfast, and then she heard a woman's voice in the background, and that was when Carla dropped the phone and Ella hung up.

What was she supposed to do now? All that day Ella waited for someone to call her, knowing they could easily redial her number from Mark's phone. She could tell them enough of the truth, that she was friends with the family, that she had given Carla her number. The rest could stay secret. But the phone never rang. She called the hotel again, but when she asked about Carla, a curt voice told her it was privileged information.

A WEEK PASSED and May slid into June. She began to search the online obituaries for a Mark Shorter, and when she found it, for a moment, it felt like everything stopped. *Beloved father*, it said. *Beloved husband.* Why didn't it say *monster*?

She called the child services hotline again, asking about Carla, but of course they wouldn't talk to her. More privileged information. She thought about talking to a lawyer, but what good would that do? Ella was shut out.

She hung up the phone, feeling a yearning so fierce, she doubled over with pain. She was so tired of taking care of things, of keeping secrets. She needed someone to listen to her, to let her lean against them. She thought about Henry, the blue of his eyes like a chip of ocean, the way he never combed his hair, but he let her comb it with her fingers. He had cooked her dinners at his place. He had kissed her neck, her shoulders, never going further unless she asked him to, as if he had known that she was being careful not to lose control. She could call him now and he'd come right over, his face serious but soft with understanding. He'd pull her against him, and he'd listen to her. He'd tell her how glad he was that she was finally opening up.

But what if she told him everything and it was simply too much?

She started to cry and then she thought about her mother, and she suddenly missed her more than she ever had. Helen's constant anxiety had made Ella want to leave, to have her own life, but Helen had also traveled two hours every weekend, each way, to visit her in prison. For over six years. She had written her letters, cheerful, full of love, never once blaming, wrote them what seemed like every day so that Ella would have something to look forward to, even when she didn't write back. When Ella had been little, her mother had wrapped her in her arms every night to tell her a story. She would make up songs and teach them to her. Every time Helen looked at her, Ella knew she was loved—there was so much wonder and adoration in her mother's eyes.

Ella picked up her cell. The moment she heard her mother's voice, she started to cry. She ached to see her. She needed to be held, to be comforted, and most of all, to not be judged.

"Baby girl," Helen said, alarmed.

"Mom," she choked out. "Please come. Please visit me. I need you. I need you." And then she started to cry harder because this time she really and truly did.

# FIFTEEN

# Ann Arbor

*June 2019*

In the cab, on the way to the Ann Arbor Hotel, where she had booked a room to keep Ella from feeling crowded, Helen was giddy. It wasn't just being able to see her daughter that made her so happy, it was being invited, being wanted. Ella had actually asked her to come! Helen had called the shop to get time off, saying it was a family emergency, letting them know she might need more than a few days.

While she was packing in Williamsburg, the downstairs buzzer had rung. She opened the window to look outside. There, on the sidewalk, stood Mouse, holding a huge package and looking up at her.

She hadn't seen him since February. Radio silence. She thought for a moment, then buzzed him in. When she opened the door, he looked so dear and familiar that for a moment, before she felt unsure, she wanted to hurl herself into his arms. Instead, she held back, but she invited him in. He handed her the wrapped package.

"This," he said, "is for you. And yes, it is a peace offering."

"For all these months of silence?"

"I'm a slow learner sometimes," he said, smiling. "I tried to, but I couldn't forget you. And I'm sorry."

"You're apologizing to me, but maybe I should be the one to apologize."

"Open it," he said.

She carefully opened the wrapping and a pour of deep blue plush fell out. She looked at him, astonished.

"I know how you love fabric. I know you love blue," he said. "It's a throw, something warm enough for you to curl up with."

She couldn't stop touching its lovely texture, pressing it against her cheek.

"I'd rather curl up with you," she said, and she saw his face relax. His eyes moved to her suitcase and his brow furrowed again.

"You're going somewhere?"

"There are things I need to—to tell you," she said, stammering. She felt her heart clamp shut.

"I'm visiting my daughter," she said finally.

"Can I come with you?"

"Next time," she said. "She's going through something, and I need to be there for her." She hadn't wanted to tell him that her daughter had been upset, that maybe she was in trouble again.

Mouse reached up and kissed her hand.

"Come back and tell me everything," he said, and Helen hoped that she could.

SHE HAD THROWN the rest of her things in the suitcase and gotten on a plane, feeling elated. Only once the plane had left the tarmac did she dare to imagine what it might mean, Ella asking her for help. Now, in the taxi, her anxiety returned.

"Music okay?" the cab driver asked. Distracted, Helen said yes, of course, of course, and kept worrying while the driver bopped one hand against the wheel and sang along with Bob Marley's "No Woman No Cry."

Sometimes she worried that she had paid so much attention to Jude, to her make-believe family with her make-believe son, that she hadn't realized the depth of what was going on with her daughter, of what terrible things Ella had been capable of doing. How funny, that you could love someone so much, even after they had done something so wrong.

Look at everything she hadn't known. She'd had to find out from the newspapers that Ella said that Jude's father beat him. The state claimed that Ella had lied. Both Jude and his father denied there had been any physical abuse. But had Ella lied? And if she had, why?

Helen blamed herself. She should have ignored Ella when her daughter told her to mind her own business—after all, they were still children. If she had known, she could have marched over to Andrew Stein's house and confronted him, threatened to call the cops and social services. What if Jude's father had gotten help, had stopped beating his son? Then no one would have needed to even think about getting rid of him.

Helen swallowed hard. All those years after the sentencing, she had driven the two long hours to the prison every weekend to see her daughter, bringing her food and books and whatever else she could, just another sad face among the defeated visitors. Jude and his father had simply vanished.

She had tried to protect Ella. Immediately after Clark told her the charges against Ella, Helen made herself go into the garden with a garbage bag, before anyone else could. *Foxglove.* It was all anyone was talking about. This garden had been everything to Jude, and by association, everything to Ella and Helen. They had all loved it.

Hands shaking, she had crouched down and had ripped out every plant and flower, all the roots and bulbs, stuffing them all into the garbage bag. The garden transformed into a messy plot of nothing. And when the detectives came by shortly after, two women with hard faces like lions, Helen pretended that there had never been any garden at all.

One of the detectives had put a hand on Helen's arm. "I have a daughter, too," she said meaningfully. *Then you know you'd do anything to protect her*, Helen thought.

In the taxi, Helen sighed heavily. She had made so many, many mistakes. But she drew herself up, letting the excitement grab her again. She was seeing her girl! Her Ella!

The music shut off and the driver pulled over. "There's the university," he said, pointing ahead of them, then pointing left, "and there's your hotel."

Helen had never been to Ann Arbor, though after Ella had left, she had spent hours watching YouTube videos of the place, trying to get a sense of where her daughter was living. She hadn't expected it to look so vivid, the way the city suddenly seemed to explode with people. She had thought it would be soothing, bucolic—because after all, it was the Midwest. But there was a pulse of energy.

Helen settled into her hotel and called Ella. Too excited to sit on the bed, she paced the room instead. She wanted to see Ella's place, but Ella said they should eat first, have a drink at this place she liked called High Dive, and she gave Helen an address that was within walking distance.

"It's only four so it won't be too noisy," Ella said.

"I can't wait to hug you," Helen said, but Ella had already hung up.

It took her ten minutes to find Huron Avenue, where High Dive was situated between two brick facades. She turned onto the street and there, standing in front of the bar, like an apparition, was Ella. "Mom!" Ella called, and then she flew into Helen's arms so hard and fast that Helen stumbled backward.

"There we are," Helen said, and then Ella pulled away and led her inside.

"It's pretty, right?" Ella said. But High Dive could have been built of diamonds and Helen wouldn't have noticed; she couldn't take her eyes off Ella. Her daughter's hair was longer, shaggier, and now the same bright red it had been when she got out of prison. Helen resisted the urge to push the mane off her face to see clearly into Ella's beautiful eyes.

The place was already crowded, but they managed to find two seats at the end of the bar, by some tables in the back. Helen was wearing a deep blue cashmere dress, but Ella was in four different shades of black. Helen kept wanting to touch her, but every time she reached over, Ella moved out from under her hand, until Helen got the message. Instead, Helen talked about the shop, about her life, and Ella was silent until Helen told her she had a boyfriend.

"Oh my God, that's wonderful!" Ella said. "You have somebody. You really do—"

"Well, I don't know about that," Helen said.

"You know. I know you know! You're blushing," Ella said, grinning. "Good for you. Tell me his name."

"I will later. I want to hear more about you," Helen said.

Ella waved to the bartender. "Two white wines," she said. "To start," she added, and Helen said nothing because maybe Ella needed a bit of wine first before she could open up.

Ella drank one glass, then ordered another, and then pointedly looked at Helen's untouched glass.

"The wine's not good?" Ella asked, and Helen shrugged. Ella knew she didn't like to drink, but Ella was watching her as if she wanted Helen to, as if it mattered. So, Helen lifted her glass and sipped.

"Fabulous," she said, and it was worth the lie to see Ella smile.

Helen kept drinking. The room grew darker as clouds moved over the Ann Arbor sky.

"Sometimes I sew messages into the hems of the clothes I make," Helen said in a rush.

Ella smiled. "What? You do?"

Helen nodded. "Bet you didn't know I put a message into that yellow wool dress I sent you, did you?"

"You did? I love that dress," Ella said.

"Go and look sometime," she said. She tried to imagine Ella's surprise after teasing out the little strip, reading the words that said Helen loved her. Ella could tuck it back in and sew a few stitches and that message would always be with her. She imagined Ella finding the earrings and wearing them every day, so that a part of Helen would always be with her, too.

"Well, I just might," Ella said.

A man in a fedora, carrying a stein of beer, eased down at a table near them, tipping his hat in their direction as he sat down. They both ignored him.

"Tell me what's going on," Helen said.

"Oh—" Ella said, as if she had forgotten that she had begged Helen to come.

"How's work going?"

"Good. It's really fun," Ella said, then whispered, "Shhh. Nobody in Ann Arbor knows I'm the columnist, which makes it kind of mysterious."

*Nobody knows you're a felon, either*, Helen thought.

A plate crashed to the floor near the entrance and the swell of voices grew louder.

"No one can hear themselves think in here," Helen fairly shouted, but Ella shook her head, putting one finger in front of her mouth.

"Baby girl," Helen said quietly, placing a hand on her daughter's. "Talk to me."

And then, haltingly, her words sliding into one another from the wine, Ella told her. Everything.

The instant she heard the word *daughter*, Helen felt herself go cold.

"What were you thinking?" Helen said, but Ella kept on talking, about how her daughter's name was Carla. About how she had made friends with Marianna, how they had all bonded. And about how everything was now a mess, because Mark, the father, was dead, and she knew Marianna was in Ann Arbor, but she couldn't reach her, and she had no idea where Carla was, and she only hoped she wasn't stuck in the system.

The whole time Ella was talking, Helen shuddered. She had thought this trip would be about her supporting Ella, getting her what she needed, sorting things out, but this—what Ella was telling her now—these were all things she thought had been buried forever. For the better.

"Oh, honey, no," Helen said finally, and Ella stared at her.

"No, no, you don't understand. You should see how beautiful she is!" Ella said. "How smart. She—"

"Stop," Helen said. "Please. Please stop."

Frowning, Ella beckoned the bartender for another drink, and as soon as it arrived, she threw half of it back, too.

"I thought you might help me—that you might even know someone who could help me find out where she is, how I could reach her."

"I *am* helping you. By telling you the truth. She isn't yours. Why are you torturing yourself like this?"

"You know, she's your *granddaughter.* Don't you want to at least see her?"

"No. No she isn't. And no, I don't. And you shouldn't either. Why are you doing this?"

"I didn't realize she'd be only six when I got out—"

"*Only* six—" Helen said.

"That's different from twenty-five! Twenty-five is an adult! Twenty-five doesn't want parents around! But six? Six does. Six needs them. Six needs to know, to have at least some sort of connection with her mother!"

"She *has* a mother. And no one is going to take a little girl, no matter what, and give her to a felon!" The word *felon* was ugly and heavy on her tongue.

"But what if she's in a foster home?"

"Is she?"

"I don't know. They won't tell me anything." Ella swallowed. "They could tell Jude!" she blurted.

"Ella, no," Helen said. "I told you he gave up his rights. You don't want to get mixed up in all of that again."

Ella's face clouded. She jerked her arm back, and the rest of her drink fell to the floor. The man in the fedora pulled his chair back and wiped at his pants.

"No problem," he said, but he was reaching for napkins, dabbing at his leg, giving them both a wary eye.

"All this time, you never said it to me, not when I was in prison, and certainly not now, but now I know how you feel about me," Ella said, her mouth a blunt line.

"How do I feel? You tell me."

"You think I did it," Ella said. "You think I'm guilty."

Helen felt her body go numb. Ella stumbled up and then Helen got up, too, but to her surprise, she had no tolerance anymore.

"Wait," Helen said, reaching for Ella and missing. "Wait—"

"I made a lot of mistakes," Ella said. "Don't you think I know that? And I paid for them. I did! But the biggest mistake was believing you still loved me. I thought maybe you could listen to me talk about my life instead of telling me how to live it."

Ella grabbed her jacket.

"Wait!" Helen cried. "Where are you going?"

"Home. I want you to go home, too."

*She's drunk*, Helen thought. *She doesn't know what she's saying.*

But then Ella was shoving her way out of the bar. Helen moved into the crowd, but she wasn't tall enough, couldn't see over the sea of bodies, could not even catch a glimpse of Ella's red hair.

The floor moved beneath her. Helen knocked against a couple, ignoring their glares, and then finally got to the door and pushed it open. But she saw only the street, sparkling in the twilight, and couples holding hands, heading into the bar. "Ella!" she called, but no one answered. People pushed past her as she stared down the block.

She leaned against the wall of the building, reeling from the wine, her first glass in months. She steadied herself, still hoping Ella would come back.

Helen sighed. She was too dizzy to walk to the hotel. Plus she'd left her jacket on her seat. She'd go back inside to get it, pay the tab, and then have someone call her a cab. She'd go to her hotel and call Ella— they would smooth it all out.

Helen went back into the noise and light, finding her stool still empty, her jacket still thrown over it. Maybe Helen deserved this punishment. She thought about the stupid secret they never told you about being a parent, how from the moment your child is born, they're moving away from you, giving you less and less of their life even as you yearn for more and more. It didn't matter if you yourself had cut your child's umbilical cord; it had never actually been cut. Not until your offspring severed that tie.

Helen had thought she would somehow always have an unshakable bond with Ella, and she knew now that was a lie. That it had never been true, not even when she had been carrying Ella inside her belly and Ella would kick hard against her, like she couldn't wait to be free.

There was so much about her daughter she no longer knew. There was the surprise of seeing Ella pull out a pair of glasses to check the drinks menu: when had that happened? Who were Ella's friends? Did she have a boyfriend? Would she stay in Ann Arbor or would she move somewhere else? How much more didn't she know? It made Helen so sad because when Ella had been young, she had prided herself on knowing everything. *You and me*, she had said. And now, Helen knew that there was going to be so much more she'd never have a chance to know. Ella was like a foreign country where Helen had once been a citizen. Now she was denied entry. It was, she reflected, similar to how she had been cut out of Hasidic life. Only this exclusion hurt even more.

The bartender, a young guy with a man bun, glided by.

"Sir?" Helen said, and he stopped. "Another, please."

Helen swirled the wine around, a tiny wave in her glass, and took a gulp—because what the hell. Here she was now, in a bar, with the noise and the thrum of music, and the heat from all the people pressed against her chest like a fist. Her daughter—her daughter!—had been here, too, until Helen ruined it. The pain was too great for her to move, to do anything. She stupidly downed one drink and then another.

She felt someone's stare, like a piece of gauze settling over her, and she realized the man in the fedora was watching her. He got up and stepped toward her. She hadn't thought anything about him before except that his hat seemed pretentious, but still she felt drawn to him. He sat on Ella's vacated stool and leaned his elbows on the bar. Here it was, another friendly male gaze, and she knew what that meant: *danger, danger*, like an alarm telling her to stop, but she moved her body closer.

"Bacardi, rocks," the man said, motioning to the bartender. His voice drifted toward her, an invitation.

Helen took another sip of her wine.

The man beside her lifted his glass and clinked it to hers. "Cheers," he said.

"L'chaim," Helen said.

He nodded, and then studied her. "You look like a pop someone shook up that needs the cap taken off," he said.

"Excuse me?"

"You seem like you're about to explode," he said. "I'm told I'm a great listener."

The alcohol was making her bold, and she ordered another. "Helen," she said.

"Jack."

She swore she saw Ella dancing in the crowd, her lovely long arms raised in greeting to a group of friends.

"Tell me what's on your mind."

Helen wasn't sure when or why she started to talk. Just that there was so much sorrow inside her, and this man's face seemed kinder

by the second. Words poured out of her. *Sip and slip*, she thought
fleetingly.

The more she talked about her daughter, the more she wanted to
tell, and the more she told, the lighter she felt, almost as if she were
watching everything play out on a movie screen and it was happening
to someone else. Jack's face softened with sympathy, and he began to
look better to her, too. She noticed his eyes, the quirk in his smile.

Then Helen told him how she had raised Ella all by herself, how she
had been kicked out of her insular Hasidic community, into another
world that maybe she had never really understood. She certainly didn't
understand it now. She told him about Jude—how her daughter's boyfriend had practically lived with them when Ella was a teenager.

"Her boyfriend," Jack repeated. "Her boyfriend lived at your
house? That must have been . . . well, different."

"It was *amazing*," Helen said. "It was a family." And then she fluttered a hand over her face because she felt as if she were about to cry.
And if she started, she'd never stop. Her stomach buckled.

"My daughter's a felon," she said in a rush. "She was in prison. For
attempted murder." Her hands began to shake. "I shouldn't have said
that."

Jack leaned closer and put his hands comfortingly over hers.

"Oh no," he said. "What a shame."

"They let her go early because they said the case was botched. Not
exonerated. She'd have to go to court for that—so technically she's still a
felon. But free." The room spun and she was sweating now, talking faster
and faster, telling him everything she could remember. Ella and Jude had
tried to kill his father, this prominent New York judge. Or only Ella had
because Jude had gone free, and it was Ella who had been in prison.

"Oh my," Jack said. "What do you think? Was she innocent? Was
she guilty?"

She'd had too much to drink, not enough food, and now she was
paying for it. "Yes. No," she said. "Maybe. Maybe I don't really know
her anymore."

And then the words kept flowing and she was telling him that Ella was a writer, that her name was Fitchburg and they had changed it from Levy.

"Imagine her giving advice to people in the paper," she said. The roaring in her chest grew louder. She was so woozy with drink. She wanted to go back to the hotel and sleep. She wanted to talk to Ella. She wanted to talk to Mouse most of all.

He cocked his head at her, his gentle smile faltering as he watched her face change. The burning in her stomach grew.

"I'll be right back—" she said.

Then she was running to the small bathroom by the door, shoving it open and rushing into a stall, kneeling, vomiting into the toilet. She retched until it seemed like she was emptied out of everything. She stumbled up and went to the sink and splashed water on her face, raising her head to see her reflection in the mirror. She tried to calm her breathing, then pulled out a lipstick from her purse to give herself some color. Then she opened the bathroom door and stepped out.

Jack was gone.

She dug in her purse for her wallet, put two fifties on the counter, which she thought should cover everything and—hands against the wall for balance—made her way outside and back to her hotel.

Her head was throbbing. Her mouth was desert dry, and though she knew she shouldn't try to talk to Ella in her condition, as soon as she got to her room, she called anyway. The call went straight to voicemail. *I'm sorry*, Helen tried to say, but she had no voice. She hung up and flopped onto the bed, the phone resting on her chest. She should call Mouse, she thought, but everything was closing in on her, narrowing into a cone of black.

IN THE MORNING, a headache raged. She pressed her thumbs into her temples, found her bottle of aspirin and downed two, showered, and then walked to Ella's. She knocked but there was no answer. She texted her, and then went to have coffee by herself. She sat in the café for two hours, waiting, and when she still didn't hear from Ella, she made a decision: she'd go home. It would be easy enough to come back.

She went back to the hotel, filled her suitcase, and called the airline about a flight back to LaGuardia. She called Ella again, but as before, it went straight to voicemail. She made one last call before takeoff, but still nothing. Ella must still be furious with her, she thought, but she could make it right. She knew she could.

# SIXTEEN

# Ann Arbor

*June 2019*

After leaving the bar that night, Ella didn't go home. She strode from one edge of Ann Arbor to the other, trying to burn out the rage, crying until she was exhausted. Nothing had gone the way she had hoped. She had thought her mother would comfort her, that she'd have answers, and instead their meeting had devolved into a confrontation.

So let her mother go back to New York City. Let her find her own life and leave Ella's alone. Ella was making more money now. If this kept up, she could rent a nicer apartment. And when she fully bloomed, when her roots were so deep and strong that no one could pull them out—then maybe she could see her mother again.

SHE IGNORED HER mother's calls the next day. Her cell buzzed constantly, so she turned it off. This silence wouldn't last forever though, because, controlling or not, Helen was her mother, and Ella loved her. Of course she loved her.

She even felt guilty that she had snapped at Helen, that she had told her to go home—and what if she really had gone? Ella waited until the afternoon, but when she called Helen, the call went to voicemail, her mother's recorded voice soft and full of light.

"Call me," Ella said. She said she was sorry, that she knew a great place they could go to for dinner.

As soon as she put her cell down, it began to buzz. She looked at the screen and there was Pearl's name. *I know, I know,* she thought. She was late on the column, but she could do it in an hour if she had to, even if her heart wasn't in it. But as soon as she answered and said hello, she could feel something like a current in the air. Something bad.

"Pearl?" she said.

"I trusted you! I gave you a chance—"

"Pearl?" she said again.

"Your column's been pulled from syndication!" Pearl yelled.

"What?" Ella said. "What are you talking about?"

"The phones are ringing. The emails are nonstop. No one wants to take advice from a felon."

There it was, the hard slap of that word.

"It's—it's not true—" Ella said.

"Don't tell me it's not true. Have you seen the papers? Turned on the local news? Your Clancy Facebook page is so filled with ugliness that I had to shut it down. We already lost four advertisers," Pearl said. "Yes, they were conservative with their money, but it doesn't matter. What else did you lie about?"

"Tell me what you want me to do, and I'll do it, I swear—" Ella braced her hands on her table, bile rising in her throat.

"You're not understanding me," Pearl said, and then Ella realized what an idiot she had been: Pearl had never been her friend, not like Marianna, not even like the checkout girl at the local grocery store who would always chat with her. Pearl was her boss. Those lunches they had shared, the occasional gossip and teasing—they were really just another veneer that could be easily torn away. Pearl had liked her only as long as the column had been building circulation.

"It's my fault. For giving you a chance," Pearl said. "I never even checked your references."

"You're firing me?" Ella said in amazement.

"You did this, not me. You should have told me the truth to begin with and maybe we could have handled this. I might have still hired you if I had known, but you kept it hidden."

"I'm so sorry—" Ella cried, but Pearl had hung up.

ELLA WEPT. WITH what she had saved, and the money left from the check Helen had given her, she had enough to keep the apartment for at least six months. But she couldn't imagine how hard staying there would be. Who would hire her now?

She thought Ann Arbor had become her home. Her safe place.

*It's all over the local news*, Pearl had said. Ella turned on the TV, and there, like a shock, was her profile plastered on the screen, the same photo from seven years ago, where she had looked like a wild thing, her eyes round and terrified, her hair blowing crazily about her face. They ran it now with a legend beneath it:

ADVICE COLUMNIST HAS SCANDAL OF HER OWN.
HISTORY OF AN ATTEMPTED MURDERESS.

To her horror, the TV news personalities were treating it like juicy gossip they couldn't wait to share.

Ella slumped into a chair, her stomach roiling. Her cell kept buzzing, and she picked it up.

"Murderer," someone said, and hung up. The cell buzzed yet again. How did they get her number? It was unlisted. She declined the call.

She looked at the news again, this time the national news, but it appeared only as a mention before they moved on to sports. Then she saw it, like a shout. Helen's name, and then hers.

EVEN MOTHER UNSURE OF
DAUGHTER'S INNOCENCE

She wrapped her arms tightly about her body. "While talking to a reporter, Helen Fitchburg, formerly Levy, described . . . ," the news-caster said.

Helen had told everything to a reporter, spilling, spilling, spilling, like a river breaking a dam. Her mother had been drunk last night, smothering her with her worries, dismissing with finality her relationship with Carla. As if Ella were ten again, misbehaving.

Andrew Stein had kept Jude's name out of the papers when it had all originally happened, but now Jude was an adult, and there it was, in print—his new name revealed, thanks to Helen. The only thing her mother hadn't spilled was the news about Carla.

*Everything that is mine is yours*, Helen had always said, but what Ella hadn't seen is that Helen had meant the opposite, too—that everything of Ella's had been hers, to do with as she pleased. And that included her secrets.

She went to her closet, rummaging around until her fingers felt wool. There it was, the yellow dress with the message her mother had claimed was in the hem. She ripped it from the hanger and threw it to the floor.

She grabbed her cell and dialed Henry at the store to explain everything to him. He picked up but as soon as she heard his hello, his voice stiff and distant, she knew that he knew already.

"I can explain," she said, starting to cry. "If I can just come to you, see your face, I can tell you the truth."

She heard him breathing. "And why would I believe you?" he said quietly.

"Because you can—because I'll tell you everything."

"My ex always said that she told me everything. Right from the start. I believed her. Right until she left me for my best friend. I told myself I'd never get in a situation like that again."

"Henry, please."

She heard something burrowing in the silence.

"I'm sorry, Ella," he said. "I truly am."

The line went dead.

# SEVENTEEN

# Brooklyn

*June 2019*

H elen got off the plane and caught a cab home from LaGuardia.

Once in her apartment, she sank into a chair, her head still throbbing. The whole plane ride home, she realized she had made a mistake, that she should have stayed in Ann Arbor and worked things out with Ella. She shouldn't have let her anxieties get the upper hand. She reached for her cell to call her daughter again, to apologize, when she heard her buzzer. She looked out her window and there was Mouse. She felt weak with relief and let him in. When he reached her apartment door, she tried to fling herself in his arms, but to her surprise, he stepped back. His face was white, a mask.

"What happened?" she said, alarmed.

"I think that's what I'm asking you—"

"Asking me what? Mouse, please, I just got back."

"Who does this to their own child?" he said. "What kind of person does this?"

"Does what?" she said. "What happened?"

"Who does this to someone they pretend to care about? To keep secrets this big! I thought we told each other the truth, that honesty was what our relationship was all about."

He paced, mapping out her living room floor until she grabbed him. "What is this about?" she pleaded, and then he stopped walking.

"You know what it's about. It's about you. You go into a bar and get drunk, and you tell some reporter everything about your daughter—"

The air squeezed around her.

"What?" she said. "*What?*"

Mouse swallowed hard. "Your daughter, the one I never got to meet. Your daughter I knew nothing about except what you told me. And it turns out you told me nothing—you didn't trust me. It turns out she's a felon, that she tried to kill someone. And you just out her to a reporter?"

Helen's legs collapsed. She fell against a chair and stumbled upright again. "What are you saying?" she said.

His face hardened. "You don't read the papers? You don't get the news on your phone? He was a prominent judge here. You think that isn't news?"

"Why would I talk to a reporter?" she said. And then she couldn't breathe. Suddenly she remembered how woozy she had been at the bar. How much she'd had to drink, how that man in the fedora had been flirting with her, urging her to talk. And she had. She had given him her real last name. Ella's first name.

At least she hadn't mentioned Ella's child.

She wondered if he had been following Ella, somehow suspecting that she might be the anonymous help columnist. It might have been a minor surprise of a story, until she, Helen, had given him something explosive instead. No wonder he had left the bar so quickly.

Helen tried to swallow, but her throat was locked. She thought of the last argument she had had with Mouse, about how things were never black and white, and here it was again. She couldn't see anything now but gray. Mouse used to look at her as if she were a treasure, as if he had won the lottery with her, but now his eyes were hard, like glass.

"I tried to tell you. But you wouldn't let me."

"Then you didn't try hard enough," Mouse said. He turned from her. "I thought I knew who you were."

She watched him leave the apartment, heard his steps going down the stairs, and he was gone.

*I did this. I did this.*

Helen finally swallowed. She turned on her computer and there it was, story after story after story. A felon writing advice columns. How the information had come from Helen, whom the story insinuated was no angel herself—a single mother who had been kicked out of the Hasidic community she had been born into. And even though it was all secular news, the gossip could reach her community and bring shame to her family once again.

*We have no daughter anymore.* She could call her mother now and her mother would probably hang up on her. But maybe her mother would just listen silently, her presence the only way she could express any love for her daughter. She could call her siblings, but who knew if they even remembered her.

Helen wept as she shut off the computer. She had lost one world and gained another. And then she'd lost this one, too.

HELEN CALLED THE dress shop to ask if she could come back early from vacation.

"Sure, why not?" her boss said kindly.

"You know why not," she replied. "I don't want to make trouble for you. You've been so kind."

"No one even knows you work here, right? You can come in through the back. You are not your daughter."

Helen drew back, stung. *Flesh of my flesh, blood of my blood.* Wasn't she her daughter? Hadn't they been through everything together?

"You're welcome here," her boss said, and there was nothing for Helen to do but thank her.

Helen tried to bury herself in work, staying in the backroom, squinting down at her tiny, perfect stitches. At least that was one thing she could get right. She sewed hems and bridesmaid dresses for breathless, goofy young women. She beaded the hem of a satin dress, each bead sewn with the care she couldn't put into words.

She called Ella every day, always with the message: *Forgive me. We need to talk. Please.* She emailed her and texted her. There was never any response.

Mouse had once told her that he loved the lilt of her voice, her faint Yiddish accent. She called him, too, hoping that hearing her voice might bring him back to her. How could she make it up to him? And how could she stand it if he didn't want to see her? He didn't answer.

The Dear Clancy column, along with the Facebook page she used to read just for the comments praising her daughter, were both gone. Another hole in her heart. Every online reference to Ella contained the scandal once again—fixed firmly in place, the torrid history of her life and her child's.

Some days she felt as if she were in a blizzard, all this anger swirling around her so that she couldn't see what was true or real anymore.

She thought about how when Ella was very little, she had sometimes had tantrums, falling to the floor, kicking her legs and banging her arms. Helen used to tell Ella about anger, how it was like a snowstorm she might feel caught in, but snow melts. "We don't have to live in that rage forever. We may be stuck in it for the moment, but poof!—then our path is clear and we can always find our way out."

But Helen didn't really follow her own advice. She had felt the same way—buried in an avalanche—when she had been kicked out of her community as a girl. Even though she had slowly dug herself out and her life had gradually changed, the inescapable yearning she still had for her past threatened like another blizzard.

If she had built a new way of being once, maybe she could do it again.

Two nights after Mouse stormed out, Helen made herself some strong oolong tea, then sat by the window. She could hear her mother's voice, confirming how every joy, how every trouble, was always from Hashem.

Well, she wasn't Hasidic anymore. She hadn't been to a religious service since before Ella was born. Her mother used to tell her that the most important forgiveness was God's, but to get it you had to first get the forgiveness of the person you had wounded. You had to ask once, then twice, and then a third time, and if you weren't forgiven by the person, then God, at least, would forgive you.

But her parents hadn't forgiven her.

Back then, Helen had been a fist of misery. She had thought that if her parents could just see their granddaughter, they would have embraced her. But she didn't have the courage to take Ella to see them until Ella was two. She had dressed her daughter in a frilly yellow dress she'd made herself. She had brushed her curls and put a bow in them. She just wanted them to know her, for her to know them. Who could resist such a beautiful little girl?

It turned out that her parents could. Her mother had stared at them from the open door and Helen could only stammer that here was her granddaughter. Then silence. Her mother blinked back tears.

"Who's at the door?" a voice had cried, and then Helen's sister Adah had flown into the doorway, stopping in shock when she spotted Helen, her eyes growing round.

"Adah!" Helen said, and then little Esti had come up behind them. Before she could say anything else, her mother firmly shut the door.

ELLA HAD BEEN sweet and solemn and precious on her mother's doorstep. But in the subway on the way home, something snapped. Ella began to scream, flailing her arms, seemingly overcome by fury. Helen wondered if she understood, if not in action, then in feeling, their rejection. The other passengers had thrown disapproving looks as though the child's distress had been Helen's fault. As though she were a terrible mother.

She had bowed her head, but she made her prayer directly to Ella: *My darling girl.* And then Ella had stopped screaming and the subway car relaxed. Helen whispered into her daughter's hair: *We will be our own family, we two. All we need is each other.* And with a start, she realized that she hadn't mentioned God, that she no longer believed in Him. No, she believed in Ella. God had abandoned her, her community had abandoned her, but her Ella never would.

Except that Ella had indeed abandoned her, and it was all Helen's fault.

Now, Helen grabbed her cellphone. She hesitated and then called her daughter. The voice message kicked in. She wondered if Ella was even listening to her messages. Perhaps Helen had been cut out completely. Undeterred, she left a message.

"This is your mother," she said, as if she had to remind her. "Forgive me." Her voice cracked. She hung up.

# PART THREE

# EIGHTEEN

# Philadelphia
*June 2019*

Jude was at work, crouching over an iMac and fiddling with the connection, when a news story about Ella popped up on the screen, along with her photo. He stood, dizzy, his heart stalling. She was out of prison. In trouble. And his name—his father's too—were in bold letters for the whole world to see.

Everything seemed to be moving in slow motion.

"Hey, you okay, dude? You look kind of green," a coworker said from the cubicle next to his. Jude, unable to speak, gathered his things and went home.

When he arrived, Angie was in the living room reading *What to Expect When You're Expecting*, balancing it on her bulging belly. She stared at him as if she didn't know him. He slumped down on the couch, bracing one hand on the end table to steady himself.

"Angie," he said. "I don't know what to say."

"How about, when were you going to tell me? I thought we were everything to each other. I thought we had trust, that nothing was off-limits for us," she said. "Why couldn't you have told me?"

"I wanted to forget—"

"*Surprise.* You can't now. And, oh joy, guess what? It's trending on Twitter."

Jude's body felt as if it belonged to someone else.

"You didn't even tell me the real reason you changed your last name! When I asked you why your name was different, you said you just liked the sound better!"

"My dad did it to keep the media away from me."

"Don't you know there are no secrets these days? Everything has a record. Secrets might get buried, but they can be found."

She picked up her phone and held the screen in front of him. Jude froze as he stared at another old photo. There she was, Ella at fifteen, flanked by two cops, her eyes terrified, her hair matted against one side of her head, her shoulders hunched. She looked so small and afraid. Everything he had buried about her, every feeling, now surfaced, suffocating him with new grief.

"She's not quoted in the article," Angie said. "But her mother is, and she mentions you."

Helen! The woman who had opened her home to him, who had given him a garden when he needed it most. Helen, whose whole world had been Ella, and who had built that world out to include him, too.

"I don't understand," Jude said.

"Neither do I," Angie said abruptly. She slipped her swollen feet into a pair of sneakers by the couch. "And I'm going for a walk. I need some time to think."

AS SOON AS she left, Jude felt the past swirling through his mind, a twister threatening to destroy him. Helen had told a journalist the whole story at a bar in Ann Arbor. Ella's boss had issued a statement about how foolish she had been to hire someone she hadn't properly vetted.

But what shocked Jude the most was the fact that the news said Ella had been released early after another journalist had taken up her cause. It had to come to light that the detectives on the case had coerced a confession. Her lawyer had had little criminal experience, and he had made mistake after mistake, going so far as to let Ella plead guilty at the arraignment. The journalist found that the toxicology report had been compromised, and evidence had been hidden. Jude had known none of this. He had held the belief firmly in his mind that she was gone from him, from his life, locked away for twenty-five years.

But Jesus, she'd been out of prison for over a year! He tried to imagine what her life must have been like, getting free. He wondered why she had gone to Ann Arbor. He understood why she hadn't reached out to him.

Had his father known she was out? Jude put his head in his hands. His dad had to have known all about this. He called him.

"We have to talk," he said as soon as his father answered.

"The Union League," his father said, his voice dry and clear, as if he knew what was coming.

ON THE WAY to the club, Jude couldn't think straight. He had left Angie a note: *My father wants to talk over lunch. I'll be home this afternoon.* He couldn't concentrate on anything but Ella, and every moment he felt a darkness growing closer and more ominous.

Jude had never been to the Union League, but he had certainly heard about it. The restaurants he frequented were casual, less fussy. This was exactly the kind of place his father loved—polished wood floors and white tablecloths, orchids on each table, the space sound-proofed so that all Jude could hear was a dim hush. The women were in dresses and the men in suits, and here was Jude in jeans and a T-shirt. He hadn't thought that what he wore would matter, but then, knowing his father, of course it would. People didn't eat here; they dined. He wondered if that was why his father had chosen it, to make him uncomfortable.

"Reservation is under Andrew Stein," Jude said to the maître-d', who suddenly brightened.

"Of course," he said. "Let me provide you with a jacket first."

He motioned to someone who brought a blue sports jacket over and Jude shrugged into it. "Right this way," the maître-d' said.

His father presided over one of the biggest tables, set in a sunny corner by a window, a menu in his hand. He was in a suit and tie, as if he were still judging cases in court rather than acting as dean.

"Well, hello," Jude's father said. He handed Jude a menu. "The steak is fabulous."

"Vegan, remember?"

"They make an excellent wild mushroom risotto."

"Sure, okay," Jude said. He waited for his father to bring up Ella, but Andrew remained silent. Jude felt everything boiling within him. Why was his father deliberately avoiding what he surely must know was the very reason for this lunch? *Say something*, he told himself, but then his father was beckoning to the waiter again, asking for sparkling water.

Andrew kept his eyes on Jude the whole time. He asked if Jude and Angie had looked at any preschools yet.

"Angie hasn't even had the baby yet. It's a little early," Jude said.

But Andrew shook his head. "Never too early," he said. "I can make a few calls for you. I already set up a 529 account to pay for the baby's education."

Jude sat back, staring at his father in disbelief.

And that was when he noticed how much older his father looked. When had his neck turned to crepe? There were wrinkles and dark circles under his eyes, and his father, usually so fastidious, had a faint stain on his dress shirt.

The food came to the table, everything served quietly. *I'll ask him about Ella now*, Jude thought, but he picked up his fork instead, wanting his father to bring it up first.

Jude talked idly about his job, but sensed his father was only half listening.

At last, he couldn't take it another second. "We have to talk about Ella," he said firmly, and his father's face darkened. "Did you know she was let out of prison early? Did you read the news about her being outed now as a felon?"

Jude's father's shoulders stiffened. "If I had known we were going to talk about this, I wouldn't have invited you to lunch."

"You knew we were going to."

"There's nothing to talk about."

"Yes, there is. Did reporters call you?"

"No."

"I don't believe you," Jude said. "What did you tell them?"

His father sighed. "Nothing you don't know."

"Did you know she was out of prison?"

"Did you think I wouldn't know?" he said quietly. "You're my son. I wanted to protect you from that girl. And now here it is again in the news. Do we really need to have a conversation about it?"

"Ella. Her name is Ella. She got out early. Why?"

"She was very lucky. And so were you."

"What? Why was she lucky? How was I lucky? I was destroyed. My whole life was."

"No, no you weren't. Are you destroyed now? No, you aren't. Look at your life and tell me it's destroyed. You have a wife who loves you. A decent job. A baby on the way."

"How long before reporters get to me?"

"They'll stop. They'll latch on to the next thing." Andrew leaned back in his chair. "Did you know that the police were ready to put you in prison? Do I have to remind you what would have happened if I hadn't stopped them?"

"This again—" Jude said.

"Okay, you want to talk, we'll really talk. Do you know how worried I was about you, about the amount of time you were spending with Ella? You two were little sticks of dynamite just waiting to go off. I always believed I was protecting you both by separating you. Don't you know that?"

"I hated you for that."

"You think I didn't know? Do you know how much it hurt? I love you. You are my son! I was so desperate to do better for you. And I wasn't going to let you ruin your life. I couldn't."

"You were desperate to do better for me?" Jude asked, astonished. "Do you hear yourself? Did that include blaming me for mom's death? Did that include drinking and then beating me so badly we had to go to the ER?"

Jude's father put his fork down.

"I'm sober now," he said. "And I regret all of that."

"Oh yeah, and you regretted it back then, too, until the next time you raised your fists to me—"

"Lower your voice," his father said quietly, glancing about the room. "I'm a different person now. The truth is I'm glad Ella was let out early. Relieved. She's still young, she still has her whole life ahead of her. Honestly, I wish her nothing but the best."

"Really. She's still a felon."

"You have your whole life ahead of you, too."

"A life you don't approve of."

Jude's father sighed. "I was wrong about Angie," he said. "All I saw was a too-young girl who got pregnant, making you a father way too soon. I couldn't come to terms with you—a young man who could have become anything you you wanted—working in IT."

"I'm happy—"

"Let me finish." Andrew put down his fork. "The world is hard. I was so broken when your mom died that I did everything wrong."

To Jude's surprise, his father looked as if he were about to cry.

Andrew waved his hand. "You don't understand. You're my son. You're the most important thing to me."

"What about justice? What about Ella? Aren't those two things important, too? I never had to go to prison, because you were rich and powerful. Ella did because her family was poor. You had all these connections, and the media just loved the story—*Poor Girl Tries to Kill Boyfriend's Rich Dad*. Remember those headlines?"

Jude's father shook his head. "No, that's not true. Not totally true. The cops were looking for someone to blame, they needed someone because of who I was, because it had all been too high-profile in the news—"

Jude put his fork down, his appetite gone.

"In the hospital, when they thought I was dying, I wasn't thinking of myself, of what might happen to me. All I could think about was what would become of you. How would you live? What would happen to the life I wanted for you? You were like a tumbleweed, and there was that wild girl, her crazy mother—"

Jude's mouth went dry. "Ella. I told you. Her name is Ella. And her mother wasn't crazy. She was kind to me. She loved me, Dad. Really loved me, like a son. Her name is Helen."

"That might be true, but you weren't hers to make into her son."

"Dad—"

"They kept asking me who gave me the tea, how did it happen. I knew the news of the incident would hit the media, but I could control the narrative. I would rather have died than see you go to prison. And believe me, you wouldn't have lasted on the inside.

"I felt sure Ella wouldn't be sent away at all. She was such a young girl, no priors, no evidence. But the police insisted on blaming some-one. And so, I told them. But then she confessed, Jude! She confessed!" Andrew laced his fingers together, now unable to look at his son.

"You told them what?"

"I told them that Ella had given me the tea. That I had seen her put the leaves in the cup—"

"She confessed. That's old news—"

"She did confess, that's true, but only after I told the cops that I had seen her making the tea, only after she had been questioned for hours. You were never questioned seriously, Jude. I saw to that. I had

Frank there, one of the most high-powered lawyers I know, to protect you, to guide you, to smooth things over with the detectives. People will confess to all sorts of things just to make the questions stop. And I didn't want that for you."

"I don't understand—what are you telling me?" Jude tried to remember that day, how Ella had gone missing. He had texted her repeatedly, but she wouldn't respond. He could still see the cup, the tea leaves, but he couldn't remember what he'd done with them, if he'd done anything at all. All he remembered was his desperate attempt to find Ella. He'd searched and searched the apartment for her, but he couldn't find her, and he had felt so betrayed. How could she have left him there alone? *I'd do anything for you.* That's what she had said, and he believed her. *Anything. I'd do anything.* Terrified, disoriented, he had run outside, searching for her, and then by the time he came back, he barely had time to look around before he saw his father hit the floor.

"What are you telling me?" Jude said again.

Andrew took Jude's hand. He breathed deeply and then sat up straighter.

"I know you think I don't love you, but I do. This has been awful for me, too. I would have done anything to make sure you were safe," he said. "Anything."

Jude felt his body trembling. For a moment he saw Ella in front of him, heard her voice. *I would do anything for you.*

"That night, neither of you brought in the tea, you just disappeared after dinner. After a while I started to clean up the kitchen and came upon the tea. I thought it might be calming, so I drank it."

"You drank it on your own then," Jude said. "She didn't give it to you—"

"You're not listening. The tea was made. That's legal intent. In the hospital that night, the cops kept asking me about you, wanting to pin blame on someone. They thought I was dying, and I knew . . . Well, deathbed confessions are always solid. Can you imagine what would have happened if they had pinned the blame on you? You would have gone to jail. It would have been in all the papers—"

"What are you talking about? It already was—"

"But that way it would have been different."

"And do you think that what happened after that wasn't 'different'?" Jude said, his voice rising. "Ella was *gone*. I had to change my name. I couldn't tell anyone anything! I was fucking destroyed!"

"Would you have survived in prison?" his father said. "I don't think so. Would you have wanted to be known all your life as the boy who tried to kill his father?"

"I called nine-one-one."

"I know that. And I know you didn't really hate me. Maybe then, in that moment, you did, but not in the wider scheme of things. You were just a kid who was pissed off about having to leave his girlfriend. You cooked up this scheme, but you were never going to—"

"Stop," Jude said. "Stop telling me how I felt or what I would have done."

Jude's father went quiet. "It's all in the past now."

"She went to prison! And it's not in the past—it's happening again, right now! They're calling our house! Calling Angie! Now we're having to relive it!"

"No, we aren't! Not if we don't want to! Why torture yourself like this? You want me to tell you something? I'll tell you something. You didn't remember anything, and that worked in our favor. Because what the cops saw was you, an innocent, loving son, frantically calling nine-one-one to save his father's life. A devoted boy who not only came to the hospital but who stubbornly refused to leave until you knew I was okay. They couldn't get you on conspiracy, and certainly not attempted murder, because legally, you hadn't done anything. You had just been a bystander. And as far as legal intent was concerned, it was your girlfriend who had foxglove growing in her backyard."

"That was *my* garden! Helen let me grow things because you wouldn't."

"You think it was all my fault? What about you, son? You let your girlfriend take the rap and admit to something she hadn't done."

Jude froze. "What?"

"It wasn't her," Jude's father said carefully.

"What do you mean, it wasn't her? You just said . . . you just told me—"

"It was you."

The words hung in the air. Stunned, Jude pushed away from the table.

"Listen to me," his father said quietly. "Hear what I'm saying. It was you. God help me, it was you who made that tea."

"How can you say such a thing? I was the one who saved you. I don't remember—"

"I know you don't, but I do. I was in the other room and could clearly see you put leaves in the teacup and then pour the hot water and stir it, though I had no idea what was in it, obviously. I was in the dining room, waiting for you two, and then I heard you calling for her. You ran out of the house after that girl to find her. You left the tea."

"You lied! You were a judge and you lied! I didn't give you that cup! Ella didn't give you that cup! You picked it up and drank it yourself. And you sent her to prison."

"You made the tea," Judge Stein repeated quietly.

"But who knows what I would have done with it! Maybe I would have tossed it into the sink! Doesn't it mean anything that I left that cup? That I went to find Ella instead? How could you lie like that?"

"The police didn't have *just* my statement; they had a signed confession, written by her."

"She was in prison because of you," Jude said, his voice hoarse with anger. "She was outed because of you. You were the one. You didn't want to be known as the father whose son hated him enough to try to kill him. You didn't want it to come out—the beatings, the alcohol. You couldn't allow any of it to sully your fucking reputation."

"No, not because of me," his father said. "And you know what? You would've heard she'd been released if you really cared. It was in all the papers and on TV at the time. Everyone was talking about it. I never brought it up because I hoped you weren't still carrying a torch for her. All I wanted was for you to heal, to get on with your life. So stop pretending like you still care about her now."

Jude felt a flash of shame. All this time he believed Ella had done it, that she was the one who had gone through with the plan, had added the foxglove, made the tea. And even though they had planned that together, he never thought it would become real. When he learned that she had confessed, it had tainted everything he felt about her. He hadn't looked for her after they moved to Philadelphia, hadn't wanted to think about all that had happened. And now he knew that she wasn't guilty. He was the guilty one, not her.

"She isn't exonerated," his father said. "And she's still technically a felon, and that's probably why that paper fired her. They felt they had to." He tried to touch Jude's hand, but his son moved away.

Jude stared at his father. "Do you realize what you did?" he asked quietly.

"I do. I saved you. I protected my son, whom I love."

"You took away the one person I loved, really loved. The one person who truly loved me. Who always looked out for me. She and Helen— they were my family, Dad. My real family.

"You have to come forward, tell the truth," Jude said. "And I will, too."

Jude's father went still. "That's not possible."

"You mean you won't admit you made a false statement to the police."

"For this case to reopen, they'd still need new evidence. We all have to just live our lives now." His father tried to touch his hand again, but Jude stood up.

"I love you," his father said. "And I'm sorry you're so upset. But you can't convince me I did the wrong thing."

"I don't think I want your love anymore. Or your money. Or anything from you."

"Jude, listen. I saved you. We have a good relationship now."

Jude gathered his things.

"You," he said, pointing at his father. "You're not welcome in my home or anywhere near Angie. You didn't just screw up Ella's life, you screwed up mine, too. You did all this, and you did it deliberately."

Jude stared at his father. Memories of happy times with both his parents flashed through his mind, followed by some of the terrible things that had come later, after his mother's death.

"I have to go; I can't talk to you." Jude pushed his chair in as his father motioned to the waiter, mouthing for him to put the meal on his tab.

"Okay, you cool off and then—"

"No, you're not listening. Don't contact me again." Jude shucked off the jacket and threw it on the chair.

"I'm your father. I'm going to be your child's grandfather."

"No. I know you think that you did it all for me, and that's what's so sad."

"Jude, I never meant to hurt you—"

"Oh no? I have the scars to prove that you did."

Jude's father was silent.

"I'm leaving," Jude said, and he strode from the restaurant.

"Jude, wait—" his father called, but Jude kept walking and didn't look back, didn't stop even when he was outside in the busy shock of the world again.

All this time, and Ella had been innocent. And he, Jude, had been guilty, a coward, unable to see the truth that was right in front of him. He hadn't even thought to question it.

Ella. She was out there somewhere. Had she made a life, the way he had? Was she still in Ann Arbor? Or back east with Helen? At the thought of Helen, he doubled over with nausea. Helen had loved him, had treated him like her son. He had loved her back. And he had betrayed her, too, and he hadn't even known it.

Well, he knew it now.

Maybe his father was wrong and Ella's name could be cleared. Weren't there organizations that helped people like her? He would find them. He could help her. Even if his father refused to testify, couldn't Jude? He would take responsibility for what he had done. He had put the leaves in the cup, he had poured the water and left it, and that, his father said, was legal intent. In any case, didn't she have a right to know? What would she do if she knew?

WHEN HE GOT home, Angie was waiting, her hair damp from the shower, a gauzy dress skating around her ankles.

"You look beautiful," he said, his mouth dry. She walked toward him.

From the dark flash of her eyes, he could tell she was still pissed. Both their cells rang, and they both ignored them. "How was lunch with Darth Vader?" she asked flatly.

He could lie if he wanted. He could tell only the parts she needed to hear, had to hear. But he was exhausted. He felt as if a chink in his life had opened, and now he wanted to widen it, to bring Angie through. He wasn't going to lie to her, not anymore. He'd had enough lies, enough secrets.

So he told her what his father had said, taking his time, watching as she didn't react. Not until he finished, and then he saw her swallow hard.

"Every time I think your dad has changed, he shows how much he hasn't," she said quietly.

"I need to tell Ella she's innocent," Jude said, and as soon as he said it, he knew that was what he had to do. He watched Angie's face, but she remained still, giving him nothing.

"Do you have her number?"

He hadn't thought of just calling her. It seemed too important, too necessary to face her. "I'm going to go see her. I owe her that."

"You know her address?"

"Someone doxxed her online. Her address is there for the world to see."

He saw her face tense with worry. What kind of asshole was he?

"I shouldn't go," he said. "Not with you pregnant."

"I'm not due for weeks," Angie said. "And look at you. You're a mess. I think you need to go."

He nodded, then watched Angie's mouth crumple.

"Do you still love her?"

The question startled him. He had locked that answer away in some parallel world. He waited a beat too long and Angie raised one hand.

"Don't answer. I don't want to know," she said. "Just do what you need to and then come back to us."

He cradled her stomach and kissed her damp cheek.

THE NEXT DAY, Jude flew to Detroit and then rented a car to drive to Ann Arbor. He didn't know if what he was doing was crazy, only that he had to do it, and he hoped that it would make things better for Ella. But he couldn't help imagining that it might make things worse. What would it be like to see her again?

He was surprised by how lively the town was, how teeming with kids, even in the summer. It had a kind of music that he couldn't place, like a low hum that moved through his body. It was the kind of place he and Ella had talked about moving to when they were planning to run away. A city, but not a big, impersonal one.

He followed the GPS to her address, then climbed the stairs to the top floor and knocked.

"Henry?" a voice said. Ella's voice. *Who's Henry?* The door to her apartment opened and there she was, looking so beautiful it crushed his heart. He couldn't tell who was more startled.

She frowned at him.

"Jude?" she asked. And he nodded.

"What are you doing here?"

She looked as confused as he felt, like the world had turned upside down. She motioned him to sit on the stairs, below her.

"I'm not inviting you in," she said. She was and wasn't Ella. He was fifteen again and wanted to crush her against him. *Do you love her?* Angie had asked. He had thought that he didn't, but here, beside her, he wasn't sure anymore.

The hair he had loved was so long now, almost to her chest, but still wildly curly and flaming red. Her freckles that he used to connect like constellations were still a bridge across her nose. She looked older, though, a woman now, not a girl. She was dressed in dark colors, not the bright ones she used to wear.

"Why are you here?" she said.

"I needed to see you—"

"Why? You never bothered to write or call me before."

"I got friends to mail you the letters I wrote, to call—"

"I never got anything from you. And I mailed you letters, too. Are you going to lie and say you never got them?"

"I never got them. And it isn't a lie."

Her mouth became a line. "Why are you here, Jude? Did you read about me in the paper, like everyone else? What is it you want?"

"Ella—"

"You used to say you loved me so much you'd die without me, remember? You loved my house so much you basically lived in it. And you loved my mom. My mom always seemed to love you. Maybe more than she did me."

"Ella—"

"Funny how nothing is as it seems, right?"

"Is Helen all right?"

There was that dry sharp laugh again. "Helen outed me," Ella said.

"I know. But she loves you. She'd never—"

"Ella, you have to hear me. You were innocent."

Ella started laughing, the sound like a bark, and then she abruptly stopped.

"Really? This is what you came for?" she said. "Nothing about me is innocent anymore. I did something criminal and I paid for it. I'll never stop paying for it."

"You aren't hearing me. You didn't do anything. My father told me. He saw it—"

Ella stiffened. "Your father. He hated me. Who cares what he told you?"

Jude pressed one hand against his forehead.

"There's something you don't know. You didn't do it. You're replaying the memories the detectives gave you. You didn't do this—" His stomach burned. "I did."

Ella didn't move. "What are you saying?"

"Me and you, Ella. We talked about killing him! That's all we did. Talked and fantasized. We were kids! That night we were so sleep-deprived that we were hallucinating! The tea, the foxglove, was all just part of the fantasy we told each other to make us feel better, to make us think we could have a life together! And that night—that horrible night—I was stuck in that fantasy, I was acting it out like I was sleepwalking."

"I made the tea," she said quietly. "I gave him the cup. It was a terrible, confusing night, but I did it."

"No, you didn't. You ran off that night," Jude said, his voice breaking. "I'm the one who grew the foxglove, who made the tea, who knew the plant's every fucking property so well I could have recited it by heart. I loathed him and loved you. And all it took to reverse my hatred was for him to almost die, for him to say he loved me. And you suffered for it."

Ella didn't move. "Why would he tell you now? He despised me."

"Because it's not about you, Ella. It's about *him*. He wanted me to know how much he had sacrificed for me, what he did on my behalf." He paused. "You have a right to know."

Ella stared at him, then started to cry, not moving to wipe away her tears.

"All this time, and I'm innocent?" She shook her head. "They kept telling me and telling me what I did, who I was, and finally I believed them." Her hands shook. "And you believed them, too—"

"I didn't know what to believe—"

She was crying steadily now.

"Want to know something funny? The cops told me confessing would make the judge go easier on me."

"I swear to you. I'm the criminal. And my father's the criminal, and I'm not seeing that bastard again. If you want me to go to the press, I will," Jude said. "We can both go. Or go to one of those places that helps exonerate people. I'll tell the truth. I'll make it right."

"I can't go through this all over again. And your father will deny it all."

"I can try—"

"With what proof?"

"Me. I'm the proof. I can try, Ella. Let me try."

"Want to know what I tried? I tried to move on and a lot of good it did. Want to know what my life is like now? My phone doesn't stop ringing. People text ugly things to me, like *murderer*. Or just *liar*. Or any other terrible word they can think of. In Brooklyn and here, I've had people slip notes under my door accusing me of all sorts of things. I've had to change my number again and again. Remember how we used to constantly text? I never do that anymore. I stay off social media because I'm a pariah there.

"I may have to move, start all over again, and maybe it won't even be safe after I move. You think proclaiming my innocence is going to change anything, make it better for me? You think people will believe me, or do you think they'll look at me and they'll always wonder? They'll make the story they want to believe."

There was silence as the truth of her words washed over him.

"What's your life like now?" she asked, still a hostile note in her voice. "Tell me."

"I work in IT."

She looked at him, surprised. "You were going to be a botanist. You had this gift with plants. It was your passion."

"Not anymore."

"I don't believe you. Things like that don't just leave you. You were born for that. What else do you have?"

"I have a wife. And a baby on the way."

He saw her flinch. "I don't remember reading that," she said finally. "Show me," she said. "Show me her picture."

Jude hesitated and then pulled out his phone, showing her a photo of him and a hugely pregnant Angie, laughing into the camera.

"You both look so happy." The tone of her voice had changed.

He tried to swallow. He thought of the promises he and Ella used to make to each other. That they'd have kids and raise them with love and compassion. That they'd live someplace where their entire back and front lawn could be one big garden, where fresh produce was always on the table.

He watched her, her mouth struggling, as if she were trying to decide whether to tell him something or not.

"Please," he said. "If you have something to say to me . . . you know we could always tell each other everything."

She shook her head resolutely.

"There's nothing," she said, her mouth a stubborn line.

He paused, waiting for more. For the first time, Ella looked deep into his eyes.

"Tell me their names. Your wife. What you're going to call your baby."

"Does it matter?"

"I want to know."

"Gus," Jude said, "if it's a boy. Giselle if it's a girl. And her name is Angie."

"Thank you."

"This frenzy is going to die down—this craziness will pass."

"Jude, stop," she said.

And for a moment she sounded the way she had when they were fifteen and she was trying to tell him not to try to slice his wrists again, to trust in the future. That everything would be okay because she loved him.

"Go home to your family, Jude," she said. "I don't blame you for anything anymore."

"What can I do? I have to do something for you."

"No. You don't. I know you want to fix this, to make things right, and I can appreciate that, but it will make things worse for me. You don't get to do that, Jude. Maybe you just have to live with this. And I do, too."

When he didn't move, she got up and reached for her door.

Jude grabbed his phone to text her his number, his email. "This is me," he said as he typed. "What's your cell number?"

"Jude, don't," she said, putting her hands firmly in her pockets. "Promise me you won't do anything about this. I can't have things made worse for me. I just can't."

"I promise," he said. Then he stood up, turning to take one last look at her, before he heard her door click shut and the lock engage.

He drove without direction, blocks across Ann Arbor, and finally pulled into a public park to get his bearings. He walked along listlessly until he neared a playground, where children's cries filled his ears. Bracing his hands on his knees, he started to cry.

WHEN HIS PLANE landed back in Philadelphia, Jude stumbled toward the cab stand. Even if he never saw or heard from Ella again, he would always have that relationship. They had been family once, he and Ella and Helen.

His mind filled with memories of Helen now. She was the last piece of this, and he didn't think he could fix that either, but he had to at least try. Her number was unlisted, but he paid one of those services to find it, and a half hour and forty dollars later, he had it and he called. He knew, as soon as he heard her voice, that it was her. He started to cry again and then caught himself. *You don't have the right to cry.*

"Don't hang up," he said. He could hear her breathing, and then she sighed.

"Jude," she said. "How did you get this number?" He used to love when she said his name, because she made him feel so safe. Her saying his name was like her saying, *I know you.*

"I paid to find it."

"Why are you calling?" Helen asked.

He told her he had just seen Ella and that it had felt like a kind of closure, something he wanted with Helen, too.

"What? You saw Ella? Why? And what closure? What did she tell you?"

He summarized their conversation and when he got to the part about his father, Helen drew her breath in sharply. "Did she tell you I outed her? Or did you read that for yourself? I didn't mean—"

"None of us did," Jude said, and then Helen grew silent. "Please don't tell her I told you about going to see her. There are things we talked about—if she wants you to know, she'll tell you. Or maybe she's told you already."

"That was all the conversation?" Helen said quietly. "She didn't tell you anything else?"

"Like what?"

"That was it? All you talked about?"

"That's all I know."

Helen blew out a breath.

"How are you now?" Jude said.

"Do you need to ask that?"

"I do."

"Tell me about your life instead," she said, and he told her about Angie and the baby, his life in Philadelphia.

"I thought you were going to be this famous botanist," Helen said. "Or do something with gardens."

Jude swallowed. "Our garden helped convict Ella."

"When I think about it now, I think that that garden was only ever innocent, Jude. It was such a pleasure. The three of us built something; we had joy in it. We all loved it. Do you know what a gift it was for me to be able to give that to you and to have you accept it? Every time I looked out the window and saw that garden, it just made me feel glad. Useful. Like I had put good out into the world. Every time something new bloomed, it was this wonderful surprise."

Jude pressed his cell against his face.

"I would love to think of you using your talent, making yourself and others happy."

"I don't know," he said.

"Well, think on it," Helen said. "I'd like to imagine all of us happy. I'm glad you called me, that we got to speak, that we had what we had. Even after everything, I still look back with wonder at that summer."

"Can I call you again?" he said.

Helen was quiet again for a moment.

"I don't think so, Jude. I used to look for you everywhere, think that one day I would run into you, that we'd have coffee and laugh and talk about our lives."

"We still can, can't we?" Jude said. "I know I've made so many mistakes—I hurt everyone."

"So did I," Helen said. "And now I know why. I tried to push the life I wanted for myself onto you two kids."

"No, no, you didn't. And I loved and wanted that life—you were like a mother to me, and I was so grateful for it."

"So was I," Helen said. "But I felt responsible for the way things turned dark for everyone, including me. I need to let that past go. And so do you."

"Please don't do this," Jude said, but already, he could feel her fading from him.

They didn't say much after that, and he knew it was probably the last time he'd hear her voice.

"Goodbye," Helen said quietly, and then, before he could say anything else, she disconnected.

Shaken, Jude sat with the phone for a minute, staring as traveler after traveler entered the long line for taxis. He called Angie.

As soon as he heard her voice, he was telling her everything about the visit, spilling out the story, leaving nothing out. When he was finished, he was afraid. "Say something," he begged.

"That's quite a story," she said quietly. "And what did the visit solve? What does she want you to do?"

"Nothing," he said. "I offered to go to the media. To go to court, because who cares if my father won't tell the truth? I can and I would. But she said no, that it would make things worse. She made me promise that I wouldn't. But I'm responsible. I did this. All of this."

"Your father did it, too," she said. "And you were fifteen."

"I was so fucked up that night," he said. "So desperate and angry and trapped—I hadn't slept, I was hallucinating. I tried to . . . I wanted to. "

"But you didn't," she said. "Right? You made the tea but then you stopped. You went to find Ella."

"But legally defined—"

"Screw legally defined," she said.

"I'm not sure who I am anymore."

"Well, I'm sure," she said, then paused. "What was it like to see her? I'm not stupid. I know people can love more than one person at the same time. Sometimes that first love always stays with you."

"I'm coming home to you. I went there because it's my fault, because I needed to be responsible, to do something."

"But you did do something. You gave her the truth. And it sounds like for her, that was what she wanted. And you gave me the truth, too."

"Are we going to be all right?" Jude asked. "Have I ruined everything?"

He could hear her breathing.

"Just come home."

# NINETEEN

# Brooklyn

*July 2019*

As the summer wore on, Helen kept calling Ella—to explain, to beg forgiveness—but Ella still wasn't picking up. Helen wrote her letters often. She sent another handmade dress in blue linen because it was getting hot. The message she sewed into the hem read, *I love you.* There was nothing else Helen could do but keep loving her and keep hoping.

Her heart, though, clamped shut against Jude. Never had she expected him to contact her, though for a while she had hoped he would, remembering how he had sparked a promise of family in her life. Well, that promise had been broken.

She knew it wasn't good for her to just sit in her apartment and ruminate, plus the sweltering heat of July wasn't really cooled by the small fan she had, so she got up, and as usual she went to walk along her old block in Williamsburg.

It always felt as if time had fractured here, with some pieces in the past and some in the present. Everything was the same and yet different, which somehow made it all the sadder. People were always coming and going on this block, kids walking to school or skipping home, girls running errands for their mothers. When she passed her old house, she stopped, as if her stare would draw someone from her family to her.

She saw the curtain flutter, a small, pale face peeking out—her sister Esti maybe, or her mother, or maybe a grandchild after all this time—but when she waved, the face vanished, the curtain pulled firmly shut. She used to know everyone on this block, the people who attended the same synagogue as her family, who had hosted one another for Shabbos dinners. She imagined she felt their stares, too. She swore she could hear the gossip.

She was still an outsider.

What was she even doing, living in Williamsburg, haunting the streets of her old neighborhood? She had moved to Bay Ridge for Ella, to make things safe. Then after Ella had left, she had felt that she should move, too, because there were too many reminders of Ella in her Bay Ridge apartment. Maybe it was time for her to move again, for herself. Just for herself. She had enough references, enough people who came all the way from Manhattan to have her tailor their clothes, and though she didn't quite understand why they did, she was grateful. Surely, she could find work on the island itself.

She went back to the real estate agent she had used before, who looked at her in surprise. "I want to know if there are any studios I can afford in Manhattan," she said.

The real estate agent smiled and pulled out a chair for her. "Manhattan!" She turned on her computer. "And so soon! You know it's going to be pricier, right? Unless you'd consider farther north. And you're not going to have the space you've had here. You okay with that?"

"Manhattan," Helen confirmed.

It would be so different, no matter where it was, she was convinced. Plus, Mouse lived there and maybe that meant something. Maybe there was an invisible hand pushing her forward, nudging her to try to make things right there, too.

The agent snapped her fingers. "Here we go. Washington Heights. Let's go take a look at this studio. Very very tiny, but affordable."

Maybe there was a God, but maybe there wasn't. She knew that the God of her childhood community was no longer hers, just as the community itself no longer was. She didn't know what she believed anymore, but maybe she'd be able to create something new.

She longed to call Ella again, to tell her she was moving to Manhattan. Her fingers curled around her phone. She so yearned to help her, not in a way that was overbearing, but maybe there was something that she could do for her indirectly. And then, thinking about Mouse, an idea began to form.

THE FIRST THING she did when she got home was to call Mouse.

"Hey," she said.

"Helen," his voice shifted. It grew stiff and she could tell he was still angry with her. She couldn't bear it. Not anymore.

"I'm moving," she said. "I wanted to tell you."

There was a silence.

"Where?" he said, and she thought, *That's a start.*

"Manhattan. I have to go look at some places."

"Are you stalking me, Helen?" he said, his voice softening.

"I would like to," she said, drawing in a breath. "And there's something else I want to tell you."

"So tell me."

"I love you," she said. "I'm sorry. Forgive me." That was her first ask.

He was silent for a moment and then she said it again, "Forgive me. Mouse. Please. You have to forgive me." She heard him clear his throat. "I'm ready to tell you everything."

"All right," he said, slowly. "Tell me. I'll listen, but I might not forgive."

Haltingly, she began to tell him everything about Ella and Jude, about the child, the prison sentence. She finally arrived at her slipup at the bar, her drunkenness and Ella's almost unbroken silence since. She felt him listening intently, and his attention was like a cloak draped around her—she had been so cold and now she was beginning to feel warm.

"I'm glad you told me," he said. He didn't sound angry anymore, but she was afraid that he would now dismiss her, say she should go and have a good life, but one without him in it.

"Could I see you, do you think?" Helen said. "I miss you. I really miss you. I miss what we had." Helen pressed her cell against her ear, waiting. *Please*, she thought.

"Well," he finally said. "Since you asked so nicely. Since I miss you, too. Yes. Yes, we can see each other." She heard the smile in his voice.

He began to talk more then, to tell her how lonely he'd been after she'd come back from Ann Arbor and they broke up again, how a friend had tried to fix him up with another woman, a gastroenterologist, and although this woman had been perfectly fine and lovely, she hadn't been Helen. He told her how sometimes he had even taken the subway to her neighborhood in Brooklyn, hoping he might run into her, but he never had.

"We'll try again," Helen said. "Tomorrow?"

He laughed and then she knew it was all right.

"How is your daughter holding up with all of this?" he asked quietly. She told him, haltingly, about how Andrew Stein had been the one to take away Jude's parental rights without Jude even knowing it. She heard his sharp intake of breath.

And only then did she dare to share her second ask.

# TWENTY

# Philadelphia

*August 2019*

Gus was born at the beginning of August, a rainy summer after-noon, with his beautiful blue eyes. Jude had stayed beside Angie, holding her hand during the delivery, sleeping next to her in the hospital, taking them both home. His family. Nothing else mattered now but this amazing little human they had created together.

And Gus was indeed amazing. He had Angie's lashes, long and full like palm fronds. He had Jude's chin; his hair, too, more than on any baby he had ever seen. Jude swore the baby smiled at him. He was sure Gus loved the rock and roll Jude played, the Mozart Angie insisted on because she had read that it made babies brilliant. Andrew sent over a child-sized wooden rocking chair that Gus was far too young for, with a note that said he'd be happy to come visit when they wanted him.

Jude had no idea if that would ever happen. But in the meantime, he spent every second he could with Gus, because the baby seemed to change every day and Jude couldn't wait to watch his son learning to walk, starting to talk, growing into his own unique little life.

He kept going to work, but while he loved being with Angie and Gus, the thought of continuing to spend eight hours a day at his IT job made his stomach roil. He began having migraines that forced him to sprawl on the couch for hours.

"Do something else," Angie told him. "You could still go back to school and be a botanist."

"I don't know. That doesn't seem right now," he said. "That was an old dream. I need a new one."

"I know you'll find it," Angie said, and dotted his forehead with a kiss.

ONE SUNNY DAY at the end of August, while both Angie and Gus were napping, Jude went out into the backyard to think. He surveyed the small space. He had never done anything with it, had let dandelions flutter through the grass, had never even tested the soil to see what might grow well there. He thought about how Helen had urged him to get back to gardening. He had created something really special in her yard—some kind of paradise.

Jude kicked at the grass, and then stooped and plucked a feather-headed dandelion, blowing on it, scattering the seeds. He made a wish for Angie to keep loving him, for Gus to be continually healthy and happy.

He had to figure something out, to untie this knot in his mind. He used to be able to do his best thinking when he was working with plants. But now he didn't even have gardening tools. Still, he went inside and got a screwdriver and a big spoon. Even though he knew it was the wrong season, he desperately wanted to do something—anything—that might feel healing. In a sunny patch at the back of the yard, he jammed the screwdriver into the grass and started tearing up the earth, feeling that familiar satisfying resistance. Maybe he could plant something. Maybe he could be responsible not just for destroying what he touched, but for growing something instead.

The more he dug, the happier he felt. The soil looked and felt good in his hands. It smelled loamy and rich. He kept digging until he had a small square cleared, and then he felt something new: relief. He realized that he was humming.

He'd spent so much time doing things for other people, desperate to make up to them for his mistakes, every action an opportunity to ask and earn forgiveness. He hadn't really thought about how he might forgive himself. But now, looking at the grass, glazed in the sun, he wanted to do what he felt he was born to do. He'd wait for Angie and Gus to awaken, and then pile them in the car and go to a gardening store. He'd buy a spade, soil and mulch, fertilizer, and seed. Here, right here, he could build a sustainable garden.

He sat back, lifting his face to the sky, shutting his eyes, at first dozy and then thrumming with excitement. Ideas buzzed in his head. It wasn't too late to plant leafy greens and carrots. And over there in the corner— corn and garlic and who knows what else could be planted now.

The more he thought about it, the more he drifted into reverie. He saw himself standing in front of a farmstand with his arms crossed, smiling because everyone was raving about the size of his zukes, the quality of his dahlias. Then he saw himself standing in someone else's yard, persuading them not to put in grass, but a native garden that would be full of butterflies and birds. It would look spectacular, and he could tell them just what to grow and how to make it flourish. Fantasy had ruined him once, but maybe now it could save him, because it was rooted in happy purpose.

He snapped up to a sitting position. That one guy at work, the one who was always asking him if he had seen some game or another the other night, was a website designer. Jude bet he could get his help. He looked across their yard and it began to transform for him. There it was, shimmering in the future, an oblong retaining wall made of perfect stones, a birdbath over in the corner. A bluestone patio. An oasis.

He heard the screen door opening and slapping shut, footsteps in the grass, and then there was Angie carrying Gus, coming toward him. He looked at her, her face half hidden in the bright sun.

"What's all this?" she said, smiling down at the patch of dirt he had dug up, the scramble of soil. "Do we have gophers now?"

He poked at the soil and gave a rueful laugh. "I keep thinking—and I know this is going to sound nuts—but maybe I could start a business. A landscaping business. Small at first. Maybe in my off hours. I could get a truck with a sign, get a website. I could build something for us.

"Crazy, right?" he said.

For a moment he couldn't read what was in Angie's face. He was worried that she might ask him how. What would they do for money while he was cutting back his hours, trying to start a business? Instead, she crouched down in the grass beside him, Gus gurgling in her lap.

"You're already a gardener, it looks like," she said. "Look at you. I haven't seen you like this since the day Gus was born."

He felt a swell of relief washing over him. Of course she was on his side. "What will we call it?" she asked.

"Dig Deep," he said, and then shook his head. "Grow On, maybe." Because that was what they were doing, growing on.

He sprawled back on the grass, looking at the sky, and then Angie did too, balancing Gus on her chest.

"Could this happen?" he asked her. "Could we really do this?"

Angie leaned over and kissed him. "You'd be surprised at what we can do. Want to know the truth? I honestly never thought about having kids. Look at what you set in motion for me, for us. And how beautifully it's all turning out." She kissed him again. "Grow On is already happening. Now you just need to believe in it."

Jude thought how every garden he built, every landscape, might make him remember Helen and Ella and their garden, the family they had made together. But all of that was over. Now he had something new and real. He had Angie and Gus and the idea for a new company that would truly be his. If he was lucky, it would grow and flourish just like the seeds he would plant.

# TWENTY-ONE

# Ann Arbor

*August 2019*

The months after Helen's visit passed in a bleary haze for Ella. Some days she found she could barely leave the apartment without feeling the crush of anxiety. Everyone she loved was gone. Jude. Her mother. Marianna. Carla. She had called child services again this morning to see if there was news of her daughter, and still they refused to talk to her. She had done search after search on the computer for news of Marianna, but what news could there be unless it was bad? She had hurt Henry so badly, she knew he wouldn't take her calls anymore.

But then there was this, a kind of spark that changed everything. Jude had given her one thing she hadn't expected: confirmation that she was innocent.

At first she didn't know what to do with that, or even how to feel. She knew about the exoneration programs, the lawyers who worked tirelessly to prove that their clients had been wrongly convicted. But she also knew there was no guarantee. And those kinds of appeals often took a long time. Did she really want to go through all that?

Her mind was spiraling.

When Jude had come to see her, she'd waited for him to bring up their baby. Helen had told her that he had signed away his rights—she was startled when Jude hadn't asked her anything about the child. She kept replaying everything he had said, and then she felt something snaking along her spine.

What if he hadn't known? What if her mother only thought he knew because that was what Judge Stein had told her?

She suddenly felt nauseous.

She was still angry with her mother, but Helen was the only one who might have an answer. Or maybe her mom was just a target for her anger and her sadness. She picked up her cell and dialed.

"Darling," Helen said, and Ella could hear the relief in her voice. She drew in a breath. "I'm so, so sorry, I—"

"No," Ella said, cutting her off. "I don't want to hear it. I don't want to talk about any of that. I just need to know something from you."

"Whatever you need."

"You told me that Jude relinquished our child. Is that true?"

"Of course it's true. Why are you asking me now?"

"How do you know?"

"Well, I heard that from your lawyer. He said he had sent the paperwork for Jude to sign, and that he had."

"Jude really signed?" Her stomach began to churn.

"What do you mean, 'really'?"

She thought of Judge Stein, how he controlled everything, how furious Jude had been with him. He never would have signed. "Did you see a signature?" Ella asked. "Was it Jude's handwriting? Would you know it if you saw it?"

Ella could hear some rustling over the phone. "No, I—" her mother said, and then she went silent, as if she was thinking about what Ella had asked.

Ella began to gasp, trying to get enough air. "Oh my God. He never knew. He never knew! How could he never know?"

"Honey, you don't know that for sure. And neither do I."

"Yes, I do. I know Jude!" Ella cried.

"Everything happened for the best," Helen insisted.

Ella felt like the air was being sucked out of her apartment. "I have to go," she said, and hung up.

She sat and clasped her arms about her body to control the shaking. She'd call Jude, she'd tell him they'd had a child together. No one could stop her from doing that. Surely he'd want to know about his daughter. He would want to understand all that had happened, the same way she did.

Then she thought about what that knowledge might do. It could create a whole new set of problems. It would hurt the family Jude was building. It would hurt Marianna, too, because now there might be someone who could lay claim to Carla.

She stopped crying and went to the sink and ran the water until it was ice cold, the way she and Jude used to when they were trying to stay awake, when just the thought of being separated seemed too impossible. She splashed the icy water on her face and leaned against the wall, shaking.

She couldn't tell Jude about Carla. She wouldn't.

The moment she thought it, she felt her body wincing as if from a blow. It was a hard choice, one that she knew she'd always question. But she wasn't going to complicate Jude's life again. She knew him well enough to know he probably would want to send money he didn't have to a child he wouldn't be allowed to know. They'd all try to make something right that never could be. And everything would feel more wrong in the process.

Let him be happy.

ALL THAT NIGHT, Ella couldn't sleep. She tried playing Miles Davis, but that made her think of Henry, so she shut it off. She picked up her knitting, falling into a hypnotic rhythm.

One row. Then the next. She felt herself going deeper and deeper into a kind of trance. When she was writing Dear Clancy, she used to tell people to go for the hard thing, to scour the broken places inside you, because that was often where the truth lay. She thought back to that night in the Steins' townhouse, about how crazy in love she and Jude had been. And then she started to remember something, the memory like a fly buzzing in her peripheral vision.

She dropped the needles. She was back in the townhouse on the Upper East Side. It was that night. That terrible night. She was moving in slow motion, the air heavy and thick around her. She couldn't keep her eyes open, and she kept rolling in and out of sleep. One minute she was in the kitchen, the next, sleeping on her desk at school until a sound jerked her away, back to the kitchen again. She was standing at the counter, looking at the foxglove, at the cup in front of her. She felt a deep, driving urge. She wanted to make the tea. She wanted to pour the water over the foxglove. She wanted Jude's father to drink the tea. She wanted him to die so that she and Jude could have their happily ever after. But then she had to pee so fiercely, she couldn't think of anything else. She had turned and gone upstairs, leaving the kitchen behind—and the empty teacup.

She hadn't made the tea. She hadn't made him drink it. But if Jude had asked her to, if he had said the words, she would have made it happen. She would have done anything to keep Jude with her.

But it hadn't been her.

ELLA SAT UP knitting until morning, and by the time it was light again she had three quarters of the front of a dark red sweater finished. She could feel the morning coming in, scrubbing the day clean, like new. She put the knitting down and reached for her cell.

Helen had texted her repeatedly, but when she tried to read the messages, the letters swam across the screen. *I'm sorry. I was wrong.* Those words jolted her. And then:

*I have a good friend, the man I told you about at the bar. His name is Mouse. We are seeing each other.*

*Well*, Ella thought, *good for both of us*. Now Helen could lean on someone other than her. But to Ella's surprise, she also felt a pang of longing. Memories, she knew, were always changing size. What held more force for her now wasn't how Helen had outed her. Instead, she remembered how Helen had visited her in prison, every week; how she had made all of her clothing in childhood; how she had rushed out to Ann Arbor when she'd called.

She put her emotions aside and searched Google, typing in Marianna's name, and then Jude's. But the news was old, familiar—links she had already explored. And then she Googled *Dear Clancy*, and there was a new column, for the same paper. It was called Dear Sara.

Stunned, Ella studied a photo of Sara, a woman who looked to be her mother's age, her hair blond and poufy, a pair of sparkly glasses perched on her nose. The first letter was about whether a sixty-year-old woman could start dating again, if she should color her hair. It was signed, *Still a Romantic*.

"Go for it!" Sara told her, and Ella sighed. She would have told Still a Romantic to stop thinking of her beauty as her best feature, to think instead about her sense of humor, her kindness, her willingness to be open to love. She would have told her that aging doesn't preclude love, that there is nothing sexier than curiosity about life. But she wasn't answering those letters anymore. No one was asking her to. No one was asking her anything.

Sunlight splashed through the window. She could shower and change, and then treat herself, get a coffee and a bagel at Full of Beans, and then come back here and look for jobs, for other places where she could live.

People were out in full force now that the weather was warm. Summer students. Faculty. Year-round families. Ella could hear the students' shouts, their rhapsodic hellos as they ran into one another.

She walked across the Diag, through the mass of people reveling in the freedom of summer. Frisbees zipped by her. Dogs gamboled and barked, sporting jaunty bandanas.

She wasn't a student. She wasn't a columnist. She most certainly wasn't a mother. And though for a while, she had loved thinking of herself as an Ann Arborite, she felt that she hadn't earned her place here. Instead, she'd had to learn to ignore the stares, the whispers. She'd be gone from here soon.

She made her way to Marianna's old housesit, and as she approached from the street, she saw a pair of boys running out the front door. Two cars were parked in the driveway—it had been empty when Marianna lived there. And she knew Marianna was gone, that Mark's old house, too, now would be empty or perhaps filled with strangers.

She couldn't handle it, these holes in her heart. There was nothing she could do about missing Carla or Marianna. She missed Helen, too, but she couldn't call her. Not yet.

Missing Henry was something different. She recognized him in the chairs at a local diner, in the carvings on a wooden bench in the Diag. She turned down the street to Wood You, her heart thudding. In the window was a beautiful carved bookcase, with real books leaning against the wood, and a sign advertising Literati, where you could buy the books—that was the kind of thing Henry did for others.

Ella took a deep breath and walked inside, but it was a woman who came to the register when the bell tinkled.

"Is Henry here?"

The woman shook her head. "He's on vacation, and boy does he deserve it. Anything I can help you with?"

"No, no, it's okay."

"Do you want me to tell him you came by?"

Ella didn't know what to say. She wanted to ask the woman her name and what she was to Henry. How long she had known him. The woman's face was open and friendly.

"Never mind, it's not important," Ella said, then turned and walked out of the store.

ELLA WAS HEADED back home when she thought she saw Marianna, standing alone outside a café, as if she were deciding whether to go inside. Ella stopped cold, hoping this really was Marianna and not just someone who looked like her. And then, as if she had felt herself being watched, Marianna turned around and saw Ella.

"Don't run," Ella called, coming closer. Marianna didn't move, her face unreadable. Ella wanted to touch her, to hold her in place.

"Marianna?" Ella said. She couldn't tell if she was angry or just stunned.

"What do you want?" Marianna said finally.

"You're still here—"

"Of course I'm still here. Do you think I'd abandon my child?" Marianna said. "Are you going to make more trouble?"

"No—no."

"I read about you in the paper," Marianna said. "Another nice secret you kept from me about your illustrious past."

Ella started to speak, but Marianna raised her hand.

"I don't want to talk about it," she said, folding her arms. "I'll ask you again, what do you want? Carla is mine now. Just mine."

Ella blinked hard. "What? Truly? I'm so happy for you—"

"Are you?"

"Of course I am!"

"A lawyer heard about my case. He took it on. Pro bono. He got Carla back to me and so quickly, too."

"You have her now?" Frantic with longing, Ella looked around. "Is she okay?"

Marianna's mouth narrowed.

"How could she be okay? Mark took her across the country to California and left her alone in a hotel room for hours. And somehow child services was investigating my capacity as a parent, not his. As fucked up as that was, there was no legal separation, no custody agreement, so he technically had a right to take her. But then he was stabbed, bleeding on the floor, and—" Marianna stopped, wavering. "Mark died, Ella. In the hotel room. With Carla. He died, right in front of her."

Ella glanced at the ground, then asked, "Do they know what happened?"

"Bar fight maybe. They found his girlfriend, but she was in Montana and didn't want anything to do with him anymore, big surprise. The police never found out who did it. They didn't even find the knife." Marianna looked past Ella for a second.

"I'm not glad he's dead, but I'm glad he's out of our lives. Carla was in foster care a few weeks and then they gave her back to me." Marianna buried her hands in her pockets. "Carla told me she called you, that you had given her your number."

"I did. I was worried—"

"I was glad she called you, that she had someone to help her."

"Where are you living now?"

"Mark never got a chance to change his will. Or he was just so certain I'd come back that he wouldn't have to. The house was left to me. And some money I never knew he had."

"You're staying in Ann Arbor?"

"What happened to me here could have happened anywhere," Marianna said. "And I've always loved this place, always felt it loved me back. Plus, I want Carla to have continuity. To be in a place she's familiar with. Her own room. A school she knows." Marianna frowned. "And anyway, you could have left, too. But you're here."

Ella drew in a breath. All this time, and she had only ever checked Marianna's housesit. If she'd gone to Mark's, she might have caught a glimpse of Carla, known that she was okay.

"Not for long," Ella admitted. "I'm thinking about moving."

"Where?"

"I don't know yet. Someplace cheap so I can coast while I figure out what to do. I won't be close enough to mess with your life, if that's what you're worried about."

She wanted to ask if Carla ever mentioned her. Did her daughter keep anything that Ella had given her? But she didn't think she had the right.

"She's yours. I know that. I just want . . . Could I see her sometime? Can I visit?"

Marianna tilted her head, considering. Ella knew that Marianna would probably tell her no, give her nothing.

"Who do you think you are?" Marianna said quietly.

"Someone who loves both of you."

"Please don't do that, don't work on my feelings," Marianna said. "My answer's that I don't know. My main concern is Carla. We'll have to see how things go with her."

"Can I see you?" Ella started to reach for Marianna and then let her hand drift back to her side. "We were friends."

Marianna snorted. "Were we ever really friends? I mean, I certainly thought so, but you lied to me. I'm still mad at you."

Ella didn't push. She thought of all the ways this could play out. Marianna might let her see Carla. She might get to play with her and watch her grow, help her fix her hair and learn to knit more complicated things, laugh at her silly jokes. She'd get to keep on loving her and be loved back. That had to be possible.

"I'll tell you something funny," Marianna said. "Something Carla loved. The lawyer said he was referred to us—convinced to take our case by someone who had a funny name. Some kind of animal."

"An animal?"

"Mouse. That was his name. Short for Mouskevitch."

Ella's legs turned to liquid. Her mother had mentioned that name. Mouse was her mother's boyfriend.

"How did you find him?"

"I didn't. That was what was so amazing. I was looking for a better lawyer, one I could afford. But then, out of the blue, this lawyer found me. Said he had heard about my case. God knows how, but I was so grateful I didn't want to jinx anything by asking. And he was taking it pro bono. He was great—we didn't even have to go to court."

Ella braced one arm against the wall. Through all those terrible years, navigating fierce first love with Jude, struggling in prison, Helen had always made sure that Ella knew what she had done for her—the prison visits, the special dresses she made for her, the way she had prodded Ella into getting an education. And yet here was something new from Helen, something perfectly orchestrated without Ella even asking or knowing about it. And it had turned out to be what she and those she cared about needed the most.

Ella reached for Marianna's hand again. "Can I call you? Can I see you again? And Carla?"

"I read the stories," Marianna said abruptly. "You're a felon."

Ella felt bile rising.

"You have a right to hate me," she said finally.

Marianna studied her. "Losing the column. Being exposed like that," she said. "That was terrible, and unfair, and it must have been horrendous for you."

Shame pushed down on her shoulders, but Ella resisted, drawing herself up.

"It was hard," she admitted. "It's still hard. But losing you, having you know I'm a felon, that's harder."

"I don't care that you're a felon," Marianna said. "I care about the deception."

Ella shielded her eyes from the sun. In the light, she couldn't read what was in Marianna's eyes.

Marianna's face softened. "How are you?" she finally said, which surprised Ella.

"I'm okay," Ella said slowly.

"Are you still with"—Marianna paused—"Henry? The guy Carla met and liked?"

Only a friend would remember something like that, Ella thought.

"I wanted you two to meet. I did. But now he's furious with me. I think we're over."

"Maybe you should tell him the truth. The way you finally did to me."

Ella thought of Henry's apartment, the chairs he lovingly made, the way he looked at her. She thought of how angry he had been with her.

"Listen," Marianna said. "Give Carla and me some time. Lots of time. Then maybe we can see you. Maybe you can come see us. I don't know what I'll decide is best for Carla, best for me. But we can see."

Ella put her hand to her mouth. She watched Marianna walking away, waiting until she was out of sight before she began to cry uncontrollably. So hard that a woman stopped to ask her if she was okay.

"I will be," Ella said, and she tried to believe it.

THAT NIGHT, ELLA called her mother.

"I saw Marianna," Ella said. "And I need to thank you and Mouse."

Helen drew in a long, slow breath.

"You don't have to do that for me, honey. Or for him. Mouse is just that kind of guy."

"I'm glad then," Ella said, and then she hesitated. "I've decided to move again. I'm just not sure where yet . . . You have any ideas for me?"

"Honey," Helen said. "I'm not going to tell you what to do anymore, but I can tell you what worked for me. When I stopped trying to reconnect with the community, another community came *to me*. I realized I didn't have to run anymore. I think, maybe, that can happen for you too. And you don't necessarily have to move again to find it."

"But everyone knows about me here—"

"No, they don't. And they talk because they don't know. Give them a chance to know you. Then they'll stop talking. And if they don't?

Well, who needs them." Ella heard a loud buzzer ring inside her mother's apartment.

"Honey," Helen said, "I have to go. I'm meeting Mouse for a show."

*Imagine*, Ella thought. *Helen with a boyfriend. Helen with her own life.*

"Mouse! This makes me ridiculously happy," Ella said.

Helen laughed. "He's going to love you," she said, and hung up.

It was the word *love* that did it. The simple fact that she could be loved, and she could love back if she were brave enough. A flash of Henry crossed Ella's mind. His kind face. The way he made her laugh. It was time. Without hesitation, she got her box of secrets and left the apartment.

STANDING IN FRONT of Henry's building, Ella buzzed his apartment, the box in her hand. To her surprise, the door clicked open. As she reached the top of the stairs, there was Henry, in a blue denim shirt, standing in his doorway.

"Come in, then," he said.

She entered his apartment and handed him the box, then sat down on his couch.

"I thought you should know everything in here now. All my secrets," she said.

He put the box aside and frowned, then sat beside her.

"Where were you?" she asked. "I went by the shop, but they said you were on vacation."

"I went away to think," he told her. "I was worried about you. And I was also mad and a little shell-shocked, if you want to know the truth."

She was sitting so close she could smell the earthy scent of his soap. She could reach out and touch his hair if she wanted. She burrowed her hands between her knees.

"I waited and waited for you to come to me, but you didn't," he said. "I kept thinking, well maybe she needs more time. Maybe I should let her be. You could have told me anything and I would have understood. I thought that was what we were moving toward."

He sighed resignedly. "But now I just don't know how I fit into your life. I don't know how I feel about any of this."

"I know."

"I mean, what has this been, you and me? I never could tell." He looked suddenly miserable. "I'm a good guy. I could ask you—oh all right, I want to ask you, why not make a fool of myself—why didn't you love me?"

"Henry—I . . ."

He waved his hand. "I know the answer. No one knows why anyone falls in love."

"I've been miserable, too."

"What is it that you want? Why are you here? I don't want that box; I made it for you. And I don't think I want your secrets, either."

"The ones I kept from you, you deserve to know."

"Ella," he said, pained. "I don't need to know them. I don't want to know them. This all feels too late."

"I wanted to tell you that I'm innocent. That I was railroaded. And if I ever wanted to be exonerated, I'd have to go back to court. But there would be no guarantee of anything other than more media, and I can't deal with that again."

"What are you saying?"

She told him more, about Jude and Andrew and that terrible night. She kept his gaze.

"That little girl you met. Carla. She's my daughter. I had her in prison, and she was adopted."

Stunned, he stared at her. "Jesus," he said finally.

"It's all true. I swear to you. And I know I fucked up. Maybe you're right, and it doesn't matter anymore. I'm thinking of moving anyway. To make a fresh start."

"I don't understand. Your child is here."

"I don't have any legal rights. And I'm still fodder for gossip here. Maybe not forever, but I don't want to be walking around in a place where everyone will be giving me the side-eye."

She expected his face to change, to show disbelief or maybe just relief, but she didn't expect compassion. She didn't expect sympathy.

"I'm so sorry, Ella."

"Please don't be angry with me," she said. "You have a right to your feelings. I know that I expect too much of people. I'm trying to stop doing that."

"Why?" he asked seriously.

"Why what?"

"I actually think you don't expect *enough* from them."

Ella blinked back tears. "I don't understand—"

"Why wouldn't you expect everything from someone you care about? Why wouldn't you want to give them everything, let them know everything? Isn't that the whole reason we're here, on this planet?"

"What if people don't want to give it—"

"Then that's their problem, not yours."

She wavered, feeling the ground shift beneath her.

"I really missed you," she said finally.

"Sometimes you have to have a little faith in people," Henry said quietly. "They can surprise you." His hair flopped over his face and he shoved it back.

"We good now?" he said, and Ella nodded.

"Good then," he said. "Will you please not even think of moving? I'm here. I'll watch out for those side-eyers."

Ella laughed and then grew serious.

"I don't even have a job," Ella said.

"But you could get one," Henry said. "I know a lot of people around Ann Arbor."

"Who would hire me?"

"People will surprise you," he said again.

"Oh, Henry, I don't know."

"So, you don't know yet," he said. "Don't you want to find out?" He reached over and put one finger in her top buttonhole. "You know, I admire you."

"What? Me? Why?"

"You were able to grow here. To be honest with me about something really tough." She heard him swallow. "You were brave. Are brave."

"That's the first time anyone's ever used me as a good example."

"Stay," he said. "We have more to figure out, you and me. And it will be more fun if we do it together."

She hesitated. She thought about what it would be like to stay here, to stand her ground among people who thought she was guilty of something terrible, who would stare at her in wonder. But she'd also be among people like Henry, people who accepted her, who rooted for her. And maybe she could start to accept and root for herself, too.

"Is that a maybe?" Henry said.

"Are you going to open the secret box?" she said, and he shook his head.

"You've told me every secret I wanted to know," he said.

She wanted to hurl herself into his arms, to take him to bed. She glanced at the door, but she couldn't move. She loved how he wasn't pushing, how he was waiting for her to make her own choice, and then she leaned against him and gave him the tenderest kiss she could. He kissed her back.

"If I stay the night, I'll never leave," she said.

"And that's bad—how?" he asked, smiling. But he got up and gently opened the front door for her.

WHEN SHE GOT home, she shucked off her clothes and reached for her robe in her closet. She really should straighten things up in here. Shirts were half off their hangers, and the yellow dress Helen had sent her was crumpled on the floor. When she picked it up, she felt something she hadn't noticed before: a lump in the hem. Something hard. She got a sewing needle to pick out a few stitches and opened the seam. There, falling into her hand, were her mother's tiny gold hoop earrings, and what looked like a scrap of fabric.

She tugged on the scrap until she could read the words:

*I will always love you and always be proud.*

Slowly, carefully, Ella threaded the gold hoops into her ear lobes, where they glittered like stars.


IT WAS THE end of August, and Ella was at one of the local markets buying groceries, at the very end of a long checkout line. She still hadn't made a final decision about whether to leave, what to do. She saw Henry almost every night now, his bright hopeful face, but he never brought up her leaving or asked her to make promises.

He had found her a job, though, at a bakery in Kerrytown, which was both something to do and a much-needed source of income. She didn't dare think about Marianna and Carla—well, not too often. Maybe she didn't deserve them in her life. But still, she kept the drawing Carla had made, the one that said *My Family at the Park.*

In line, Ella was admiring the panache of an older woman in front of her, dressed gaudily in bright shorts and a red T-shirt, her hair punked up and white, when the woman's groceries dropped from her hands and spilled onto the floor.

"My God, I'm such a klutz," the woman said, crouching, picking up grapes and apples and a few lemons. She rose to smile ruefully at Ella. She was wearing huge, mirrored earrings that Ella admired.

Ella picked up a stray lemon and handed it to the woman.

"Thank you!"

"No problem," Ella said, and smiled. "I like your earrings."

"I just wear them to deflect from how old I am."

"What? You don't look old at all." *This woman is strikingly lovely,* Ella thought.

"Oh my God, yes I do," the woman said. "I worry that the first thing people think when they see me is why is that woman so *old*? Why doesn't she take better care of herself? She could color her hair. But if I did color it, then they'd think, who is she fooling? It just goes on and on." The woman hesitated as if she were making a judgment call. "I'm sixty-seven," she said finally. "What a tragedy."

"Okay," Ella said calmly. "You're sixty-seven. And you have beautiful skin."

"What? Look at these lines. I would get those injections people keep telling me about, but I hate needles."

"You don't need to do that."

"I do. I feel that people don't respect me because of my age."

"Do you have proof of that?" Ella said. "Did anyone ever, ever say that? Or hint at it even?"

"Well, no," the woman admitted.

"That's because it's simply not true."

Here was the kind of face-to-face moment that resonated, the kind that she hadn't had since she was a peer leader in prison. Getting people to realize that what they were most afraid of just might not be real. The woman's face relaxed into a smile.

"Maybe," she said, and then, impulsively, she moved closer.

"Wait," she said. "I know who you are."

Ella grew rigid, but the woman touched her arm.

"You're Ella Fitchburg, right?"

"I need to go—" Ella said, looking around, but the people in line in front of and behind her were lost in their own worlds. No one was listening. The woman touched her arm again gently.

"No, no, I don't care about all that tabloid stuff," she said, and Ella flinched. "I want to talk about your column! I used to read it religiously. Dear Clancy. Loved it! Just so appreciated your advice. You're good at this. Have you ever thought of being a therapist?"

"Me? A therapist?" Ella said.

"Well, why not?" the woman said.

"I would need a license. A graduate program. It's expensive."

The woman shook her head. "Not always. There are scholarships, loans. If you're a resident, it's so much cheaper. Are you a resident? Been here a year at least? That's all it takes."

Ella wavered. "Yes," she said. "I guess I am."

"And there's other cheaper colleges than U of M. I took courses at Eastern myself."

"I don't know if anyone would want to come to me," Ella said.

"Why not? I would."

This woman wasn't frowning. She didn't hum with that vibration Ella had grown to recognize, that excited wanting-to-know-every-sordid-detail she encountered so often in strangers now. This woman's eyes were clear and focused on her.

"Why?" Ella said.

"Because you've been through so much and you're still here. Because you never gave up. Because you just helped me a minute ago with a few casual words. And believe me, I have more issues than I can deal with. I can't help thinking that someone like you would understand anything I might say. And that you wouldn't judge me."

Ella stayed very still, listening, thinking.

The woman stepped forward and Ella drew back as a reflex. But something about this person made her quick to relax.

"My name is Melody. Melody Strong." The line had inched forward and suddenly it was Melody's turn.

"Go do it," Melody said. "I'll be your first client."

"You would?" Ella said, astonished. She felt her heart kickstarting, her breath quickening. Dizzy, she braced a hand along the checkout belt. She could feel Melody smiling at her, all that encouragement and warmth like a sun.

"Do it," Melody repeated, and then she picked up her groceries and was gone.

ELLA WALKED HOME in a daze.

"Hey, smiley!" a random guy called out to her, and she laughed, realizing what she must have looked like. She felt as if a sparkler had been lit inside her. As soon as she got inside her apartment, she dumped the groceries on her chair and began to research graduate programs. Eastern Michigan had some. So did Wayne State. Her hands trembled over the keyboard. Both had two-year programs, and then training. Both had scholarships. She could take one course at a time, as she could afford it. She could get work-study, too, to help her finances. Maybe it would take forever, but it wouldn't matter because she'd be working toward a goal. An extraordinary goal.

*I can do this. I can be this.*

Clancy was a costume she had put on every day to pass. But this— this was truly her.

HER HANDS GRIPPED the edge of her chair. *Breathe*, she told herself. *Breathe*. It was just an application. She could do this. She could stay in a place she loved. She could eventually even set up a practice here.

*I can do this. I can be this. This is who I want to be.*

Everything now was a leap of faith, she thought, including Henry. How she needed him. How she might love him. How she owed it to herself to find out.

Her hands reached for her cell. He answered on the first ring and she instantly felt his sense of calm washing over her.

"Hey," she said. "Remember you said I should consider not leaving—"

"Oh my God, you're staying?" he said.

"I'm coming over."

And then she did.

THE FRIDAY AFTER Ella had made her decision to stay, to go back to school, she went outside, feeling restless. Shouldn't she be happier? Maybe she could be if some things didn't still tug at her, things that felt unfinished. She didn't know when, how, or even *if* she'd have a deeper relationship with Marianna and Carla, though she desperately hoped she would. She was anxious about going back to school, too: how she'd do there, if she'd fit in and have friends, and if she did, what she'd share with them about her past.

She told herself she had done the tough stuff already. She'd earned a degree from Bard while in prison. She had held a job that people respected. And, at long last, she'd found out the truth—discovered her innocence. If she could do all that, she could do anything.

Her hand unconsciously moved to the tattoo on her arm, circling the hummingbird she had gotten all those years ago with Jude. It had faded, the wings blurred, as if the bird had dropped all thoughts of flight and had given up. When she had seen Jude, she had spotted his arm, bare of his tattoo, and she'd felt the absence like a slap. She hadn't needed to ask him why he removed it. She knew. Getting those tattoos was the kind of reckless thing crazy kids do, but they were both older now. Jude had lasered his off, along with his past. Maybe it was time for her to get rid of hers, too.

Determined, heart thudding, she headed over to Rose's Tattoo. Rose was there alone, and she smiled when she saw Ella. Her eyes gravitated to the tattoo.

"I want to get rid of it," Ella said emphatically. "Laser it off." She couldn't wait now to get it removed, to be free of it.

Rose arched a brow. "Really?" she said. "You sure? It's so beautiful."

"It doesn't belong on me anymore."

"What a shame."

"I need it gone," Ella emphasized. She couldn't bear the imprint of it on her skin anymore. She wanted her arm bare and clear, the final piece of her past zapped away so that she could move forward.

Rose patted a leather chair. "Sure. Have a seat."

Ella sat, but instead of feeling relieved, she felt a flutter of panic. At first she wasn't sure why, but then she looked around the tattoo parlor, at the photographs of people and their tats. Some people had commemorative dates on their skin. Others had hearts or words, like *Mary, Forever.*

Rose pointed out a picture of a young woman with two tiny stick figures. "See that? At first it was just one, for her baby. Then she had another three years later! Tattoos can always be adjusted."

She looked down at her tattoo again. It was hazy, as if the bird didn't really know what it wanted to be yet. It represented her past. But maybe she could clarify it, see it in a new way. Maybe she could even make it beautiful. Maybe she wouldn't have to hide it anymore.

Something was happening. She felt it rising up inside her.

"Maybe you could change it," Ella said. "Could you make it fly again?"

"Attagirl," Rose said, and picked up the needle. She winked at her. "Let's see how big and beautiful it can be."

A wave of excitement washed over Ella. She sat up straighter.

"I'm ready," she said.

And now, finally, she was.

Ella sat still, alert, oxygen rocketing through her. *I'm doing this,* she thought.

And then, just for a moment, before Rose's needle even touched her skin, she swore she heard the flapping of wings, like a new, glorious life, ready to take flight.

# ACKNOWLEDGMENTS

I've been so incredibly lucky to have Gail Hochman as my agent, friend, brilliant editor, lunch companion, and style consultant. Huge thanks to the first editor for this book, the kind, patient, and very legendary Chuck Adams, and I owe just about everything to my genius new editor, Evan Hansen-Bundy, whose care, talent and extraordinary suggestions made me sure I had ascended to literary partnership heaven. I also want to thank Algonquin Books and Hachette for taking such good care of me: Betsy Gleick, Michael McKenzie, Lizzi Middleman, Brunson Hoole, Ashley Mason, Sue Wilkins, Debra Linn, Stephanie Mendoza, Katrina Tiktinsky, and everyone. Thanks, too, to my beloved personal publicist Laura Rossi.

I actually love the research stage, and so many wonderful people helped in the writing of this novel. I am the granddaughter of an orthodox Jewish rabbi, and I grew up on my mother's stories of what that kind of life was like, and why and how she left it behind even as she still yearned for her lost community. Orthodox is not Hasidic, like one of my main characters, and to ensure I got those differences right, I interviewed many people. Huge thanks and love to two remarkable women who left the Hasidic community to forge new lives: Leah Lax, the author of both the book and the extraordinary opera *Uncovered*, and author/activist Beatrice Weber, who sued her son's yeshiva for not providing adequate secular education.

I lived in Ann Arbor while going to college there and loved it so much, I refused to leave for a few years. To help me get modern-day details right, I relied on Vicki Honeyman, who was my friend so many years ago and who still is. And thanks to Hilary and Michael Gustafson and bookseller Shannon at Ann Arbor's fabulous Literati Bookstore, whose T-shirt inspired me while I wrote.

For legal issues I have to thank attorney Gregg Rosen, first husband and always friend, who calmly untangled the law to fit my plot. Kudos also to the hilariously funny and smart Peter Barton, Staff Attorney at Queens Defenders, who spent hours talking to me and also gave me excellent suggestions for legal movies. And as always, thanks to my friend Hersh Katz for his spot-on and wise counsel.

Child custody issues change from state to state, so I am totally in debt to the patient, brilliant explainers-of-all-things—Ryann Kaplan, Lysne Beckwith Tate and Kimberly Green.

I had the help of the famous Poison Lady, Luci Zahray, for figuring out that foxglove was the answer to my plot, but I also made friends with emergency room veteran Charlie Goldberg, who helped me figure out symptoms and timing, and who was so funny, I wanted to talk to him for hours. Thanks also to author Ellen Meister.

Prison activist, author and friend Jean Trounstine changed my life by inviting me to the Changing Lives through Literature classes she held for women on probation. Thanks to Maria Medeiros and Priscilla, who opened up to me about their former lives in prison.

Thank you, too, to the writers who read and reread my drafts. Hillary Strong, brilliant writer and beloved family, was writing her novel at the same time I was writing mine, and our long and delightful daily talks sustained me. So did Gina Sorell's pep talks and careful readings. I also cannot thank the incredible Stephanie Gangi and Leora Skolkin-Smith enough, as well as Clea Simon, Jeff Lyons, Jean Kwok, B. A. Shapiro, and Andrea Robinson, who tamed my timeline and made it work.

And to my tribe, Thrity Umrigar, Mary Morris, Clea Simon, Sharyn November, Jane Praeger, Linda Corcoran, Robin Wolfson and Cliff Tisdell, Larry and Amy Rossman, Sally Beth Edelstein, Sara Divello,

Jonathan Evison, Susan Henderson, Ilvi Dulak, Rochelle Jewell Shapiro, Nicole Bokat, Zibby Owens, Annie O'Brien, Victoria Zackheim, Pamela Klinger-Horn, Ron Block, Robin Kall, Barbara Gale, Laura Rossi, Jennifer Banash, Gina Barreca, Mary Webber O'Malley, Jessica Keener, Rachel Cantor, Bethanne Patrick, Christina Baker Kline, Dawn Tripp, Thelma Adams, Jen Pastiloff, Meg Waite Clayton, Jo Fisher, Amy Ferris, Pulpwood Queens, Carolyn Zeytoonian, Tom Frueh, Lindy Judge, Nancy Lattanzi, Jenny Halpern and Marike Jainchill.

These last few years have been crushingly hard for everyone. There were shocking way-too-early deaths and I still deeply mourn my best of friends: Jimmy Lambros, Peter J. Salzano and Jana Conn. When the pandemic hit, my whole book tour was canceled. I sent the video I had made of the speech I was to give librarians, complete with hand motions, to my team at Algonquin, who liked it so much they sent it out as a publicity tool. I invited writers to make small videos, shouting out an indie bookstore and an author, and I would feature them on my Facebook page as part of the "Nothing is Cancelled Virtual Book Tour" series. I was soon inundated! And then Jenna Blum called me asking if I needed help and A Mighty Blaze was born. We started with just the two of us flying blind, and now we have a staff of over thirty passionate volunteers, and I adore every single one, including Mark Cecil, Laura Rossi, Mary Webber O'Malley, Julie Gerstanblatt, Rachel Barenbaum, our Authors Love Bookstores team Kimberly Hensle Lowrance and Joseph Moldover. And thanks to the many writers and independent bookstores who let us interview them for A Mighty Blaze.

Thank you to the UCLA Extension Writers' Program for their everlasting support of the writing classes I teach, and, of course, to the indie bookstores that champion writers and readers every single nanosecond.

As always, I couldn't have written a syllable of this book without my partner-in-crime and best beloved friend and husband, Jeff Tamarkin, who made me laugh when I despaired, even as he made sure that my characters were traveling the right routes and listening to the right music. And to my favorite horror movie aficionado, my smart, creative, funny, talented son, Max Tamarkin. Love you both forever and forever.